THE SURGEON'S HOUSE

THE SURGEON'S HOUSE

JODY COOKSLEY

Allison & Busby Limited
11 Wardour Mews
London W1F 8AN
allisonandbusby.com

First published in Great Britain by Allison & Busby in 2025.

First Edition

HB ISBN 978-0-7490-3172-5

Typeset in 11/16pt Adobe Garamond Pro by
Allison & Busby Ltd.

By choosing this product, you help take care of the world's forests.
Learn more: www.fsc.org.

FSC
www.fsc.org
MIX
Paper | Supporting
responsible forestry
FSC® C171272

Printed and bound in the UK using 100% Renewable Electricity at
CPI Group (UK) Ltd, Croydon, CR0 4YY

EU GPSR Authorised Representative
LOGOS EUROPE, 9 rue Nicolas Poussin, 17000, LA ROCHELLE, France
E-mail: Contact@logoseurope.eu

For Matt

1

St Michael's Mortuary, Putney Burial Ground, 1883

It wasn't my first corpse. Something George appeared to forget. He disappeared with the magistrate to identify the body, asking me to wait outside as though I were delicate. Shielding me after everything we'd suffered. It was not his place to choose. Rose may have been our cook, but she was my friend and the closest I'd had to a mother figure in many years, perhaps ever. If I didn't see her, I'd never believe it was true. Poor Rose spent her life helping others, dishing out love and wisdom with her generous plates. Who could possibly wish her harm?

Banished to the corridor, I heard the urgent voices of men discussing things they believed a woman shouldn't hear. Why must I stay outside? I shifted uncomfortably on the waiting room bench; damp stone smudged with lichen and rust-stained in odd patches, as though bodies were examined there, too. Cold seeped through my cotton skirts and I stood, paced impatiently, my heels striking against the flagstones. Before they showed me her belongings, I'd prayed for a case of mistaken identity; another woman murdered on her way home. Such violence was common, after all. But they'd found her silver locket, the only item of jewellery she ever wore, chased on both sides with a pretty pattern of ivy leaves hanging from curled tendrils and engraved with her own initials – *RCP* for Rose Caroline Parmiter. Distinctive. Unmistakably hers. And she would never have relinquished it without a fight. If the thief was disturbed, forced to flee the scene, then someone must have seen something. These were thoughts *I* should be sharing with the magistrate. George didn't know her half so well, and he was always so deferential to authority that he would never think to ask.

Small, high windows lined the corridor, barred with stripes of lead to stop the ghouls that risked their souls for the chance of a ring or a gold tooth – whatever the morticians hadn't already removed. Through dirty panes, half covered with branches of yew, I saw the light fading, evening drawing in. What could be taking them so long? Pacing closer to the door, I knelt awkwardly to peer through the hole. A heavy key blocked my view. They'd locked themselves in. What did they imagine would frighten me? I pressed my ear to the rough wood.

'My first time back,' said George. 'Doesn't get any prettier.'

As a boatman, George used to clear the river of all its strange flotsam, delivering to the mortuary regularly. I'd almost forgotten. No wonder he took charge so swiftly.

'There are similarities. The rock to the back of the head.' The voice waited for a moment. 'Could be a surgeon's orders again? Something fresh for demonstrations? You know they don't always wait for the formalities.'

A pause before George replied. 'Those bodies came from the water. We just . . . We didn't really examine them.'

A chill ran through me like a spectral sword. The doctor was always straight there to collect the cadavers for lecture demonstrations when his hired thugs had been busy along the river. Were they talking about him? I thought his ghost had left our lives a long time ago.

'It's a common weapon,' George added, his voice firm. He

8

didn't want to recall that man any more than I did.

The magistrate sighed loudly. 'And you can't think of anyone who would have wanted her out of the way?'

'Rose? Heavens no. Everyone loved Rose. I never heard her say an unkind word to anyone.'

'Outside of your household then? Did she have family on bad terms?' The magistrate coughed. 'A gentleman caller, perhaps?'

'No-one we knew of. Though she had plenty of friends in the Half Moon.'

'We'll question everyone who was there last night.'

'Whoever killed her must have watched her leave.'

'Unless he already knew her habits,' added the magistrate. 'He could have waited outside.'

Rose only drank once a week, on her night off. Always said she went to the tavern to 'forget the wickedness in the world', and who could blame her? It was a wonder she didn't drink daily.

'Her pocket's been slit. There was no money on her.'

'She'd probably spent it.'

Why would a thief target a woman like Rose? A plain domestic servant, long past her prime. Even if he hadn't intended to kill her, who would waste time for the chance of a shilling when there were better marks to be had? I conjured a mental image of her, dressed in the blue gown and red-patterned shawl she always wore on her night off. Bonnet ribbons loose – she never bothered to tie them properly – and large green umbrella over one arm. Key chain hanging from the loop she'd made in her skirt. That huge set of irons fit every room in Evergreen House and they never left her pocket. Had the police found them, too? I certainly hoped so. It wouldn't do for those to get into the wrong hands.

'May I show you something?' asked the magistrate. A rasping noise, like rough cotton being pulled back. 'The rock may have brought her down, but it seems that her assailant wanted to make sure she didn't survive.'

'Saints preserve us!' George spoke in a low whispered voice. 'Whoever you're looking for is going to have some marks on him.'

Good for her. Rose was a large woman and fit for her age. Even after a few gins she would have put up a fight.

'The police think it likely to have been a smaller man, someone with weak upper body strength using the element of surprise with the blow from behind before he cut her throat.'

Oh, poor Rose! To survive all we'd been through, only to meet such a terrible end.

A scraping sound, like furniture moving, before the key rattled in the lock. I jumped back, began to pace again and whirled round to face them as soon as they opened the door. George looked shocked, as though he'd forgotten I was there.

'Rebecca, you needn't have waited.'

As if I would leave without knowing the truth. 'Is it her? Our Rose?'

'It is.' George put an arm around my shoulder. Exhausted from the day, I burst into tears, leaning against him as my knees gave way. It felt good to be held, to breathe his comforting scent of rosemary and earth. Perhaps, if we tried, something good may come of this nightmare. We had loved one another deeply once, and we would need each other now.

By the time we left the mortuary, it was early evening and purple clouds gathered, spreading like a bruise across the sky. We walked home in silence, unable to speak, watching costers starting their rounds. People bought twists of paper filled with nuts and sugared apple and then went about their business – finished work, arrived at clubs, joined families. They would return home and eat together, enjoying the company of their loved ones while we walked around the hole in our happiness. Evergreen would not be the same without Rose and I dreaded the sight of the kitchens.

We took the back stairs, treading lightly as thieves, unwilling to risk questions. How would we find the words to tell the rest of the household? They'd be hungry soon, looking for Rose and finding a cold stove, an empty chair. Along with the ten unmarried mothers that lived with us were almost as many of their children. Rose was special to every one of them. It would be difficult enough to share the news without them asking questions first.

In the upstairs drawing room, George slumped in his chair fully dressed, boots on, his face drawn. I pulled the curtains across the window and removed my cloak before taking a low seat beside him.

'Was Rose . . . was it bad?' I took his hand in mine and, as he pressed it to his face, I felt the tracks of tears he would deny shedding. 'George,' I said softly. 'I heard them asking questions . . . about the old doctor.'

He raised his head to look at me, eyes dark with fear. 'Dr Everley is dead,' he said. 'They both are.'

My sister, Maddie, had been married to Lucius Everley – a match my parents forced in a bid to repair our name when I brought shame on our family. A doctor every bit as bad as his father, hanged for unimaginable crimes committed in the Everleys' clinics, and in their private home for fallen women. Poor Maddie was so cruelly treated by her husband and his evil sister, Grace, that she wanted nothing to do with their legacy, handing over the running of Evergreen to George and I when she escaped. We'd done our utmost to make it a peaceful place for women and girls failed by society and abused in the very house that was supposed to help them. But now Rose was dead, brutally murdered, and I felt a creeping suspicion that the family was somehow involved.

'It feels as though they're back,' I said.

'How can they be? I watched him hang myself, and she'll never be released. Nor should she after . . .' George cradled his head in his hands. 'It feels like yesterday.'

'You must try not to think of it.' He should never have spoken the name aloud. What curses might such carelessness invoke?

'It's not something you forget.'

George was always so strong for me, for Maddie. But it was he who'd dug the garden to get proof for the court, he who'd found the bones of those poor children. He did it for us, to make sure Lucius and Grace didn't get away with it. And he'd stayed silent all this time. We should speak of it; *he* should speak of it. Memories lodged like splinters in his mind, and they would hurt him slowly. He needed to grieve, for the souls of those babies and the thoughts of the ones we would never have. It would free his mind of dark thoughts. Threlfall himself was fond of the talking therapy and he was always explaining it to anyone who'd listen.

'Perhaps you could talk to Dr Threlfall?' The man was vain and shallow, and his botched testimony in court had almost resulted in Maddie's wrongful conviction. I didn't like him any more than George did. But he was permitted by law to work from the clinic in our basement and, since his presence seemed to please the Charity Board, there was little we could do about it. He might as well be put to use in helping us.

'I'd rather go completely mad than spend a minute in the company of that arrogant dandy.'

I knew better than to argue. I'd have to find a way of putting them together that seemed accidental.

'Stay here and rest. It must have been hard for you today. I'll tell the girls myself.' I could do that much for George. And for

Rose. She was never anything but strong. No doubt she was badly treated by the Everleys too, but she'd remained the whole time they were proprietors of their house for delinquents, and she stayed when George and I took over, helping us return it to a sanctuary. 'We can talk about how we manage in the morning.'

George, pale as bone, didn't protest when I laid a blanket across his lap. 'Spare them the details,' he said, catching hold of my hand.

Could I? Such news travelled fast on the street and even now I might be too late. Better they hear it first-hand than through gossip from strangers. I closed the door gently behind me. Though my heart ached to help him, George would have to wait.

2

Evergreen House, Putney Heath

Sounds of early evening rose and hung in the air. Happy chatter as the women finished their work producing willow baskets or wallpaper in the drawing rooms we'd turned into studios. Our aim was to help everyone we could and for years we'd succeeded. They spent mornings with their children, walking in the parks or playing, and afternoons working while the little ones took their lessons with one of the visiting tutors. Those women who couldn't read or write took lessons too. It *was* a happy place. We had achieved that much. But in the process George and I had changed. And we had left it too long to mention. At first it seemed easy to look forward. There was much to do – our wedding, redecorating the house, teaching the women, gaining their trust. We had to convince the Board inspectors that we were worthy, because we couldn't pay to bribe them like the Everleys did. And all the while we hoped for a family of our own. We expected one. In a house full of infants our lack of children hung between us like a hex, and our conversation tiptoed around it. In unspoken ways we threw blame for the children we wanted so badly, and with each year that passed we lost faith in ourselves.

Shaking the dinner bell, I walked to the kitchen where the air was cold, the stove unlit, the smell of baking faded. No longer a cosy sanctuary, just a room with a red-tiled floor, a huge picture window and walls of shelves filled with jars of preserves and pickles. The sight of the handwriting on the labels brought tears to my eyes and I blinked them back. I must be strong for all of us. Sending the children to wash, I placed the bell on the refectory table. Sensing trouble, the women leant on the backs of chairs, throwing anxious looks at one another, waiting for a signal. In many ways I was a mother to them all, and some days that was enough. If I thought that George felt it too, it would always be enough.

I took a deep breath. 'I'm very, very sorry to have to tell you that Rose passed away yesterday.'

Shocked silence broken by Sophia's anguished sobs, followed by cries of disbelief. 'She was fit as a flea yesterday!' 'I spoke to her as she left!' 'She was never unwell.'

'What happened?' Amy's voice carried clearly. One of our longest-staying residents, she was respected by the others, who often looked to her for guidance. Noise in the room abated as they waited for my response.

'She was . . .' There was no easy way to explain – I'd have to shock first and console after. 'The magistrate believes she was murdered. Her body was found on Briar Walk, at the edge of the park, where she must have been attacked on her way home. She'd been robbed.'

Little point in mentioning the keys. It wouldn't help matters if we all feared intruders and, besides, Rose may have left them at home. I'd need to search her rooms. Should I ask the police before doing so? Possibly there would be evidence that a trained eye could spot, some clue about her life outside the house that could lead us to the perpetrator. When the women were calmer, I could ask them too, but not yet. Almost everyone had begun to cry. Most of them had been cruelly treated by their own families and Rose, with her broad shoulders and big heart, may well have given them their first kindness.

'Who would want to hurt Rose?' Felicia's eyes were bright, and she held her fists in tight balls, as though she planned to seek revenge. If anyone could, it would be her. Five foot nothing of muscle and Irish grit.

'Nobody who knew her. I am so, so sorry and you know I will feel her loss just as keenly as all of you. But you mustn't worry. The streets are dangerous at night, and she had been robbed. There can be no-one who deliberately wished her harm.' Felicia gave me a sharp look. She didn't trust my words. 'The children will need to be fed. Amy, could you light the stove? Yesterday's bread will bear heating and I can make soup.' Turning my face away, I bit my lip hard. I couldn't face the thought of finding another cook, and the kitchens would not organise themselves.

After soothing the women, feeding the children, and settling them to bed with stories, I was exhausted, and disappointed to find George already asleep. I'd hoped to sit with him into the night as we used to. A glass of brandy would be welcome for my nerves, but we'd sworn to run a temperate house and there was nothing of the kind to hand. Too restless to settle, I picked up the parcel of Rose's things that still lay in the middle of the table and untied the string. Her patterned shawl, torn on one side in a way that wouldn't bear mending. Two hairpins with jet bead ends, a halfpenny coin and her battered felt bonnet, ribbons loose as always, bent out of shape by something heavy inside. I was surprised by the weight of the locket, which I'd only ever seen around Rose's neck. Close up it was lovely. A beautifully worked pendant with a thick-linked chain, much admired by the women, perhaps coveted by some. It wouldn't be unusual for light fingers to pocket another's treasure.

But murder? Our girls were tough – Felicia, in particular, enjoyed a brawl before she came to us – but they would never harm someone deliberately and especially not their beloved Rose.

Only one woman I knew was capable of slitting someone's throat, and she was safely locked away. Grace Atherton, sister of Lucius. A clever actress, beautiful enough to charm the court and, with Threlfall's help, slippery enough to evade the noose. Cruel and unfeeling when she ran Evergreen, treating us like property with little choice but to obey or face worse on the street. I was always convinced it was *her* hands that hurt the babies. She showed no remorse at the hearing, no emotion for her brother or the servants that hanged with him. Sometimes I wondered what her life was like: if she managed to charm the wardens too, or if she led a brutal existence of cold baths and thin food, restrained by the wrists for her own safety. I hoped so. She'd done far worse to others.

Pressing the locket to my cheek, I thought of all the ways that Rose had saved me, pushing me to be stronger, helping me to live with grief, absolving me from the guilt I felt over my part in our history. '*We all have to love deep and fall hard. It's the reason we're here on earth. That's how things are.*' Could I find the words to heal us now?

'I'll never forget you,' I whispered into the cold silver. Much as I'd have liked to keep it as a constant reminder, it wouldn't be right. Rose had worn the locket every day I'd known her, and she should be buried with it. I would take it back to the mortuary, for whoever performed her last offices after the autopsy, but first I should look inside in case there was anything that held a clue to her death. As I prized it open, I found a folded piece of paper, a cutting from a newspaper article about the death of an army captain. Above the print was a linocut of a young man in military dress. For the first time I realised Rose had another life before Evergreen. All of us so wrapped up in our own troubles that no-one ever thought to ask. Her brother? A tragic love? Had she been seduced like the others and been one of the first when old Everley set up this house? It would explain her endless patience, the reason she stayed for so long. It would explain her wisdom over joy and pain. Now we'd never know. In the silence of the night, George sleeping in the chair beside me, I let my tears fall unchecked.

Dawn came slowly, pale and subdued, as though the sun itself was in mourning. A necklace of dewdrops draped the web across the kitchen window, quivering in the breeze, the movement fooling its spider. She scuttled back and forth, empty-handed, returning to the edge. Clever thing to weave such a home. Her body, fat with young, pulsed as she hunted and worked, her back lined with three broken white stripes. I should be working too, lighting the stove and readying the kitchen for breakfast, preparing the words that would tell the children that their Rose would not be back. But it was early, my heart was heavy, and I opened the door to the garden, hoping for a moment of peace.

A chill mist rose from the lawn. Long-tailed tits perched on branches of hornbeam, little pink bellies puffing out as they sang. Below, in the bare border, blackbirds tapped their beaks to the earth, drawing worms. Only corvids gathered when the Everleys were in charge; crows and jackdaws waiting for Grace to feed them scraps of meat. She especially loved ravens, like the pair on her family crest. Slick, black thieves that came for scraps and foraged nests until no others were left. It had taken a while for the small birds to return, and I still found joy in their song. I would buy some seeds from the grocer and scatter them across the grass. Spring was late, the food of winter scarce, and the birds would need nourishment as they began to nest. Pulling the shawl tightly around my shoulders, I misted the air with my breath. George and I no longer spoke of nesting, though it was all we planned once. He wanted *three, four, seven children* he would say, and we'd list their names, two each for boys or girls because both were wanted. All were wanted. But every month I hugged my flat stomach and silently understood that I'd failed.

The door banged suddenly, making me start, and I turned to see Amy, holding her daughter's hand.

'I didn't mean to startle you, Rebecca. Neither of us could sleep. I thought I'd bring her outside for some air.'

'We had the same thought.' I smiled. Sensible Amy was one of my favourites, and I was glad to see her. I patted my lap and little Evie clambered up, kicking against my leg with her boots. She nestled against me, twisting a strand of my hair in her hot hand, and I felt a surge of love and longing.

'Cold out.' Amy clasped her hands together and breathed warm air onto them. 'Are you thinking about Rose?'

'We're all thinking of her.'

'See Rose?' Evie struggled to get down, as though she could run into the kitchen and be seized in a floury embrace, given milk and shortbread while she sat on the table.

'Not now. Later.' Amy's eyes met mine. 'Go and see if there are eggs to collect.' She handed the little girl a basket and Evie ran to the coop on stiff, chubby legs, ribbons sliding down her hair. 'What will we say to them?'

'What can we say? Children must meet death at some point. We'll explain after breakfast.' Amy threw me a look of alarm. 'Not the whole truth. There's no need for detail. But they must understand she is not coming back.' There were funeral plans to make, people to inform. Perhaps Amy would help with that. She

19

was a practical girl, not given to flighty behaviour and gossip like some of the others.

'What if they hear something? People talk. There'll be rumours.'

She was right. But if we told the older children then, sooner or later, they would take great delight in terrifying the younger ones with the gruesome story. There were enough ghosts at Evergreen already. 'We will cross that bridge when we come to it,' I said firmly.

We watched the birds peck and fuss. Streaks of pale sunlight threaded the grey sky and striped the boxwood leaves.

'It's nice out here.' Amy leant against my shoulder.

'It is,' I agreed. The garden was tranquil, the place I was drawn to whenever I needed peace. George and I had worked as hard to change the grounds as we had to brighten the rooms inside. We'd cleared the filthy pond and set waterlilies, planted bearded irises to bring the damsels and butterflies in summer. Replaced the huge stone greyhounds with troughs of scented hyacinth and jasmine. A labour of love for the women who stayed and a sign we were safe for those to come. A sanctuary.

Evie ran back and thrust her basket at us, almost spilling the contents.

'Clever girl!' said Amy. 'Look how many you found.'

Five pale, speckled eggs rolled together, perfect ovals. After so much brooding effort the poor creatures must wonder why their nests were always empty.

'Should be a few more,' I said. 'Why don't you go back together and see if you can find them? They don't always leave them in the nesting boxes, and we could all do with a good breakfast today.'

Watching them skip to the end of the garden, hand in hand, I felt a surge of pride for what George and I had achieved. We kept babies with their mothers, where they should be, not starved and beaten for their burden of sin in homes for deserted children. I'd heard tales of those places – some of our women were raised there themselves – and if we saved even one child from such a life, it should make us happy. It was selfish to wish for our own family when we could do so much for others.

I tipped the dregs of my tea onto the grass and a robin hopped over to inspect them. Tea leaves clumped into the outline of a bird, black with a puffed chest and large beak, wings folded and crossed behind it. Instinctively I looked up to where the Everley crest was carved into the stone above the doorway – two long, crossed swords below the pair of ravens. George had tried to remove it, but it was deeply set in the cornerstone, the foundation of the wall, as though the entire house was built upon it. Inscribed underneath was their family motto – *spectemur agendo*, 'let us be judged for our actions'. Our actions bore judging. We'd worked so hard to rid our lives of the stain of murder, to build a happy home for those in need; now we must fight to do so again.

3

All Saints Asylum, Hanwell

Hair slips down my shoulders and onto the floor, where it's gathered in bunches by a slipshod girl. Hands red and chapped from scrubbing, knees and elbows sticking out from her patched cotton dress. She eyes me nervously as she darts back and forth, expecting a kick in the ribs or a pinch where the bruise won't show. I won't hurt the little mouse. If I move now, the warden's scissors will slip.

Mr Varley cut well, close to the scalp, leaving long enough strands to be dressed. Cold air settles in the places now uncovered, my ears and neck exposed. I resist the temptation to touch my head. After ten years in here, I still have my vanity; still miss the feel of eyes upon me as I enter a room. So much power in beauty, the admiration and the jealousy. A knowledge I should be passing to my daughter. Eloise would be old enough now to use her looks to her advantage, and I would have enjoyed teaching her the many ways to raise or ruin men.

Once it's washed, my hair will fetch an excellent price from the wigmakers. A rare colour. What my dear brother, Lucius, called 'burnished' as he wound it round my bare throat. My weak fool of a husband used to brush it with a hundred strokes every night, before he disappeared for good. Such pretty hair. Would my daughter's be the same? I push a strand of it aside with my toe, turning it to catch the light, and the mouse withdraws her hand. I bare my teeth.

Edward Threlfall, with his covetous eye for beauty, adored my hair. Pity nothing could match his self-love. His passion for me has not lasted, yet the more he withdraws, the more I desire his attention because, though he is weak, he is handsome and clever. An expert in his field. His efforts brought about a second trial, for me alone, and between us we were brilliant, both born to charm. We convinced the court that I was no accomplice but an unwitting bystander; that the knowledge of my brother's wickedness, especially the murder of my husband, had unhinged my mind. '*She is an innocent, ill served by life and family. A good mother. Imagine the effect on her children if she is murdered in the name of the law for crimes which were, in fact, committed by her brother.*' Oh, Edward was gullible. And I was grateful. After the trial, after he released me from the noose and condemned me to a madhouse, he could not wait to apologise. '*It was all I could do. And it is better than death.*' Perhaps. But my thoughts are dark in my solitude, and his visits are scarce.

'Lay it flat. We'll need to douse it before it goes anywhere. Probably crawling with lice.' Varley takes a bottle from his pocket as he bids the girl to smooth the strands of my hair across the floor.

A throaty growl escapes me, and he throws a sharp look. 'If you can't behave, I'm happy to fetch the binding chair.'

I scowl at his bursting buttons and plump soft hands, thinking of the knife hidden under my mattress, smuggled by Threlfall in the early days when he still carried out my wishes. It would be easy. Varley is slow, fattened on the food the staff save for themselves, gorging while we starve. Tempting to stick my knife into that fleshy neck, but a waste of opportunity and likely to get me restrained.

I've seen what they do to the violent, and I don't wish to become acquainted with leather straits and French chairs.

'Perhaps you should let us wash more often.'

'A bowl of hot water a week should be enough to keep clean.' Varley throws prussic acid across the hair and a strong smell of bitter almond rises from the floor. 'You don't help yourselves. You should be thanking me for getting rid of these.'

A lie. My hair is clean. They've been dying to get to it and only now do they dare. Threlfall's patronage went some way to protect me once. But he's been absent for a long time judging by the marks on my wall, little lines in the bare plaster like rat scratchings. Soft and damp enough to use my fingernails to mark the passing of every night.

Gathering up the poisoned hair, the mouse flinches as it burns her skin, and Varley begins to shave my head in long, rough strokes. Without Threlfall I am just another inmate. Shut away from the world, called a lunatic, forbidden to own the property I worked so hard to defend. This place has benefitted from the sale of my house, the rest kept in trust for my children, adults now – Eloise with her new life overseas, denied the difference I could have made to her beauty. Perhaps she is like me after all. Daniel and Edmond remain in their nursing home; I am made to write to them twice a year, receiving terse replies on their progress and health. As though I care.

'I would like a bowl of water now,' I say, as Varley wipes the razor on his apron and closes the blade. I try to keep my voice pleasant, though I would rather draw the blade across his throat. 'Please. The hair itches my skin.'

'You'll have to wait until tomorrow, like everyone else. Probably scabies. I'll send matron in to have a look at you.' Varley douses my scalp with pale brown liquid from another bottle. Sharp-sour, like vinegar, it burns as it gathers in the nicks and cuts left by his blade. A chemical odour that is strong enough to draw tears. By the time Varley and his little mouse leave, I can barely breathe.

Surprisingly soft bristle greets my inquisitive fingers. Will it grow back differently? Does it change me? If I was permitted a looking glass, I would know. Asylum rules forbid them. Mirrors drive lunatics to frenzies, pecking and scratching at their reflections like caged birds. But I have everything else I need. Threlfall made the room as comfortable as he could with its cotton mattress, its lack of buckles and restraints. He brought pillows and cushions, my own gowns and slippers, because he needed my permission to fund his work. My share in Evergreen House is loaned to him until such time as my children need it, a covenant to carry on Father's research. He is no match for Father's intellect, but then neither was my brother. Lucius was always too weak for medicine. A certain cruelty is what science requires. Does Edward have it? He is certainly vain, and selfish vanity can render us cruel. Whether it will be enough to serve the legacy remains to be seen. I need his visits to resume.

The sound of heavy footsteps echoes in the corridor. For a brief moment, I imagine Varley has brought the water I requested. Then the key clicks as they lock my room for the night, caging me like an animal. My head and neck feel itchy raw. My need for vengeance burns.

4

Evergreen House

George didn't rise for breakfast, and I left him sleeping, wishing he looked so peaceful awake. Long eyelashes shadowing his cheeks, mouth curled at the edges as though love greeted him in dreams. It was the way he looked at me once. How he looked the very first day I met him, in The Cut, on my way to meet a gentleman. Not the worst kind – Lord Phoenix threw lavish parties and spoilt his 'good sports'. Even so I walked slowly, enjoying the solitude of the street, wending my way through the back alleys by the river. The Thames was ripe that day, shrouding the lanes with a thick, greenish mist that clung to clothes and flattened curls. My hat, newly trimmed in ostrich, drooped its fine feathers in the damp, and I stopped to remove it, so absorbed in inspecting the damage that I didn't notice the figure until he was in front of me. An apparition from the mist. I rammed the hat back onto my head as though he'd caught me naked and he burst out laughing, the best-looking man I'd ever seen.

'I'm sure I'm pleased to give you such amusement,' I said haughtily, trying to push past. 'If you've quite finished.'

'Forgive me.' He spread his hands, took a step back. 'I'm sorry I startled you. Can't see your own limbs in this fog.'

His particular limbs were nicely muscled; firm arms with

the defined dip and curve of a boxer or one who worked with his strength. A docker, perhaps, though his waistcoat and cap suggested he was a boatman, a type I'd been warned not to trust.

'You seemed so cross about your hat,' he said, 'I couldn't help but laugh. You look better without it.'

His smile reached his eyes, which twinkled with mischief, and when he held out his arm I took it as though I never had the choice to do anything else. By the time we reached my party we were laughing together, leaning into each other. It wasn't until after he left that I realised he'd changed direction for me. I was late for Lord Phoenix that night, which wouldn't have mattered had Grace not already been there, a storm cloud on her beautiful face. The next time I met George I bore the marks of her rings across my cheekbone, and he began his campaign to set me free.

Trying not to wake him, I moved quietly as I dressed, choosing a dark-grey gown for respect and adding a green wrap because Rose loved colour. I brushed and pinned my hair, added green ribbons and then swiftly removed them. Sometimes I forgot I was no longer a girl. Best not to be thought frivolous at such a time.

The kitchen was still dark and cold, though I heard others stirring. Children springing awake with the impatience of the young, mothers shushing and soothing for another five minutes in bed. The stove was temperamental, taking several matches before it lit, and I couldn't find the oats. I set a pan of water to boil, counted the eggs that Amy had left on the table. One each for the children. What was left of the bread was hardening, and I doused the tough crust with drops of water, placed it on a tray in the bottom oven. I'd gathered a posy of snowdrops with some twigs of red-flowering quince, and I arranged them in a glass, set them on the table in the middle of the crockery. It was important to order things nicely, showing we would manage. They'd all look to George and me for guidance, and we mustn't fail them.

At last, I found the oats, protected from mice on a high pantry shelf, and shook them from the tin, stirring in water mixed with milk for the women's porridge. It would be necessary to write some instructions, share the tasks until we could find a new cook. Though I felt guilty for even thinking of replacing Rose, we had a busy house to run and without routine things would easily slide. Had I thanked her enough while she lived? We would never have got the house running without her help. I hoped she knew how much we loved her. Blinking back tears, I watched the children rush in, jostling and scraping chairs to sit by their favourites. Albie almost upset the vase and I leant over to right it, the white and red flowers a sudden image of blood on snow.

'Good morning, Mrs Harris.'

'I made these.' Evie pointed to the eggs that sat in their blue striped cups.

'No, you didn't,' scoffed Albie, 'chickens made them.'

'She means she collected them for me, didn't you, dear?' I planted a kiss on the top of Evie's head and Albie scowled. 'You were very helpful this morning.'

'I want to get the eggs tomorrow.' Albie scuffed his feet against the chair leg.

'Thank you. I will hold you to that,' I replied.

'You'll never get up in time,' said Sophia, his mother. She yawned, covering her mouth half-heartedly, and sat down heavily.

'I will,' said Albie, 'I'll get up before the sun rises and I'll find a hundred eggs.'

'You won't find eggs in the dark. Poor chickens probably won't have laid them by then.' Sophia reached over and took a piece of bread from Albie's plate.

I hovered by the table, burning with bad news. They should eat first. Some of them might spoil their appetites with tears and then breakfast would be wasted. Where to start?

'Where's Rose?' said Albie suddenly, looking around the kitchen with a suspicious expression. 'Why are *you* cooking?'

'Well, there's something I need to . . .' I began, before Sophia interrupted, her mouth half full of the tough bread.

'She's dead. Killed. They found her in the park yesterday.'

'Sophia!' Amy began to shush and comfort the children who had set to wailing. Some of them had not understood and carried on cramming eggs and bread into their mouths as if nothing had happened.

'May I speak with you outside?' I struggled to control myself. Sophia was one of our youngest mothers, barely a child herself when she had Albie, but I wouldn't tolerate such insensitive behaviour. Silly girl dreamt of being an actress, and she was fond of drama of all kinds. Probably dying to spread the news as far as she possibly could.

Sophia rose reluctantly, taking another finger of bread, and met me in the hallway.

'You've upset the children. That is not how I wanted them to hear.'

She gave a sulky shrug. Despite her constant misbehaviour, she disliked reproach. A long silk scarf hung from her neck, and she twisted and flicked at the ends of it.

'I want you to promise that you will not breathe a word outside this house. Rose was a friend to all of us. She doesn't deserve her fate to be a subject for tavern gossip.'

'You can't stop people talking about it.'

'I can ask *you* not to talk about it.' I almost mentioned the keys to frighten her, but that was something I must keep quiet. I couldn't risk her sharing it with the other women. 'May I remind you that you are here as a guest. You and Albie are fed and clothed in return for a small amount of work and the utmost loyalty to our community. It will do none of us good if you spread rumours about Rose. Am I understood?'

Sophia sucked in her top lip like a child and gave a barely perceptible nod. I disliked such threats and reminders; our women had already been poorly treated and should not be made to feel permanently grateful, as they would in some charitable institutions. But she tested my patience too often, and now I would have to deal with the children as well as the kitchens. My visit to Rose to return her locket would have to wait.

'Perhaps you can take the children into the garden to find something for the door wreaths? It will give them something to do.'

'But I've to learn my lines,' she protested. 'There's only an hour or so left this morning and the troupe is holding auditions next week. I need to be ready.'

'What troupe?'

'The actors! They're at the mission hall looking for new stars of the stage.'

Really, she was impossible. Who did she think would look after Albie? I drew myself up to full height and spoke in my sternest voice. 'I'm disappointed that you don't seem to share our burden of mourning, and I will hear no more of this today. Go and cut some thin ends from the blacking curtains in the paint room, for hanging the wreaths. I will take the children to gather leaves in the garden. *You* may not care, but we are watched here. There are plenty of people willing to criticise us for bohemian ways. And those people are more than capable of closing our doors.' Inspectors from the Charity Board were always looking for signs that we were less than respectable. Mr Lavell, newly risen to chief inspector, seemed to visit with increasing regularity since his promotion, always with an excuse – a new law, some irregularity to check. Sometimes he visited to interview new girls. Sometimes he simply claimed to be passing, though there were few other institutions under his jurisdiction anywhere nearby. I would have to find a cook before his next visit or he would make it his business to keep checking.

'I would never call this place *bohemian*.' Threlfall's kid boots fell softly on the rugs, and he startled us both, though Sophia recovered quickly enough to bat her eyelashes at him, rearranging her scarf and patting the plaits of her hair.

'I'm sure you would know more about that than us.' Sometimes I forgot that he held keys to the kitchens, coming and going as he pleased. He occupied the basement rooms that once housed old Dr Everley's clinic, seeing patients from the separate side entrance after we walled up the door and passage that linked it to the house. Still, he was often to be found on the ground floor, looking for treats from Rose or talking someone into taking part in his endless research into women's health. Much good he did my sister. Maddie couldn't bear the sight of him after he took her husband's side and then spoke for Grace. It was all I could do to tolerate him, as I knew I must.

'I lead a *blameless* life, Mrs Harris.' He lifted my hand with a flourish and planted a kiss that pressed slightly too long. Sophia giggled, and he turned to seize her hand too.

'True gentleman,' she said coquettishly. 'I'll wager you enjoy the theatre, Dr Threlfall?' She threw me a sly, sideways look.

'Of course. If a man tires of entertainment, then he must be tired of life itself. Why do you ask?'

'Dr Threlfall doesn't wish to be bothered with your nonsense, Sophia. Run along and do as you were asked.' I stared until she moved, reluctantly, to fetch the scissors. I was not convinced she wouldn't find some excuse to bother him again. His vanity was dangerous, his looks and manners easily turned heads. He was just a student when he spoke in court, a budding young alienist. But he was powerful now, a sought-after psychologist, his reputation enhanced by his performance at the Assizes.

'I'm afraid you will find us in some disarray. We have been struck with terrible news.'

'I have heard. I came to offer my condolences. Rose was a wonderful cook, and a wonderful woman. I was very fond of her.' He pulled a solemn face, drawing his chin down to the layers of lace at his neck. Under his raven-black jacket was a waistcoat of red, scarred with neat black lines of stitching. His breeches and stockings were black sateen and the overall effect was of theatrical mourning, a handsome actor pretending bereavement.

'Thank you for your concern. News certainly travels fast.' How did he know? I had hoped for time to collect myself before the rumours began. 'May I ask how you were informed?'

'My work takes me often to the constabulary. Many criminals would feign to be listed mad these days. How are you faring?'

How could he complain about that? He had practically started the trend and there was one woman, at least, who should be brought to trial for her crimes without the cloak of insanity.

'As well as can be expected.'

'If you'll permit a doctor's licence, you do not look well.' Threlfall placed a hand on my shoulder and warmth from his elegant fingers spread through the fabric of my dress. The diamonds in his ring caught the light and I noticed a new, large cabochon ruby; his business must flourish. 'Your beautiful bloom is quite faded. If I can be of any assistance, you know where you may find me.'

Such easy flattery. 'I'm simply tired. There is much to do.' I should remind him that George was my steadfast, but I couldn't say so in honesty at that moment in time and Threlfall would notice. He would find me out, because worming himself into people's minds was what he did best. 'The women are much affected, and the children of course. I'm sure they'll be grateful for your offers of assistance.'

'Sophia is a strong girl. She will be a great comfort to you.'

'Indeed.' Had she already fallen for his charms? She was so very young, the thought was troubling.

'I'll pause my work for a while, as a sign of respect to the house. You won't want patients trooping through my clinic. But I will call on you, as a friend.'

'I have little time for calls.' Wriggling my shoulder away from the press of his hand, I gestured to take my leave. 'And I must see to the children.'

Threlfall raised a manicured finger to his chin and stood in a gesture of deep thought. 'It's my belief that you work too hard, Mrs Harris. It is not good for women – for anyone, but women especially. Do take care of your health.'

5

Evergreen House

Despite my best efforts, the kitchens ran poorly with little routine. Some of the women were willing to help but few displayed culinary talent. Unsurprisingly, since they were the ones left behind. The Everleys' housekeeper had been instructed to train the 'good' ones, teaching them domestic skills before they were sent into service as maids and cooks. Others, like me, considered too pretty, slipshod, or talkative for such roles, were trained for the streets by Grace.

'Rose taught me,' said Tizzy. 'When the Everleys chose me for service. She showed me how to wash clothes, and scrub steps. I already knew how to cook, because I worked in a tavern, but she showed me how to manage in a kitchen.'

Dear Tizzy could manage anything. The Everleys' former housemaid. She'd been sent from Evergreen by Grace to Lucius' household when his hideous small museum frightened his existing maid away. Tizzy was made of far sterner stuff. Grace, expecting loyalty, couldn't imagine what she was capable of, or she would never have introduced her. Harriet Tisman, always known as Tizzy, had immediately struck up a friendship with Maddie that soon turned to love, and was fearless in standing up to the Everleys and helping my sister escape. She faced beatings, restraint, a courtroom and a madhouse before their case finally won and she was freed. Without her, Maddie might still be living in solitude and terror. Instead they lived together in a commune of artists, visiting Evergreen to teach the women crafts.

'Didn't Rose help some of the others?' asked Maddie.

I shook my head. 'None that are left.' Grace always said I was one of the lucky ones, selected for a life of 'pleasure' to earn my keep. Nausea rose at the memory.

'Then I have even more cause to be grateful to her,' said Maddie, taking Tizzy's hand. 'Without Rose you would never have come to work for Lucius, and we would never have met.'

Embarrassed at such a show of affection, I turned away and began to busy myself with the willow strands and painting equipment, smoothing the brushes and ordering them by size.

'She didn't teach the others,' I said. 'And neither did we. We thought they were better off learning crafts. Taking pride in what they make.' Our baskets sold well at the markets, and we were gaining such a reputation for fine painted wallpaper that it was hard to keep up with demand. None of that helped when baking was needed. We were all quite miserable with soggy pies and loaves that wouldn't rise. Yet I still couldn't face advertising for a replacement cook. It would feel too real, too final.

'Don't set those out today.' Maddie stayed my hand. 'We thought the painters might like to go outside this afternoon. It's a fine day and I have some designs I'd like to practise. It will do them good to walk to the park and paint the leaves as they look in nature.'

It would. And the morning's cold fog had warmed to a beautiful fresh day. Clean air would take their minds off grieving for a while and Maddie, who knew Rose the least well of any of us, would be a cheerful companion. An empty house would also give me the chance to look for Rose's keys.

'Thank you. Let me see the design.' My sister was a skilful artist, able to render flowers and plants as beautifully as they grew in life. Expert, too, at simplifying nature's patterns for the women to copy and print.

Maddie drew a sketchbook from her carpetbag and handed it to Tizzy, who opened it and proudly turned it to face me. Full-length sketches of women in Greek dress caught my breath, reminding me of photographs I'd rather forget. Grace setting up her camera in the garden, by the stone dogs, posing us for gentlemen's collections. We wore diaphanous shifts with no undergarments, the material clinging and stretching across our bare skin. My cheeks burnt at the memory. Another secret that I kept from George because there was something so shameful about standing still while it happened, allowing the images to be taken and shared.

'They are certainly striking.' Surely, Maddie didn't intend for these to be copied?

'Not those! Hardly a subject for wallpaper.' Maddie laughed, tried to retrieve the book, but I held it and began to turn the pages. The sketches were beautiful, rendered in languid, sensual lines. On closer inspection, her women didn't look the slightest bit passive. They wore fierce expressions, eyes burning with power intense enough to ignite a room.

'Amazing, aren't they?' Tizzy beamed as proudly as though she'd wielded the wax and charcoal herself. 'Maddie's been painting them too. Classical figures and depictions of *wronged women*.'

I raised an eyebrow, enquiring, and my sister shuffled awkwardly.

'I can't just draw flowers for wallpaper. I've been trying to take commissions for portraits, but nobody seems to want a female artist.' She tilted her chin; a gesture of defiance learnt from Tizzy.

Good to see her grow bold. 'I wanted to paint something for myself, and I decided, after . . .'

Those skilful evolutionary drawings she'd made for Lucius. The ones that sketched flesh to bones and helped him to imagine his horrible chimera. The 'fish with feet' that he built from the bones of murdered children, that she eventually recognised and worked to expose. As with the garden photographs, it wasn't her fault, but she must feel the shame.

'I decided to learn something new. Figurative painting. There's no shortage of models at Hamblin, and the others have been very kind about them, which made me want to paint more.'

'You're far too modest!' said Tizzy. 'You'll be the best-known female artist in London soon.'

Pink crept across Maddie's cheeks, and I noticed how pretty she had become. A late bloomer, her looks enhanced by happiness.

'Some of these are on canvases already. They're women from Greek myth,' said Maddie, 'all the ones that we're taught to think of as villains and witches. The evil ones. Really they're just cruelly treated. I was reading them again and it gave me the idea to do a series. Wronged women.'

'Who's this?' I ran my finger down the sketch of a beautiful young woman, her expression wide-eyed and distraught, bearing the weight of terrible news. Like the Pre-Raphaelites in Kensington Museum, their beautiful colours and serene maidens at odds with the squalor of the artists' lives. I met them on more than one occasion whilst working for Grace. Maddie was just as skilful, more so, yet if she made lovers of her models and drank away the afternoons she would be vilified not celebrated.

'Pandora.'

Of course. 'How is she wronged? She did open the box and release misery onto the earth.'

'She was set up to fail. Given to humanity as a gift, a curse and a punishment to humans for acquiring fire. Zeus made her curious deliberately, knowing what would happen.'

'Women are always to blame,' muttered Tizzy.

'And she did manage to save hope,' Maddie added.

'I'd like to see the paintings.' They would be beautiful. I was as proud of Maddie as Tizzy was. I hoped she knew.

'You're welcome at Hamblin at any time.'

'Is this the one for the new paper?' A repeating pattern of snowdrops and ivy covered the page. It would look fresh and clean on walls, easy for the women to paint on rolls. 'It's lovely. Thank you.' Curled ivy like the deep engraving on Rose's locket. I should take the necklace to her. Perhaps, if I had the chance to see her laid out, I would be able to look forward.

'You seem restless. It would do you good to join us outside.' Maddie's eyes were wide with concern. She shouldn't be worrying for me. After everything she'd suffered, she deserved a peaceful life.

Tizzy looked anxiously between us. 'Is there something we should know?'

Weariness made every muscle of my face ache as I tried to smile. 'No. Rose is gone, and everything is sad, but there's nothing to fret over. Take the work outside today. I'll settle the children with their lessons and then perhaps I might lie down for a while. I haven't slept well.'

'Do rest, Rebecca, please. The whole house relies on you,' said Maddie.

'And looks to you for guidance,' added Tizzy. She understood how easily a house full of women was given to flights of fancy. It didn't take much to upset.

'I'm just tired. I'll mend.'

Maddie looked as though she didn't believe me. 'Where's

George?' He was her favourite now, though his rough manners had startled her when they first met. He'd risked his life to obtain the proof the courts needed to absolve her and convict Lucius instead, and she would always be grateful. We all would.

'He's gone with Anne, to register the birth.'

'But he was born weeks ago.' Poor thing was starving when she arrived, little Thomas the most underweight child we'd seen.

'They're only just able to venture out.' George took money to bribe the clerk not to alert the authorities about the delay. It was the kind of thing that Mr Lavell would make it his business to investigate, logging every discrepancy in his ledgers as he looked for reasons to bring us under his management. Thomas still looked small enough, but if persuasion was needed it would be easier for a man to make the case, to sign the papers. Even over something so firmly in a woman's sphere as the birth of a child, it was men who arranged everything. It must be hard for George to do so. Taking child after child for their legal recognition. A time when a man would usually be congratulated, praised for his vigour, for fulfilling his duty in society. And all he did was accompany the mother. The fathers were never to be seen.

'I wish them both well. And you, dear Rebecca. I'm always willing to share your burdens.' Maddie threw her arms around me. 'As is George. You know how deeply he loves you, sister.'

'I know.' It made nothing easier to bear.

Announcement of the outing was swiftly followed by a flurry of clothes and shawls, questions over which boots were whose, whether there were enough sketchbooks and small brushes for everyone to share. By the time the house was quiet, and the children were scratching letters onto slates in the kitchen with their tutor, I'd almost decided to rest as I promised. But with the house empty there was no better time to search, and I went straight upstairs to satisfy my curiosity over the missing keys.

Rose's bedroom was at the top of the house. A large attic with an inset window that looked out over the street. I'd rarely been inside. Rose spent most of her time in the kitchen, holding court by the stove, surrounded by people who'd gathered to rest in her warmth. Clothes were strewn across the chair, the dressing table in disarray. Different to the kitchen with its jars and tins in ordered rows. Nothing was organised here. The air smelt of lavender and coal tar soap, a slightly musky sweat. So deeply her that I felt like a trespasser and tried to move noiselessly.

I swept a hand under the mattress, feeling for the keys. Touching something cold I drew back, raised the sheet, found an empty gin bottle that I placed on the floor. I'd throw it away later. If the police, or the Board inspectors, needed to search, then it would be best to keep her character upright. It didn't take much for Mr Lavell to try closing us down; he was constantly prying and arriving unannounced, attempting to catch us at something unholy. He must have received my letter by now and would likely revel in the news.

Nothing under the pillow, below the bed, or hanging from the frame. The chest of drawers was full of linen, things I'd never seen before, sheets and pillowslips, nightgowns, baby clothes – even a shroud – all hemmed, sewn and monogrammed with R and W, as though intended for a trousseau. Rose was a dark horse indeed. There was intention in the way these things were put together, the shroud a sign that she'd pledged her whole life to another once. Had she planned to marry the soldier in the locket? What happened to him? A whole life hidden away, lived in service to others.

Every drawer was opened and swept, the curtains drawn, the

wardrobe checked. Two pairs of felt boots were found empty, a small vase turned upside down. There was nowhere left to search – Rose's huge set of keys was most definitely missing. A long chain, hung with a key for every room in the building. If her assailant knew where she worked, he could rob us whenever he liked. Why did she have to take them with her that night? At the very least we should change the outside locks.

Sitting heavily on the patchwork coverlet, I traced the places where the stitches had pulled, the fabric worn and dulled. I breathed in the scent of her, trying to catch and keep it before it faded. Soon the room would be needed for another cook. Unwilling to break the spell of the afternoon, I walked carefully down the attic stairs. If the girls were still out and the children occupied, I might yet have the chance to rest. Just as I reached the landing, I saw George looking up.

'Did you manage with Thomas?' I asked.

'All done. It costs six shillings now to register without a father.'

'Another tax on misfortune.'

'Everything alright?' George looked up to the attic floor.

'I was checking the gutters. The rain's been gathering by Amy's windows, and I thought they might be blocked.'

A poor excuse. It was hardly the kind of work I would normally bother with.

'Were they blocked?' George gave me a searching look.

'I removed some moss. I think it will stop now. We can check next time it rains.' Another secret wedged between us.

6

St Michael's Mortuary

Two days passed before I found the chance to slip away unnoticed. The afternoon was brightly cold, in the stoic cheerful way of early spring, and I decided to walk to the mortuary. Fixing my bonnet like carriage-horse blinders, I looked straight ahead to avoid eye contact with anyone who wanted to gossip under cover of asking after the household. Hands pushed into a wool muffler, warming the silver locket against my fingers. Cloud puffs hung in a pale grey sky. Tiny buds sprang, surprised, from bare branches.

''Ere's one for you, lady.' A man stepped into my path, waving an illustrated paper and pulling a further stack of them on a little dogcart, overloaded and fit to topple. Gruesome woodcuts appeared below the title – *Feast of Blood* – and I shrank back in horror. Penny dreadfuls. Who on earth would want to read them?

'Don't pretend you won't devour this when you get home.'

A smell of cooked onions emanated from his tweed jacket, which was streaked with grease. No doubt he shared a single room with others. I knew too well the depths that could be reached to make a living and I had no wish to judge, but I would never understand why people saw such tales as entertainment. If their lives ever knew real horror, they would shrink from them too.

'This one's a true crime.' He blocked my way with his cart, and I held the locket in my muffler tightly, shook my head. 'It's about an evil doctor who sets about murdering babies to make into museum pieces. Like nothing you've ever read before. 'Orrible it is.'

Flecks of spittle flew onto my sleeve, and I raised my muffler to push him backwards, taking the chance to dodge around the cart and make my escape. What he described was our story, Lucius Everley's crime, the title page covered with ravens in case the connection was not clear enough.

'You're missing a cracker,' he called after me.

As I hurried away, I glanced over my shoulder to see a crowd already gathering around his cart, men and women of all ages clamouring to hear more. Dark tales of twisted nobility with insatiable urges. It drew them in. Sensational stories to titillate readers. No creativity needed from the writers, a gift to the illustrators. All those missing babies at Evergreen. All those souls without rest. Would we ever be allowed to forget?

No-one answered the sound of the heavy brass knocker as it fell against the mortuary door, and I almost turned away. But without knowing when I would have the chance to return, I determined the afternoon wouldn't be wasted. Rose should be buried with her precious locket, and I'd also like to know how things proceeded so I could start to plan the arrangements for her funeral. She deserved a decent burial. I leant against the door, and, to my surprise, it gave way with a low groan as though it ached from years of use. The lobby was empty, dimly lit from the high windows, and no lamplight or sound suggested anyone was at work. My footsteps echoed around the stone walls as I crossed the floor to the waiting chamber where George had left me before. A voice came from the lying room, high and wavering, like someone singing a hymn. Who was I disturbing?

Before knocking, I coughed to announce my presence. Abruptly the singing stopped, boot leather clattered, and the door was flung open to reveal a stout woman of perhaps fifty years. Eyes opened wide with surprise. She looked me up and down like I had no business in such a place.

'How did you get in here?' she asked, incredulous, as though she suspected me of having arrived on a magical carpet.

'The door was open. I'm sorry for intruding. I wanted to speak with someone.'

'I'll forget my head one of these days,' she muttered to herself, 'could have had anyone in here. Wait there.' She stomped off the way I'd come in, and I heard the sound of a key as she locked us in.

'Who did you want to speak to then? Don't get many social visits. Can't offer you tea I'm afraid, not safe to eat or drink in here.' As she smiled, I caught the glint of a gold tooth and in the low light it gave her a crafty look. Plain clothes, a navy dress with the sleeves rolled to the elbow like a factory girl, overlaid by a dirty yellow apron. A pair of men's work boots stuck out from under her skirts.

'My friend is here, my cook, Rose . . .' I became flustered and she patted my arm with her large hand, waited for me to finish. 'She was murdered. I think she is still here. I came to bring her locket, so she could wear it when . . .' I drew the locket from my muffler and held it up. It turned and twisted on its chain, glinting where I'd cleaned the silver.

'Pretty.' The woman took it, and I was pleased she didn't open it or ask questions. 'Do you want to see her? I'm getting her ready now.'

'Is she . . .'

'She's alright now. I've been here all day. Might do you good to come in.' She offered her hand like a gentleman on business, and I was too surprised to refuse. As she gripped my fingers, I noticed a softness to her skin that I hadn't expected. 'Martha Rawlings. Call me Martha.'

'Mrs Harris. Rebecca,' I replied.

On three sides of the room, rows of candles lined up along the base of the walls, throwing long-legged shadows. Their light was comforting, church-like, and I moved towards the table in the centre, noting the crate of ice beneath.

'Keeps them cool while I work on them,' said Martha. 'Bit much sometimes otherwise.' She wrinkled her nose. 'You can go closer, nothing to hurt you in here.'

Rose's hair had been brushed back and pinned into a neat braid that circled the top of her head. A waxy sheen lay on her skin from the embalming fluid, eyes weighed down with two dark pennies and arms crossed over her chest like a tombstone knight. Relieved to see her at peace, I leant over and kissed her cold forehead.

'Thank you,' I said to Martha, 'for what you've done for her. I'm truly grateful.'

Martha bowed her head, clearly unused to gratitude. Giving last offices was a vital job, and yet she worked alone and unacknowledged. Administering care to the dead, who wouldn't notice, creating her peaceful space with candles and singing soft hymns to them. I would find a way to thank her properly.

'You can put it on.' She handed me the locket. 'It was good of you to bring it. She will know. She's still here, somewhere, until her soul finds rest.' Martha raised her eyes towards the ceiling, as though Rose might be found there, floating over us with her big arms outstretched. 'It's why I keep the lighting soft in here, to calm the souls.'

I unhooked the clasp of the chain, holding it out awkwardly until she lifted Rose's head just high enough for me to slip it under and fasten it around her neck. Her skin felt cold as marble, her features smooth and unlined. Death had taken away the years and cares. A wad of cotton underneath her head was stained in rusted rings and I was glad that Martha had arranged her hair over the wound. As I settled the locket on her chest, my hand nudged against her lace collar. Before I could avert my eyes, I saw the deep red scar that ran across her neck, the wound closed in neat, even stitches. Martha was a skilled needlewoman.

She saw me flinch. 'It would have been quick for her.'

'You'd make a good surgeon. If only such work was not felt to be the preserve of men.'

She gave me a look that showed she thought the same. Women were only allowed to operate on the dead, sometimes the dying. And yet, at one time, all healers were female, the herbalists and midwives, fever nurses and bonesetters.

I drew Rose's collar up over the scar, stepping back from the table.

'They've already done the report. You'll get your copy soon,' said Martha gently, 'and try not to remember her like this.'

7

All Saints Asylum

Mr Varley starts to announce Edward's visit when he brings my breakfast, but I already know. The tray reminds me of the early days of my confinement, before these walls grew up between us. An egg, buttered toast, hot coffee. Linen napkins and a cloth. All the things his patronage once bought me daily. Such luxuries disappeared some time ago, replaced by regulation gruel, and as soon as I see them, I understand.

'He is coming.' I say, tucking a dried flower into the page of my book before closing it and placing it on the floor, taking care to show the title. One of Father's surgical texts, bound in hide and lettered in gilt like the others on the shelf. The feel of their pages is comforting, a reminder that his research is important, that his legacy must be finished. Cooking fat clings to the warden's uniform, mixed with the scent of cheap hair oil and sweat, making me gag as he leans over to place the tray next to it.

'Put it on the table.' Emboldened by the promise of renewed support, I make my voice imperious. He jumped to my bidding once and he'll do it again. Too fat to move quickly, he bends awkwardly to retrieve it, the back of his jacket straining at the seams. Coffee spills into the saucer as he bangs it down. 'When you bring a fresh cup, you can fetch me some other things. Or send the little mouse, I don't care.' I do though – I prefer her humility, the way she skitters from my gaze, flinching at the slightest raised voice. I like to watch her squirm and see the wide-eyed sideways look that shows I'm still powerful. 'I'll need hot water, a towel, some oil for my skin. And a scarf for my head. I don't think Dr Threlfall will be too pleased to see what you have done to my hair.'

Face impassive as he listens, Varley stands with arms clasped behind him, so his enormous stomach sticks out even further. Enough to suppress my appetite, though the miserable porridge has kept my figure trim enough to fit into the smallest of stays. My lavender velvet will be perfect. It still hangs with the others on the rail behind the length of damask in the corner, unworn for months. There seemed little point in dressing up for myself. But I will make the effort today, ensure that Edward realises what he misses. He has always had his share of female attention; the simpering clients and the girls that fall for his outrageous style. He pretends to be unaware, but even in the courtroom there were women in the gallery who vied with one another for a glance in their direction. I'm sure he isn't lonely. But I held his whole attention once and I can do it again. When the mouse comes, I'll make her lace the stays tight enough to stop my breath. Already I feel the warmth of Edward's hands on my waist, the way he will spread his fingertips around to see them meet at the other side. With a little persuasion I can ask for his influence again. Excitement rises at the possibility.

'Will that be all, milady?'

'I do not like your tone, and neither will Dr Threlfall. You should take care. He will certainly be interested to see how I am treated.'

'He doesn't seem terribly interested.' Varley walks over to the door, draws out his heavy chain. 'He's already left,' he calls back over his shoulder. The key twists and clicks in the lock and, as he walks away, he begins to whistle a tune I do not recognise. Something new. Something else I am denied in here. Footsteps echo in the corridor. Trembling with rage at the sound of his flat feet walking to freedom, I sweep the breakfast tray and its contents from the table and send it crashing into the wall. Yolk drips yellow slime-trails down the plaster, shards of china stud the rug. They won't clean up, they never do. Even when the inmates throw slops, they make them live in their own excrement. A lesson never learnt – buckets are overturned daily.

The flower I used to mark my place has fallen from the pages of the book onto the floor. A violet. From the bunch that Threlfall placed on my nightstand the first time he visited me in here. He was so contrite that day. So malleable. It didn't take long to persuade him to make me happy by continuing with Father's research. How far has he developed it? We haven't discussed his findings in almost a year, and I begin to suspect that he hasn't the stomach for it. Does he stay away because he is nervous to tell me? I bend to retrieve the violet and see that the edges of its petals are withered, its vibrant colour faded to grey. How many years before I, too, fade to nothing? When that happens, there will be nothing left for me in this world. By now I should be training Eloise. How old would she be now? Sixteen? Seventeen? The age I was when Father described my face as having '*the cold, sharp beauty of a row of silver knives*'. Delightful. Lucius thought I'd be hurt by the phrase. Poor Lucius. I shouldn't allow myself to think too much of him or I may really lose my mind. I loved him. Too much. But he was weak, like Mother. Why else would she have died whilst giving birth? She wasn't strong enough to bear another after me and Father knew it. He never shed a tear. '*All that matters, Grace, is not to be weak.*' I *will not* be weak.

I imagine Eloise with a face like mine was at seventeen years old. A cold, sharp beauty. Already beginning to show when she was six years old. Too trusting then. Too taken with Lucius' wife and her silly fairytales. Such nonsense. Children need discipline, manners and ambitious social goals, not elves and faeries. When she was taken from me, after the trial, I had barely begun her training. Eloise was obedient, of course, but wholly unaware of her role. My daughter was to be my triumph. Someone I could train to manipulate men in the way that always worked for me. Easy enough to teach a girl the tricks of a coquette. Did she turn out as a femme fatale anyway? Was it in her blood? For her own sake I hope so. This world is cruel to the weak and to weak women especially. I *will not* be weak. I will get myself out of this place one day, but first I must attend to my appearance. If Edward came back once, there is every chance he will return. A sign that he's close to understanding the research and is returning to my side. I know from the breakfast tray that he's thinking of me. He has not forgotten.

8

Evergreen House

M r Lavell pressed together the tips of his gloved fingers and surveyed the line of boxwood and laurel wreaths that hung along the front wall.

'One is usually enough.'

George had said the same thing, always careful not to draw unwanted attention. But all the children wanted to make them and how could I choose when they'd taken such care? Black ribbons waved like cat tails in the breeze. Unlucky.

'Not enough for Rose, Mr Lavell,' I said brightly, 'we were all very fond of her.'

He removed his hat and looked me up and down, slowly, with an air of disapproval.

'It is equally unusual to wear mourning for a domestic servant. Especially one who is . . . loose in her personal ways.'

'Rose was here for a long time. She was like a mother to some of the girls and women we help.' She was like a mother to me, though I didn't say it. My position as proprietress depended on the utmost respectability and I mustn't alert them to my past. If Lavell reminded the Board that a former delinquent ran Evergreen, they'd excuse him to visit more often. He already took issue with George, always questioning about his life on the river, reminding him of his place. As luck would have it, George was already out.

'A strange sort of mother who would abandon her charges to soak herself in gin.' Lavell raised an eyebrow. He might have been handsome if he ever smiled. Instead his face, florid with fine wines, was always straining to see things he could take, his small eyes narrowed by greed. 'I understand that your cook was thoroughly in her cups when she brought this trouble upon herself?'

How tempting to strike a slap across his fleshy face. He barely hid his contempt, and I was certain he knew the effect of his words. I balled my hands into fists, nails digging into my skin as a reminder to be careful. His reputation was grim. In his recent rise to power he'd already claimed an orphanage and a home for retired soldiers, both for what he called 'running soft'. One was now a lucrative laundry business, the other a factory making new rope from picked oakum.

'We keep a temperate house, Mr Lavell. Rose was in the habit of going out to take one drink a week with friends at the Half Moon.' I took licence with the truth. One or two drinks that she paid for, but there were always people to stand her more. 'I'm sure you would agree that a working person needs rest and relaxation with friends. It seems that street talk has rather escalated the circumstances of her tragic death.'

'A working *man* is welcome to such pleasures. I need not remind you that a woman's place is to provide comforts at home.' He rose to his full height as though daring me to contradict. A tall hulk of a man, suit straining with muscles that had long ago succumbed to the temptations of good living. Still, he could throw me to the floor with little effort.

'Indeed. And that is how we train our girls, as you know.' It stuck in my throat to agree to such folly, and I gritted my teeth. 'But I do believe that ours should be a town in which everyone is safe to walk home without fear of violence.'

'That is quite beyond my control. Though the Half Moon is hardly a place for a woman of good reputation, and neither is Briar Walk.'

Why would he mention Briar Walk? My letter said nothing of where she was found. Perhaps the Board had to be informed? I made a mental note to ask George to check with the magistrate.

Mr Lavell coughed into his glove. 'Perhaps I might be invited inside? My domain is a small one, but I can, at least, ensure that standards are kept high in the institutions I inspect.'

'Of course.' I stood aside and he walked through the door with a ginger step, perhaps expecting to find we had kitted out the house as an opium den in the three or four weeks since his last visit. Many times I'd asked him not to refer to us as an institution; we were a house, a home for our girls, a phrase he seemed to dislike as much as he disliked me. Although the house was perfectly warm, he kept his gloves on and drew his cloak around him, as though delinquency might be contagious.

I hovered before closing the door. 'We weren't expecting you until next week.'

'I came to express my condolences.' He ran his gloved hand along the hall table, inspected his fingers for dust marks with a look of contempt.

'We run a decent house, Mr Lavell. The women clean in the mornings and work at their crafts in the afternoons.'

'I'm glad to hear it. And recent events have not upset the order of things? It wouldn't be right for routines to change. Those with a propensity to lapse in their moral duty will always be looking for excuses to do so.'

To whom did we owe a moral duty? And what did he expect? We'd lost a cook, a dear friend – of course the house was upside down. I hesitated a moment too long and he rounded on me, waiting for an answer he could approve.

'As you can see, we have kept order. It's kind of you to come out of your way to offer sympathy.' I appealed to his better nature. 'May I offer you some refreshment?'

'Tea would be welcome.'

I tried to usher him into the front drawing room with its indigo curtains and velvet-covered stools. It was the smartest of the studio rooms, where we finished off the baskets with coloured willow stripes and twisted handles, storing them in high piles in each corner ready for loading onto the market cart. Amy would be managing the tasks inside and I could trust her to hold a conversation with Mr Lavell while I fetched a tray.

He stayed my hand. 'I will accompany you. Since I'm here, I may as well look around and perhaps I can file my report early.'

'As you wish.' I made my tread as heavy as possible on the bare wooden stair boards, hoping the sound would act as a warning to anyone below. Usually such visits were announced, giving us time to dress the children neatly and make sure the women were not quarrelling over some imagined slight. Raised voices travelled clearly up the stairwell. The inspector raised an eyebrow, and I fixed my gaze in front. 'I do hope your colleagues are well. It's been a cold winter and we're not yet past the risk of grippe.'

Mr Lavell paused. 'Does someone ail here?'

Tempting to say we had something contagious, to persuade him to disappear, though it would only mean increased visits of a different kind. 'We're quite well, thank you. We take great care to protect ourselves.'

On the ground floor, he walked behind me, touching every door and trying the handles as though checking to see we were secure. The voices stopped briefly, then resumed even louder. There was nothing for it but to burst in, and hope that whatever was happening would be easily resolved. Sophia shrieked, and well she might. She lay on the floor wearing nothing but a long white petticoat, her hair loose and stuck through with leaves and flowers as though she had escaped from a madhouse through a hedge. Pots and pans were strewn across the worktop and table, whether left out from lunch or arranged to start supper it was difficult to say. Henrietta and Felicia sat on chairs, watching her. Both jumped from their skins as we entered.

'What is the meaning of this behaviour?' Difficult to keep my voice from wavering. This was all we needed.

'It does not *seem* as though routines are being kept,' murmured Mr Lavell. His piggy eyes were fixed on Sophia, a look I recognised and didn't care for in my house. I took off my wrap, covering her shoulders for modesty. Something she seemed to lack.

Felicia and Henrietta began to speak at once.

'Amy asked us to do the food, to help you out.'

'But Sophia was learning her lines.'

'For the play.'

'We were going to start supper as soon as she finished.'

'She was very good.'

Sophia still sat on the floor with her legs drawn up and bare feet showing, toes smudged with dirt. At the last comment she perked up and smiled. 'Was I really? Good?' She looked over to where we stood. 'I'm to be Ophelia, in *Hamlet*.'

'Then get thee to a nunnery,' smirked Mr Lavell.

'You know it!' She jumped up, the shawl slipped to the ground, and I fixed her with what I hoped was a withering stare.

'I will hear no more of this. Go and change into some respectable clothes and spend ten minutes at prayer in your room.'

Sophia pushed past me, and the others began to tidy the

kitchen in silence. I'd heard of *Hamlet*. A Shakespeare play. Though I didn't know the plot and I wondered what kind of character she was supposed to be. Like any mother I was half proud to hear she was good at acting and half horrified at her wilful disobedience. To be dressed in such a manner on the kitchen floor. In front of a gentleman from the Board! And if that costume was what she would be half-wearing on stage, then it was a very good thing I was prohibiting it.

'On second thoughts, I believe I will forgo the tea.' Mr Lavell drew a bone-white handkerchief from his pocket and mopped his brow, though the kitchen was quite cold with both stove and fire unlit. 'It seems to me that you require some help. We have considered it before; now it strikes me that it's high time we appointed someone to manage things here.'

Someone cold and cruel who would dress us all in workhouse clothes and demand we were grateful for every small favour. The children, those incarnations of their mothers' sins, would be beaten and forced to work instead of learning their lessons. Our pretty workshops would be dismissed as vanity and the women would be forced to take in laundry for their bed and board. Exactly as other houses for fallen women were run. But we'd made a special place here, something good from the Everleys' poison. How could I allow the Board to take it from us?

'We are much affected by our loss. Permit us to restore order and, when you attend on your official visit next week, you'll see us much changed.' I took his hand, and he leered down at me.

'Very well. I will just see to the locks at the back, to be certain you're safe, and be on my way. But you are clearly in need of domestic help. It seems your delinquents do not change their habits so much. You leave me no choice but to order a full visit.'

9

Evergreen House

George handed over the envelope as carefully as if it contained live ammunition. Anything that looked official made him uncomfortable – bills, inspection notices, reference requests. He could read perfectly well, I taught him myself, but the threat of authority made him anxious, and he always passed such letters to me. The seal was smudged, the initials impossible to decipher. I took a kitchen knife and slit the paper quickly, cutting the letter inside in my haste.

'From the coroner's office. Looks like an autopsy report.' The inquest had been held in the Half Moon, where Rose had been drinking just moments before the attack. The only place big enough to hold the slab and all the jurors, and probably plenty of uninvited guests as well. I couldn't bear the thought of people treating it as entertainment. She deserved respect.

'Come on then, what does it say?'

I gestured to the door and George closed it, checking the corridor for eavesdroppers first. The paper was large, stiff, folded in several places, and it dropped down like a proclamation.

'Looks detailed.' I began to read from the beautiful copperplate script.

Record of autopsy on body of Rose Caroline Parmiter, aged 56 years, Thursday 15th February 1883 at 12.30 p.m. Two days after death.

The autopsy was performed by Dr Thomas Bellingham, Medical Examiner, assisted by Dr Henry Taylor and witnessed by Frederick Waites and Matthew Anstey.

No women present. Normal for such events, but Rose lived her whole life in the company of women, and it seemed wrong to end it like that. At least she had Martha to take care of her afterwards.

Body that of a female, well nourished and fleshy. 5 feet and 2 inches in height. Stiffness of limbs from rigor mortis. Artificial teeth in upper jaw. Marks of violence on front and back of body. Front: incised wound across lower neck 5 inches in width and 2 and a half inches in depth. Contusions on upper arms, numbering 8. Back: crushing wound to skull, contusion, 6 inches wide, 8 inches high and 3 inches deep. Wound to skull did not expose brain. Lungs normal for age. Heart enlarged. Abdomen: stomach normal, spleen and pancreas normal, kidneys, liver, bladder and intestines signs of disease. Womb small fibroid tumour. Lower bowel empty, upper bowel containing undigested food.

Cause of death: suspected murder by incised wound to neck and subsequent loss of blood.

George took my hand. 'It contains nothing we didn't already know.'

'I didn't know she was ill.' *Signs of disease.* Would her time with us have been short? To know might make things easier to bear.

'Does it matter?'

'Perhaps.' I wanted to know if it was quick, if she would have felt pain and fear or whether the sudden blood loss would have swiftly rendered her unconscious. Threlfall would tell me, would likely relish the task, but I'd rather ask someone sympathetic. Martha, perhaps, with her knowledge of pathology. She was at home in the mortuary and wouldn't flinch at the report.

'It wouldn't change the fact that Rose is gone, that you loved her.'

'Don't you think the way it happened . . . it feels like something bad is returning.' My throat caught on the words, and I felt George release my hand, unable to bear crying of any kind. A weakness, prohibited in his harsh childhood and former work. He was still unused to a life surrounded by women. Still ignorant of the healing power of tears.

'You're upset. You've lost a friend. But these streets are full of thieves and cut-throats. It's a nonsense to think you can link every bad thing to what happened before. They're gone, unable to harm anyone.'

Sounded to me as though he was also attempting to convince himself. 'You're right.' I breathed deeply, tried to refold the report, and found I couldn't make it sit neatly back in the envelope. 'We need to talk about Sophia.' I relayed the scene discovered by myself and Mr Lavell. Was George hiding a smile behind his hand? Our situation was tenuous, our relationship with the Board was strained, and he found her antics amusing. He did not have to bear the contempt on Lavell's face. 'She has asked to attend rehearsals while we are preparing for the wake. I've refused, of course, but I anticipate her usual behaviour of coming to wheedle a different response from you. I would appreciate a firm reply.'

'I don't see the harm. There's plenty of us to help and the church will be packed with Rose's friends. She was fond of Sophia.'

'Everyone is fond of Sophia. It's how she gets away with it. In this instance she must support the house and forget such frivolous concerns. She has responsibilities.'

'If you say so.'

'I do. Having favourites doesn't help us.'

'I don't have favourites.' George gave me a strange look. 'You've been too much concerned with propriety. Don't you remember the conversations we had when we set things up? The ways you wanted to inspire the women. The freedom you wanted for them?'

'Before I realised the power of the Board.' A sudden image of Lavell's expression when he looked at Sophia made me flinch. He was powerful enough to behave as he pleased and I dreaded his influence at Evergreen. The odious man stood much to gain from our misfortune.

'It's late. And I've no wish to argue.' George placed his hand on my shoulder as he left the room, and I missed its warmth as soon as he'd gone. What did he know of the Board or Lavell? He always disappeared when they arrived, running errands to avoid their condescending remarks on his accent, the comments on his past. I knew it must grate on him. But I was left to deal with it all. And Lavell had little more time for a woman than a boatman. We all fell into his category of *unsuitable*. It took effort to earn his trust and respect, and I would not let a flighty girl help to bring down everything I'd worked so hard to achieve.

I took the report to hide from others, realising the letter wouldn't fit back in the envelope because another piece of paper was inside. A small sheet, unlined, folded in half. Inside, the same handwritten script read *Addendum: Suspected murder weapon recovered from blackcurrant bush on Briar Walk.* The rest of the words were streaked with what looked like tea, but I thought I could make out the words *silver* and *bee*. Was I imagining them? Is that what I'd expected, to see the symbol of the House of Everley?

Everything at the house on Arlington Crescent that Lucius had shared with Maddie was covered in thin silver bees, from the dining service and cutlery to the combs and brushes in the bedrooms. Maddie herself had kept a letter opener in the same design that she'd once tried to use in self-defence.

For now, I'd keep the weapon to myself, but I would have to get a clean copy from the coroner and, at some point, I would need to show the report to Lavell. Since he had been so knowledgeable about Briar Walk, perhaps he already knew about the knife; he certainly seemed to realise our keys were missing with all the rattling and trying of doors. As I placed the papers in the bureau drawer, I felt the weight of secrets hanging heavy as a locket round my neck.

10

Holy Trinity Church, Putney Bridge

'There are rather too many women for such an occasion, if I may say so.' The man from Cassells threw a look black enough to match his suit and tails. Removing his top hat, he raked his long fingers through sparse strands of hair that stuck to his pate with cheap oil. His skin was parchment pale, so deeply creased and lined that he might have undertaken funerals since his firm began.

'Too many?' I questioned.

'In my considerable experience, too many women at a funeral will simply end in mayhem. Weeping, wailing.' He leant in towards me. 'Some of these women are very young.'

'The children won't be attending.' Amy had volunteered to look after them all. Though she was close to Rose, she hated church and took any excuse not to go. The children were all dressed in their best clothes, completing their lessons quietly while they waited for the tea and cakes that were promised after the funeral.

'I should think not.' He wrinkled his nose, and I resisted the urge to defend them. It wouldn't help any more than it helped with Lavell. They were good children, raised well. Everyone expected their start in life to turn them into miniature demons, but they'd known love and kindness at Evergreen and it was all they needed.

'The young women outside? Some of them are dressed as if they plan to join the procession.'

'They will. Rose was our cook and our friend, and they'll wish to pay their respects.' We couldn't afford mourning dress for everyone, and I would not have him slighting the girls for their clothes. There'd be plenty of Rose's associates from the Half Moon for him to look down his nose at later.

'I'm afraid young women are not to be recommended. Too much imagination for such occasions. Any excuse to push things to a more dramatic turn.'

This snobbery was all my fault. I should have listened to George and given Rose a standard servant's send-off, but I wanted to show what she meant to us and, somehow, try to mitigate the horror of her death. Cassells were a middle-class funeral directors and I wanted the procession done properly. I wanted people to see us going past and take off their hats, to show her the respect she deserved on the way to her final resting place. It wasn't much to ask. 'These women are practically family for the deceased, and they will *all* be attending.'

'But *not* family?'

'As far as I'm aware Rose had no family. None that she would have wanted to invite. And I've been tasked with carrying out her wishes.'

'I see.' Finally reminded that I was responsible for the payment of his not inconsiderable fee, the director replaced his hat, turned to leave, and was almost knocked down by Sophia. The girl had appalling timing.

'May I be excused, Mrs Harris?'

'Are you quite well?'

The director hung by until I bid him check on the cart, which was watched by the sad-looking mutes who would lead our procession. We should be leaving shortly. It was a good twenty-minute walk to the church at normal pace, heavy going with a loaded funeral cart and motley mourners.

'I am more than well! I'm to be in the play. *Hamlet*.' Sophia hopped from one foot to the other, her shawl slipping down her shoulders and her dress completely unsuitable for the day.

'What does that have to do with anything? This is an important day for the house, Sophia.' A chance to show that we could do things well, respectably. She was always letting herself and others down.

'It's today. The casting and the costumes. I'm to make some silk flowers for Ophelia to throw when she says the lines about remembrance, and it's funny because Rose helped me learn the lines and I know she wouldn't mind . . .'

'That is enough.' I made my voice as icy as I could manage, and Sophia stopped chattering. 'Go and put on your dark wool dress and be back down here in less than five minutes. This isn't a circus. It's Rose's funeral, and we are all needed for one another.'

'But it's today.' Sophia whirled round to appeal to George, who had just come over to call a ten-minute warning.

I replied before he could speak. 'Today, of all days, you can think of something other than yourself. Go and change.'

My hands shook as I pulled on my gloves, and I had to ask George to fasten the black ribbons on my bonnet. I couldn't meet his eye. He tied them awkwardly and they sat on my chin in a clump.

'I know you're sad for Rose,' he said, 'but Sophia is young, she's excited.'

Was I not still young? I didn't feel it. 'She's pretty and can twist you around her finger.' I should not speak so, but sometimes the strain of holding everyone up made me sharp.

64

'No. There's only one woman who could ever do that.' George's voice sounded sad, as though he no longer meant it. Before I could reply, the bearers lifted the pall, and we were bidden to walk in silence.

'Two women. Mary, the holy Virgin, pure and good, willing to sacrifice and to be made an instrument of God so that He could bring us his son to show us the light. Or Eve, the temptress, seduced by the Devil himself, swayed by the way of flesh and sinfulness, who failed to obey the rules of law and order, who caused the fall of man. Eve, who expelled us all from Paradise. There is choice in life, choice in death. Rose Caroline Parmiter chose to devote her life to caring for women who chose the way of Eve.'

The reverend slammed his hands at the edges of the pulpit, shaking the stand. It rested on a giant gold eagle, its outstretched wings and fierce beaked face in permanent hunt. Their expressions matched. The congregation was hunted. I gripped the hymnal tightly and looked straight ahead. If I caught the eye of Maddie or Tizzy my anger would get the better of itself, and what good what that do any of us?

'As we contemplate the last and final resting place of Rose Caroline Parmiter, we must see her life as a beacon to guide us, and we must ask ourselves, what *is* a woman's place?' Appealing to the congregation, his gaze travelled the pews. The front row was empty, no-one willing to get close enough for accusation. Our group had taken the next two rows, all women except for George and his friend Albert, who was as fond of Rose as anyone who knew her. All looked down at their laps. We were used to the words, had come to expect them, but I never attended a sermon without wondering where the compassion went. When did fire and brimstone replace the lamb? As Rose always said, a little kindness goes a very long way. Most of our girls could have done with more of it than they found in life.

'What *is* a woman's place?' he repeated, the gold threads and silver beading shining from his surplice in the candlelight. Jewels glinted in the rings he wore on every finger. A peacock showiness he would likely despise in girls who wanted pretty shields against the dreariness of everyday life.

'It is in the home. Caring for family. Caring for the household. Creating a peaceful sanctuary to which men will want to return.'

And if they didn't want to, what then? If a woman did everything she was asked and her husband still chose to drink all day, or strike her children or lie with other women, was that to be her fault too? For not creating a warm enough home? It had taken months to persuade Amy she was not to blame for her husband's fists, and I was glad she wasn't there to hear the peacock spouting such nonsense.

'In the home, away from bad influence and those who would tempt them like snakes bearing fruit. Cultivating the softer graces. Becoming dutiful and submissive, modest in dress and behaviour.'

Pausing for effect, he narrowed his eyes towards the back, where a group of what I assumed to be Rose's tavern friends were muttering to one another. It was a cold church; they were older and thinly dressed in what might pass as respectable. No doubt they were passing tots of liquor to keep the freezing draughts at bay. For the third time in as many days I found myself craving the taste, and I conjured the sudden image of a serpent with a bottle of brandy curled in its outstretched tail. Grace had preferred us all to drink when she ran Evergreen because it kept us docile. It took time to get the liking for it out of my system.

'As our dear departed Rose knew, meekness, cultivated on Christian principles, is the proper consummation and highest finishing of female excellence.' He glared, singling me out for his words as though he read my thoughts. 'Without it, women have no course but to bring down sin upon themselves and the others in their community.'

It was a long sermon, detailed in its advice, and by the time we followed the glittering reverend from his stand the rain had set in. Choir boys strained on tiptoe to cover him with a vast black umbrella. He studiously ignored them, lifting his heavy robes away from the mud to reveal shiny boots of black leather, embellished with tooling and rows of buttons like the ones Grace used to have sent from Italy. When we reached the churchyard, the curate took the umbrella, standing solemnly by the reverend and holding it high to protect their clothes. Wet grass slipped against the smooth soles of my best boots as we gathered around the grave. As I righted myself, I caught Sophia's eye and received a sullen scowl in return, though it looked as though she'd been crying. Hopefully for Rose and not her missed appointment.

Rain fell into the open ground, spattering mud and making it difficult for the bearers to hold their footing as they lowered the heavy coffin on its ropes. We'd chosen a stout design, lead-lined to protect her from theft and rodents. As she'd protected us. Rose never liked the girls to quarrel, ruling that no-one should sleep on an argument. Sometimes she'd sit up for hours to listen to their tales of slights and misdemeanours, urging them to see the other side, often making them laugh in the process. She was right, it *was* important that we behaved with respect and understood one another's stories. Small irritations would fester into full-scale war if we let them. Keeping the peace would become another of my duties, and I already knew I would find it difficult.

I leant over to throw in my flower, a white narcissus like the others. Rose's favourites were roses, of course, especially yellow, impossible to find at this time of year. Even these had cost a small fortune, but it was important for us all to make the gesture. We'd already been told there were too many of us to throw earth, and the wet weather had clumped the ground into clods that would sound like rocks on the lid. Rain poured onto the casket, running down the sides of the open grave, foretelling more deaths within a year. George would dismiss such thoughts as superstition, but I knew how many of the old tales rang true. He took my hand in his own, rough and warm despite the weather and his lack of gloves, and I leant against him for a moment, his body solid as rock. Perhaps I should tell him about the knife with its silver bee, my wild suspicion that Rose was another victim of the Everleys. It would send me half mad to keep such a thing to myself. If I voiced my fear, would it spread like wildfire? Could speaking it aloud make it true? Mournful bells rang a warning from the steeple as though tolling for the death of happiness itself.

11

All Saints Asylum

Threlfall leaves the door open, just like the mouse does when she comes to fetch my bucket. As though he also fears attack. Surely he hasn't forgotten what we were to each other? He may be free – no doubt he has kissed a dozen women since we last made love – but he is bound to me in ways we both know cannot be undone. Then why does he look so nervous?

'I bring news.' Reaching into his jacket pocket, he removes an envelope, opened at the top, a sheet of paper poking through.

'Please close the door.' As he obliges, I move to sit on the bed, motion for him to take the chair. At least I am dressed to receive surprise visitors. My instincts were correct: he is returning to me, and I am eager to know why. 'Mr Varley said you were here last week. Yet you did not visit.' I tilt my head, widen my eyes.

'Forgive me. I have kept this news for a while because I did not know how to deliver it without breaking your heart.' A lock of hair falls across his brow, his expression is sincere. Does he imagine me to be in love with him? I bite my lip to stifle a laugh at the very thought. I never loved him like I loved my brother. It simply made me feel beautiful to have a man that others wanted. Later I liked the power of his influence, and I need it still, more than ever now. I feel under the mattress, reassured to touch cold silver. Something wicked whispers that I should give him the knife, ask him to do my bidding, Father's bidding. I uncurl my fingers and release it, leave it hidden, wait for him to speak. He is nowhere near ready to listen to my plans.

'The news concerns Daniel. And Edmond.'

'What of them?' I'm made to write to my sons twice a year, receiving stilted lines in return, in childish letters written so roughly that they make holes in the paper. Edmond and Daniel reside in a private nursing home, paid for from the sale of our house because the criminally mad may not own property and there is no-one else to care for them. Twins. Damaged at birth. Both weak-minded and Daniel also physically limited because of the cruelty of his brother. Still, they'll be enjoying a better life than mine in here. They were left enough money to cover the necessary bribes, to ensure they eat well and sleep in soft beds with padded restraints instead of chains. I still write to Eloise, too, through her new family, receiving brief replies that could either indicate that my wish to raise her cold and heartless has worked, or she is deeply unhappy and ill-treated. Either way, it is hard for me to care, though I would like to know how she looks, whether she has taken my advice and kept her figure, made the most of her cold, sharp beauty.

'There's no easy way to say this, so forgive me if I speak bluntly. In any case you are a doctor's daughter and I know you will not flinch.' He has remembered that much, at least. 'I'm afraid they passed away. Both of them.'

Dead. Whatever our relationship, a parent should never outlive their children. My first thought is to tell Lucius, another reminder that he is gone. As for the boys, they were always weak. Unloved. Unwanted in society. 'How did it happen?' I ask, disliking the tremulous note in my voice.

'It seems that Edmond attacked his brother. They were left alone for just a moment while the nurse changed their beds, which were soiled, and he . . .' Threlfall pauses, takes my hand. I press it lightly. 'The matron said that he truly seemed to want to hurt Daniel. I don't want to distress you . . .'

How little Threlfall knows me! I take his other hand, an excuse to draw him further towards me. 'Please – a mother should not be left to imagine.'

'The staff have seen other episodes pass between them over the years, though they explained that Edmond seemed to have been much calmer recently, which is why the nurse felt it safe to leave them for a moment. They can't be completely sure, but they believe that Edmond strangled him. With such fervour that his own heart failed. When the nurse returned, she found them lying together, Edmond's arm around his brother's throat. I am very sorry, Grace, for your loss.'

Poor Daniel. Leaving the world as he entered it. At birth the cord was wrapped around his neck, starving his oxygen. Lucius delivered them himself and there was nothing to be done. Edmond determined to survive at all costs, leaving Daniel without breath, a damaged brain. How can I weep for them? Daniel's was half a life, shut away in his condition, and Edmond made everyone nervous, myself included, because we always knew he was capable of violence. A murderer. He was in good company with our family. I feel no sadness at their death, but I do recognise a chance to seize the moment. I stare at the blank wall until tears well in my eyes, then turn to Threlfall, pleading, release his hands and wait for him to fold me in his arms. Gently I shake my shoulders, as though holding back unbearable grief, and smile to myself as he bends his head over mine, as I feel the familiar touch of his hair on the nape of my neck. What news to bring us together again.

71

There will be much to say, much to use to my advantage.

We stay entwined until the light from the high window grows grey and shadows slant across the floor. I pull myself away. 'I have kept you long enough. I know you are too busy for me now and I don't wish to be a burden, despite what we were once.'

Threlfall sighs deeply. 'I have neglected you, dear Grace. And I am truly sorry.'

Raising my head, I take care to show the effort it takes to pull my tear-stained cheeks into a smile. 'I'm sorry too, Edward. I had hoped that together we might complete Father's research.'

'We have plenty of time to do that.'

'Do we? Since you left, they have not remembered me. I am treated the same as the others.' I cast down my eyes. 'I may not have long.'

'I will visit each week and make it my business to see that Varley treats you well.'

'And Father's research?'

He hesitates. As I suspected, he doesn't have the stomach. 'You are right, Grace. Dr Everley's papers must be finished. We'll start as soon as I can find an assistant.'

12

Evergreen House

When our party returned to the house, we were wet through. Rose's friends and our girls all threw off their shawls and coats in a steaming jumble in the hallway, and I hadn't the heart to admonish them. We could sort out the mess later. For now, we needed warmth and cheer. Amy had thoughtfully lit fires in the downstairs rooms and for once the kitchen was welcoming. It seemed fitting to crowd inside.

'Bessie, thank you for coming.' I clasped the hand of the Half Moon's formidable landlady, her faded beauty flattered by her black silk and jet beads. She wore a black net veil that she lifted to dab at her eyes with a black kerchief.

'Did my heart good to see such a turn-out for her.' Bessie removed her leather gloves and began to rummage through her many pockets, finally uncovering a brandy bottle which she waved cheerily. 'Want me to put this in a cup?'

'We don't have liquor in this house, I'm afraid,' I replied.

'No bother,' she replied, pushing the bottle into the arm of her coat before lifting it up to take a not-so-secret swig. 'For my nerves,' she said sweetly.

'You'll miss her.'

'I will that. She's been coming in for as long as I've had the pub and lord knows how many years that is, I've lost count. Once a week, regular as clockwork, never any bother. She was a friend to everyone.'

Something the magistrate asked came back to me. 'Did she have any special friends?'

Bessie gave me a saucy look. 'A *gentleman* friend?' She laughed so hard she seemed to shake, took another swig. 'Not Rose. Too clever for that sort of bother.'

I'd already guessed the answer. If Rose ever had a great love, it was years before.

Bessie craned her neck to look around the kitchen as though searching for someone. 'She didn't have a relative or someone come to visit recently?'

Rose never had visitors. I shook my head. 'Why?'

'She was talking to a youngster I'd never seen before, all skin and bone. Looked like they might have been arguing. Thought it could have been a relative.'

Before I had a chance to ask questions, Albie came over with a plate of cakes and Bessie hid her bottle in her pocket, bending down to make a fuss of him before he dragged her off to see the rest of the spread that he'd helped to make. Circling with the plate, I tried to speak to everyone. Rose's friends were enjoying a change of scene, and it was generally so busy that I didn't notice Threlfall for some time. Maddie clearly had. I only spotted him because I wondered who she was eyeing so warily. She and Tizzy muttered together, bonnets in hand as though planning a swift departure. When I followed their gaze, I found him holding court in the middle of a group of women, Sophia and Felicia hanging on his every word. The first no doubt bad-mouthing me for standing between her and her dreams.

'He has no right to be here, as though he was Rose's friend.'

Maddie's eyes flashed. 'He didn't even come to the service.'

'I asked him not to, Maddie, because I didn't want you upset. I wasn't aware he was going to join us this afternoon. But it is his usual day. I can't stop him.'

'Does he always spend time in the kitchens?'

I thought for a moment. 'Actually, yes. Rose seemed to find him amusing and, like any young man, he was fond of her cooking.' It annoyed me, too, when I saw them together, laughing over one of his ridiculous jokes, his dainty boots propped up on a chair as he polished off a plate of scones or a thick ham sandwich. She made fun of him, and he seemed to enjoy it. He seemed to care for her. I had not yet found time to show him the autopsy report; perhaps it would be helpful for us both to know the truth about her condition. Or perhaps I should ask Martha, who seemed both knowledgeable and kind.

'A lapse in her usual good judgement.'

'Rose had time for everyone.' Always said everyone had a story, never felt it her place to judge. It made her perfect for Evergreen but left her vulnerable, and was it possible that her sweet nature had led to an untimely end? Had she known the person who attacked her, realising too late that they intended harm? 'Besides, he works here. You know we can't prohibit him, even if we wanted to. He's allowed to be here by law.'

'The Everleys' lapdog.' Maddie's hands shook against the teacup. 'You know he's not to be trusted.' Was she suggesting he'd had something to do with Rose's death? 'He's an alienist. He'll say anything he's paid to say.'

'I know. But, while Grace remains at All Saints, he has her share in the house. The basement rooms are entirely his and she has gifted him the right to remain until her release.'

'She'll never be released.' Tizzy took the cup from Maddie,

placed it gently on the table and then held her hands until they calmed.

'Tizzy's right, it's unlikely.'

'It's where her father worked.' Maddie spoke slowly, as though remembering something from long ago. 'The basement at Evergreen, I read about it in his research papers. They were all in Lucius' library. Horrible papers. Pain research. He used to administer pain to dogs, measuring their response, and he started to do it to humans too. Under the guise of medical research.'

'Shhh,' soothed Tizzy, 'it does you no good to dredge all this up.'

Albie ran over with a handful of biscuits that he pushed at Maddie and Tizzy. 'I made these,' he said proudly.

'Thank you, little man.' I smiled at the crumbs smeared across his face and waistcoat. How had he managed to get such a dirty face? His mother still flirted with Threlfall on the other side of the table. What would happen to Albie if she got her wish and left us? That would be something she hadn't considered at all.

'*I* made them too.' Evie ran up, dragging Amy by the hand. 'Do you like them?'

'They're delicious,' I said. 'Rose would be proud of you both.'

'She's in heaven.' Evie pushed another biscuit into her mouth.

'Can she see us?' asked Albie. 'Now, through the roof, or only when we're in the garden?'

'I expect she can see us all the time.' It had seemed that way when she was here too. She always knew what was going on, usually before I did.

'I'm so sorry about these two.' Amy took their hands. 'You know not to interrupt when people are talking.'

'Women are always talking,' said Albie, earning a thump from Evie. Where had he got that from in this house?

'Who told you that, Albie?'

Albie screwed up his face as though trying to remember. 'He came the other day.'

'Mr Lavell? The inspector?'

Albie nodded, dragging his sleeve across his mouth as Amy led him away. When did Lavell find the time to talk to the children? I did not like the idea that he visited when I was out. Making such foolish comments. He shouldn't be with the children at all. The conditions of the Board certainly didn't allow him to wander all over the house. I would have to keep a closer eye on him.

'He's carrying on what that man started. Old Dr Everley,' said Maddie, and Tizzy shuddered. My head full of inspectors, it took me a moment to realise she was still talking about Threlfall. 'Portraits of him hanging everywhere, as though he was a great man of science. He tortured people. It was the reason he set up this house in the first place. Not to help women but to hurt them. Women no-one else wanted. Women whose families rejected them or who were too scared to tell them their stories. He knew he'd get away with it.'

'Well, the Everleys didn't get away with it, in the end, did they?' I'd had enough of this conversation. Already melancholy and exhausted from the day, if I thought too much about our own family I would despair.

'*He* did. And his papers were never discredited.' Maddie rounded on me. 'Do you *know* what Threlfall is doing in those rooms? Have you ever checked?'

Such vehemence was unnerving. 'Some of the girls visit him. The ones that want to talk about themselves, about what happened to them. Julia said it did her some good.' Did the children visit him too? It may not be safe to do so. I would speak to Amy, warn them away.

Maddie looked doubtful. 'Don't take your eyes off him. Don't trust him, Rebecca. You don't know him.'

Was Threlfall still acting on the Everleys' behalf? And if he was, why Rose? What could that hope to achieve for him? She was the only one here on his side.

Threlfall finished his tea and strode towards us as though his ears burnt with our words. Sophia giggled with Felicia behind his back, copying his upright walk, hands clasped importantly behind her back. Good. She cared more for making her friend laugh than impressing him, so at least she wasn't in thrall to the man. Maddie stiffened, and Tizzy began to gather their things, making ready to leave.

'I trust the service went well this afternoon?' Threlfall gave a fussy little bow of greeting and I inclined my head in return, watching Sophia laugh at the pair of us.

'Thank you. Reverend Stone gave his usual strong address.' That was true enough. I'd barely heard him give a sermon where the Fall wasn't mentioned and began to suspect he spoke entirely for the benefit of our house.

'He's an excellent orator,' Threlfall nodded sagely. 'You look well, Mrs Everley. I do hope you're not leaving on my account.'

Maddie would not like being addressed by her married name, nor would she care to explain that she'd taken back our maiden name, Brewster. The comment hung in the air.

'Is that your sketchbook? May I see? I was always very taken with your artistic skills.'

The sheer nerve of him! Striding about as though he was untouchable. Maddie had told me of the excruciating interviews she was made to have with him, her husband using them as evidence against her, questioning her state of mind, convincing the court of her guilt in murdering her own child. She'd been terrified to speak, in case one wrong word was used against her. I went to take the book, intending to open it at the flower designs, but he intercepted and began to leaf through the pages, propping it open on the table.

'Beautiful.' He ran his elegant finger across the drawing of Pandora. Soft hands with neatly groomed nails, French lace at his cuff, every inch the man of luxury and culture. 'These are Greek in design. Sketches for painting I imagine? Are you planning a series? Perhaps for the walls of this house?'

'She's begun to paint them already and they're quite brilliant. Wronged women from myth and legend.' Tizzy spoke with a dangerous mix of defiance and pride. Maddie gave a little shake of her head.

'Indeed? Let me guess.' Threlfall affected an air of intrigue as he examined Maddie's work. 'This must be Helen? Such a beautiful face. A self-portrait perhaps.' He smiled, delighted by his own charm. 'But wronged? She started the War of Troy!'

'Did she fire the first arrow?' Tizzy stepped in. 'Or was she kidnapped and treated like stolen property in a fight between two silly vain men? One who took what he wanted and the other who'd rather kill a whole army than see his property tainted by another?'

'Interesting. And this one?'

Tizzy nudged Maddie, clearly enjoying the debate. She should be careful. There were plenty of men and scholars who wouldn't listen with interest in the same way as Threlfall. Who knew his connections these days? His patients came from everywhere, all rungs of society. If he mentioned this to the wrong person it could be dangerous for Maddie, especially with her history. Their commune of artists was already barely tolerated. It wouldn't take much to have it closed for good. Lavell would certainly take against it and he seemed to get more powerful by the day; who knew where his influence might reach?

'Clytemnestra,' Maddie whispered.

'Come now. A jealous wife who killed her husband? Poor Agamemnon. And he a war hero too.'

Tizzy nudged Maddie again. Perhaps she'd forgotten this one. I had certainly never heard of her.

'Agamemnon sacrificed their daughter. Killed her, to appease the goddess Artemis. After which he brought his mistress back to live in his marital home. Clytemnestra's response was wrong. But she was wronged originally, yes.' Maddie sighed.

'And was murdered in turn by her own children. Am I right?' Threlfall looked up, pleased with his knowledge, and Maddie nodded reluctantly. 'Oh come, is this Medusa? What a wonderful drawing.'

'Medusa was the most wronged!' cried Tizzy. 'She was violently taken by Poseidon in Athena's temple, yet blamed by the goddess and transformed to this.'

'Is that true?' Threlfall stroked his chin. 'If I ever knew that, I had certainly forgotten. You must show these. Why not enter them for the Summer Exhibition? It's open now.'

'I don't think so.' Maddie took the book and folded her arms across it.

'If the paintings are anything like as skilled as your sketches, then you stand a good chance. You deserve it.'

As close to an apology as she would ever receive, and it was all I could do not to strike him. I determined to visit the mews, to see the paintings for myself. But I should warn Maddie that if she did decide to show them, she should do so under a male name. Such subjects would be torn apart if it was suspected they were delivered by a woman.

13

Cut-Throat Lane, Putney Embankment

Though I found it difficult to believe my sister's theories of Threlfall, they worried me enough to keep my distance. If I showed him the autopsy report and drew him into my confidence, it would be awkward to explain to Maddie. She was already shaken by Rose's death, a reminder of her tragic past, and I didn't want my actions to contribute to the way she felt. Instead, I took the report to the mortuary in the burial ground, hoping to find Martha.

'Hardly the place for a decent woman to pay afternoon visits.' The same magistrate who'd prevented me from seeing Rose's body peered out from a small, shuttered window in the mortuary door. His presence indicated another unnatural death – why else would he be here? Murders were common enough, as I kept repeating to reassure myself that recent events had no connection with the Everleys.

'I was hoping to find Martha Rawlings here.'

'You were here before.'

'Yes. With Mr Harris, Rose was our cook.'

'Mrs Rawlings won't know any more than you've already been told.'

'I understand that.' Through rising irritation, I tried to make my voice pleasant. 'I have something I'd like to give her. For the care she administered to Rose.' Partly true. The basket I carried was a gift from our workshop. I didn't mention the autopsy report secreted in my pocket.

'I will make sure she receives it.'

'That is most kind. But I would rather give thanks in person.'

Sighing deeply, as though I bothered his soul, the magistrate slammed back the window shutter and I stood in front of the closed door, unsure whether he would return. I had almost decided to leave when I heard the sound of the bolt drawing back. He thrust at me a small card with the words *Martha Rawlings, Body Preparation and Funeral Services* on the front, a line drawing of a lily above. Turning it over I read *c/o The Stonemason's Arms, Havelock Street, Putney Embankment.*

Taking it back with a look that implied I'd be unable to remember the address, he disappeared into the mortuary gloom and I walked to the park gates, turning left towards the embankment. A thin drizzle of rain quickly misted the air, collecting in branches and dropping against the brim of my bonnet until the mourning ribbons were soaked. The weather suited my mood. I wasn't sure what I hoped to find, but I'd felt a connection with Martha; her solid frame and quiet dignity reminded me of Rose, and I walked to see her because I needed some kind of comfort. By the time I reached the Stonemason's it was past midday and its snug was half filled with drinkers. Their conversation seemed to lull as I entered and I raised my head, clutched the basket more tightly, took a moment to consider my words.

'I am told I may be able to find Martha Rawlings here.'

Wiping a wet hand on his filthy apron, the barkeeper held my gaze for a moment too long to be comfortable, then jerked his head towards a door on the right.

'Through there?'

Heavy pouches of florid skin hung from his jowls and the whites of his eyes were dandelion yellow. He looked as though he tasted every drink he poured and then took one himself for good measure. Nodding, he added, 'You might not want to see her though,' before turning to collect the tankards that his potboy had piled on the bar top. The boy grinned, revealing a row of teeth as brown as brick dust.

What was she doing? I'd been in enough public houses as rough as this one and plenty worse. It would take a lot to shock me, though I dressed more respectably these days. Shaking the drips from my basket, I pushed at the door and was inside the room before I realised what was happening. A sharp smell filled my throat, and I placed a hand across my mouth and nose to mask it. The body of an old man lay stretched over three tables pushed together, his head lolling back to show shrunken gums and a large, pale tongue. Running from his neck to his abdomen was a wide slit and his innards bulged up and over the sides of the open flesh. The cloth below had slipped and I could clearly see his shrivelled genitalia, the sight of which was somehow worse than the butcher's mess above.

A man in a frock coat stood by the makeshift autopsy slab, bloodied hands holding a long scalpel knife.

'Women are not permitted to watch.' An incredulous tone to his voice.

Chairs were seated in a ring around the body, a motley collection of men. Some dressed in the black coats and white collars of university students, some well-dressed and upright, observing keenly. Others were clearly from the Stonemason's general clientele, there for free entertainment and taking ghoulish pleasure in the sight. One leant against the wall, fast asleep. Finally, I saw Martha, standing at the back by the other door, a look of astonishment on her face.

'I'm sorry, I . . .' I floundered as Martha shook her head quickly, perhaps warning me not to draw attention to her presence. She jerked her head towards the front door and I backed through the entrance behind me, through the noisy main bar and onto the street, relieved to be out.

Martha was already on the pavement. 'I take it you're looking for me.' She didn't looked pleased.

'The address was on your card at the mortuary.'

'I live nearby. It suits me to hold business away from my home. Not everyone understands what I do.'

Of course she would need to protect herself. Women always must. But there were people who wouldn't want to understand why a woman would work in her field, who would make her life hard if they could.

'I do,' I said, 'and I wanted to thank you properly for what you did for Rose.' I held out the damp basket. 'The women make these in the workshop. I asked them to make a special one for you.' It was pretty, with strands of three colours woven into the willow and felted flowers tied to the handles. I felt suddenly silly. Why would Martha want this to go with her serge uniform and men's boots?

'It's lovely,' she replied. 'And you are wet. Would you like to come and dry yourself?'

'I couldn't go back in there.'

She raised an eyebrow. 'I should think not. They barely tolerate me, and I could do the work faster and more neatly than any of them. Come on.'

Gripping the basket in one hand, a leather bag in the other, she steered me along the street away from the tavern, eyes fixed straight ahead as though she expected to see no-one she wished to meet and would not pass the time of day if she did. The streets by the embankment were black with soot from the trains and the soap factory, pavements running with filthy water. A group of dirt-streaked children jumped in the stream, shrieking obscenities at one another as the foul liquid splashed up. I curbed my instinct to admonish them. They couldn't help the lives they led. It made me think again of how important it was to care for our infants at Evergreen, to give them hope. There were children not much older sewing leather for shoes on the cramped stools of a sweating den. A ripe smell of urine from the tanning emanated through its open doors as we passed.

Martha's home was at the back of a ground-floor terrace. One room, with nothing to screen the bed. Freshly swept and laid, the small grate held a single pot that she took to fill from the handpump in the yard before setting it on a trivet while she took a match to the kindling. By the single chair, a half-plank was nailed to the wall, a makeshift table hung over with a short cloth. I imagined her sitting there by candlelight, carefully cleaning the tools of her trade before placing them neatly in her bag. Nothing feminine here, no sewing or craft, no samplers, not even a quilt on the rough wool blanket that covered the bed. On the shelf sat a single plate and cup, confirming she lived alone, though I already knew. I was drawn to her air of self-sufficiency. Tempted by such a life myself. The monastic simplicity of Martha's room reminded me of where George had lived when I escaped from Evergreen to join him. A similar air of pride in its cleanliness and frugal furnishing. Martha placed the basket on her shelf and I was pleased to see her smile as she twisted it to show the flowers. Strong women may still like fancy; perhaps we could support one another. It would do her some good to spend time with our community, just as her strength would help me.

'You didn't come all this way without a reason.' Martha set down a mug of strong tea.

'I hoped you could help me.' I drew the autopsy report from my pocket.

'That's all in order, I wrote it out myself.'

'Signs of disease,' I said. 'What signs?'

Martha looked to the floor and breathed deeply before replying. 'You want comfort, I can see that, and I'm not good at such things. If you want reassurance that her time would have been short, I can't give you that because I don't know and I won't pretend. It's likely she had stomach ulcers or something similar that may or may not have shortened her life.'

Tears sprang to my eyes and I willed myself not to cry in front of her.

'It wouldn't help,' she said more softly. 'What happened to your friend was terrible and only time will heal your thoughts of her.'

Perhaps. We had already learnt to live with horror. I was reminded that I still needed to know about the knife, whether it was an Everley blade, and I fished out the addendum from the bottom of the envelope.

'Did you write this up, too?'

Martha nodded, took the slip and began to read, '"Curved silver knife, chased thin blade, well worn on both sides. Stained with blood of various ages. Handle silver, decorated with thin silver bee."'

Like everything else at Arlington Crescent, the Everley design. When Maddie sold the house and effects, she'd wanted the silver to be melted but some had been sold intact. Could some ghoulish collector have purchased an Everley surgical knife with the intention of causing harm? Martha wouldn't understand, not yet, though already I could see myself drawing her into my confidence. I couldn't risk Maddie or George fearing for their lives again. For now, I would have to keep this knowledge to myself.

14

Evergreen House

True to Lavell's promise, it wasn't long before the Board arrived heavy-handed. Another man as large as himself and a woman so thin and sharp I feared I could cut myself on her edges. They kept their cloaks and hats, though the woman removed her gloves to write in a heavy book. Unsure of what exactly she was noting, I was as fearful of saying something wrong as I was worried at seeming unwelcoming, and I veered between silence and chattering like a madwoman.

Lavell was forced to raise a hand to silence me before speaking.

'Have you thought to change the locks for security? I'm not suggesting you should, just wondering if that has happened.'

What a strange question. Not for the first time I worried that he somehow knew about the missing keys.

'We have not. Would you recommend that we do so?'

'I wouldn't have thought it necessary. But after something like this, a houseful of women can become quite hysterical.'

That word again. He sounded like Threlfall. And what if we were anxious? One of us had been murdered in cold blood. I said nothing as he made a point of checking all the doors again, taking special interest in the side door to the garden where Sophia and

Felicia skulked, taking their time over hanging sheets. I watched through the window, disliking how close he stood to them as he talked, worrying how they would answer him. Sophia didn't seem to be simpering and preening as she did with Threlfall, which I took as a good sign. When he came back inside, the woman, introduced as Mrs Beckwith, ran her hands along the kitchen surfaces as though she found everything filthy and contagious.

'You must excuse us. It's barely a week since the funeral and we still grieve.' It was not unclean, just unwelcoming. None of us had mastered the art of breadmaking and a sad pair of flat loaves sulked under a cloth on the table.

'You have clearly not done as we asked and secured domestic help.' Mr Lavell clasped his hands behind his back and leant over me in a way I disliked. 'What are the children eating? Do you have a plan?'

'I have placed a notice in the window of the greengrocer and on the post office counter.'

'And no replies?' He moved so close I felt his hot breath on my neck.

'Not as yet.' Since I'd only posted the day before, it would have been surprising if any applications had arrived.

'You must place an advertisement in the *Gazetteer of London*. That is where *steady* servants can be found.'

'Evergreen is not in the *Gazetteer*, so I'm not sure they would allow it.'

'*Not in?* My dear woman, how on earth do you hope to attract benefactors?'

Did I hope to? I wasn't sure I wanted anyone else poking their noses into the way I ran things; it was bad enough having to deal with him.

'We manage for money. The baskets and wallpaper sell well,

and the women cultivate little gardens in the summer for exercise as well as for our fruits and vegetables. If you look in the pantry, you'll see that we've saved a lot of the produce. We even sold jars of apple sauce and redcurrant jelly.'

'Playing house.' Mr Tovey puffed out his chest. 'They should be doing laundry, Mr Lavell. You were quite right, and I agree that this house should take a leaf from the Magdalen Hospital – they run a tight ship there.'

So Lavell had turned the Board against us already. 'I'm sure they do. But we are small, able to manage in the ways we have. And the women are becoming skilled, they support themselves. They're not wanted in domestic service, as you know, and short of marriage . . .'

'Who would take them in marriage!' Tovey snorted.

I bit my tongue. Men like George were out there. Men who understood enough to know that a woman is not to blame for everything in her history. Though the facts would always be there, ready to be pulled out at the first sign of argument. He had never said so, but I suspected George blamed me for our lack of children. My body had been treated poorly and there were consequences.

'Would you like to see the schoolroom?' For once, knowing the inspectors' time of arrival, I had tidied the children and set them to their lessons. It would surely cheer the Board to see them hard at their letters, trying to better themselves. I had peeped in before answering the doorbell, comforted by Amy's command of the room and the determined looks on their clean little faces. 'The children would be happy to read to you.'

'Do you know what you are educating them *for*?' Mrs Beckwith licked the end of her pencil and hovered it above a fresh page in her book.

Of course I knew. But it felt so like a test I became flustered.

'For their futures.'

'And what do you expect their futures will be?'

'I don't know,' I said honestly. 'But I know they'll be happier if they can read and write. And so will the women. It will give them more choices and make it harder for people to trick them.'

Mrs Beckwith gave a humourless laugh, as though she believed misfortune was always the fault of the victim. Perhaps she did. It seemed to be the general consensus. But I wanted to help them. To make up for everyone I couldn't help when Grace was still here. When they arrived these girls had been slipshod, anxious, starving. Under my care they stood taller, their cheeks bloomed, they knew themselves. Some of them found positions, making space for others to join. Aveline had been wed last year, to the owner of a tavern who was well acquainted with stories like hers and little perturbed by them. She was thriving. Able to tackle the business accounts as well as life upstairs. If anything happened to her husband, she would manage. Caroline, who lost her child not long after she arrived with us, had taken a position as a station mistress on the London to Brighton service. I opened my mouth, intending to tell their stories of success, but was quickly interrupted.

'You have no real help here. No philanthropic management, no expertise. It would not be shameful to admit you were unable to continue.' Mr Lavell patted my arm as though I were a child, and I felt heat rise in my chest. How dare he? 'I am personally very happy to oversee the transition of Evergreen to a Board that I would head up and manage. It is an excellent house in a convenient situation and could be a force for good in the right hands.'

It was the second time in as many visits that he'd expressed a wish to run the house. What on earth did he want with us? Was the Magdalen model so lucrative after all or did he just hate to see women overcoming their fates?

'It is my belief, Mr Lavell, that the house is already a force for good. We have suffered a setback, but we will recover.'

'How long it takes for you to recover is of the essence.' Lavell's teeth were long and yellow. When he smiled, he looked ready to bite.

'Why *do* you feel such a need to help these creatures?' asked Mrs Beckwith. 'Why put yourself out? You could pass this house over to be run as an enterprise tomorrow.'

Because I was one of them once. I knew how it felt to have no love, no certainty and no trust of my fellow man. Though I could read and write very well, and much good it did me. I was tricked anyway. Abandoned, deserted by my lover and then my family. Mother still refused to write to us after everything we'd been through, thinking only of the shame on the Brewster name. The indignity she allegedly suffered, while we had been frightened, degraded, abused and even, in Maddie's case, thrown into jail. But it would never do to remind Mrs Beckwith of that. Neither would it be prudent to mention what might happen to the children if Lavell got his wish and took over the house. Orphanages wouldn't take illegitimates, and if their mothers were still alive then the foundling homes wouldn't take them either. They'd end up in the workhouse, picking oakum and rags at three and four years old.

'I believe that our system works well for the women here. I can tell you our success stories. Show you the skill they have at their crafts.'

'These women have already lost their characters,' said Tovey.

Only because they were made to feel such all-consuming guilt.

'It's my belief that I can make them better situations,' I said, 'and I intend to do so.'

Movement through the window caught my eye as two ravens flew down to land on the edge of a stone urn. Wings folded behind them like the arms of inspectors. Eyes like funeral beads. One turned to look up, head on one side, and stared unblinking into the house. Their arrival felt ominous. A shadow fell across the birds, and they flew down to the lawn. Threlfall must have been sitting on the bench. As he rose, he caught my eye and waved, then came in through the kitchen door.

'Sorry, wasn't aware you had visitors.'

'It's quite alright.' Something told me the group would approve of his presence. Though his shirtsleeves were rolled to the elbow, his waistcoat unbuttoned, it was clear that his clothes were expensive. Leather boots shining like the chain of his watch and thigh muscles straining against new moleskin breeches, he seemed bursting with power and vitality. He moved as self-consciously as if he knew it. 'Allow me to introduce Dr Threlfall, whose clinic operates from our basement rooms. He's a psychologist and researcher.' I turned to the inspectors and they introduced themselves.

'Why have we never met before?' Mr Lavell almost bowed in his haste to shake Threlfall's hand. 'That lends an excellent edge to the house.'

And makes it even more attractive to Lavell. I cursed myself for not ushering him away.

'What are you currently researching?' Lavell asked.

'I specialise in hysteria. Though my patients come for quite a range of therapies.'

'One might imagine you have a steady stream of subjects here.' Lavell gave a pompous laugh.

Threlfall laughed with him, as though they were members of the same club. Oh, he was good. A natural charmer. I could learn from the way he slipped in anywhere like he belonged.

'The therapies are for my paying patients. My research is quite different. I'm attempting to understand pain.'

Just as Maddie said. Was he continuing Dr Everley's work? I didn't like to think of it below our home. Threlfall carried a roll of baize under his arm, a tool wrap. He must have taken them out to clean them. Were they Everley tools? Decorated with thin silver bees? If they were, it was possible one was missing. At the first chance I would try to find out.

'There is much being done in the field, I understand?' Mrs Beckwith had pushed lorgnettes onto the blade of her nose, to get a better view of Threlfall as he spoke.

'Much indeed. Though most of it in Germany. We're in danger of being left behind.'

'Then England is lucky to have you. I would like to hear more, when you have the time.'

It seemed his charm was not limited to young women. She was positively simpering.

'I am always delighted to talk of my work, especially with intelligent colleagues.'

'Don't let us keep you,' said Mr Lavell. 'Although I will just ask whether you have been affected by the domestic situation here? This unfortunate business. It seems it has quite turned things upside down. We are looking to see where we may help in the administrative side of things.'

Threlfall pulled a sorry face and hung his head, so the curl of his fringe fell over one eye. A sigh escaped Mrs Beckwith.

'I am much affected by the loss of Rose. She was a constant in this household and a source of great comfort to me.'

'Do you know anything that might shed light on the incident?' Mr Lavell asked.

'I've heard nothing.' Threlfall shook his head firmly. 'It's unlikely to be anything other than an unhappy coincidence. But we'll find out soon enough. The murderer will confess, they always do. Such deeds weigh heavy upon men and sooner or later they must unburden themselves.'

As he spoke, I studied his face carefully. His expression gave nothing away. If he had wielded the weapon, then he was absolutely brazen. I would expect nothing less of him.

'Let us hope you are correct.' Lavell seemed slightly shaken by the intensity of Threlfall's words. Perhaps the idea of murderers confessing was too much for a man with such a taste for soft living. Perhaps he himself had something to hide. He was certainly keen to use Rose's death to his advantage. For a moment I eyed his huge frame with a new mistrust before shaking my head. I should get a hold of myself and stop indulging in silly fancies before Evergreen was taken from under my nose.

'It's my great belief that deeds and words unspoken prey heavy on the minds of men. They are dangerous to the mental faculties and must be appeased. Confession is a healing thing,' said Threlfall.

'As is a well-run household,' said Mrs Beckwith, dragging her attention from Threlfall reluctantly.

Lavell turned to face his colleagues, his earlier bluster dampened. 'What is our recommendation to be?'

15

All Saints Asylum

Strengthened by Edward's visit, I've begun to take care of my appearance. Little point in beauty if no-one's there to admire and reflect it. But since he has returned, I have mended my dresses, grown my hair. Its texture has changed, and it reaches my ears in loose waves, thicker and more luxuriant than before. I will not let them cut it again. They wouldn't dare. Varley walks warily around me, nervous to displease his patron, unsure of the position I hold since Threlfall brought his news. It suits me to have him compliant. When I ask for bathing water and essence of rose, he brings them, placing the basin down carefully on the floor with a soft, folded towel. Leaving the room to afford me privacy while I wash. He sends his little mouse and she watches with quick, bright eyes while I soften my skin and rub the scented oil along the length of my newly bright hair. Unsure whether she should still fear me or whether I'm as changed as my appearance. Her presence is growing on me the more admiring her gaze becomes.

Bowls and spoons bang against bars and doors, a cacophony of sound. It rings in my ears the whole length of the corridor, punctuated by obscenities. I am called a whore, a slut, a filthy bastard, and I do not mind because I know that means they think I'm a visitor. Outsiders are always treated as such – abused, vilified, spat upon. As though the inmates know they have no hope of escape and want to punish those who walk free. It's just a ritual, but it pleases me that I'm subject to the same, that in my newly tamed appearance I have separated from the others completely.

Greedy for air, I speed my step until I'm level with the mouse, clamouring for my hour in the garden. Outside I breathe deeply, holding lungfuls of air. It's vaguely scented with lilac from the bush that overhangs the perimeter wall, overlaid with the dull cabbage smell emanating from the kitchens. I take the short bench, spreading my skirts to force the mouse to perch at the end. Every now and then she throws anxious glances, her fingers plucking at a tendril of clematis she's pulled from the bush.

'Why don't you gather a bunch?' I throw her a sly look. 'You could give them to your lover.'

The mouse jumps up as though bitten. She doesn't like the word, but she's blushing just the same. A flush spreads across her scrawny neck to the tips of her protruding ears.

'The kitchen boy, is it? Or Mr Varley?' Her face! It is the warden. This is too good. 'Isn't he a little old for you? Perhaps his wife will not mind.'

I watch her retreat to the opposite side of the garden, where she stares at me balefully until I close my eyes and Lucius appears, as he always does, wearing the secret smile he kept for me. This time it's half sad, in sorrow for our sons, as much for their existence as their demise. Edmond and Daniel were tainted from the start, born of true sin, unlikely to lead normal lives. Incredible to have been born at all; so few twins survive. Daniel was always weak and Edmond always stronger. Only Lucius' skill brought them into this world, saving me in the process, and I could tell by his face he wished they hadn't survived. In the end, Edmond's furious anger finished them both. It's hard to be sad for them, but the news has made me melancholy, wistful for Father, aching for Lucius, for family. Eloise is all I have left. It's been months since she replied to my letters, but I should let her know about her brothers. If nothing else, it will mean there's money for her. Their care was expensive, their nursing home underhand in what it stole from them. If Edward ever comes back, he can help me to recover the rest.

He is taking his time to return. I tell myself that he's researching, waiting until he understands Father's work before we start. I know from the scratches on my wall it has been over a week already, despite his promise. Why do I seem to need his approval? There may be others who could take on Father's work, but none that know me so well, none that are bound so closely. I'm unlikely to ever be allowed to leave this place, and who else is there to play with? At least he is pretty. Varley would be easier. And, now that I know their secret, it would be fun to see what that did to the mouse, but I know I couldn't bear his touch. It would achieve nothing. I must have Edward.

Reaching over to the fence I pull a flower from the vine, one to press as a replacement for the violet I tore to pieces, and spread it out against the blue skirt of my gown. It's more beautiful than I remember. Soft velvet with silk-embroidered starflowers along the neckline, down the length of the deep bodice. A flattering fit with hundreds of pleats at the waistband that flared out the skirts when I was free to dance. The last time I wore it was the wildest ball, three hundred people at the Guildhall with ice sculptures all along the tables: carved swans and rearing horses. A whole bowl of pineapples seated in the centre, carved for eating not display, and I tried them for the first time. Even in the best homes they were usually rented, returned, displayed again elsewhere. They tasted of seduction, forbidden pleasures, like goblin fruit. I swore I would never eat anything else ever again and the Duke of Devonshire professed himself in love, placed squares of it in my punch. I was free as a bird. A beautiful young widow. Free to ignore the advice of my late husband and father — '*make sure you dance with everyone who asks, don't whisper while you're dancing, don't flirt, don't attract attention*'. Lucius sulked while I spent the evening with the Duke, hands on my bare arms, hot breath on my neck. Indian sapphires at my throat, studded on the slides in my hair, glittering under the gaze of my lovers. Is that the life Eloise is leading? The life I wanted for her. I can't imagine it.

Closing my eyes, I find myself back at the Guildhall, swirling to a polka before a sea of faces, all turned towards me. Flames flicker from chandeliers, the light fractured in diamond cuts. Cellists swing their bows, the music reaches a crescendo and we dance as though the devil cannot catch us. Reaching up to my face, I press my fingers hard into my eyes until the colours bleed together in a spray of fractured rainbows, like the glitter of candlelit crystal.

16

Evergreen House

The inspectors conferred for so long that I began to feel faint. Waiting for judgement. Since Threlfall left they had all stopped posturing. The men no longer pulled in their stomachs and affected a knowledge of science. Mrs Beckwith, no longer simpering, was poised like a gin trap as she listed all the failings of our home. I could barely stand more when Mr Lavell adopted a formal stance and began to speak.

'Mrs Harris, you are certainly fortunate to have such an upright, professional man as Dr Threlfall working here. It makes your situation less grave, for the time being. However, you have not made a genuine attempt to manage the domestic situation, and I'm afraid you give us little choice but to place your establishment under closer watch. I will personally supervise everything, so I will need a room allocated from which to work when I need it. We will also send a cook, along with an assessor to work out what needs adapting should the transition to laundry be—'

At that moment the doorbell rang and, as I had no wish to understand what his team of staff would do, I left the inspectors in the kitchen and rushed to answer it. A room for him to work from! Where would we put him? The idea that Lavell would be here daily chilled my bones, and I determined to put it off for as long as possible. Standing on the fifth step, as though she'd changed her mind after pulling the bell rope and decided to flee, was a young woman with pale skin and large eyes the colour of deep water. She was painfully thin, with cheekbones like a barber's razor. Bony fingers gripped a soft cloth bag in front of her like a shield. Despite her pitiful figure, her expression was bold and gave me the impression I wouldn't like to cross her. I imagined her temper to be as fiery as the colour of her hair. She looked different to the kind of girls that usually came looking for help – self-contained and defiantly dignified. Unbroken, and certainly not with child. I waited for her to speak.

'I've come about the position.'

Good cooks were usually rounded, well fed. She was as little like Rose as it was possible to be. Still, we could never replace Rose, so what did it matter? The girl tilted her chin expectantly and pursed her thin lips to a line.

'Our advertisement for a cook?'

'And housekeeper.'

Had I put that in the advertisement? I didn't remember. And she didn't look old enough to have the experience. Her accent was unusual, harsh with jarring elongated vowel sounds.

'Do you have references?'

She nodded and I ushered her inside, where she stood by the umbrella stand, opened her bag and removed a folded piece of paper. Unmoving, she held it out and I was forced to take a step to reach it. In the dim light the writing was hard to decipher, scratchy, as though it had been written with a cheap pen or makeshift quill. Here and there were patches that were difficult to read, either faint or blotched with spots of ink, and the whole thing smelt oddly of something I couldn't quite place.

To whom it may concern

This is to say that Angela Browning has been employed by me in the capacity of working cook-housekeeper. I found her honest, sober and temperate. Her cookery, both plain and fancy, is of a good standard. She is quiet and discreet in the house and clean and tidy in the kitchen.

Mrs R. J. Featherstone
Emelyn House
Flint Street
Co. Cork
Ireland

Ireland. I could hardly take up the reference. It would be weeks before I received a reply. Should I take a risk on this strange, plain girl? Lavell and his cronies waited downstairs, desperate to claim our house unless we recovered. In reality, I had little choice but to hire her.

'As I am unable to follow this up quickly, might I suggest that we start you on a month's trial? That will allow me to confirm your papers, as well as giving you a chance to settle and discover whether you could be happy here.' I gave a smile that wasn't returned. The girl didn't look as though she'd be happy anywhere. 'Why don't I show you the kitchen?' It would be good for the inspectors to see her before they left. 'You can leave your bag there if you like?'

'It's not heavy.' She drew it further towards her as though I'd reached to take it. Personal things. Likely to be sentimental. From what I'd heard of the situation in Ireland, she would have faced difficulty; she certainly looked as though she'd starved. I'd give her time to come round to talking about it.

'This is Miss Browning.' I threw open the kitchen door with a

101

flourish. 'She has answered our advertisement. Her papers are in order.'

'Like the poet,' said Lavell, with a deep bow. He looked so disappointed at her lack of response that I was forced to hide a smile behind the folded letter I still held in my hand.

'Or the method of cooking meat,' Mrs Beckwith smirked. 'A suitable name for a cook.' Her face also fell when Angela failed to laugh at her joke. 'No doubt you've heard that before.'

'Yes, ma'am.'

She hadn't addressed me as such. Since I'd only just noticed, I could hardly correct her now. I'd probably ask her to stop after a few days anyway. If she stayed that long.

'What a very strange accent.' Mrs Beckwith loomed in to examine Angela's plain features with her lorgnettes. 'Where are you from?'

She hesitated a little too long and I jumped in to help. 'Angela has come from Ireland.'

'Let the girl speak,' she snapped, 'that is not a Dublin accent.'

'I'm from Kilkenny,' Angela looked at me, 'though I've been working in Cork.'

'And what is your experience?'

'I started at the big house when I was twelve and I worked my way to housekeeper and cook. We managed from the estate at first, the kitchen gardens, but the blight is bad. It affected everything. They had to let me go and I came to England with the money I saved. I've been staying with my aunt, by the bridge.'

Lack of food might have stopped her growing much, but she certainly didn't look over twenty. She rattled off her story as though she had learnt it word for word. Perhaps we were not the first house to which she had applied.

'Luckily for you, Mrs Harris appears to enjoy a sad story.' Mrs

Beckwith snapped shut her notebook and tucked her pencil into the pocket of her jacket. 'She will no doubt look after you well.'

'We will see ourselves out.' Lavell's small eyes narrowed further as he stared at me. 'You have another two weeks. And we've decided that this house needs a chaplain, a discussion you missed whilst out of the room. We have agreed on Reverend Illingworth. Experienced in charitable matters and not afraid of ruined souls. We will send him to visit next week.'

Ruined souls. What would Angela think of us now? I wanted to explain in my own words what Evergreen aimed to be, how we helped our girls. After that introduction she'd have the wrong impression from the outset. Mr Lavell and his cronies flounced out like actors walking stage left after a thrilling twist of plot. I clapped my hands together in a bid to look more decisive than I felt.

'Inspectors from the Charity Board,' I said. 'They visit every so often. To make sure things are in order.' And to wait for the money that my predecessors handed out for them to look the other way. Lavell always lingered in the hallway as if giving me a chance to hand over a fat envelope, as Grace used to give the old chief inspector, but I refused to let the girls' hard-earned money go that way. Today's events made me realise it may well be time to capitulate. Something else to discuss with George when he returned. I certainly couldn't have Lavell here on a daily basis, sticking his nose into everything.

I waited, to give her time for questions, but she seemed wholly incurious. Had she already been told about us, or did she simply not care? 'We take in women here, and their illegitimate children. We look after them and train them for jobs, sometimes marriage. Our craft rooms are upstairs, I can show you tomorrow. Some of the women stay long term and some we help to move on. Do you have any questions?'

Angela shook her head, her face impassive. A woman who wasn't easily shocked. Usually that meant a woman of similar experience, but it was hard to tell. Her slight figure showed no sign of motherhood, though her eyes, ringed with shadows, held the depth of experience.

'Would you like to go back to your aunt's to collect your things?'

'I have my things here.'

She must have been sure of securing the position. Or, more likely, the aunt's house was fictitious and she'd been living on the street. If the latter was true, it was little wonder she wasn't bothered by our reputation. The cloth bag was small and half full. She must rely on the clothes she stood up in. Rose's dresses would certainly not fit her but there would be plenty of material there to alter.

'I'll show you to your room.' As I spoke, I remembered it was still full of Rose's belongings. Skirts still hung in the press and her sheets were unwashed. 'Perhaps you could wait a moment while I see to arranging it comfortably.'

'Will I not sleep in the kitchen?' she asked.

Before I could answer, Felicia and Sophia appeared, arm in arm and giggling.

'Has he gone?' asked Felicia, looking around. 'He was supposed to come out and talk with us again.'

'If you mean Mr Lavell, yes, he and his colleagues have left.' Why was she so keen to see him? I wouldn't mention the threats – the girls would meet the new chaplain soon enough, and by the looks of them they could do with some guidance.

'You new?' Sophia held out a hand of greeting, which Angela stared at until she lowered it again. Sophia tossed her head. Pretty and vivacious, she was popular with the women and unused to such treatment. 'You don't look very *full*, if you don't mind me saying.'

When would she ever learn to think before she opened her mouth?

'Angela is our new cook. Angela, please meet Sophia and Felicia.' All three nodded their heads warily.

'Don't look much like a cook.' Felicia eyed her new housemate's bony frame.

'Angela has just arrived from Ireland. I need not remind you, Felicia, of the situation there.' She'd come over from Dublin as a child, soon left to fend for herself when her father and brother found work on the railways.

'Does she speak?'

'I do. But I don't enjoy empty chatter. Unlike most of my countrymen.'

Felicia raised her eyebrows theatrically. 'Where did you say you were from?'

'Kilkenny. Though I've lived in Cork for a long time.'

'Really. What part?'

'You wouldn't know of it.'

'Try me.'

'That's enough, Felicia. You've been in England a long time.' I threw her a warning look and she pursed her lips, as though she hadn't quite finished. Poor Angela wouldn't stay if she carried on and then we'd be without help again. 'I do hope you will *all* make Angela welcome. Why don't you make some tea while I see to her rooms?'

As I turned to leave, Angela picked up her bag and followed. I didn't protest. Who could blame her? Those two could be difficult if they took a dislike. We had just reached the stairs when Angela tapped my arm.

'What was that door?'

I glanced behind me. In the short corridor between the kitchen

105

and the lobby was a butler's pantry that we used as a storage space for the women's craft materials. 'It's just a closet. I can show you later.' Angela had already walked back and was trying the handle. Wilful. Perhaps she would get along with Felicia after all.

'It sticks sometimes. But it's just a cupboard.'

Angela pushed her shoulder against the door, and it swung open, catching on the stack of willow canes inside. She edged around them, and I stayed by the entrance, watching her inspect the space. It was bigger than I remembered, two narrow connecting rooms, the first lined with wooden benches for polishing silver and brushing hats, the second fitted with a wooden cabin bed and ancient mattress, a hollow space beneath for storing valuables. Everything was covered in a thin veil of dust. Evergreen, the last place to hold fancy dinners, hadn't needed a butler in many years.

'This will do nicely.'

Angela was almost smiling. Surely she didn't mean to sleep in there?

'I'd rather be close to the kitchen than upstairs with . . .' She paused, as though she thought better of what she was about to say. Had those silly girls coloured her impression of us? 'I'll just need a blanket.'

Both wood and walls were painted grey and neither room had windows. A hiding place, not a suitable room for a young woman. 'Are you quite sure? The room upstairs is light and airy.'

She began to fuss with moving the stacks of canes. I'd have to find somewhere else to store them. Rose's room, perhaps, though it would be inconvenient to drag them up and down the stairs every time they were needed.

'We could paper it with something pretty?' George had become adept at such tasks. At the very least I should bring down Rose's colourful quilt.

Angela shook her head and placed her bag on the mattress with such an air of propriety that I felt like an intruder. 'It's fine, just needs a clean.'

'If you're sure?'

'I'd a cot next to the oven before. This is grand.'

'Then we'll need some soap and hot water.' We could make it clean and spartan, like Martha's house. I began to point out where things were stored in the kitchen.

'I don't need nurse-maiding, I can find things myself.' Angela peeled the cloth from the sunken loaves and raised an eyebrow. 'That's if you have anything in the pantry.'

I gave a laugh that came out nervous. 'As you can see, we need your help. The pantry is here, and beyond is the door to the garden.' I beckoned her over and opened the top of the stable door. 'It's a pretty garden. I'm sure you'll enjoy sitting out here. Perhaps it will remind you of home.'

'I hope not,' she replied, with a look of distaste.

Maybe her story was worse than starvation. She'd tell us in time. The air outside was damp and close, another fog coming. A raven hopped backwards from the flowerbed, dragging something behind. As it reached the lawn, I saw it was a fledgling chick, its stretched body barely feathered, its head lolling from its neck, firmly clamped in the raven's velvet beak.

17

Cut-Throat Lane

Martha took the mug, enamelled the colour of harebells, without comment. If she recognised the gift as a sign that I intended to visit often then she didn't say, which meant she didn't mind, and I was pleased to think we might be friends. She was straightforward, honest and capable, and exactly the person I needed to reassure me that my anxious fears were unfounded. The story of my sister's nightmare marriage and her husband's grotesque small museum took two rounds of tea to complete and she listened without interruption, an impassive expression on her weathered face. She must have seen much in life not to shrink from such a tale.

'So when you told me about the murder weapon, it seemed as though the Everleys had returned,' I finished.

'How many of them are there?'

A sensible question, reassuring in itself because the answer was easy. I knew from the Assizes that Grace's children were the last of them, and they were far away.

'Grace resides at All Saints in Hanwell, her sons in a secure nursing home and Eloise, her daughter, was sent to Australia I believe. She was young enough to start afresh without the stain of her family name. As far as I'm aware, they are the last of the Everley line.'

'Then how *can* they have returned?' So matter-of-fact. For Martha life and death were always black and white. I had allowed myself to become more fanciful in a house of women.

'But the knife, the bee on the handle. Surely it must come from the house of Everley?'

'Perhaps. But you said yourself that the effects were sold. It could have passed through a dozen hands on its way to the street.'

Still an extraordinary coincidence. Though her words were comforting, I couldn't shake the feeling that the shadows of the past crept closer. Should I tell her of the keys? I had no wish to burden her with my problems but there was no-one else to trust who wouldn't be worried by the news. I stood, relieving the ache in my lower back from sitting so long on the hard chair, slightly shamed to have left Martha perching at the edge of her bed, upright and uncomplaining. George and I had lived like this once, thrown together in the press of a single room. Would our lives have been different if we hadn't taken on Evergreen? If we'd stayed there or found a cottage to rent? We could have been happy with a quiet life. He would still have his friends on the water, I would have managed for some kind of work. A cosy dream. But it wouldn't change the way my body worked, and without children the two of us would grow apart just the same. More so in a house of two. At least there was life at Evergreen. And we had wanted to help. At the outset we shared the dream to build better lives for everyone, staying up late to agree every decision. Now things were busy from dusk until dawn, with George always finding a maintenance job to deal with and me left to the accounts, the constant needs of the girls and the strained conversations with Angela.

'You're right. I'm imagining the worst. There are too many worries at the moment and it's making me anxious about everything.'

'I can give you some extract of passionflower. Calming, like chamomile, if you add it to hot water.'

'You are kind, Martha. I'm so very grateful to have met you.'

To my surprise she blushed at the words, and began to busy herself filling up a small triangle of muslin with a scoop of powder coloured lavender grey. I saw the open chest with its rows of drawers and neat labels, like a miniature apothecary. She was a healer for the living as well as the dead.

'You need to stop thinking about things you can't change.'

'I can't find Rose's keys. A chain of dozens which opened every door in the house. They were not in her room, or the kitchen, and I can only assume they were on her when . . . do you remember seeing such a thing at the mortuary?'

Martha screwed up her face in concentration. 'Bodies are usually picked clean of any effects by the time I get to them. I don't remember seeing anything like that. But if anyone planned to rob you, wouldn't they have done so by now? And if they were lost during the attack, then whoever found them wouldn't know where they were from.'

Unless that person knew exactly what they were and the keys were the reason Rose was killed in the first place. But why would strangers imagine we had wealth to take? And who could want to hurt us? The missing keys turned in my thoughts in the middle of the night and I still had no satisfying explanation, just a restless feeling that someone wished us harm. We were vulnerable. There were plenty of men that might seek revenge. If Amy's husband had found her, or Henrietta's father . . . such men were capable of violence; and what if it was someone closer? Maddie mistrusted Threlfall already and Mr Lavell had shown such an interest in the doors that I half suspected he knew all about the keys himself, something that was impossible for an innocent party to know.

Martha, who looked after herself alone, would know nothing of such fears. Responsibility for the women weighed on me more heavily than ever.

'I know it will do no good to tell you not to worry,' said Martha, 'so why not just change the locks?'

Our front door was so weathered, the wood stretched and swelled against its frame, that the new slide bolt didn't quite sit straight. The shaft would only slip into the catch if the whole thing was lifted slightly, allowing the edges to meet.

'We can fasten them together,' I said, 'a new routine after bedtime. I know I'm overcautious but it's important that I know we're all safe.' I could hardly voice my real fears to George. Since Rose's funeral I'd caught him more than once leaning on his tools just staring into the air before him, and when I'd tapped his shoulder by the flowerbed he'd jumped half out of his skin. Her death, the circumstances around it, had brought things back for him. I knew that. Changed our world back to one where bad things happened. 'You've been sleeping badly too.' Slipping from the bed like a thief in the hours before dawn.

George shrugged. 'Be alright when the weather's better. Too much time indoors doesn't suit me.' Holding up a metal elbow lock, he added, 'Want this one on the front as well?'

'Or the kitchen door?' More chance of unseen intruders padding across soft grass than climbing the steps. And it was the kitchen door in which Lavell seemed to show the most interest.

'Gets used too much. If I fit this someone's just going to lose the spindle.'

'Should we leave it?' I could hardly voice my fears about Lavell.

George reached up to tuck a stray lock of hair into my plait. 'If it makes you happier, I'll fit them to all the doors.'

For a moment I wanted to catch his fingers, hold his weathered skin against my face. Yet I could hardly bear for him to touch me, because every night of closeness meant another time of hope that was destined to end in tears and disappointment.

'I just didn't like knowing that a stranger could let themselves in, if they chose.'

'Well, they can't now. As long as we remember to slide these across, we'll be fine.' George opened the door to sweep out the wood dust and a tendril of creeper caught his cheek. 'I only cut these last week.' He looked up, grabbed a handful of vine and pulled it roughly, scattering buds of soft, rolled leaves.

'That's why they're called creepers.' He was right though. The more we cut it back the more it seemed to grow, covering the attic windows and darkening all the glass across the front of the building. It was hard to destroy. Pretty in spring with its pale green bursts but in autumn the leaves were blood red, dripping down every wall.

George wiped his hands on his thighs, packed his tools into their crate. I wanted to keep him with me.

'Have you spoken much to our new cook? I'm worried that the work is too much for her with so many mouths to feed.' Though the stoves were always going, the fires lit, the kitchen felt no warmer. When we worked through the deliveries and menu each morning, Angela always had a pan about to catch or some tins to fill that required her attention.

George looked down at his feet for a moment, chewing his lip like a child with a difficult sum. His boots hung open, tongues loose and unbound because he hated lacing them to the top. 'She's not Rose,' he said. 'And it's going to take a while to get used to that. But you need to give her time. This place is bound to be different to anywhere she's lived before.'

'You're right. As always. And we're eating well again.' Her taciturn demeanour annoyed me more than it should – if she wanted to keep her past private, it was her own choice. She didn't owe me her story so I could play mother.

George patted his stomach. 'We certainly are. Have you had a response from her reference?'

'Not yet. I don't know how long the post will take.' I was less worried about that than whether she would stay. I wasn't at all sure our house was what Angela wanted. More than once she'd told me she couldn't stand gossip, rolling her eyes at Sophia and Felicia and their constant chatter. 'It would have to be very bad news to let her go now, anyway.'

Delicious smells of baking dough reached the room beside the garden where I kept the books. I lifted my head from the ledger and breathed in a scent like warm floury arms wrapping round me. My stomach growled. Unable to sleep, I'd been working since dawn, making sure things were up to date for Mr Lavell, and I realised I was hungry. Angela had been busy. She must have been up early, too, to bake fresh for breakfast. A sign that she really did like us.

Stretching my shoulders, I snuffed the lamp and closed the ledger, placing it in the bureau drawer with the others. So many notes. Outgoings, market takings, the costs of materials for the workshops – everything was accounted. Every outing was logged. Every haul from the kitchen garden. Every progress test for the children. And, in a heavy hardback scrapbook, a detailed write-up of every girl's story since I'd been in charge at Evergreen, my own at the front to encourage them. They all made sorry reading. Harriet, who ran from the clutches of her stepfather and only found work by the docks. Charlotte, a small girl with feline eyes who worked long factory shifts, seduced by the apothecary who continually increased the price of the medicines she needed for her mother. Emily, the eldest of nine children, sent to a work as a parlourmaid by parents who were delighted she'd found a good position. Raped by the 'gentleman' of the house, thrown out when her stomach grew, too disgraced to return home. She was fourteen. Emily was gone now, one of our success stories, a good presentable girl, young enough to hide her past and grown fierce enough never to repeat it. Housemaid to a doctor's family and likely to be promoted. There was always hope if society allowed these girls to move on.

At the end of each entry, I left two blank pages to fill with their futures. Happier words. Some, like Emily's, were filled. Others, like Amy, who might never leave for fear of being found by her violent husband, had some paragraphs of achievements and things to make us proud. Like the time she nursed little Charlie through the croup, or when she went straight out after Felicia to bring her home safely after an argument. The pages on Angela were blank. Was I right to have made them? She didn't come to us for help. We employed her fairly. Yet she had a story, I knew it, and I knew that telling it would help. The girls were encouraged to talk openly about their past lives in order to understand and empathise with one another. Giving them words made life easier to bear and allowed them to move on.

I locked all the books safely in the bureau and made sure to lock the door behind me. I wasn't worried about the accounts, but the girls' stories were given in confidence and not mine to share.

'What have you made, Angela? It smells wonderful.' I crossed the kitchen to stand by the stove and she stiffened, replied without turning.

'Fruit bread. With currants and dried apple. I thought the children would like it.'

'They certainly will. How wonderful.'

Angela's apron straps stuck out from her back on the points of her shoulder blades. Her shoulders themselves were hunched halfway up to her ears, as though she cringed from life itself.

'Have the children come in to help you yet?'

'Kitchen's no place for children.'

'They like to bake. You could teach them.'

'I can't be watching them all the time and they'll just burn themselves. They always do.'

'Very well. The kitchen is your domain.' Perhaps she would teach me, and then I could help them. It seemed a shame to deny Albie and the others the pleasures of creating food to share when they enjoyed it so much. Angela busied herself slicing the loaves and stacking them onto plates. She still wore the stout men's boots and plain wool dress she'd arrived in, despite the clothes I'd made her from what remained in Rose's wardrobe.

'You haven't worn your new yellow dress yet. It's perfect for spring.' I'd hoped the cheerful colour would bring a smile to her face. She stayed silent. 'Angela? Do you dislike the dress?'

'The colour is for whores.'

Though she spoke quietly, the violence of the word echoed round the room. Shocking to hear it, especially from a young girl in such a house as ours. I breathed deeply, remembering the blank page of her story. Something unknown and terrible.

'We don't use that word here.'

'What do you call them then, women who've disgraced themselves?' She turned and fixed me with a stare.

'We call them women,' I said firmly. 'And we do not judge.'

18

Evergreen House

It was hard to shake the sound of the word, which rang in my ears all day. Most people, like Mr Lavell, spoke of bad characters, pollution and disgrace. Others, like Bessie, affectionately called us ladybirds, judys and dollymops. *Whore* was a dangerous word. To hear it said with such venom by a young woman was troubling. What had happened to make her think so? Did she despise herself? Was Ireland an even harsher place to make a living than London? I would have to work harder to bring her round, make her welcome and coax out her story. Better out loud than festering in secret.

'Does something worry you?' Amy touched my arm gently and I gathered my senses.

'I was just thinking. Have you finished?'

Amy passed over the book for me to check. She perched on a three-legged stool by my desk, as she did every Wednesday, while she learnt how to run the accounts and manage the household expenses, copying grocery lists and matching bills and receipts for provisions.

'A worry shared is a worry halved,' she said, and I smiled to hear my own phrase returned to me.

'It's nothing. Really. I miss Rose sometimes, that's all.' It was true, and something I knew Amy would understand. If I mentioned what Angela had said, it would only cause upset among the women. They already found it difficult to warm to her.

'I think of her too.' Amy wiped her pen on a cloth, replaced it in the holder. 'And one day it will be happy to think of her, but it isn't yet, is it?'

Amy would run Evergreen one day, I saw it clearly. Full of empathy and a kindness that was firm enough to sympathise and then set people on their way. Not dissimilar to Rose, though with a good head for business in addition. I felt a sudden rush of fondness for her.

'How are you finding Angela?'

'She's a good cook. The children loved her currant loaf.'

'They did.' Albie had made it his business to count the dried fruit in every piece and even up the tally across the plates. I caught Angela rolling her eyes at him, though all I saw was the bossy fairness of an older child with too many siblings. At least I could ask whether she was an only child. It might explain things. 'Have the others mentioned her?'

'They don't know her well,' Amy replied. 'She's not one for talking.'

'I would also like to know her better,' I agreed. 'But we don't know what she's suffered in Ireland. We must give her time to settle.'

'Felicia seems to think that she's been away from Ireland longer than she says.'

'I hope Felicia isn't making trouble?'

Amy opened her mouth and closed it again, as though changing her mind about what she was going to say. 'Angela is terribly thin.'

'Does she eat?'

'Not with us. But she's in the kitchens all day, so maybe she eats early.'

117

'I know I can trust you to make her feel welcome. And if she does talk to you, it will do her good.' I began to pack away the ledgers. It was coming to the end of the free hours before supper and would soon be time to call the children in from the garden.

'She said Rose was weak,' Amy said suddenly.

Rose wasn't a weak woman – loving and trusting certainly, but never weak. And Angela had never met her. 'Why would she say that?'

'We were helping with the plates, Sophia and I, and remembering Rose. Sophia said she was one of the strongest women she'd ever met and Angela said she must have been weak to be attacked like that. I thought Sophia was going to cry.'

'She wouldn't say that if she knew Rose.'

'Why would she say something like that at all?'

'Who knows?' Why would she call her gift a whore's dress? 'I think she's awkward. Perhaps she feels uncomfortable replacing someone like Rose, who was so loved. Like we said, she needs time to settle.'

Just as I opened the door to usher her through, a short high-pitched scream echoed along the corridor. We exchanged glances.

'The children,' said Amy, and we hurried to the garden, where the children seemed to be playing a game of blind man's buff, running away from Albie who wore a handkerchief across his eyes. They were laughing and shrieking but not screaming.

Amy counted them. 'They're all there.' Her words were broken by another short scream, clearly coming from the basement.

'We should go and see what's happening,' I said. Neither of us moved. The clinic was out of bounds, a separate space from the rest of the house, and Threlfall would dislike us interfering. It would be wrong to upset him, especially since Mr Lavell seemed to like him so much.

'Some of his patients have special treatment. Physical treatment for what ails them in their minds. Shocks. I overheard him talking to Sophia, and I've seen some of them leaving.'

So had I, arms pinned by their husbands or fathers, marched to waiting carriages. All in various states of disarray.

'Why was he talking to Sophia?'

Amy gave me a curious look. 'She's taking part in his study. So is Felicia. I thought you knew?'

Did I? It was possible she'd mentioned it when I was distracted. It happened often lately. But I didn't like the thought of Threlfall at home in my house, talking to my girls and behaving as though he owned the place. It was bad enough that Mr Lavell seemed to come and go as he pleased.

'I'll ask him to explain.'

'He's quite happy to talk about it. He's trying to prove that unmarried mothers can't help it. How did he phrase it?' She screwed up her face with the effort of remembering. 'He said there's a correct *social order* to things. He's been measuring the girls' faces, writing down things about the size of their noses, and the shapes of their chins. That sort of thing.'

Another scream, louder and longer. A chilling sound, filled with fear. 'That doesn't sound like measuring,' I said.

I'd never heard any noise from the basement previously, though Threlfall brought a steady stream of patients through his back door. The rooms were self-contained, with a small bathroom and two bedrooms in addition to the clinic, laboratory and waiting room. I'd seen them when we first moved in, when I'd hoped to refurbish and purify the space. More than a decade since, I gave birth there too, my child delivered skilfully by Lucius Everley, removed and murdered while I lay drugged, like the dozens of others killed by him and his evil father. Little bones used in their horrible museum. What was happening? What did it mean to hear such sounds from those rooms? We'd stopped them, I knew we had. Terrible images were conjured by the sounds of another scream. Waves of nausea rose and I reeled, faint, leant against the wall.

Someone called my name. I struggled to focus, as though dragged from a dream, and saw Threlfall's face looming over me, close enough for his curled forelock to brush my cheek.

'Mrs Harris.' A sharp scent of ammonia filled my nostrils and I sat up, pushing him away. He fastened the lid of a small blue bottle. Mr Lavell stood next to him. How did that man always appear when we were at our worst? I took a deep breath.

'That's better. Salts usually do the trick.' Threlfall was remarkably cheerful, as always, his expression habitually delighted with himself. Was Maddie right? Could he torture someone and then smile about it?

'You fainted, Rebecca.' Amy looked concerned. 'You should try to eat something.'

'We heard a noise.' I remembered that much. But I could hardly elaborate in front of Lavell. What would he make of that? Screams coming from Threlfall's rooms. I'd struggled to make myself investigate, terrified of what I might find. Had Amy been forced to go instead? She was pale; her fingers plucked anxiously against the cloth of her apron.

'*Mea culpa.*' Threlfall pocketed the little bottle and clasped his hands to his heart in supplication. 'Please forgive me. It was such a beautiful day, I was working with the windows open.'

'I heard screams.' Maddie's warning. He's carrying out Old Everley's research.

'Sophia and Felicia were helping me to finish a paper.' He turned and gestured for them to come forward and Felicia shuffled towards me, her expression sulky and her clothes dishevelled, like one of his patients.

'Are you well, Felicia?' I asked.

She nodded, though she rubbed the top of her right arm as if it hurt. I bid her straighten herself and call the children in to get washed, and she threw a baleful backward glance at Threlfall. He gave a cheery wave, and I felt a sudden urge to slap his youthful face. His neckerchief was satin, woven in threads of crimson and orange that licked his neck like flames. Would Angela call that a whore's choice? Such rules would never apply. The scarf was pinned in place with a huge amber stud, dotted with tiny, trapped insects in flecks of black.

'Felicia has told me of your research,' said Lavell. Is that what they were discussing at his last visit? Surely even he could not approve of such cruelty.

'Ah yes, they are all intrigued by my theory of delinquency as a mental disease. I believe it is fixed at birth by the alignment of humours – that there are, quite literally, some people who are born to sin. Well established in men, of course, through phrenology and the prison studies. But this is the first that shows how phenotypes predicate the lives of women.'

Long words intended to impress. An educated man, schooled in scientific thought and given all the advantages of understanding that his class and sex had gifted. Surely he could find more pressing work. Lavell hung on his every word.

'It's coming on well,' he continued, 'though I need more subjects.'

Mr Lavell nodded vigorously. 'Mrs Harris will be pleased to assist, I am sure.'

'The women are still in my care,' I said boldly, 'and what I've heard this afternoon would make me reluctant to send them downstairs.'

'Those two were helping with a different study. I'm also researching pain. To assess the cumulative effects of treatment for mental diseases.'

'Can you treat what is divined at birth?'

'An excellent question. Not all maladies are so predicated. Hysteria, for example, can affect anyone. Any woman, of course.'

And most of the patients dragged to see him had nothing of the sort. More likely they were brought because their husbands wanted them submissive, or their fathers disapproved of their behaviour, and Threlfall obliged by hurting the poor things until they complied. I held my tongue. Threlfall was a blight that must remain if we were to keep our respectability with Lavell and his Board. But I liked the fact less and less. I was as trapped as the creatures in his tiepin.

19

All Saints Asylum

Edward stands back, watching, while his assistant works. Another handsome young man, with a fondness for fine clothes. A secretary from the Society, perhaps, like the ones Father used to have perform the parts of his research he liked the least – note-taking, blood-wiping, bringing round the subjects with caustic salts. He had to pay his young men well. This one also looks well paid. Fine lace spills over his satin waistcoat, as white as his shirt and fixed with a large ruby pin. Soft hands, a crested signet ring on one and a seal ring on the other. An old family, paying for their son to be trained as a mind doctor. Would he turn on them as soon as he qualified?

'I'm sorry, this might be cold.' Cut crystal rings in the young man's voice. 'Keep very still.' He draws a measuring tape from a leather reel and presses the steel end to the bridge of my nose, pulls down the tape, counts the notches. Placing it on the empty chair, he jots the number into a table that's been hand-drawn in his notebook, then measures the width of my forehead. Several times he repeats the process – on cheekbones, eyebrows, ears. Slow, deliberate movements, checking each figure with care to make a good impression. It must be his first time. I doubt whether he's more than eighteen years old. A rash on the skin under his chin shows where he's scraped a blade to encourage his beard.

'Open your mouth please.' I hesitate, and he smiles encouragement as though I'm a simpleton. 'I need to count your teeth.'

I pull back my lips and he seems surprised to find my teeth complete. He writes down the number in the last column and checks along the row. Looks from my face to the numbers with a puzzled frown that wrinkles his nose and narrows his eyes.

'Perhaps you could check? This patient's measurements are not consistent with your theory, and I fear they may very well skew the results.'

'And what is your theory?' I address Threlfall directly in a clear voice. The assistant jumps back as though I've bitten him. 'Are you proposing a taxonomy of the lunatic physiognomy?'

'In a manner of speaking.' Threlfall holds up a hand to silence the young man, who's become excitable at the idea a lunatic might be able to articulate a knowledge of complex science.

'So you have decided to start with "The Delinquent Mind".' One of the studies that Father started at Evergreen House, with its steady stream of fallen women to examine. Disposable patients. Too weak to withstand the treatment. Once he knew they wouldn't cope, he used his blood-letting fleam to release them from life and swept them away to the dissection tables of the operating theatres at the Royal College. How much has Edward guessed? How much could he be persuaded to continue?

'An excellent paper,' he replies, 'and the impetus for what promises to be exciting further work. We are attempting to ascertain whether the slide of the mind is predicated in the make-up of the physical body, as your eminent father proved with the criminal classes. Our work will lead us to many institutions such as this.'

'And what do your findings show to date?' As I hold his gaze, I run the point of my tongue slowly along my bottom lip. A brief flicker of hunger shows in his eyes, and I feel the familiar warmth of stirring desire. Exactly what I hoped for when I dressed so carefully in low-cut silk, tightly fitted on the bodice. My hair has begun to grow, enough to pull back with my silver slides, its shortness emphasising the shape of my face. I know exactly what effect I am having on these men. I could have trained Eloise so well. Anger flashes at the reminder that I am denied a mother's greatest pleasure – watching her daughter grow into her own feminine power. Eloise could have wound this little boy around her elegant finger and kept him as a lapdog. I'm reminded that I haven't yet written to notify her of her brothers' fates. Perhaps I could spare the detail. But she needs to know. Indeed the news may bring her home, if only for a brief time away from her new family, because the money used to keep those two alive will now be hers to dispense with as she wishes. And bring her as many lapdogs as she chooses. I will write as soon as I can. It will be good to see how she compares to my younger self; and if she hasn't turned out the way I wanted, then it won't be too late to bring her round. She's still young, still possesses the intoxicating power of youth.

'This woman doesn't belong in here.' Wide-eyed and unsettled, the assistant looks to Threlfall, who has obviously not allowed him into our secret. He clearly has no idea of the Everley story, or the pact we made to keep me from the noose.

Deliberately I slow my speech, calm my anger. 'Oh, but I do, don't I, Edward?'

'Gather the instruments. I wish to speak with this patient and will meet you outside.'

Slowly, with more care than necessary, the assistant does as he is bid, replacing tools in their cases and packing them into a large leather bag that looks very much like Father's. As he moves I can see that it is: the brass initials still sit just below the clasp. Does it contain the same tools? A thrill passes through me at the thought of those cloth-wrapped silver blades. The young man throws sideways glances as he works, as though I am a mermaid or some other freak of nature, then takes the bag and goes to stand outside.

'He's certainly handsome.'

'He is little more than a child.'

'A handsome child.'

A flicker of annoyance crosses his face at my words.

'I'm teasing, Edward. He is dull next to your light.' Threlfall flicks a lock of hair, his pride returned. 'And perhaps not ready for the other streams of Father's work. Have you engaged him for this study only?'

'At this stage, yes. He's my cousin, on Father's side, just down from Oxford and hoping to be accepted into Golding's Medical School. Still wet behind the ears, of course, but this is interesting work and straightforward enough.'

A sudden memory of Edward at the trial, still green himself but full of the strength of his own words, his convictions. So keen to show that alienists should be accepted as respectable medics that he was blinded to the truth of the case.

'That would explain the family resemblance,' I murmur, thinking. 'How long do you expect your involvement in this study to last? A good Threlfall brain like that should be able to manage a simple measurement theory.' I touch his arm, conspiratorial, feel the thrill of flesh beneath his shirt. 'Why not leave him to the delinquent minds while you explore Father's true legacy.' Reaching to the line of hide-bound texts I remove the third, run my index finger over the gilded letters of its title, *The Source and Manifestation of Nervous Pain*. Father's work on isolating nerves and their role in pain, the precursor to the study he started on continuous pain. In particular, the way overuse of a pain stimulus seemed to cause the brain to shut out the signals. What he called his *work on weakness and resilience*. A masterpiece. The pain rooms are in the basement clinic at Evergreen. If I can persuade Edward of the worth of this research, it will finally be completed.

'Send your cousin away, and sit down to read. You can have Varley bring us some tea.'

20

Hamblin Mews, South Kensington

'This is absolutely good enough for the exhibition.' I stepped back from the canvas to admire Maddie's work. Medusa towered above me, eyes glowering, snakes writhing around her head as if they were alive. How had she caught such a sheen to their skin? Coppery, glistening and burnished with patterns of light. Maddie's Medusa was no green-skinned monster. Deep amber eyes burnt in a gold-peach complexion, their expression both anguished and threatening. 'She is beautiful and terrifying. I feel as though I shouldn't look at her directly lest she turn me to stone.'

'She wouldn't do that to you,' said Maddie, 'she wouldn't hurt any of us. She's a protector.'

'Your painting is incredible. These must have taken years.'

Maddie shrugged. 'I've learnt a lot from the others here. I used to be better with charcoal, but I've worked hard at the oils. I knew exactly how I wanted these to appear.'

'You are far too modest!' Alice struck her playfully on the arm. 'She's a formidable talent. Far too good for the rest of us.'

'That is hardly true,' I protested. Alice, like the others at Hamblin Mews, was a skilled artist who made a good living illustrating books. Botanical guides or medical texts, and beautifully drawn plates for fairytales. All of the artists in their group were charming and generous, though bold enough to make me nervous. Alice, her long hair caught and pinned with knitting needles, was dressed in trousers and a man's smock, and no-one but me seemed shocked.

'You are always so serious, dear Rebecca.' Alice sat down on a red velvet love seat and patted the cushion next to her. 'Come and sit here while we look at the rest of your sister's work. We're all very proud of her, Tizzy especially. See how they glow with the passion of youth! Does it not delight you?'

Maddie's happiness was everything to me, but I still considered it dangerous for her and Tizzy to live openly as lovers. I wasn't used to their bohemian friends and frank conversations. Alice beamed, offering a pouch of tobacco she knew very well I would decline. She pushed hers into a long clay pipe, leant back and blew rings with the smoke. Sincerely I hoped Maddie wouldn't take up such habits.

'They certainly made the right choice moving here,' I said. Alice had welcomed them after the trial, nursing them back to reality in her commune of unmarried artists, and I was grateful to her for it. A sweet home, in one of five studio cottages, and they all ate together in the evenings, taking turns to cook and host in their kitchens. I'd joined them for supper before, but this time I realised just how much their new friends had changed them. Tizzy and Maddie spoke confidently of books I hadn't read, politicians I didn't know, recounting tales of marches for suffrage or bills for factory workers. A different life to mine, but we all helped others and I loved them dearly, both of them. It struck me that such feelings might be the reason for Martha's single life, though I certainly didn't know her well enough to ask and she seemed content enough with the way she lived.

Maddie stacked Medusa against the wall and heaved another canvas to the stand. Equally impressive, this was an elegant brushwork depiction of a dreamy medieval maiden, in a long, belted gown with a faraway, vaguely fearful look on her face.

'I recognise this one from your sketches. Pandora?'

'Yes. I wasn't sure if I should add the box, but I thought it was better without. I wanted to paint her as a person rather than an idea. To be seen for herself rather than her act.'

'It's like a Pre-Raphaelite painting.'

Alice rolled her eyes. '*Them*. I'm amazed they get any painting done at all. They seem to spend most of the day in bed.' She narrowed her eyes at the canvas. 'It is a bit. I like the style. I think it adds a bit of ambiguity to have her dressed differently. Without the nymphs and togas.'

Maddie laughed. 'I sketched them in Greek clothes, then decided I'd update them. It gives the chance to add more colour rather than a line of women in white robes.'

A sudden memory made me shiver, in a way that Rose would say was someone walking on my grave. A line of us in thin white robes or nothing at all. Remembering the cold air on my bare skin, the shame of my nakedness, Lucius and Grace behind the camera.

'I hadn't expected these paintings to be so huge,' I said. Pandora was far bigger than life-size.

'I wanted them big. The canvases cost a fortune. I think they're about a third larger than standard size. It seemed important to make them look powerful.'

'They'll certainly be noticed at the Academy.' Alice looked around for an ashtray before tapping her pipe into a potted palm. House-proud Tizzy scowled.

Maddie turned to me. 'Do you think I should show them?'

It was touching to see how anxious she was for me to like her paintings. Despite her considerable skill she'd never been proud, or been encouraged to show off her gift. Mother hated her drawing, admonishing her for the time she spent sketching with the boys and criticising such unladylike behaviour. Much good it had done her to push her daughter into a hasty marriage with Lucius Everley. And where were she and Father now? Even after the trial they refused to contact us. I wasn't even sure they were still alive. Our sister, Isabel, had formally disowned us, returning letters unopened until we stopped writing. Without a family's love and support, and after everything she had lived through, Maddie had a tendency to self-doubt. I understood that she didn't want to put her paintings up for exhibition and risk criticism; she had chosen an artist's life, thrown everything into it, and where would that lead if she wasn't accepted as a painter?

'I think they're wonderful, sister. But I'm not an expert.' I'd visited the Summer Exhibition the year before, with Maddie and her friends. To me, these paintings looked perfectly worthy of the Academy's coveted eye-level hangings. 'What do you say, Alice?'

'Get them submitted immediately! If I could paint anything half as good, I'd carry it all the way there myself.' Alice folded her arms as though the decision was made. 'How many will you enter?'

'You're allowed to submit up to eight.'

'Medusa, naturally,' said Alice, crossing her legs. Trousers certainly looked comfortable to wear. 'What do you think, Rebecca?'

'I couldn't choose. They are all lovely.'

Maddie considered the stack of canvases. 'Helen, I think. And Pandora. They seem to go together.'

Helen, painted against a backdrop of war, sinking ships and bloody swords. Her expression was beatific, as though the violence was nothing to do with her.

'Use your initials, Maddie. It will help them get accepted.' I couldn't imagine the Royal Academy accepting these if they thought they were painted by a woman. 'Once it's on the wall you can reveal yourself.'

Alice snorted and muttered something dark about male conspiracy.

'Rebecca is probably right,' said Maddie. 'Would George take them for me? I'd give him the fee.'

'You have to pay for entry?'

'For each item, each painting or sculpture. Then they are assessed by the Selection and Hanging Committee.'

'I expect he would take them if you wrapped them.' George had a liking for art and would enjoy the subterfuge.

'Better use your sister's address then.' Alice picked up her pipe and tobacco and stood to leave. 'They'll know the Mews, it will be hard to hide if they see you live here.'

Maddie stacked the canvases in a line, and I saw how powerful they would look on the walls at Burlington House. Pandora's outstretched arm seemed to reach for Medusa, a picture of compassion and sisterhood. Though beautiful and richly coloured, the paintings made me melancholy. These were fictional women, conjured from Maddie's imagination, but they were so lifelike, and the wrongs against them so universal that I could weep for them all.

'You seem sad.'

'For your heroines. Who would not be?' I replied. 'You'll delight the committee.'

'It's more than that.'

Where to start? I could tell her that the ravens had returned and know she would understand. I could say that I feared intruders after the lost keys, despite the deadbolts, because whoever killed Rose had used an Everley knife. I worried that Threlfall would hurt the girls, that Lavell also had dark designs on our household, that George and I were tearing apart from each other. I was losing my grip on the house.

'It's been hard to settle after Rose,' I replied.

Maddie gave me a searching look. It was difficult to fool her. Isolated from family, we'd grown to understand each other very well. I changed the subject.

'Sophia is troublesome.'

'Isn't she always?' Maddie smiled.

'She takes turns with Felicia. Who's on my side in this instance. Sophia wants to join a theatre troupe.'

'Wasn't she on the stage before? I seem to remember her talking about it.'

'Near the stage. The mistress of a stage producer. Who set her up in an apartment in Kensington with *trompe l'oeil* walls and a bedroom full of empty promises. She never got as far as an audition and when she fell with Albie, he threw her out. Doesn't seem to have put her off walking the boards.'

'Is she good?'

'She seems to think so. She's got herself a part in a play.'

'Then we must go to watch! It will be fun, and an outing will do you good. You work too hard. We'll go together, with Tizzy and George.'

'I'll ask. But I don't want to encourage her.'

'I thought you were fond of her.'

'Her head is quite turned. And there's Albie. Travelling theatres are no place for children.'

'I can think of plenty worse.'

'I *am* fond of her.'

'Then perhaps that is the trouble.'

Without replying I moved to the stack of canvases, leaning them forward to take a final look at Medusa. She was majestic, terrifying, beautiful. And I realised that she reminded me of Grace.

21

Evergreen House

Maddie understood me too well and she was right about Sophia. The girl was one of my favourites. For all the trouble she caused with Felicia, for all her outspoken ways and foolhardy stubbornness, she had a kind heart and a smile that could light up a room. A natural flirt, with men and women, and endlessly curious. The girl's sheer love of life stopped our routine becoming boring. No wonder poor Felicia couldn't bear the thought of her leaving; she relied on Sophia's light to guide her. I had no such excuse. It was mean of me to want to keep her just because she reminded me of myself in happier times, before responsibility weighed me down. We should go to see her play, Maddie was right about that too. It would do us all good to be absorbed in something else for an evening.

With a sigh, I finished updating the accounts book, blotted the page and closed it with the tissue paper still inside. '*This is my work and I love it,*' Martha had said when I asked her about the autopsy room. '*It makes me feel useful, and there is very little else that interests me.*' My work may be less extreme but I was proud of what I'd achieved at Evergreen, the sanctuary we'd created. I had taught myself to manage a household of tasks and I knew I could never go back to a life without purpose. I slotted the book into the space next to the previous year's log, ensuring everything was in order for our new chaplain's arrival. He was unlikely to be as thorough as Mr Lavell in looking for discrepancies, errors and signs that we weren't operating properly. But he was certainly working for him, and it didn't hurt to be ready. I had made my peace with the plan, convinced myself his presence would be beneficial. A little religious instruction was missing in our lives. It was hard for us all to go to church together, difficult for any church to welcome us into their congregation, and it would do some of the girls good to have moral guidance, kindly meant. I remembered the case notes and decided there was no need to keep them in the office and risk them being read. I would take them up to my bedroom and push them far into the space between the mattress and the wall. The women had trusted me with their stories, and I could not let them fall into the wrong hands. Most of their notes contained details that would horrify a man of God, and I was keen to make a good first impression. If we could start well when he arrived, we might get along and, if we did, that could help to keep the Board happy, and prevent Lavell from moving in as he threatened.

Sliding the case notes under my arm, I rested them against the wall as I fumbled for the key and noticed a waft of something strange. Sweet and rotten, like an uncleared pond or a decaying pile of leaves. I checked the round vase in the hallway, but the water was fresh, the stems of narcissi barely wilting. George had mulched the borders – it could be carrying from outside. But the garden doors were closed when I checked, the windows fastened against the rain. The weather would damp it down in any case. And it seemed to come from inside the house.

Carrying the book of case histories, I checked the scullery to see if any laundry had been left soaking. It wasn't the day for sheets, but it was possible that one of the children had soiled their bed linen or been unwell in the night. With so many little ones it happened reasonably often, and the stains were sometimes soaked in sour milk or lye to remove the ammonia. The room was fresh, unused. Both stone sinks were empty, the floor scrubbed clean. The smell grew stronger by the kitchen, and I hesitated outside for fear of what I might find. Angela butchering dinner, or binding sweetmeats in thin strips of tissue. I hadn't the stomach to witness it. But the kitchen was empty, too, a lull between the clearing from lunch and the start of preparations for dinner.

Through the old glass of the picture window, the garden looked drab. Rain soaked. White fingers of birch spread over the cowed heads of early daffodil. Creeper had sprouted on the back wall too, its tendrils curling along the sill and up the wooden frames, half covering the stairs to the basement. George should cut it back on the first dry day. Threlfall's rooms must look respectable for his patients. According to Maddie they paid a fortune for his treatment. Surely the smell could not come from his clinic? The internal door had been sealed for years, but I stood by it anyway, felt along the edges for gaps and breathed against the wall. Could it be my imagination? Such an atmosphere of brimstone would raise suspicion in the chaplain, and I wanted the whole house clean and tidy before the morning. As I turned to mount the stairs, intending to hide the casebook, I realised the smell was worse outside Angela's rooms. I knocked softly on the outer door, pressing my ear against the wood to listen. No answer. A louder knock brought forth a muttering, someone annoyed at being disturbed, and with a final firm rap I heard footsteps clumping on the floorboards. Angela wore boots at all times, even in the house. A further sign she didn't feel at home. With her light bag and her heavy boots, she was ready to flit at a moment's notice.

She opened the door and peered out.

'Is everything alright?'

Angela nodded. 'It's my free time.'

'I know – forgive my intrusion, but I'm investigating a smell.'

'What smell?'

I waved my hands around. 'As though a dog has rolled in a dead fox.'

'It's the basement.'

Threlfall. What was he up to down there? My stomach tightened. Whatever it was, I would need to be brave. I couldn't risk the inspectors noticing the smell.

Angela still held the door but as we spoke it was opening further. I hesitated, unsure whether I was being invited inside.

'If you want to come in, you can.' She jerked her head with a small movement that could not have been less inviting.

Inside was spartan compared to the cheerful jumble of the rest of the house. I sat on a hard stool and placed the casebook on the rug beside me. No pictures hung on the walls, no samplers or photographs of family. She'd turned over Rose's quilt so the bright patterns were hidden, and the plain cotton backing uppermost. What sort of life had she had before us? There was still no reply from the house in Ireland and I worried that she'd left on bad terms.

'I can find you some things to make it more comfortable in here. If you would like.'

'I'm quite comfortable,' she replied, unable or unwilling to meet my gaze. What could occupy her? No sewing or books were laid out. She seemed so sad most of the time that we should help her do anything that made her happy.

'Would you like to join me for some tea?' I felt as though I intruded, even though she had invited me in. If she was to really settle at Evergreen, then we had to get to know her. I was about to ask how she was feeling when a high-pitched giggle in the corridor announced the arrival of Sophia and her gang.

'The fruitcake you made was delicious and there's plenty left.' Angela bit her lip but I could see she was thinking about it. 'Come on.' I held out my hand. 'Let's go and see what they're finding to giggle about.'

When we reached the kitchen Amy was admonishing Felicia. 'Really, it's not seemly for you to be talking like that.'

'Like what?' I asked.

'She was telling us about the pleasure boats at Putney Bridge,' said Amy quickly.

Sophia pulled a saucy face. 'About the *captain* of the boat.'

'He wasn't the captain and you know it. Anyway, that was a long time ago, before I came here and became *respectable*.'

Sophia fell about in peals of laughter. Amy threw me a helpless look.

'So what did *you* do, before you joined us and became respectable?' Felicia rounded on Angela.

'Angela hasn't had that sort of life,' I said quickly, busying myself with the tea things. I was going to remind them that she was employed as our cook, but I worried it would come out wrong and seem as though I was reminding her of her place, just when I'd coaxed her to take part in a conversation.

'Why don't you tell us then, about Ireland.' Sophia stared.

'I wasn't back there long,' she mumbled.

'What do you mean?' asked Amy gently. 'You don't have to talk if you don't want to. But it can help. It helped me. It still helps to hear other people's stories.'

Amy always knew the right things to say. Angela's expression softened. I poured the tea and we waited.

'I got sent abroad when I was young. I don't know how young, I can't remember much but the churning sea. Decks slick with vomit. It was dark below deck, and hard to walk from one place to another in the dark.'

'What were you sent for? Stealing?' demanded Felicia. 'Why would they let you walk about?'

'Let her talk,' said Amy.

Angela's hand shook as she replaced her cup in the saucer. 'I was with a nurse. She was kind. But when we got there she left me at the dock, in the queue. They matched me with a family that needed help and I was taken straight to their farm. We walked a hundred miles to reach it, men on horses and women on foot beside.'

'What was it like?'

'Dreary. A wasteland of rocks and sand and scrubland plants covered in thorns and spikes.'

Felicia and Sophia sat with pursed lips of disbelief. Though I would never be so unkind to Angela, I struggled to believe her myself. Ships left for the colonies every week, always full of tales of the wondrous country that awaited.

'And the farmer was horrible. Huge and angry with hair all over his arms and hands. His wife and sons barely spoke to me except to order me to do jobs.'

'Was it a big farm?'

'It wasn't really a farm at all. Just fields of rocks and sheep because the land was infertile. I was too young to help. I couldn't hold the sheep still or lift the axe or pull the plough or ride the horse. They regretted taking me on and reminded me of it every day. They put me on stone picking, shifting the rocks out of the fields so they could try to grow crops in heat without water.'

'That sounds like a pointless exercise.'

'It was. And I broke my wrist lifting a rock.' Her face clouded. 'They put me in the kitchen, and I cooked with one hand while his wife worked the sheep. I took her place for everything. Everything a wife should do.'

She looked directly at me, as though daring me to contradict her. That part of her tale, at least, was easy to believe.

'How did you get away from them?' I asked.

'I stole. Begged rides until I reached the dock, then hid between barrels and bags on the first ship I found. Night watchman knew I was there. He fed me in return for favours.'

Amazing she'd escaped motherhood with such a tale. I ran my eye over the flat board of her stomach, and she read my mind.

'Two children at the farm.'

'Where are they then?' Felicia leant forward and suddenly Angela shut down, her face hard and pinched as an oyster. Her mouth became sulky again, her sharp angles returned. She refused to answer any questions and I began to regret trying to draw her out. Whatever her story was, it can't possibly have been so far-fetched as the one she spun in the kitchen. It was clear that the others didn't believe her, despite her obvious fury. Angela was possibly the most complicated of all the women at Evergreen and I was determined to find out why.

22

Dr Threlfall's Alienist Clinic, Putney Heath

I pulled the bell rope a second time, half hoping no-one would answer. What would I say to Threlfall? I'd checked every room upstairs and the smell must be coming from the basement. With Mr Lavell constantly visiting without notice, I had little choice but to investigate, though my stomach tightened at the thought of what I might uncover. Footsteps could be heard inside. Was Threlfall avoiding us? Just as I was about to ring the bell again, the door swung open with a low creak and, for a moment, I thought no-one was there, my head raised to a man's height in anticipation.

'The doctor's not in.'

I looked down to see Hester, his maid, barely taller than Albie, with large hands and feet that stuck right out from under her black dress. She peered around the door with the look of a woodland creature, a mole perhaps, her whole face drawn tight around her eyes as though she strained to see. Too long spent underground. I leant across, trying to see into the gloom behind her. Would she let me in without him present?

'What a shame, he should have expected me. It's just a routine look around, before our inspectors visit.' I affected the tone I reserved for authority. 'It won't take long.'

'You don't usually come in.' Hester still gripped the edge of the door with hands large enough to dig through soil.

'It's a new policy. The Board will have to look at the whole house to sign us off.' I decided to take a risk; even if she could read and write, which was doubtful, it was unlikely Threlfall trusted her with his correspondence. 'I believe they sent a letter about it last week.'

Hester relinquished the door and took a step back, her feet invisible beneath long skirts. Without a word she turned, disappeared into the murky corridor and I followed, the ripe scent catching in my throat. It was clear the basement was the source. There'd been a smell like this when we cleared the rooms before, like dead flower stems left too long in water, or badly stored meat. A slime scent. Rotten sweet. It had taken weeks of clearing and airing to rid the rooms then; there wouldn't be time to remove it before Lavell returned. I would have to hope there was something we could do to mask it, though I began to dread what I might find.

We walked past cabinets in the waiting room, a closed door that I knew led to the place Threlfall saw and examined his patients. In the dim light of the side room, the smell became almost unbearable. I hadn't been aware that Hester lived down here, but the wooden cot told me otherwise. On top of its folded blankets were a Bible and a book of psalms, bound in matching purple cloth. A gift from her anxious mother, perhaps, fearful of the company she kept. I would certainly not like a daughter of mine to be working in such a clinic. The books were laid out neatly, side by side, for show or protection. Hester scuttled to the other side of the room, and I saw objects spread on a low table, hardly trusting my eyes. Knives of varying sizes sat in neat rows next to what looked like the parts of an animal. Was Threlfall practising rituals? Was Hester? There were tales of gypsies from overseas who sliced the throats of chickens, to read the future in the shapes made by their blood as it spilt to the ground. Predicting fate like Rose's tea leaves. But Hester wasn't dark-eyed and wild; she was pale as bone, her movements painfully slow.

Ordinary objects lined up beside the blades, waiting to be used. A stout wooden reel of strong waxed shoe thread. A strangely shaped lump of wood, polished to a deep patina. Hester seized up something caked with dried blood, a sort of feathered skin, and stretched it out wide. She gestured to a row of stuffed creatures on the top shelf of the plate stands. Two mice, both standing on hind legs with pale pink paws outstretched and tails curled round their hind quarters. A squirrel, slightly lopsided, its tail thin and sad. And a raven, the most lifelike, staring out in judgement with its glass bead eyes. The work was crude, jarring, a showcase of dead creatures nothing like the slick taxidermy of the Everleys' small museum.

'Is this yours, or Dr Threlfall's?'

'Mine.' She gestured at the sad menagerie. 'He doesn't like me to work on the fresh ones when he's here.' She picked up the raven in her huge paws and I saw that her fingernails were long enough to cut thread.

'You have been busy.'

'Never liked sewing. Trying to keep my hands occupied.'

'What do you use to treat the skins and stop them decaying?'

'I put some turps on it. Seen the doctor do that.'

'I think perhaps you need to use more.' A milking pail sat under the table, half filled with flesh and congealed blood. 'And you need to find a better way to deal with that.' I pointed and wrinkled my nose. It was definitely the source of the smell.

'I'll burn it.'

What did Maddie say Lucius used for his creatures? Lime? It couldn't smell worse and it would melt the flesh down.

Hester pushed a stool towards me, and I sat, transfixed, as she stretched what look like the skin of a mallard around a crude metal frame and began to stuff the insides with hay and wads of cotton.

'Where did you get it?'

She didn't answer. Probably killed it herself. Much more of this and she'd bring rats into the house too. She began to sew the skin over the padded frame, pulling it tightly and checking the stitches met before puffing the feathers over the join. A skilled needlewoman, like Martha. Transfixed, I watched the thread weave in and out, the duck's flesh pulsing with the rhythmic movement of her fingers, and my mind returned to the neat line of stitches across Rose's throat. Could Hester wield a knife as easily as a thimble?

'Did Dr Threlfall teach you?'

'Dr Everley.' Her needle became unthreaded. It might have been the action of licking the end of the cotton to guide it back through the eye, but I thought she smiled at the mention of his name.

'Did you work here with him?' I looked at her more closely. She was the size of a child, and I'd assumed she was young – but the hair below her cap was partially grey, the skin of her neck wrinkled and dry. It was possible.

'For a while. He was a great doctor.' She worked on her stitches without looking up, but I could sense the obvious pride she had in working for someone so well known.

'Dr Threlfall also enjoys a good reputation. I'm sure you are kept very busy in the clinic looking after all the patients that come and go.' Did I sound patronising? I didn't mean to but she unnerved me, sitting there in her pile of animals, sewing the dead back to life.

'Mind meddling,' she muttered. 'That's what Dr Everley called it. All this nonsense with treating people who've lost their minds.'

'He's very well respected. I believe he's often in the journals.'

'I expect he is.' Hester raised her head and I saw that her left eye drooped slightly, pulled by a poorly healed wound at the top of her cheek. 'But it's not surgery. Not proper medicine, is it?'

Hester finished the duck's torso before she put down her work to show me out, and I stood by the side gate for several minutes to regain my composure so that I could return to the house. I had certainly not expected to find the clinic in such a state of disarray. Threlfall would be horrified to hear her speak of his work in such a disparaging manner. He was immensely pleased with his own achievements and must imagine her in thrall to him, as he evidently believed the rest of us to be. It was hardly my place to tell tales. Dr Threlfall's relationship with his staff was none of my business. And yet the encounter left me unsettled, in no way reassured as to the respectability of the clinic in our basement. The knowledge that Hester had worked for the Everleys was a particularly unwelcome surprise, and I determined to find out more when I could.

Angela banged pots and pans around the kitchen, barely acknowledging my presence. She'd been colder since sharing her strange story, as though she resented our disbelief. Many times I'd wondered if it could be true, but there were too many unanswered questions. It seemed highly unlikely that she would leave children of her own in such a place, or that she could have escaped from her situation without money or help. As for her descriptions of the country, they seemed imagined from depictions of hell in her illustrated Bible. Nowhere on our green earth could there be such a place.

'Is that supper?'

An almost imperceptible grunt of affirmation.

'What are you making?'

'Stew of seafood.'

That certainly wasn't what we'd planned and it wouldn't be popular with half the women, but perhaps she knew and didn't care. She must have made a special trip to buy the ingredients.

'Did you visit the fishmonger?'

'He came here. His boy did, anyway, selling it off half price.' She threw a handwritten receipt onto the counter and I pocketed it to add to the ledger, edging closer to the stove.

'Is this a recipe from Ireland, or perhaps somewhere else you've lived?'

Angela made a noise of disgust and filled a fish steamer with boiling water.

'Would you like to talk more, without the others here?' I owed her the chance to tell her story.

For a moment she stopped working, but before she could open her mouth to reply I was distracted by the sight of what looked like Mr Lavell's cloak lying across the kitchen chair. Charcoal grey with a double collar and epaulettes, both edged in white, that connected in a sort of run-off for rain. Unusual in style, and unlike him to leave it so carelessly instead of hanging it in the hall.

'Do we have a visitor, Angela?'

'He went to look round.' She opened the stove door and pushed the fish kettle inside, slamming it again with such force that I feared the hinges might break. I should find out what was troubling her, but I did not know how long Lavell had been inside the house; he could have been anywhere and he may very well be talking to someone like Sophia, which would do none of us any good.

'I must see to him. Has he been offered tea, Angela? I'll be back as soon as I can, and we will have our talk.'

Without waiting for a response, I dashed out of the kitchen and along the hallway, listening for voices. The downstairs rooms were hives of industry. Some women wove baskets or pots, stretching and pulling the strands of willow, packing it tightly between the uprights, their hands protected from the rough ends of cane with white cotton gloves. They chattered as they worked, eyes fixed on the weaving to make sure each line was neat and straight. They hadn't seen visitors and sent me to the paper room, where Henrietta and Sophia stood either end of a paste table, stretching a roll of lining paper while Caroline dipped and pressed a carved block of wood, pressing it down carefully to leave the outline of an oakleaf. She spaced them out in rows, leaving room for acorns to be hand-painted below them. A pretty pattern that was popular with customers.

'Mr Lavell asked to speak with some of us.' Sophia's tone was sulky. 'And Amy wouldn't let me go with Felicia. She took him off herself.' She moved a hand to pat her hair and the paper moved slightly.

'Do concentrate, Sophia, this roll is almost finished,' Caroline admonished. 'They're upstairs in your drawing room, Rebecca. They're taking tea up there.'

At least he was with Amy – I could trust her to mitigate any unwanted prying. 'Did he look into the workrooms?'

'Only to ask for you.'

'May I be excused now? I've to learn my lines and my arms are aching.' Sophia pouted.

Would she ever think of anyone but herself? 'We have an important visitor, Sophia, you may break at the allotted time. And please remember how much we rely on one another to survive.'

I knew from Caroline's stifled giggle that Sophia pulled a face behind my back. I'd expect nothing less. One day she would understand; for now, there were more important matters to attend.

Knocking briefly, I opened the door straight away. Both Lavell and Felicia, on facing chairs, flinched as thought they'd been caught at something. Amy, sitting slightly apart on the ottoman, smiled with a look of relief.

'I'm sorry, Mr Lavell, I wasn't aware of your visit. Forgive my absence, I was attending to something with Dr Threlfall.'

'Important work,' he nodded sagely.

Hester didn't seem to think so. 'Did you wish to see us about anything in particular?'

'Professional interest, Mrs Harris, to see how you are managing.' Lavell gave a slow smile that looked anything but sincere.

'As you can see, we manage very well. Did Amy show you the workshops? The women make great progress in their work. We're very proud of what they achieve.'

'Yes, I saw the crafts downstairs. They certainly looked as though they were enjoying themselves. There is a side room by the paper room that will do very well for my office.'

Was he talking about *my* study? The idea of him in there every day while I hid upstairs was almost too much to bear. With a start I remembered the casebook. What had I done with it? In all the excitement of Angela's fictional story, I couldn't remember where it was. I certainly didn't recall hiding it in my bedroom as I'd planned.

'I look forward to reviewing the accounts so we can see how to move things forward.' Lavell leant back in George's good chair and laced his fingers together. 'I also came to inform you that Mr Illingworth will start with you tomorrow. He will be my eyes and ears when I can't be here in person.'

'I trust that Amy and Felicia have made you comfortable?' He looked far too comfortable, boots up on the tapestry footstool to gain the best of the fire.

'We've had a lovely talk. Mr Lavell has been asking about what I did before Evergreen,' Felicia said proudly.

My heart sank. Aside from Sophia herself, she was the last of the residents I'd want talking to anyone from the Board. Lavell was clear about his designs on our house. Any whiff of scandal and he'd get his wishes sooner. Amy picked at the skin around her nails, as she did when she was nervous. Fervently I hoped he had not asked her questions too; she was terrified of her husband finding her but equally worried about lying. If he'd asked directly, she would have told the truth.

Lavell nodded. 'Indeed I have – it's been most enlightening, but there's always more for me to understand. Felicia tells me that you sometimes write stories down? If you have such a casebook, I would very much like to see it.'

23

All Saints Asylum

All night they call, with the moon's full light falling through the bars, through cracks in the bricks. Even the worst of them in their windowless rooms lined with straw pads. Even those hidden in the shadows feel the moon. It darkens their minds, calls their demons, throws their bodies into shapes. They reach for knives, sharpen their nails on the wall, scrabble for shards of wood or brick so they can hurt whoever comes near. So they can hurt themselves. Pulling hair in clumps. Reaching to the backs of their mouths and pulling out their own teeth in bloodied stumps, yanking until their shrunken gums give way and the metal taste of blood satisfies their cravings. Until the next month, when the lunar energy renews their strength. Lunatics. The moon lends its name. A monthly curse that shows I'm not like them. Such wildness. Sometimes I wish my demons were the same.

Edward won't come until they're calm. He never comes on days and nights like these, never comes on the days they drill. Varley has stopped threatening me with the pain relief tool, maybe because he knows I have no hope of leaving anyway. What would be the point of trying to cure my affliction? I've seen the holes it left in other women, heard the noise as they turn the handle to push the blade into the skull, holding it in place with a spike. I know what they do, and so does Threlfall, but he prefers to pretend that the work he carries out has nothing to do with this primal, violent urge for chaos and the equally violent cures. He likes to stay clean. Sticks with his fashionable talking therapy for wealthy clients. In reality, it's little different. Those gentlemen grip their wives' arms all the way to the clinic. No matter. Edward tells me his work is gaining attention and I've read the summaries, have taken part too, subjected myself to their prodding and screening. All my ideas, developing Father's. By rights my name should sit alongside his, but even if I was out of here, even if my name had not been blackened by the Brewsters, it would never be allowed. A woman's name in science. Unthinkable.

The mouse scurries in, an open letter in her little paws. Nervously she holds out the ragged envelope and I take pleasure in covering her skin with mine, slowly drawing it from her grasp. Her nails are bitten to the quick, striped with dried blood, and the sight of them turns my stomach. Touching anything must give her pain. Perhaps she likes that. Perhaps the sharp stab of pain dulls the screech of everything else, just for a while. That I can understand. My own thighs are crossed with silvery scars, delicate kisses from the knife under my mattress.

'Who is it from?'

She shakes her head so vigorously that her whole body moves from side to side, like a docked puppy trying to wag its tail.

'Don't be shy. I know you read all my letters – everyone's post is opened here, is it not?'

'In case it is upsetting, Mr Varley says. It's for your own good.' Her voice is thin, high, nervous.

'Everything is for our own good, isn't it? Would you agree?'

She raises a little paw to her mouth and begins to nibble on a shred of nail. Terrified of everything, and little wonder after what she must witness.

'Why don't you read it to me then? In case it is upsetting. You wouldn't want me to become distressed, would you?'

She draws out the letter and begins to read in a stilting manner, stumbling on almost every word. Extraordinary. I had assumed she was illiterate. Little mouse is stronger than she looks.

'"*Dear Mother*"' . . . From Eloise. Even if it was a much-delayed note from those poor boys, they wouldn't start a letter like that. Edmond used to launch straight in with complaints about the food, asking when they would get out.

'"*Dear Mother, thank you for your letter. I was sorry to hear about my brothers, I'm sure you will be sad. Thank you for your invitation to come home. I would like to come back to see you. I'm not yet sure when I can be spared but do ask Dr Threlfall to send money for a ticket, as you suggested. Please send it to the postbox below and I will collect. I hope that I may see you again one day soon. Your affectionate, Eloise.*"'

A short letter. Brief and lacking emotion, like her childhood. *Affectionate.* She was never that, neither was I, but there is something about the tone of this note that worries me.

'Thank you.' I dismiss the mouse, eager to be alone with thoughts of family, and she hesitates, drops an awkward half-curtsey. She's impressed with me, increasingly so. I should use that to my advantage. If she ever gets an afternoon off, I might be able to persuade her to spy on Evergreen House. 'You should try some curl papers my dear, it would lift your face.'

She reddens. 'Thank you, ma'am.'

'Do call me Grace.' I beam a dazzling smile and she backs out, flustered. I like it when she comes without Varley.

The letter is a single page and I turn it over, to check whether the mouse missed something overleaf. If Eloise's new family are censoring her letters, they may only look at the front. A postbox collection, too. If money was sent to her address, would someone take it? I don't like to think of her as vulnerable. As I suspected, there is another note on the reverse, small, scratched letters so faint they don't show through the vellum. I hold it up, narrow my eyes and read.

Do send the money. Your letter has brought back so many memories of the time before we were all forced apart. A sadness for my brothers, though Edmond was never kind, and I miss you and Uncle Lucius.

Does she know he was hanged? After the trial, everything to do with the children was managed by Threlfall, who worked with the magdalens to arrange their care. Would he have sheltered Eloise from the truth? Possibly. He can be deeply sentimental.

I miss our comfortable home – so do I, my dear – *and I would very much like to live with you again.*

So her new life hasn't claimed her. All may not be lost. I doubt she's really pining for her childhood; it will be the money that's struck such a change of heart. But, if she still carries her cold sharp beauty, I can set my plan into action nevertheless. Aim her at Edward's cousin, perhaps, or even Edward himself once I'm ready to give him up. Two of us. The poor boy won't know what has crept up behind him.

24

Evergreen House

Thunder rattled the eaves for most of the night, creeper tapped its stemmed fingers against the windows, and every violent noise made me fear intruders with the faces of Lavell and Hester, armed with Rose's keys and my missing casebook. I slept as lightly as a new mother. George, too, was restless. Twice I woke to find him out of bed, the sheets on his side creased and cold. In the morning I was slow with lack of sleep, but the new day brought calm skies and I hoped the rain would hold off long enough to show the chaplain our garden. That part of our endeavours, at least, should meet with approval. The women had worked hard in their free time to clear the vegetable patch from last year's dried stalks, digging out the clumps of winter weeds and raking the soil into furrows ready for planting. The glass house was neatly stacked with seed trays and swept of dried earth. Hazel twigs were stripped of climbing beans and piled against the fence, ready to be pushed together and tied with twine to form a frame for the new crop. A season for new starts and fresh hopes.

I lay in bed longer than usual, watching the sun rise fully through the open curtains. I'd come round to the idea of the chaplain and was determined that his first visit should go well. He'd be a positive role model, a source of kindness and someone in whom the girls could confide, as I confided in Martha. The right person could restore us after Rose; he might even help Angela. Yawning and stretching, I smoothed the bedclothes, drew up the quilt and plumped the pillows. Another half hour would be bliss, but I could hear the others moving around and knew I should be there to supervise. I chose a dark brown dress with no decoration, adding a plain grey wrap against the morning chill and forcing my curls into plaits that I pinned at the back. The woman reflected in the looking glass was every inch the respectable proprietress.

I'd scarcely descended the stairs when a sharp tug on the bell rope set off the cacophony of inside chimes. Our visitor was early. I smoothed my clothes, lifted my chin and went straight to answer the door, worrying that I'd have no chance to check the rooms first, and no opportunity to take breakfast. My stomach rumbled at the thought as I lifted the latch and opened the heavy door, surprised to see him standing on the very top step. Without waiting to be invited he pushed through the door and held out his coat and hat.

'You can fetch your master now.'

Slim build, with a steeply receding hairline and small, folded ears. A starched white collar and a darned patch on the sleeve of his jacket. He peered around, as though his eyesight might be poor. It wrinkled the skin on the bridge of his nose and sharpened his features, giving him the look of a weasel about to pounce.

'Good morning – Mr Illingworth, I presume?' I took his things and placed them neatly on the hallstand. 'Mrs Harris. I am the mistress of the house.'

'And where are the rest of your flock?'

'They're breakfasting.' I guessed from the noise. 'Would you care for anything?'

He emitted a short barking noise that might have been intended as a laugh. 'I ate two hours since and have already done my rounds of visiting the sick.'

I took a slight step backwards, hoping none were contagious.

'And is this the usual routine? To start the day so late?'

No point in misleading him. He would only ask the others and that would be another black mark against me. 'Yes, quite usual. You will find us very productive throughout the day and evening, and breakfast, like all mealtimes, is a chance for the household to gather. An important time.'

'Do you not gather at prayer?'

I hesitated. Only on Sundays, and I imagined he wouldn't like to hear that. 'Of course. But in a big household there's always much to discuss, and prayers is a reflective time.' He could not disagree. 'Shall I show you the rooms on this floor?'

'Why don't we begin downstairs?' He gestured for me to lead the way and I smiled brightly as I stepped in front, hoping nothing would be out of order.

Everything was cleared, the plates scraped and stacked ready for taking to the scullery. Angela was kneading dough on the huge wooden board by the stove. The children stood in line, waiting for Amy to clean their faces. George sat at the table with Henrietta, our newest addition, twisting willow into shapes as he showed her how to make handles for baskets. It was a picture of neatness and industry. I breathed a sigh of relief. George winked at me, and I hoped that it went unnoticed. Mr Illingworth lifted his chin and sniffed the air suspiciously. The rotten smell lingered, and I couldn't shake the image of Hester smiling at the Everley name. At the next opportunity I would ask Threlfall how long she'd been with him, to set my mind at rest about her grisly creatures and whether they were practise for more sinister work. As I looked around for something to distract my guest, Sophia and

Felicia walked in, holding either end of the empty crockery tray, chattering furiously. When they saw us, they set down the tray and dropped theatrical curtsies. Both were dressed garishly, despite my warnings. Mr Illingworth's beady eyes narrowed further as he peered at them.

'And who might you be?'

They introduced themselves, giggling and casting their eyes to the floor, while his expression grew stern.

'Then you are dressed in a style that is plainly beyond your honest means.'

'These were Sophia's when she . . . before she came here.'

'And such tawdry finery is not suitable for the situation you are in now. Mrs Harris, you do these women an unkindness by fostering in them a love of showing off beyond their stations.'

All the girls had something. Paste jewels or pretty hair slides, some lace or a silk flower in a straw hat. It hurt no-one and it cheered them. Gave them a bit of colour in an otherwise difficult life. What did it matter?

'If God hadn't wanted us to wear colours, he wouldn't have made them,' I replied.

'That is exactly the sort of answer I expected.' Mr Illingworth folded his arms. 'A giddy love of dress can have ruinous consequences. God has allotted to each their correct place in society and to live outside of that is blasphemous. My first recommendation will be a uniform dress. Something serviceable and plain, the same for every one of your . . . what do you call them?'

'They are our guests here. And we're happy to have them.'

'Guests.' He almost spat the word. 'Little wonder they think it appropriate to swan around in cheap satin and paste jewels. How can they work like this?'

George motioned for Amy to take the children out. He opened his mouth as though about to argue with the reverend and I shook my head quickly at him. It wouldn't help if we both fell foul of the man's temper.

'This is my husband and the second proprietor of the house.'

George held out his hand and Mr Illingworth brushed it with his fingertips. 'Where did you send the children? To their lessons?'

'The children take their lessons in the afternoon, while the women work.'

'They do not look fittingly dressed to hear the good word.' He paused, looking from myself to George while Sophia and Felicia gawped, still holding the tray.

'You can take the rest of the plates,' I said to them. 'Now, thank you.'

'I take it their lessons are based on the scriptures?'

'Of course,' George agreed. He knew very well that Amy told them stories, made their learning fun.

'Their daily instruction in the Christian religion may of course be supplemented with other teaching as may fit them for service and train them for habits of industry, usefulness and virtue. I'll test them on their scriptures at the next opportunity.'

'Well, they are very young. Amy will be dressing them for the garden. Perhaps you'd like to see that now? We've been clearing ready for spring planting. It's wholesome work and allows us to grow more than we require, so we're able to deliver surplus locally where it's needed.'

Mr Illingworth assented, unfolded his arms, and George went to open the doors, returning almost immediately.

'Do you have the key?'

I patted the pocket of my skirt without really expecting to find it there. I wasn't in the habit of taking it from the lock, though I couldn't promise I hadn't lost it. Lately I'd been too distracted for certainty about anything.

Angela still pounded the dough, punching and kneading with the strength of a prize fighter. I had to call her twice before she wheeled around to face us, holding her floured hands up away from her apron.

'Those two had it last,' she said, pointing at the girls as they returned with the plates tray, turning back to her worktop immediately.

Why would they remove the key? Fearful of intruders perhaps. A conversation for later.

'Felicia, could you please give George the key to the garden door?'

Mr Illingworth began to tap his foot, showing us he was a busy man, unused to being kept waiting. Felicia's cheeks coloured an unbecoming shade of pink.

'It's in our room, I'll fetch it.' Sophia looked uncomfortable.

'Then I will take the opportunity to view some of the bedrooms,' Mr Illingworth pounced. 'Lead the way.'

Sophia and Felicia hung back, nudging each other and whispering as he and George left the kitchen. Whatever was causing them to behave like children? Something told me that Angela knew. As soon as Mr Illingworth was out of earshot, she began to sing happily to herself. I hurried after them, taking the stairs two at a time, almost tripping on a piece of carpet where a stair rod had come loose. Sophia and Felicia occupied a bedroom on the third floor – a nice room, large and airy, its green walls painted with apple blossom. They shared it with two other women, both reserved in comparison. I hoped they hadn't been doing something that would get them all in trouble.

I needn't have worried; the room was as neat as could be. Beds made, curtains looped back, drawers and wardrobe fastened shut. No dirty clothes lying on the furniture. Shoes neatly paired in rows. A large, leather-bound family Bible sat on the table.

'This all seems in order.' Mr Illingworth looked pleased.

'The women keep their rooms well. They're all the same, so there's no need to go into them all. Pass us the key, Felicia, it's time for your chores.'

Neither girl moved. We waited. George tried to steer Mr Illingworth away but, sensing trouble, he brushed away his arm and stayed put.

'If it's lost, then say so.'

Felicia's face was miserable. She reached over to the Bible, and I saw that the key was stuck between its pages. What on earth had the foolish things been doing? Something harmless, the kind of mischief young girls find together. But the chaplain would not find it so.

'What is the meaning of this? A desecration of the word.' His voice was dangerously quiet.

'It's nothing.' Felicia scuffed her slipper against the rag rug. 'You put a key in the book of Ruth, and say letters out loud, and if the book moves it's the name of your husband. Everyone does it.'

'Do they indeed.' Mr Illingworth turned to glare at me, and I knew our cause was lost.

The rest of the visit was disastrous. He declined to inspect the kitchen garden and found the children wanting in their knowledge of the scriptures. In the workrooms, he made note of everything the women wore. The skilfully painted wallpaper was dismissed as 'frippery', the baskets were 'overly decorated'. All my careful bookkeeping was overlooked. He could barely contain his fury at Felicia's brazen use of the good book and the detrimental influence it had, accusing her of nothing less than devil worship.

'You have run a lax household, Mr and Mrs Harris, and such behaviour is the consequence.'

George and I sat before him in the front parlour, side by side, heads bowed like bad children.

'If you would look at the accounts, at the way she has thought through the plans and brought them to routines,' George pleaded. 'Rebecca works hard, really hard, to provide a living, and a family, for girls and women who have nothing.'

It warmed my heart to hear him say it. For so long I felt I'd failed my duty as a wife, and it was good to know he was still proud of what we'd achieved. His words made me bolder.

'We all work hard,' I said. 'Felicia's mistake was unfortunate. But she's a young girl, cruelly treated by life, and like all young people she's eager to know what her future holds; if it will be happy.'

'These girls have lived lives of pollution, and that pollution is evident in their ways.' Lavell's words again; I don't know why I thought it would be different. 'It is unclear to me why you have refused to follow the recommended routine of prayers and laundry. It would keep them busy rather than turning their heads with fancy goods and time for leisure that allows their minds to dream above their stations.'

'They wouldn't stay long in a laundry.' I spoke calmly, retaining eye contact. 'The work is gruelling and would soon send them back to the streets or into unsuitable places.'

'I will organise a visit to the Magdalen Hospital for Penitents. They run an excellent programme. If you follow their model, under the guidance of Mr Lavell's Board, not only will the laundry bring in income, but you will also be able to access the alms fund to help with their food.'

He'd made his decision before he even came. Primed by

Lavell to push his cause. Another temporary prison to further punish women who had suffered enough. A continuous file of downtrodden souls moving through without hope of changing their situation. Lining the pockets of Lavell and his cronies. And what would become of the children? Would they be expected to work too?

'I've been to those places. And I would prefer to provide an establishment that does not expect humiliation in return for bed and board.'

'There's nothing humiliating about a life of service.' He gave me a stern look. 'It is the life I have chosen for myself.'

'That's not what I meant. We have an opportunity here to transform the lives of a few women who can become part of a community and live meaningful lives. I want the women in my care to be able to look on their children and see something other than shame or fear.'

Mr Illingworth made a strangled noise. 'Your penitents are unlikely to reform while their sin incarnate acts as a reminder of their transgressions.'

Where would the little ones go? They'd be farmed or put to work. Wherever they went, they'd be miserable without us.

'Children should stay with their mothers, in a place where both can be educated and given a second chance.'

'I can see that you think you are helping, Mrs Harris. But there's little point in educating these people.'

My fingers itched to slap his pompous face. He could not be more pleased with himself. What did he know of life and what it did to the powerless and vulnerable? His opinions were built on theory and good wine.

'I believe there's a strong link between lack of education and crime. And I intend—'

'What is *your* opinion on this matter, Mr Harris?' he interrupted, rounding on George. 'Is your wife correct? I'll wager you're a man who has been well acquainted with the underworld. I have been told of your previous . . . *occupation.*'

A deep flush ran across George's neck, and he shifted in the hard parlour chair. To sit in such a manner was torment for a practical man who hardly ever spent the day indoors.

'I wholeheartedly agree with my wife. London's class of unfortunates grows at an alarming rate, and I would rather help to change their lives than punish them.' He sat back, slightly breathless with the effort of impressing. I could not have loved him more.

That night I made a full round of the house, visiting the children's two big dormitories and the smaller room where Albie slept. As the eldest child he enjoyed the privilege of his own space, though he still came to join the others for stories and prayers, and I wondered if he felt unsafe without company after so long together. When I asked him if he'd rather stay in the dorm, he agreed, sharing happily with Henry.

All the women were quieter than usual, worried, perhaps about the results of the visit. I didn't explain our conversation with the chaplain, though they all knew about the book and key. Amy told me, reluctantly, that Sophia had also encouraged Felicia to perform the same blasphemous trick to ask for the name of Rose's killer to be revealed. Thank heavens Illingworth didn't hear that. What if they imagined a name was revealed, or made assumptions about who was responsible for a heinous crime? What would they have done? Such speculation could ruin reputations.

Drained by a day on best behaviour, I was tired and irritable by the time I reached Felicia's room. Her eyes were wide, contrite, but I did not sympathise. Neither did I explain how I'd defended her to Mr Illingworth. I wanted her to be sorry. 'It was reckless and foolish behaviour. You have set the chaplain against us and given him cause to file a disastrous report that may very well close us down. I am deeply disappointed in you, Felicia. I don't want you in your room tonight, you have not earned the right to speak with anyone. You can take Albie's bedroom and stay away from everyone until I tell you otherwise.' Isolation was the worst punishment for such a social animal as Felicia. Some time alone would help her to think.

25

Evergreen House

Amy stood in the doorway, her face bone pale and serious. Evie, held up on her hip, peeped round at me and then buried her face back in the folds of her mother's shawl. Her hair was wild, unbrushed. Dirt and tears stained her cheeks.

'I need to talk to Rebecca now,' said Amy quietly, bending to set her down. The little girl snuggled deeper, clinging on with her fingers and knees. 'Come on.'

'What's happened?' I mouthed above the tousled head.

Amy pulled a grim expression.

'Would you like to help me set out the plates for breakfast, Evie?' I began to play hide and seek with her, bobbing round and down behind Amy until she started to giggle and loosened her grip. I transferred her weight to me and felt the warmth of her chubby limbs, hot breath on my neck. 'Do you know which ones are the blue plates? The ones we use for our eggs?'

Evie nodded solemnly, one thumb pushed into her mouth.

'See if you can count how many we'll need.' I set her down and she tottered towards the cupboard where they were kept.

'What is it?' I whispered.

Amy closed her eyes. 'It's Felicia. She's in the garden.'

I glanced at the clock. It was early for anyone else to be up, especially Felicia. Other than the three of us and Angela, the house was usually quiet until well after seven.

'What's she doing?' My first, rather uncharitable, thought was that she was drunk and had somehow managed to stay out all night. That was all we needed to enhance our reputation.

'Nothing.' Amy's eyes widened. 'I think she might be . . . dead.' She mouthed the last word with a warning look to the other side of the room, where Evie was busily lifting plates from the cupboard one at a time and spreading them across the floor.

'Could you help Evie?' Angela would be up soon and wouldn't like to find children in her kitchen. 'I'll go and see if she's alright.' Felicia was a difficult girl, her flightiness not helped by Sophia's current mood. It wouldn't surprise me if she'd planned a night out and found herself unable to get back in once we'd fastened the new deadbolts. Though Amy had plenty of experience managing such episodes; she would have known what to do with her. And Felicia wasn't the sort to do things alone – she would surely have dragged one of the others along if that was her intent. Fear quickened my breath. I heard the thump of my heart in my chest. What if Rose's killer had returned? By the time I stood on the lawn, I dreaded what I might find. No-one was asleep on the bench, or the low wall by the sunken grass. No-one sat on the edges of the urns or slumped against the fence. I was about to go back inside, to tell Amy that the silly girl had probably woken and would need strong tea, when I saw a flash of dark red by the lily pond. Skirts, crumpled and caught on the edging, revealed a muddy pair of house slippers. Felicia would not have gone out at night in those.

Even as I rushed across the garden, I knew I was too late. The angle of her body was unnatural, arms flung up and torso twisted so that her legs pointed in a different direction. Her face was completely submerged in the water, hair hanging in loose wet strands around her head, like Medusa's snakes. She was heavy in my arms, difficult to turn over, her skin as cold as marble. When I finally pulled her free and turned her over, I stood back and looked at her for a moment, half expecting her to sit up and cough the dirty water from her lungs, berate me for letting her fall in, demand to wear my shawl. Nothing happened. Her eyelids were open, eyes rolled backwards showing too much white. Weeds were stuck to her hair, droplets ran from her forehead to her ears and neck then dripped onto her dress.

How had she come to such an end? In her own garden? The grass by the pond was slightly scuffed but there were no real signs of a struggle. Guilt for the way I had spoken to her flooded in, and I knelt down to counteract the sudden light-headedness. Was this my fault? I'd defended her to Illingworth, knowing her crime was just high spirits, and then punished her anyway, scolding her harshly enough to draw tears. Had she taken her own life? Beyond the silly key incident, had she really been meddling with spirits? If she had, it may have frightened her. But this was Felicia, bold as brass, strong and determined. A fighter. She'd set fire to her bed because she wanted to be let go from service, and it had worked – she'd ended up on the streets and that's where her further trouble began. Despite everything Felicia had endured, she'd never broken. I couldn't imagine anything being bad enough for her to do such a terrible thing. Impossible, too, to drown oneself in a pond like that. Still, there she was, lifeless, in the very place I promised everyone would be safe, and at that moment it seemed there was no-one to blame but myself.

I stood, walked around the pond, looking for any indication that she'd tripped. But the edging was all intact and her face bore no obvious signs that she'd knocked herself out. Neither did she smell of liquor. There was no explanation except that Rose's murderer had returned. What did he want with us? Would he pick us off one by one? The gate was still locked, though the side door to the basement was open. Someone who knew the place well could have slipped away without notice. Hester could easily hide: Lavell wouldn't raise suspicions. How could I work out what happened? I couldn't bear to touch her again to see if there were marks of attack. Lying there, cold on the grass, she looked a sorry figure, younger than her years. A child I should have protected. My tears came then, great tearing sobs of sorrow for the life she wouldn't have, the future I'd wanted for her after everything she'd been through. Felicia was a mixer, one of the most wilful girls we'd housed, but she was a loyal friend to all of us and Sophia would be lost without her. This was my fault; I was a bad person, a wild girl who'd brought shame on my family and entangled us with the Everleys. Now their evil was returning to haunt us.

For too long I sat on the damp grass, unsure what to do. The others would be up by now, the children hungry. They needed routine and stability. A dead girl in the garden would prove Lavell and Illingworth right, would undermine any attempt to keep things going and allow them to take over in the way they wanted. This nightmare needed managing with the minimum of fuss.

Swinging with a sudden creak, the side gate opened and a man in a greatcoat and oversized hat let himself through, fastened it shut behind him. Threlfall. He was a doctor and could surely help. Though I was certain she was dead, it needed someone to confirm, and he could stay while I fetched the magistrate. As I called his name, ran to meet him, I remembered the scream, the way she had behaved when she left his rooms. Was this somehow linked to his research? It was too late to change my mind; he was already holding my arm in a gesture of concern.

'The pond, quickly.' Breathless, I struggled to explain.

'Are you quite well, Mrs Harris?'

'It's Felicia. I think . . .' I couldn't bring myself to say it, but my face must have told him. He was already hurrying across the lawn just as George arrived.

'Is it true?' George put his arms around me, and I leant against him in relief. I needed him there. Though I would not be sent away from the magistrate again; this time I wanted to hear everything that was said.

'I think it is. Threlfall is checking but she was face down in the water when I found her.' My throat caught on the words, my voice rough and sore from tears. 'We'll need the magistrate.'

'I'll fetch him.'

'You will catch your death like that. Put a jacket on, and a hat.' If he understood that I was warning him to look respectable, he didn't show it. 'How are the others?'

'Everything is calm inside. Amy sent me out. Did she find . . . ?' George looked over to where Threlfall was kneeling beside the pond, and we both walked towards him. He was holding her left hand, lace cuffs falling on her arm, his head bent over in prayer or sadness.

'Nothing.' He looked up. 'No vital signs at all. I'm so sorry for your loss. She was a spirited girl, and the household will be the poorer for her absence.'

Fresh tears blurred my vision. I would have to send for Martha, though she'd have her work cut out to mask the marks around poor Felicia's neck. Threlfall pulled a tragic face, dabbed his eyes with a mauve silk scarf and pressed his hand over her eyelids until they stayed closed.

* * *

'It's *not* your fault, Rebecca, please stop saying that. Death happens.'

Maddie was right. Young women did pass over every day. They died of typhoid, fell in rivers, caught colds and scarlet fever. They died giving birth, or afterwards. They were beaten, starved and strangled. But they didn't die at Evergreen. Not any more. It was the first time that someone in my care was lost, and I couldn't explain to Maddie how that made me feel.

'Sophia is distraught. She blames herself too. That silly game with the book and the key. She used to play it with her sisters, and nothing ever happened. But when Felicia said the letters . . .' With a shiver, I realised I hadn't asked which game, the future husband or the murderer's name. 'When she said the letters, the book really seemed to move, and it frightened them. That's why they forgot to replace the key.'

'Sophia must know it can't really have moved?'

'She has convinced herself.' She refused to sleep in their room, or little Albie's room where poor Felicia had spent her last night, and the pair of them were squeezed together in a nursery cot in the children's dormitory.

'Have you given any more thought to her request?'

'The theatre?' I hadn't. But it may help. Sophia was too fond of drama and her presence wouldn't help the house to move on. It might be for the best if she spent some time away. 'I'm inclined to allow it. We'll go to watch, too – it will please her.'

'Was there anything else unusual? Other than Felicia being up early, of course.'

That was unusual. Generally, she was the last to wander downstairs, her head still full of dreams. But she'd been sleeping in a strange bed, isolated from her friends at a time when she was nervous of what she'd conjured and worried about being in trouble. Little wonder she'd been wandering. I closed my eyes, willing my mind to stop finding more reasons to blame myself.

'I found her deep in conversation with Mr Lavell not a week since. He seemed very interested in her for some reason.'

'A gentleman from the Board is hardly suspicious.'

That was a matter for discussion. 'And she'd been seeing Threlfall.'

Maddie stiffened. 'Was she suffering, in her mind?'

Felicia was the least likely to suffer so. 'She was helping him. With his research.'

'It's not wise to let him close to anyone.'

'I don't know.' Lifting the green glazed pot, I poured tea into matching cups, and did not comment when Maddie added a tot of gin to each from a small hip flask. It couldn't hurt this afternoon, though she'd picked up such habits from Alice as to make me think she should not be encouraged here when Mr Lavell visited. Or the chaplain. With a jolt I realised that I had informed neither of Felicia's death. It wasn't a conversation I relished and yet they should know before the news was reported. Lavell knew her better than any of the other girls, and I already suspected it wasn't wise to let *him* get close to anyone either. 'Threlfall was helpful this morning. And he seemed upset.'

'Well, we all know what a wonderful actor he is.' Maddie held out her flask to deliver another slug, and I placed my hand over my cup. Steadying nerves was one thing. Afternoon drinking quite another.

'You're not in your commune now,' I admonished.

'It's been a difficult day. None of us may judge.' She shook her head and placed the flask back in her pocket. 'What research was Felicia helping with?'

Explaining the scream and its strange aftermath, with Sophia dishevelled and Felicia sullen, would only cause Maddie to worry even more. 'He said he was measuring responses to pain stimuli.'

'Have you been downstairs? It sounds like a good idea to do so. You're subjected to enough inspection here.' Maddie looked thoughtful. 'Old Everley did pain research. Viciously tortured animals. People, too, probably, but he didn't put that in his papers. Ask Threlfall what he's up to. Promise me you'll send George in there?'

George kept as far away from Threlfall as possible. If it would help to find out what happened to Felicia, I would go there myself. Wouldn't hurt to see what Hester thought about it all either.

'I will.'

Trailing a black crêpe ribbon, the kitchen cat pushed itself through the small crack in the doorway. It turned, pounced, and trapped the end between its front paws, rolling over onto its back to pummel its catch with its hind legs.

'Did you tie that?' Maddie picked up the creature, remaking the bow as it struggled and fussed to get away.

I nodded. I'd fastened a black ribbon to every live thing in the household: the dogs, the children's wrists, even the chickens were dragging bows from their legs as they scratched in the dirt. To protect us from deaths spreading further. An old wives' tale, but I'd do anything to ensure nothing else happened here. Two funerals in as many months. Our world felt like it was crumbling.

'You're really worried?'

Murders, ravens and missing babies. Gruesome clinical research. Taxidermy in the basement and bodies appearing all these years later. Why would I not worry? There was no telling where it would end. But Maddie was the last person in whom I should confide. She and Tizzy had worked hard to rid themselves of the past. They had changed, moved on. I shouldn't be filling their minds with memories they'd burnt.

'I feel as though I'm no longer in control,' I said carefully. 'When I was in the workhouse, before Father came to find me and bring me here, my life wasn't my own. I woke, and ate, and worked when I was told to, and I never knew when someone would come and take me to another room, make me work on something else. I'd be moved from the kitchen to the laundry to the yard. Without explanation or reason. Always feeling watched and never knowing what I did to displease whoever observed. I am beginning to feel the same.'

'You run this place beautifully! When I think of what it was before.' Maddie shuddered, instinctively reached for her hip flask. Perhaps the past was still close for her after all.

'Between Mr Lavell and now Reverend Illingworth, I don't know how long we have before they will turn us into another hospital for penitents. We'll be forced to take in laundry and the children will all be sent away. They're happy here, Maddie.' Felicia's child was, thankfully, too young to understand the full horror of the morning's find. He'd look for her a while, toddling from room to room, without words, his whole face a question mark. And it would tear my heart to see him searching. But he would grow, and he would forget. Provided our little family was allowed to stay together.

'I know. You do so much to help them.'

'They help one another. Yesterday, when Albie fell, Evie rushed over to him and kissed the scrape on his knee. They're like siblings.' As we were years ago, roaming the garden at Lynton, before my foolish choices brought first shame and then horror to my family. Was it my punishment not to bear children?

'The children's happiness is not entirely your responsibility.' Maddie's voice brought me from my daydream. 'I wonder, sometimes, if you take on too much.'

'I love them like my own. Maybe I shouldn't say that. But they do bring me joy. And it's been hard, for me and George.' There, it was out. I willed her to understand, because how else could I explain? It hurt me more and more to look at him, to feel the empty promise in his touch and ignore the vacant nest that hung between us.

'You are so sad, sister.'

She came to sit beside me on the sofa and placed her hand on my face, her eyes searching, her silk sleeves brushing my cheek. Around her neck was the amethyst locket that had belonged to Lucius' mother, a lock of her own murdered son's hair inside. Dried and red-brown, a baby's first curl. I hadn't seen the necklace since she first left their family home and I'd never seen her wearing it before. The stones flashed shades of purple in the light from the fire.

'What was her name?' she asked.

I knew at once what she meant. My child of shame and sin, the one that pushed me to the workhouse, then to the Everleys. The baby girl they never let me see. I had to imagine her face, the colour of her hair, the shape of her fingers. Not a night went by when I didn't. I knew that Maddie had named hers Arthur, that Tizzy's own stolen child was to be Rose before she, too, was taken. Had they talked of it together and shared their pain?

'Elisabeth,' I whispered, her name searing my throat. 'I would have called her Elisabeth.'

174

26

Evergreen House

Hovering in the hallway, I waited for Maddie to arrive, fussing over the vase of dried flowers. Some were still bright and cheerful, but last year's lavender had lost its bloom, and I removed the grey stems, pushed them into the pocket of my apron. Later I would place them in the grate, to wring the last scent from the dry stalks as they burnt. It was a bright day, and the light from the door's stained-glass panel threw haloes across the floor, patterning the black and white tiles that Mother would have called 'grand'. She'd have liked this place; its elegant rooms and sweeping stairs would appeal to her snobbishness. It was everything she'd pushed us towards – the Everley name, their beautiful houses. I loved Evergreen too, each room filled with memories – the women we'd helped, the children we were raising, the way we managed without anyone else. It tore my heart to imagine it being taken from us.

Furious knocking broke my reverie. Freezing air blew through the doorway as I answered and Maddie burst in, pushing the table against the door to prop it open for the delivery men.

'Sorry I'm late. I couldn't decide which to bring.'

One by one the men heaved in the canvases, wrapped in layers of brown paper for protection in transit. Maddie flitted across the hall, giving instructions. Dressed like an artist with ruffled petticoats and loose stays. Russian boots in soft brown leather, heavily embroidered in red and green thread, flashed under her skirts. It did my heart good to see her so restless and pretty.

'Careful.' I reached out to steady the vase as it caught on her sleeve. 'You're like a trapped butterfly today. Do let them work.'

She whirled round to face me, flushed and smiling. 'It's too exciting.'

Prevented from using her talent by Mother, forced to waste it on Lucius' horrible evolutionary drawings. Little wonder she was pleased with her painting now. Her skill was remarkable. But if she didn't take care, the opportunity to exhibit would be snatched from her too.

'It is exciting.' I waited until the men had stacked the last parcel and taken their leave before continuing. 'You never know who's listening. If you want this to succeed, you'll need a bit less fuss.'

'When will he go?'

Having promised to enter Maddie's work for the Summer Exhibition, George was already preparing. I wanted the paintings out of the house before the girls started asking questions. Certainly, before Mr Illingworth arrived. I was already dreading hearing his thoughts on poor Felicia and I didn't need to explain why a series of controversial paintings were cluttering the hallway.

'He's getting the trap ready now.'

'The trap?' Maddie looked crestfallen. 'It's nowhere near big enough for these.'

'It's all we have! How else did you think he would get there? We can start getting them to the garden door, out of the way.' I bent my knees and attempted to lift one of the parcels, unable to shift even one side. 'What have you done to them?'

'Framed them. Tizzy helped. Alice has been showing her how to stretch the canvas properly. We found some beautiful gilt ones.

I thought it would help to get them chosen.'

'I'm sure it will, but we're going to need George to move them.'
I stood back, considering the bulk of the parcels. 'I think we can
probably fit about five in the trap.'

'You're allowed to enter eight.'

'Do you think they'd take that many?'

Maddie shook her head, and the string of tiny copper bells
she'd sewn to her neckline jingled prettily. 'No. They don't often
take more than one or two per artist. Unless they're already very
famous, of course. Turner had three once.'

'You should take Helen. Her backdrop is very like a Turner.'

'Helen, Pandora, Medusa.' Maddie read out the names she'd
written on the paper wrapping. 'I need one or two more . . . how
about Cassandra?'

'The fortune teller?'

'Sort of. She understood the gods, through birdsong mostly.
I've painted her in an aviary.' Maddie ripped a long tear in the
paper and held it open for me to see. Cassandra sat on the floor
of a cage, legs curled to one side in a fold of sky-blue material.
Colourful birds perched along her outstretched arms, their feathers
painted to look as though a light breeze ruffled them. Intricate and
beautiful.

'Her eyes are weary.' I indicated the mauve-grey shadows that
matched my own. They drew the gaze and gave the portrait a
wretched-looking beauty.

'She angered Apollo.'

'How?'

'Rejected him.'

'I thought the gods took no notice of that.'

'Zeus certainly didn't. Apollo decided to curse her instead,
making sure that no-one would ever believe what she said. She

predicted the Trojan War and tried to prevent it, but her father had her locked up as a madwoman and the war went ahead anyway.'

A story close to Maddie's heart. 'Women speak but we are not heard,' I murmured. 'Did she die in an asylum?'

'No. She was kidnapped and killed.'

'Goodness. I think she deserves to go. There could be many interpretations of your composition and the birds are beautiful.'

Maddie tucked the torn paper behind one of the lines of string that held it fast. She lifted another.

'What's all this?' Sophia called as she walked downstairs.

Maddie dropped the parcel as though it were on fire.

'Maddie's sold some of her paintings,' I replied. 'George is delivering them to their new owners.' How easily the lies dripped from my tongue. 'Sophia, you're surely not going onto the street dressed like that?' A long white nightdress, with full sleeves and cutwork at the cuffs and neck, the stitching stretched and uneven.

'It's my costume,' she said, holding it out with a sad smile. 'Felicia helped me to make it.'

How could I scold her? She'd lost her dearest friend, and such memories would tinge everything she touched for many years to come. I made a show of checking my pocket watch. 'Shouldn't you be at work?'

'I'm to rehearse. I asked Mr Harris.' She looked down at her hands, wreathed in silk flowers like the ones stuck in her loose hair. Felicia probably made those too, she was skilled at craft. What a waste of her young life.

'Did you indeed. And he told you to wander the street like a . . .'

'Madwoman. I'm meant to be a madwoman. That's the point of the costume.'

George appeared, dressed in his overcoat, a sheepish look on his face. 'It can't hurt,' he said. 'She's had . . . we've all had . . .' He flapped his arms helplessly. 'It can't hurt.'

I knew he was right. But I felt things slipping away from me.

'You can drive her in the trap, when you deliver these paintings that Maddie has sold.'

'I thought—'

I silenced him with a look. Something I was getting rather good at. 'Sophia, go and fetch my cloak. You will need to cover yourself.'

'You're letting me go!' She threw her arms around my neck and kissed me, artless and trusting, and my heart ached for her safety.

'You'll need to let us know when George can bring you home. And lift your skirts.' Dust and rain would soon soil the pure white of her dress. She ran upstairs, taking two at a time, to fetch the cloak.

'She'll be missing Felicia,' said Maddie. 'Is there news?'

Nothing had arrived from the magistrate. No news, information, condolence. I half believed they wouldn't even follow it up – just another dead delinquent, brought to her inevitable fate.

'Nothing. They performed the autopsy on Thursday, but we haven't received the report.' I hadn't chosen her clothes for the burial. I should take them to Martha. Perhaps Sophia would like to be involved? It might help her, and we couldn't use what Felicia was wearing when I found her in the pond. It was covered in mud from the lawn. She certainly couldn't be buried in it.

'Am I supposed to be taking all of these?' George hefted the weight of a parcel, holding it by one edge in a way that I feared might damage the frame. Maddie indicated those she'd selected, and he began to take them to the trap by the back gate.

'One more . . .' Maddie frowned, looking at the packages as though she could see through the paper. 'Pythia then, the oracle.

Actually a group of women, blamed for the messages they deliver, either not giving them quickly enough or interpreting them wrongly. I painted them with sort of milky eyes that see in the next world.' She moved as though to unwrap it.

'Don't tear it. I'll look forward to seeing it hanging at the Academy.'

'You can have this one as a gift. Hang it in your room.' Maddie pulled the parcel open. 'Penthesilea, leader of the Amazons.'

One breast missing, spear drawn back, arrows in a holster on her back. I was struck by her warlike expression, eyes narrowed as she set her sights. 'Is that how you see me?' I asked.

Maddie considered, her head angled to one side. 'A little. You're certainly brave.'

To call me brave, after all she had suffered. I *would* hang it upstairs. I would look at it every morning to remind myself what bravery could achieve.

27

All Saints Asylum

Eloise has not replied to my last two letters. Just when I thought she would be mine. Perhaps her new family read them and took fright. I try to remember my words and I'm sure they were meant to sound loving, encouraging. No mention of Father's research, or my plans for her future, just the promise of money and family – good family. Perhaps they have simply been instructed to deny her contact while I rot in here. The suspense is excruciating. What has happened to my child? Mine and Matthew's. Eloise lost her father young, though she never knew it, because we pretended that he worked in India. Did the details of his murder ever reach her? If I have any chance of bringing her back, then I must hope they did not.

Matthew was a fool. A wealthy one, but foolish nevertheless. Lucius despised his lack of intellect. We knew Father would expect me to marry, though I'd always imagined myself as a surgeon's wife, living in a medical house. Helping with research. It was all I knew. So, when Father brought home a merchant and placed him in front of me, at first I showed little interest beyond my usual bid to ensnare his attention. Not bad-looking, respectable, well-cut clothes made without show and a splendid pair of Italian boots in oxblood leather. His family fortune was built on silk, an astronomical sum, and as the heir he was expected to make constant visits overseas to inspect trade. Our suspicions that his family sent him away to keep him occupied were well founded. He was ignorant of science, disinterested in music, and lacking the understanding of wit. Such a crashing bore at parties that our friends insisted I had married him to punish them. Still, his personal allowance was enough to keep both Everley houses running in the style we preferred. Several times a year he took trips overseas, so when he started asking questions – about the small museum, the clinic, Evergreen – well, it was easy to explain away his absence. I wanted to keep those beautiful oxblood boots. But, because he wore them all the time, Father insisted they were buried with him, so as not to raise suspicion.

Eloise never really knew her father because he was hardly in the country, ideal in a husband. She was fonder of Lucius. Closer to him than me. Children bore me with their questions and whining. She would interest me far more as a young woman, but she was small when I was thrown in here and later I was told she had been sent halfway round the world to a new life. Barely eight years old. The age I was when Father brought me into his research.

Even as a child I showed more aptitude than Lucius, though Father rarely allowed me to do more than carry his tools and tidy his desk. Education was for boys only. Still, I stole his books, read them in secret, and my brother shone more brightly in the glow of my ambition. We learnt together, he explaining the tricker elements of biological theory and I pushing him towards the darker side of medicine, winning Father's approval for both of us. Lucius needed me by his side. And Father needed my compliance, my participation in the experiments he set up to understand pain. The research that began with Mother's spaniels and quickly moved to delinquent women, though Father went through *them* rather quickly. He was close to proving his theory, the one I want Edward to finish. Threlfall just needs the right subject, someone strong enough to cope with the stimulus the way I stopped the pain affecting me. Over time, I learnt to separate my mind from my body, something which has served me well in recent years. The ability to raise my thoughts above my feelings is invaluable in here.

Lucius was never strong enough to help. He cried at the slightest bruise. Like Mother, he was beautiful but flawed with weakness. I might have inherited her beauty, but it came with Father's steel. We would have won together, Lucius and I, if it hadn't been for his wife, Madeleine. We underestimated her and her sister. Thoughts of revenge keep me strong. I will find a way to finish them, and Edward will help me. I am sure of it. He is close by in their basement, close enough to worm his way inside the house and fill the teapot with prussic powders. On his last visit he assured me that his clinic under Evergreen House is thriving; he won't want the threat of losing it.

I reach under the mattress and touch the cold blade, run my finger along the Everley bees that decorate its shaft. Edward loved such objects once. I made him gifts of our silverware: a mustard dish, a trinket bowl, a sword-sharp paper knife like this one, and he jested that he would own the House of Everley one teaspoon at a time. It isn't far from the truth. He's the last of us in many ways, the only person on the outside I can trust like family. He may still be trusting enough to believe my story, but I can see from the way he carries himself that he has changed. Become more worldly. Dressed in luxurious clothes that evidence his pride. He has a lifestyle and a reputation to maintain, and he won't want anything to threaten that. Soon I will ask him to use the knife. And he dare not refuse.

28

Evergreen House

When George returned, I was hovering on the ground floor, restless and preoccupied. Unable to settle at the accounts, or work on chores. Since I'd realised the casebook was missing, I'd searched all over the house and found it nowhere. How had I mislaid such a precious thing? I remembered the plan to hide it in the space beside my mattress, before the chaplain was expected, but when I searched there it was empty. Retracing my steps didn't help. I couldn't recall whether something had happened to keep me from using the hiding place, or if I'd managed to secrete it, in which case someone had found and removed it. With the keys already missing and another death in the household, it didn't take much for me to worry that might be true. But who would want such a collection? Secrets that could only hurt their keepers. That Mr Lavell had expressly asked to see it was troubling. The book wasn't in the study, or the parlour, or the trunk on the landing. It didn't appear to be in any of the bedrooms, but searching too closely without permission felt wrong, and how could I explain my carelessness? All those stories, freely given in trust that they'd be safe. Heartbreaking stories of wronged women. They could wreak havoc if caught in untrustworthy hands.

'Were you waiting for me?' The arms of George's coat were

covered in dust; a rolled cobweb hung from his shoulder.

'Not really.' I couldn't bring myself to admit why I was restless. I'd search everywhere first. 'You look as though you've been in a cellar.'

'I have. Sort of. They make you take your paintings to the storerooms. Which could do with a clean. It's a good job Maddie wrapped them so well.'

'Was it easy?'

'They asked me no end of questions about painting. I don't look the type, evidently.' He tried to brush the cobweb from his shoulder, grimacing as it stretched and stuck along his sleeve.

'You should have borrowed some of Threlfall's scarves.'

'Not likely!'

We shared a smile for what felt like the first time in months.

'Did you manage to answer their questions?'

'Think so. Said I was dropping them for a friend, a self-taught painter, and I didn't know what size brushes they use because they had to make do with ones that they found in the rag carts.'

How much I underestimated him at times. 'What name did you give?'

'For the painter? M. V. Brewster. They didn't ask for the full name. Didn't ask my name either.'

'What did they say about the canvases?'

'They just put numbers on them, didn't even look at them. They had an awful lot in the store already. You might want to prepare her, in case they don't get chosen. There's only so much wall space in there.' George removed his coat and hung it on the newel post. 'Some of the canvases being delivered were enormous. Hers were heavy enough.' He bent and removed his boots, picking them up by the laces. 'I'm going to boil some water for a bath.'

'Would you help me with one last thing first?' I indicated the remaining canvas, leaning against the hallstand.

'If Maddie wants that back, she can come and fetch it. I've put the horse away now.'

'It's a gift for us.'

He looked doubtful. 'Where's it to go?' Reaching out, he pulled back the paper where Maddie had ripped it earlier. 'Who's this supposed to be?'

Me. She had said so. I felt a swell of pride that my sister might compare me to the warrior she had painted. A huntress, leading a group of armed women into what looked like a dangerous battleground, with a look of fierce concentration on the fight ahead. Maddie's Amazon had no room for self-doubt and fear.

'It's Penthesilea, the legendary Amazon warrior queen.'

George squinted. 'She looks a bit like you.'

Dark curls tumbled below her helmet; had Maddie really thought of me all along?

'Fierce?'

'A little. I like it, I think.'

'Good. Because it's going to have to hang in our bedroom. I don't think the inspectors or the chaplain would approve.' I could just imagine the conversation.

'Weren't the Amazons supposed to hate men?'

'They didn't hate them, they pitied them, apparently. Penthesilea thought male politics were ridiculous, and that men were often wrong and wouldn't admit it.'

'She might have a point there.' George hefted the painting onto his shoulder and began to lift it up the stairs. 'Going to frighten me to death looking at this every morning.'

'It will keep you on your toes. Did you remember to collect Sophia?' I called up the stairs after him.

'She came in with me.' He leant the painting against the

bannister as he called down in reply. 'Must have stayed in the kitchen. She did say she was hungry.'

Actors were no doubt above such earthly routines as lunch. Or proper clothes. It would be typical if the chaplain decided to pay a call when she was sitting there in a nightgown. I made my way to the kitchens, intending to ask her to change. Voices carried into the corridor, and I nudged the door further to better hear what they were discussing. Eavesdropping felt underhand, but I was worried at the mood of the house and concerned the women weren't always honest with me about their feelings. We all missed having Rose to confide in.

'It wouldn't surprise me.' Angela's voice, unmistakable with her thick accent.

'I can't begin to think it.' Sophia, sounding as though she had a mouthful of cake. 'But it's been going round and round in my head. I don't understand how anyone could have got into the garden without being let in, or managed to lure her outside so early. She hated mornings.'

They must be talking about Felicia. Poor Sophia. They were inseparable.

'Did she, perhaps, have a lover?' That sounded like Amy. Sensible thought. Someone she would have arranged to see, perhaps indignant over the way I'd punished her and wanting some reassurance.

'Definitely not.' Sophia was adamant. 'I would have known; she would have told me. She was my best friend in the world.'

Too young to know that sometimes friends kept secrets to protect each other.

'It must have been him.' Angela again. I had to strain to understand her words. 'She trusted him, you said that. She would have done what he asked her. And he's got a past. Quite a chequered one. He could have had a hand in things before.'

Did she mean Lavell? No, Threlfall – she was accusing the doctor of murdering Felicia. I'd already considered the possibility, remembered the screams from his basement. But Threlfall's standing was such that we'd have to be very certain of the facts before making accusations.

'What things?' Sophia, eating again.

'He was a boatman, wasn't he? It's a tough job. Full of crime. He would have seen bodies all the time.'

Angela was accusing George!

'That doesn't make him a murderer.' A man's voice, with an accent like a cut chandelier. It could only be Threlfall, increasingly at home above stairs.

Stepping louder than usual on the tiled floor to announce my presence, I pushed open the door and levelled my gaze at Angela.

'Nobody is above suspicion,' I said firmly. 'Two victims, innocent women, no apparent motive for their deaths and the only link the fact that they both lived here. Naturally the instinct is to assume it was someone they knew. The police will want to speak with everyone. It is *not* helpful to speculate and spread rumour about one person. Do you understand?'

Angela gave a sulky nod. Threlfall stood, stretching like a cat. He must have been sitting on the hard kitchen chair for a while. He took up his jacket and both Angela and Sophia watched as he slid his arms into the burgundy velvet. Neither seemed to imagine him to be capable of murder, but his profile matched more closely than George's. I held my tongue on the matter, determined to investigate.

'Sophia, I'm disappointed in you.' My voice wavered slightly as I realised that was the exact phrase I'd used on Felicia. 'George has shown nothing but kindness to you and Albie. Go and change out of your costume or you won't join us for supper.'

She rose from the chair and shuffled off with a baleful backward glance, like a scolded puppy. Artificial flowers fell from her hair and Amy began to gather them up.

'Forgive me.' Threlfall held out a hand in supplication. 'The conversation may have been sparked by something I said. Sophia was telling us about the play – she did very well by the way, you must ask her about it, she was proud and excited to tell you. Anyway, she was telling us about it, and about Ophelia, who suffered in her mind.'

'I thought all the characters in *Hamlet* suffered in their minds.' I'd been reading it in secret.

'That is a matter for discussion. There's a world of difference between self-doubt or experiencing a reaction to traumatic events and the descent into hysteria and madness. Women are closer to madness than men, and it's easier for their minds to fall ill because their bodies are weak; they cannot hold up. Women also suffer in the mind from the nature of their very physiognomy, it is constantly changing.'

He was lecturing us, again, on things he had never experienced. Making a living from writing papers about women, their predetermined lives, their responses to pain. 'And how is this linked to Felicia's untimely death?'

'Ophelia, you may recall, drowned herself. I made the, I realise now ill-chosen, suggestion that dear Felicia may have committed self-murder. And I apologise, profusely, for any upset it may have caused.'

If she had, then Threlfall was to blame. I would not forget the chill of the screams that came from his basement. But I'd already ruled out suicide. Impossible to imagine from the way she had lain. No-one could hold their own head down in such shallow water.

'I'm sorry, too, Rebecca.' Amy at least looked genuinely contrite. 'It was an interesting conversation, because Sophia was so happy and because I've seen the painting of Ophelia by . . . I can't remember who . . . and I got carried away.'

'Millais,' said Threlfall. 'It is beautiful.'

Muddy dress, eyes rolled to white, hair clumped in wet ropes around her face. Felicia, never beautiful in life, was certainly not so in death.

'Sophia is a fanciful girl,' I said sternly, hoping to warn him away from her. 'And such conversations are not to be encouraged.'

29

Holy Trinity Church

The day of Felicia's funeral began with promise, bright sunshine masking bitterly cold winds; red weals streaking clouds. By the time our procession assembled, thin drops of rain fell as vicious as needles on cheeks and ungloved hands. We left the front door slightly open, to counteract the bad luck that might befall a procession prevented from returning, and turned the casket to ensure she left the house feet first. The mirrors had been covered all week, the photographs faced down. Everything designed to ensure that Felicia really left, to prevent her ghost from tormenting us. If only spirits were all we had to fear.

As we lined up, the director beckoned me to one side. 'It is difficult, we understand, to plan for these things. But we are here for the second time in as many months, and you have not spared expense.'

In my guilt at failing to protect Felicia, I'd chosen an elm casket with brass trim and a deep lining in purple velvet. She'd always hated cold and any kind of discomfort.

'You know that you can trust us to settle the account.' We'd paid in cash the day after Rose's.

'I merely wished to suggest that you may choose to establish a burial club. We offer excellent terms for weekly payments, and all costs are payable from the moment of joining. You are a very large household, and the expenses may grow.'

He'd removed his top hat to speak with me and was twisting it between his hands. Sleet ran along his leather gloves and dripped onto the brim. His advice seemed kindly meant, delivered with eyes downcast as though the matter was too delicate to watch my response. Still, I could not help but take offence. Did people think I was careless with my charges? Did they know something more than I about the danger we faced? I resented the insinuation that the bodies would keep coming, even though it was what I feared.

'We will think on it.'

I turned to find Amy waiting with an umbrella. She held it over me with a comforting gesture, dabbing the rain from my forehead with a lace-trimmed pocket handkerchief.

'George asks if you're ready to begin?' Amy's eyes darted nervously back to the house.

'I know you don't like leaving the children with Angela.' I looped my arm in hers and we walked along the line. 'But it's not for long. The others all wanted to be here, and she barely knew Felicia. She can manage for a short while.'

Amy looked doubtful. 'She's not always kind to them.'

'She makes them all kinds of treats. Her manner is brisk, that's all. When she's cooking, she doesn't like to be distracted.' I was keen to convince, but I trusted Amy's judge of character. When this was over, I'd keep a closer eye on Angela. She had no idea how to speak to the little ones, and no patience with their noise. Warning them all to be on their best behaviour, I'd promised we'd blow eggs for painting at Easter if they were good.

'She made Albie stand facing the wall for the whole of teatime because he took an extra slice of bread.'

'We don't know what hardships she faced in Ireland. I can only imagine. She would have gone without food for a long time.'

Both sides of the street were lined with people. Solemn families in work clothes with rows of children like steps, their faces serious as they chewed on crusts of bread.

'Here we are,' I said brightly. 'We can talk about Angela later. Isn't it good to see so many people turned out?'

Men smeared with factory grime, arms folded, mouths clamped on clay pipes. Groups of women in cheap finery, the paste jewels and feathers so beloved of Felicia, all turning and preening and tipping their hats to catch attention. They would know her from the inns, before she joined us. She often threatened to go back but she rarely did. Something told me it wasn't as fun as she made out. I should speak to them, discover what they thought about the murderer. Everything pointed to the fact that it was someone she knew. I should ask, too, if the police had interviewed them – because from what I could make out, they had been slow to do so. And every week lost was another week we were unsafe.

'They're just here to gawp.' Amy set her jaw and we slipped in next to George, behind the pall-bearers.

They hefted the casket to their shoulders, and I was pleased with the way the wood shone, the gleam from the brass of the finishings. A good ending. A respectable sign, belying the reality of the corpse. Martha had done her best, had covered the marks so the women could pay their respects. But I knew they were there. Deep red strangulation marks, the shade of her dress. Imprints the colour of wine where fingers had pressed until the air was choked from her throat. Felicia's death was not an accident, or a suicide, despite the constant references to both. My mind raced with murder. There were so many suspects I imagined to be capable of hurting Felicia. Hester, with her creepy hobbies and her large strong hands, was probably too small to dispatch such a fighter. But she'd been close to both Lavell and Threlfall and neither were above suspicion.

Such thoughts weighed heavy on my heart as we began the slow procession to the church, Martha leading the way, the only woman in a set of mourners. She'd insisted on paying proper respect because the whole time she'd laid Felicia out, I told her stories of the poor girl; and when she was done she claimed a kindred spirit. I suspected she was here more for me than anyone else, but her presence was calming and I was grateful. The gathered crowd relaxed, dispersing as we passed. Children tripped, wailed, stretched out their arms to be lifted. Mothers gathered them together. Men stamped their feet, suggested a warm-up and a toast to the dead; women swished their skirts in agreement. Hawkers drew forth trays of chestnuts, apples dried in slices and paper twists of sugar. I recognised the seller of penny bloods with his painted cart, his pile of papers with their grisly linocuts and horror headlines, and I closed my eyes so I wouldn't have to read them. Our stories could fill dozens.

Ordinarily delighted by such scenes, the women stayed silent. Each one no doubt quietly imagining her own demise. A friend's life cut cruelly short. And if any one of them had asked me whether they'd be safe, I wouldn't have been able to promise it.

Mr Illingworth threw toys into the wicker laundry hamper, muttering crossly to himself. Mr Lavell stood beside him with a pious look on his face. He held a large leather bag that I half suspected contained my casebook.

'They're just children,' I protested. After the sadness of the funeral, we had allowed them a day of play.

He paused, holding up a toy duck made of velveteen. It made him look slightly ridiculous, and brought to mind an unpleasant memory of Hester stitching up the dead mallard in her makeshift workshop.

'We are halfway through Lent. Do you believe it to be fitting that any of the Lord's disciples should be playing with toys, or otherwise enjoying themselves while He is lonely and fasting in the wilderness?' He threw the duck into the box, and pulled a wooden train engine from Evie's hands.

'We *are* observing Lent, Mr Illingworth. Eating plain food and praying together after breakfast, as well as before bed. It's Evie's birthday, and you're upsetting them.' On cue, Evie, initially surprised, set to wailing at the loss of her plaything.

'Marking such celebrations is inappropriate to a season which should be devoted to deep humiliation and mourning. There are many such things which should be spared. Forty days of deprivation is hardly comparable to the sacrifices He made.' He glared at Evie, who hid behind my skirts and began to twist the material around her chubby fist.

'Surely not the slates? The children require those for their lessons.'

'For what remains of the fasting time, they may learn their scriptures by heart. I will prepare a list of suitable verses.'

There was little use in responding, his mind was already set, but his idea of a routine for children was cruel. Worse was his insistence that the women stopped their cottage industry for the same period. If we were unable to fulfil orders, we'd gain a reputation for slipshod work that would upset the business we'd worked so hard to build.

Illingworth finished confiscating the slates, threw them into the hamper with the last of the toys and pushed the lid shut, squashing the arm of a rag doll which hung loose over the side. Evie howled again.

'Children, if they are seen, should most definitely not be heard,' snapped Mr Lavell.

Amy stepped forward and gently released my skirts from Evie's grip, taking her back to the others who sat in a circle on the floor. Her face was a picture of such loathing that I was taken by surprise – until I remembered that her husband, a drunk and vicious wifebeater, was also a lay preacher. She'd come to us for sanctuary, and though she wasn't fallen in the same sense as the others I had promised to protect them both. This would make her feel unsafe again. It suddenly struck me that if Mr Lavell knew her story, he may very well send her back to her husband. How could I have been so careless with the book?

'Start with the scriptures, Amy. We're grateful to you for correcting our observation of Lent.' I gave Amy a meaningful look as I ushered the men out of the room, hoping she understood that I meant her to tell the children one of her stories to cheer them. 'I'd be most grateful if you could explain a little more about the observations. As you know, I was raised in the country, where religious matters merge with the cycle of country life. Farmers may not stop milking, or sowing.'

'You were raised on a farm?' Illingworth's lip curled slightly, and I wondered if there was anything on the earth he actually liked.

'Father was a doctor, work which never stops of course, but our home was surrounded by farmland.' I felt a stab of sickness for the innocence of that time, and my hand in destroying it.

'What is the point you are attempting to raise?' Lavell barely concealed his irritation.

Careful not to appear to challenge his authority, I said, 'I merely wished for guidance, as someone who has not had the lifelong benefit of strict observance.'

Mr Illingworth puffed his chest and pressed his fingers together in front of him. 'The Lenten abstinence before the three holiest days of the liturgical year is a time of fasting and repentance. The avoidance of anything self-indulgent allows us to focus on our sins and to repent. Your cook, well versed in such matters, has already assured me that you are avoiding meat and dairy in accordance with the advice.'

When had he seen Angela? I'd barely left his side. 'So no-one is prevented from working?'

'There is no reason for daily work and chores to stop while fasting.'

'Thank you.'

'Unless,' Lavell added, 'such work involves fripperies and self-indulgence. I cannot imagine that anyone would condone taking part in such *work* as painting flowers onto paper for the unnecessary adornment of homes.'

'If we cannot paint our papers, we'll lose business.' It had been hard enough to find buyers willing to patronise our enterprise in the first place. Customers, initially curious to see what fallen women looked like, were taken by the quality of work and recommended others to order. 'There are many factories that will continue to open.'

'I have no jurisdiction there. But I am employed to spiritually guide this house. And I need not remind you that there is much for this household to repent.'

My fingernails dug crescents into my palms. If we let our waiting customers down, we'd be ruined financially and end up relying on the alms fund. Is that what Lavell wanted after all? It would certainly make it easier for him to take over our house.

'Please understand when I say we do not criticise everything,' Lavell condescended, his bag tightly gripped in both hands. 'You are a diligent record keeper, and your books are up to date. But you have neglected the spiritual instruction these young women require. I found no mention of such matters in your rules of conduct. And it is imperative if they are ever to hope of repentance.'

Such interest in the books. I prayed he had not got hold of the case notes. There was little more to say without accusing him, and

I was grateful when Angela appeared to interrupt the conversation.

'Pardon.' She bobbed down. 'I thought our visitors had left.'

'We are on our way,' Lavell said. 'Don't let us stop you.'

'Only Sophia left this in the kitchen, and I thought she might have need of it.'

Angela handed over the creased volume of *Hamlet*. It was as much as I could do not to strike her with it. Her face was a picture of innocence, but I suspected she knew exactly the effect it would create. Sulky, perhaps, at being caught out for blaming George. Unusually, her dress was smeared with flour. Her appearance was generally as neat and plain as her room. And then I remembered. I'd been distracted there when I carried the casebook. If it was anywhere, it may still be on her rug.

'This is certainly not appropriate reading matter. Now, or at any other time in the Christian calendar.' Illingworth's face reddened.

Nudging the door with my foot, I tested to see if it gave way without risking the telltale rattle of the handle. It moved. I slipped in quietly. Just a few moments to look inside, to satisfy myself that the book wasn't there. The three of them were deep in prayer and would be occupied for a while, but it felt uncomfortable to be in someone else's private space without their knowledge. An action that transgressed my own rule for the household. I'd always been sure to impress upon the women the need to respect one another's privacy. Now I had not only lost their stories, but I'd also broken my own code.

Disorientated by the dimness, I ran my hands carefully along the wall, judging the distance to the table. I dared not light a lamp or candle, or risk the noise of tripping, and was forced to wait while my eyes adjusted to the gloom.

Angela's bed was made tightly, the sheets and blanket tucked in so far that it was hard to run a hand inside to check if the book was hidden there. The rooms were sparsely furnished, leaving few spaces to search. Cupboards mostly bare except for some spare stockings and aprons and a home-made doll sewn from rags. Nothing in the space between the wall, or underneath, or in the gap behind the warp of the wainscot. I lifted the pillow, pushed my fingers in and felt the hardness of a book. Heart racing, I pulled it out, only to find it was a textbook of some kind. A collection of essays without illustration, theories of science and medicine. A brief glance at the list of contributors revealed Everley's name among them. Angela must have found it in the rooms somewhere, lost and forgotten, and decided to keep it. A beautiful volume, bound in dark blue leather with gold lettering. Tempting for someone with so few possessions, even if she found the words impossible to read and understand.

As I searched, I became increasingly aware of the sensation that someone was watching me, a prickling of the skin on my shoulders and neck, like the light brush of insects' legs. My mind playing tricks. There was nowhere for a person to hide. I'd opened all the cupboards and drawers, lifted the curtain that covered the empty clothes rail. I should leave. The casebook was clearly not there, and if Angela arrived, I wouldn't be able to explain my presence. My feet scuffed the rug and its rags of fabric bunched up, their colours faded. I would have the older children make another one, to give to Angela as a present. I had plenty of scraps of fabric for them to use, in all the colours of the rainbow. They'd enjoy it and a pretty rug would make these rooms more homely – everything in them was grey. As I bent to smooth the crease, prevent another trip, I felt something under the material. Hard edges, rectangular, solid. Before I even drew it out, I knew it was the casebook. That Angela had gone to the trouble of secreting it in such a fashion meant she knew what it was. What she wanted with it, I had no idea.

30

Dr Threlfall's Alienist Clinic

Hester held up a lopsided fox, its jaw stretched into an improbable shape. One eye was higher than the other, a little like her own. She looked expectant, clearly waiting for approval. Perhaps she assumed my visit was on account of her taxidermy.

'Very good, Hester, is that your first fox?'

She nodded proudly. 'Biggest animal I've done so far. It was hard to get the legs right.'

'So I see.' The poor creature appeared to have five, its tail hanging as miserably as its limbs. She turned on her heel, dragging the fox by one leg, and disappeared, presumably to fetch Threlfall for me. What a strange life she lived down here with her misshapen menagerie.

I sat on my hands to warm them and protect my thighs from the wiry horsehair that poked through the seat. Three more chairs were pushed against the walls; a wispy Aspidistra sat on a tall wooden plinth, drooping and in need of water. Four stuffed songbirds perched on stands inside a metal cage, their glass eyes unnerving. So realistic they must have been bought. Magazines lay piled on a low woven stool – *The Examiner*, the *Modern Review*, *The Observatory*. Popular science to amaze and horrify. Claims to cure diseases, sketches of dissections, photographs of freaks of nature. Fossils too, great lizards and prehistoric elephants. Since Lucius Everley's fake creatures, I found it difficult to believe that any such things were true. The Society had accepted his papers, the small bones he categorised as evidence of changeling creatures. If Maddie and George hadn't risked everything to expose him, he'd be murdering still, using newborn babies to make his chimeras. Poor George had barely recovered. A family was supposed to heal us. Maddie had Tizzy and her art to think of, but I hadn't given George what he needed. I had failed, first as a wife and now as a guardian to the girls in my care.

'Mrs Harris, are you quite alright?'

A voice roused me from my thoughts, and I looked up dazed, slightly surprised to find myself in a strange room.

'Can I get you some water? Salts?' Threlfall bent over, his expression exaggerated concern. Expensive cologne filled the air. Vetiver and violet, heady and enticing, quite at odds with my idea of a doctor's rooms. He was freshly shaved, hair falling forward, unfettered by oil, and his shirtsleeves were rolled to the elbow. Four rings glittered on his fingers. Surely such jewellery hampered his work? I felt foolish in my plain serge and pinned hair, underdressed for visits.

'I was elsewhere, in my mind, forgive me.'

'Memories spring from strange wells sometimes.' He sat on the chair next to mine, legs apart, muscles straining against his breeches. 'A chance word, or a scent from childhood, and we can disappear into our thoughts. I hope you were in a good place.'

'There are few good memories for me here.' Why did he always pretend our past was nothing to do with him? Regaining focus, I sat up straighter, clasped my hands together. I had a message to impart. 'I came to see if Sophia was here. She's been missing for hours. And to ask if it was strictly necessary for your research to involve my household. There must be plenty of women willing to take part for a fee.' I knew full well he wasn't paying them, but I wished to make a point.

'Sophia is in the clinic – forgive me, I didn't know she was needed, or I wouldn't have kept her so long.' Threlfall's teeth bared in a smile. White and tipped with neat points like those of carnivorous beasts. 'She's been helping me today. With my research. And I hope I have, in turn, been helping her. She was most upset about her unfortunate friend and very keen to talk about it.'

How could he speak of Felicia without faltering? His eyes, the bright blue of forget-me-nots, were clear. Could he mask it so well if he was responsible? Maddie certainly blamed him, hinting it may not be his first, though she had no proof. He was too clever to leave traces, too boyish and handsome for many to mistrust.

'The incident has left us all upset.'

'Of course. I have heard it may have been self-murder. What are your thoughts on the matter?'

His gaze was bold, searching, as though it could pierce right through my skull. I wouldn't let him read my mind.

'My thoughts are irrelevant. It's a matter for the police now.' He didn't flinch at the word, as I might have suspected.

'Sophia tells me they have not been forthcoming in help.'

'Sophia has a taste for drama. I'm grateful to you for listening to her, and it has likely done her good to talk. But she's highly imaginative, and her inventions are not always good for the rest of the house.'

Threlfall folded his arms. 'She's a grown woman, and adults do not like to be treated as children. Perhaps you might think of that?'

Then they shouldn't act like them. I opened my mouth to reply, then thought better of it, warning myself to be more guarded around him. He had the ability to draw more of your thoughts than you wanted to share.

'She is unhappy,' he added. 'I know she wouldn't mind me saying that.'

'We are all unhappy. We've lost two dear friends.'

Threlfall rose, began to pace the small room with his hands clasped behind his back. I sat, cornered, a hare before a terrier.

'I don't know how much you are aware of the progress we make in psychology. Much is learnt and written each day.' He drew a copy of *Mind* from the pile of magazines. 'If you're interested in such matters, I have plenty of reading material to lend.'

'I thought you believed education to be taxing on the minds of women.'

He stopped pacing, stiffened, unused to being challenged.

'In very small doses some factual education can be invigorating. Stories and novels, however, are not to be recommended. Some of my most difficult patients are habitual readers of serial novels and the worst kind of sensational literature.'

First inspectors and chaplains and now doctors telling us what we may read, how we may live, what was appropriate for us to do with the bodies we were given. Women's bodies and minds were objects of fear, and scientific research was obsessed with them. The satin back of Threlfall's waistcoat was crossed with pintucks in neat narrow rows, a great extravagance for hidden material. I hadn't seen such clothes as Threlfall wore since I entertained the Everleys' aristocratic clients. Our girls may not be paying him for his listening services, but plenty of people clearly were.

'As I was saying, we make much headway in diseases of the mind. Unhappiness, unchecked, can soon spill over into something more dangerous. Hysteria, melancholia and so on.'

'Are you suggesting that Sophia is unwell?' I felt my throat constrict. The air was thick with Threlfall's cologne.

'I'm merely pointing out that she's in danger.' He stood by my chair, forcing me to look up at him. 'She is brooding on dark thoughts, imagining threats and missing her friend. Were you aware of her fears about Mr Lavell?'

I felt a sudden chill. What had he done now? Had Felicia told Sophia something about his visit? I struggled to compose myself before replying. It wouldn't do to let Threlfall see my discomfort.

'I was not. Sophia barely sees the inspectors.'

'It's a well-established fact that women are more vulnerable to insanity than men, because their reproductive systems render them less able to control their emotions. Diseases of the mind are just like diseases of the body. In a sense, women's brains lie in their wombs and giving birth is their true and natural purpose. All those emotions are going unchannelled in Sophia and alongside everything else, unless she finds a purpose outside of herself her mind will drag her under.'

Then I was failing in my true and natural purpose. Pointless in society. Such words could seem like hatred for the female sex and yet they were so plausible from the mouth of a doctor, a scientist, a *specialist* of the mind. How much did men pay for him to silence their wives?

I rose to match his height and we stood close enough together to feel the warmth of each other's skin. 'It sounds as though Sophia has been petitioning you to persuade us to change our minds. To permit her to follow her dreams of acting.'

'Not at all. I am genuinely worried for her state of mind. Though she did speak of it. And I would urge you to reconsider. It could be just the distraction she requires.'

How dare he lecture me? And as for Sophia, she would regret running downstairs to get Threlfall to argue her case.

'George and I will discuss it.' My tone was firm enough to

indicate that avenue of conversation was closed. Though he had done his work, and a thread of doubt already crossed my mind. Perhaps, after all, it would be good for Sophia to leave, though not for the reasons he listed but because every time she stepped into the garden, she would see the wax-white face of her friend on the grass. Whether her leaving would be good for Albie was a different question. 'You've told me how you helped her – now perhaps you would explain how she, and the others, are helping you?'

'A slightly more delicate matter,' he began, and was immediately interrupted.

Sophia crashed into the room, wearing a thin muslin dress and a sulky expression.

'Why are you wearing summer clothes, Sophia?' She rolled her eyes and I realised I'd done it again. Spoken to her as though she were a child. I felt like one myself, close to tantrum in this stifling waiting room. I'd had enough of Threlfall and his patronising science, and it was time I asked Sophia what she knew about Lavell. Without a word I took Sophia's arm and ushered her towards the entrance. Threlfall leapt in front of us to open the door, sweeping his left arm out in an expansive gesture.

'Thank you, ladies, for your generous time. Sophia, do remember my advice. Plenty of rest and fresh air.'

She simpered, patted her blonde curls. There didn't seem much wrong with her now.

'I like your lion, Dr Threlfall.' She stroked the nose of the doorknocker and dropped the ring against the brass backdrop. It made a loud thudding noise that brought Hester hurrying to the lobby, before stomping out again with a huff.

'Sorry, Hester,' he called, with a conspiratorial glance at Sophia. 'I'm very fond of lions. They embody much that we should strive for.'

It was my understanding that the males of the pride did little but posture, leaving the hunting and family groups to the females. I didn't make the point. Sometimes the posture was necessary for real life to continue unobserved. Besides, there were more important conversations to be had.

Blossom from the early-flowering plum blew down in flurries, spoilt by the sharpness of the breeze. Tufts of white down, like the feathers on Hester's table, spilt from the songbirds she trapped and stuffed. Linnets and bluetits. Tiny things with weightless bodies like the ones in Threlfall's waiting room. So many petals had blown from the tree it was almost bare, buds exposed to the elements, and I was saddened to miss its display. A cruel spring. Bad weather buffeting and breaking the fragile flowers as they attempted to push through the earth. Stems of daffodil bent by gusts bowed face down into the grass around the pond, their yellow skirts caked in mud. I breathed deeply, icy air hitting my chest and waking my senses.

'Cold?' George rubbed my shoulders. 'We should go back inside.'

'I feel better out here.' I'd sent Sophia to change, so I could talk to George without her interrupting, and I didn't want to waste the chance. 'Sophia has been seeing Threlfall, and he is concerned for her. As am I.' I proceeded to explain, using Threlfall's description of the descent from unhappiness into melancholia and worse. Adding my own worries that such behaviour might ignite the household. Hysteria could, apparently, be contagious in a house of women and I did not want further upset to ensue. As I spoke the words, I felt anger rise. First inspectors and now doctors. 'Things already begin to fall apart,' I added.

'You sound as dramatic as Sophia,' said George. 'Nothing has fallen apart. Everyone is sad and anxious, and understandably so, but we'll get through it.' He took my hand. 'We've got through worse.'

I didn't quite believe him, but the words were good to hear.

'Sophia though, will she pull through if she stays here? She's lost her friend and there's little to keep her. I just worry for Albie. I'm not sure life on the road is good for such a young child, and his nature is so sweet I would hate to see it spoilt.' I couldn't imagine him as a child of the travelling theatre, rough and dirty, left to his own devices for many hours on end or put to work hauling scenery.

George held my gaze. 'Does he have to leave too?'

I hadn't considered the possibility that they would separate. But he'd be fine with us, with his friends, with all of us to look after him. Knowing Sophia her adventure wouldn't last long, and she'd soon return complaining of some slight, or lack of attention.

'Why don't we go to watch her play? See for ourselves. If she's as good as she thinks she is, then there will be no further debate. She can come back to visit, and Albie will be fine with us.'

George had a soft spot for the boy, as did I. Albie was full of kindness, fond of everyone.

'We'll go,' I agreed. 'It will do us some good.'

Sophia was waiting in the kitchen, looking at her hands like a child anticipating a scolding. When she saw me, she scowled. Had I become so harsh? Despite Threlfall's advice she was still just a child, and all I wanted was her safety and happiness. I gathered her to me in a long embrace and then laughed at her look of surprise.

'George and I have decided that we must see this marvellous acting for ourselves.'

'You may come the week after Easter! To the first night.' She clapped her hands together, eyes bright, no sign of the predicted melancholia.

'Excellent. Maddie and Tizzy would like to come too. Can you get four tickets?'

She nodded eagerly, then threw her arms around my neck and kissed me. 'You'll be so proud.' She ran to kiss George, who turned red. 'You will too. I must practise my lines!'

I went to fetch her copy of the play from its hiding place in the drawer of the kitchen table. 'Luckily, I rescued this from Mr Lavell. Don't leave it lying around the house.'

Angela coughed deliberately, trying to catch attention. At first, I imagined she wanted to stop me telling Sophia it was she who'd handed over the script, as if I would. There was enough trouble without me adding to it. But as I turned, I saw that Mr Lavell stood by the back door, as comfortable as if he owned the house already, a roll of papers under his arm, tied with a red ribbon. I recognised it immediately as Felicia's. Only one woman here would be so bold as to deck herself in red ribbons. A coincidence, surely? There was one haberdasher on the high street, one stock of ribbons. Lavell could easily have purchased the same, but it was not the time to ask.

'Forgive me, I wasn't aware that you had come to call.' I tried to hide my surprise with manners.

'Don't worry about me.' He waved a hand at the room. 'Just go about your business as though I weren't here. I've brought a few of my things to move into the office so I can be on hand much more often to help.'

Had he indeed. At least my casebook had been found. It was safely underneath my mattress. Though if he really intended to move in, I may have to move it out of the house altogether. I couldn't be sure he wouldn't turn us upside down looking for information to close us.

'Someone has been busy in the kitchen,' he said approvingly. How long had he been here? If it was anyone else, our taciturn cook would have thrown them out of her domain.

Angela held out a tray of biscuits, iced with almond paste in yellow and pale green. Some bore spring flowers and some letters, all neatly written to fit in the circles.

'They're beautiful, Angela, thank you,' I said.

Amy arrived just as she placed the tray onto the table, followed by the children, who rushed forward to gawp at the treats.

'Look, a flower!' 'Biscuits!' they chorused.

'Thank you, Miss Angela,' Albie said solemnly.

'Excellent manners,' said Mr Lavell, his tone more of a comment on the unruly conduct of the others. He passed me his roll of papers to hold, and I surreptitiously stroked the ribbon. Same colour, same thick crossed edging. Exactly like Felicia's. If I could think of a way to ask that was seemly, I would question the haberdasher on sales.

'My letter!' said Rubina, snatching up a biscuit iced with *R* in green paste.

'That one is Rebecca's.' Angela looked horrified at such a lack of manners.

Before Amy could stop her, Rubina had crammed the biscuit into her mouth.

'It doesn't matter,' I said, 'they're all lovely. Well done on recognising our letter. Rubina and Rebecca are the same, aren't they? I can have one with a flower instead.'

'Manners do matter,' muttered Angela.

'They do,' I agreed, fixing her with what I hoped was a meaningful stare. With Mr Lavell watching intently, it was the wrong time to mention the book she had taken and hidden beneath the rug in her room, but I determined to ask when I could. If she knew I'd taken it back she did not say, and we were playing a waiting game to see who would mention it first.

31

All Saints Asylum

Edward slides the magazine across the table, open at the first page of his paper. *The Delinquent Mind: A Study of Fallen Women*. He's eager for praise, pawing like a puppy dog, eyes shining. I scan to the credits; there are none. No acknowledgements for the people who set up Evergreen, for Father's brilliance, for me who made the place such a rich source of research. It's well-written, with a certain flowery overlay to the eloquence that is typical of his hand but out of place in a scientific journal. The central hypothesis is based on the physical assessments he had his cousin collect: the measurements from Evergreen supplemented with the shape and size of lunatics and other women thought best off out of sight – prodded, dressed, undressed, limbs stretched out, teeth counted. All adding to the proof that a certain type of woman will always turn out bad, her destiny predicted in the stars and in the measurements of her face, the shape of her torso. It isn't true, of course. Most of them turn bad through poverty, or cruelty, but it suits polite society to think differently. It suited me well once. What would Edward say if he knew about Lucius and me? How far could he imagine a 'fall'?

'Congratulations.' I pat the bed, inviting him to sit beside me, and he complies, purring at the praise. My nose fills with rich cologne, vetiver and musk, that makes me want to bite into his skin. Likely a present from one of his patients, or their long-suffering husbands, unaware they were paying a premium for their wives to fall in love.

'It was, in the end, an easy sell to the Society. No-one else was carrying out such a study on women. There have been, of course, quite a few phenotyping papers based on the male physique – Hawton, Angelfield and so on – but no-one has carried out the same investigations into the female body. The editor has called it "a fascinating paper."' He reaches over to point at the introduction, as though I'm unable to read it for myself, and I could kick myself for fanning the flame of his arrogance. Flattery was essential to encourage his compliance, but it has changed him for the worse. He's starting to believe in his own abilities. 'I must thank you for suggesting it.'

At last. Acknowledgement. I incline my head with submissive grace, biding my time. He's wearing the signet ring I gifted to remind him of his place, his debt to the House of Everley. Twin ravens and crossed swords. A crest to be feared. Yet my placing of the symbol doesn't seem to have worked. He appears to be forgetting his position.

'And what of the pain study? Father's study? Is it near to completion? I hope you followed his conclusions, he was close to breakthrough when he left us.'

He blushes like an adolescent, high spots on the apples of his cheeks.

'I have begun. But it seems as though he's suggesting a few things that inure recipients to feeling pain. An overload of the stimulus, for example, which would mean continuing to inflict pain long after the sufferer has felt it first.'

'That is correct. And effective, I believe.' I still bear the scars, mostly invisible. Administering pain is a highly effective way of controlling the body to control the mind, especially via the methods Father used – electric pulses, needles, knives. His beloved mechanical fleam. Blunter objects to compare with the sharp points, measuring the impact of their wider range and force. Lucius dropped out in the earliest stages, a useless subject according to Father. Weak. Perhaps. But I was happy to protect him by taking more of the sessions. And Father was so pleased with our progress. He called it a breakthrough. An exceptional response. Once I learnt to overcome the feelings and control my mind, he used me as a constant, an experimental control. He should have worked with others slowly, over time. But he was too impatient, pushed too far.

'It killed the dogs he used. I don't believe it could be proven in humans.' Lucius shakes his head, as though he dares to disapprove. What if he knew? Father was so keen to show what we discovered that he moved too fast on all his subjects. Mother's spaniels were the first to go. Dispatched so quickly it must have been intentional. Then the girls he paid off not to disclose where they got the wounds that landed them in hospital, or those that ended in asylums with wardens bribed not to note the bruises. Even the girls that were taken to the college theatres, or the ones that Barker had to bury. Father didn't write that up.

'Father certainly believed it could be proved in humans.' Can I tell him I was the subject? I badly want to impress him, but I suspect it may simply frighten him more. 'In fact, he did prove it. You will have read his notes on Patient C?'

Threlfall runs his fingers through his hair. 'As I was reading, I began to gain the impression that even Dr Everley found that particular patient's response an anomaly. He seems to have spent years trying to replicate such an extraordinary response well enough to draw an adequate conclusion.'

An anomaly! If he's read the notes, then he has not read carefully enough to understand. All our hard work. All those hours in the pain room.

'It also seems as though he's suggesting that starvation or fasting provide anaesthesia to pain?'

'That is correct. What he was unable to see was how that interfered with pain signalling. Whether it weakened or strengthened the subject.'

I will him to understand. But the look of horror he gives me tells me that he isn't ready.

'I could never subject a patient to such a study.'

Too weak for medicine after all. Maybe there will be time to change his mind. And he is greedy enough to manipulate, vain enough to flatter. If only Eloise would come back, we could both work on him together. What a sight that would be.

Stroking his cheek with the back of my index finger, I sweep it slowly across his mouth. He clutches at my wrist; I take a sudden, gasping breath and slide my other hand inside his shirt, feel the warmth of his chest, the strong beat of his heart. Is he still drawn to the danger between us?

'Soon you'll be able to design any study that takes your fancy. You are making a name for yourself.'

His chest swells as he smiles. 'I think there's much more to say about the female delinquent mind. I've only just begun with the facial types study – there must be commonalities of thought and temperament. Shared propensity to anger, certain humours. Even a link between the type and the stages of motherhood and abandonment. It could keep me busy for years.'

And keep him from the real prize. Our name could be restored if he'd only finish the pain research. I edge myself closer, feel the shudder in the muscles of his thigh. 'And at Evergreen you have a ready set of subjects. Case studies. As well as Father's equipment.'

'Not such a supply as I'd hoped. They don't seem to come and go as before. Hardly any have left lately, which means there's a finite cohort.'

'Rebecca plans to make good citizens of them?'

'She tries. Though the Board are always watching. Mr Lavell is a constant visitor.'

My ears prick at the mention of a name I had forgotten. Lavell. Another man pleased with his own achievements, eager for flattery. He was new to the Board when I took over Evergreen, and very useful to me once. Could he be so again?

'Apparently he threatens to turn Evergreen into a hospital for penitents.'

Then his power must have increased in the time I've been in here. Even better. I will find out what I can. 'Which means you may not have long to use the women for research.' Father's signet ring catches the light, throws gold across the magazine still open on the table. I think of the knife, still hidden under the mattress. It is time. 'Imagine. If Rebecca weren't there, you could have it all to yourself.'

32

Evergreen House

Easter weekend, late that year, brought an end to the rain. Pale sunlight edged the clouds, drying the lawn and drawing the children outside. Amy picked flowers – lilies and tulips – and sent for George to cut boughs from the trees and shrubs in the lanes. Work he enjoyed. He followed behind her in thick gauntlets, with a pocketful of knives, pushing a wheelbarrow that he filled with branches. White blossom from the spiked hawthorn and bent boughs of lilac, their blooms too heavy for the tree. Tiny flowers of white and purple bunched into points, scented like spring. We arranged them all in pots and jars until the house looked happy.

We'd saved the eggs for blowing and painting, or dyeing, and hiding in the bushes for children to find. It was just as much fun for the women. Sophia and Rachel made bowls of dye from oranges and cranberries, filling the kitchen with the smell of Christmas. Whole eggs were hard-boiled with lemons, colouring them bright yellow, or beetroot to make them purple-red, colour that stained cloths and fingers in shades of bruised skin. The children spent an afternoon carefully pushing pins into eggs and blowing the yolks into a dish that we used to make custard pudding, before painting the dried shells in stripes and spots of colour and arranging them in a bowl.

Angela seemed unhappy at the invasion of her kitchen. 'This is a holy weekend, remembering a time of execution, not a party.'

'It's a celebration. A resurrection. And a time to welcome new life and spring,' I replied, pushing aside the nagging doubt that Mr Illingworth would not approve of our celebrations. No need for him to know. 'And it is teaching the children.'

Angela's piety didn't stretch to traditional Easter foods, and I took over the mixing of raisins, spices and candied peel for the hot cross buns, helping Albie to roll strips of flour paste for the lines on top. Angela made a fruit base for the simnel cake, as requested, watching carefully as we rolled the marzipan and grilled it golden. It toasted unevenly; the marzipan balls decorating the edge were of different sizes, some flattened and misshapen where the children had rolled too enthusiastically. They recited the names of the disciples as they placed them, eleven minus Judas the betrayer. When they were satisfied, they carried it over to Rubina who had refused to join in.

'She seems to have caught a chill.' Henrietta placed a motherly hand on the child's forehead. 'I should take her up to bed. We don't want everyone coming down with it.'

Scarlet fever was always a threat, especially with so many visits from inspectors and chaplains who went from place to place. 'Do you feel hot, Rubina?' I asked, and the child shook her head. She was pale as a lily, her eyes dull and staring. 'Don't you want to paint an egg?' A fat tear welled until it spilt down her cheek. 'We'll save some for you until you feel better.' I passed her a glass jug of pansies. 'You can take these up to your room, to cheer you, and I'll put an egg aside for you to paint tomorrow.'

Rubina didn't smile, as I'd hoped, but she clasped the jug, solemn and careful, holding it against her chest with both arms as she slid down from the chair and followed her mother upstairs.

Too much excitement probably. I'd seen similar behaviour when long-anticipated parties suddenly proved too much for the birthday child.

It was nice to have everyone together, all working to make the house cheerful and mark a time of new beginnings. The year's strange sadness, far from uniting us in sorrow, had led to a spate of bickering and quarrels that weren't easily resolved. We'd never lived like that before. I could have counted the disagreements on the fingers of one hand. Now, things were less happy. Partly we were still missing Rose, who had the knack of getting the best out of the women by appealing to their better natures, getting them to look out for and help one another. It was my job to keep them in line, the tough parent, and Rose's to listen to their woes and cajole them into seeing one another's points of view. She never wanted the women to go to bed unless they were all friends again, so that each morning started well. Now some of them were at each other's throats continually, taking small possessions and fighting over ownership when once everything was shared.

Under the chair where Rubina had been sitting was a magazine, half rolled and slightly ragged at the edges. I bent to retrieve it, almost recoiling when I realised it was a penny blood. A crude linocut cover showed a woman cowering from a soldier as he tried to push her in front of a moving train. Without reading it I recognised Henrietta's story. How had it got into the hands of the papers?

'May I ask who has brought this into the house?' I held it up, trying to hide the fact that my hand was shaking. Everyone looked at me blankly. 'This is not suitable reading matter for a family environment. If I find any others of this nature there will be serious consequences, is that understood?'

With some difficulty I tore the pages into pieces, opened the door of the stove and threw them on top of the burning wood, watching the ink-green smoke swirl and hiss for a moment. None of the women protested. Had they brought it inside? It struck me briefly that George may have bought it, to show me, once he recognised the theme. I would find the chance to ask him before questioning them further.

Angela muttered something as I slammed the stove door shut.

'Did you have something to say?' I asked sharply. She was fond of muttering, and it annoyed me. She seemed to imagine herself above the rest of the women. It would be better if she tried to fit in, especially since none of them believed her tale.

'I said they're true stories. They get them from the courts, or from people just telling their history. They pay well for them.'

'They are not good stories to repeat. Did you buy this one?'

'No.' She tossed her head back and her white cap slipped back slightly, showing a bright orange slash of hair. 'I was given it.'

Was she indeed. Who would give such a thing to a young woman? 'Who gave it to you?'

'The seller.' She gave a sly look from the corner of her eye, and I remembered the casebook. If she'd found time to read it, then she was one of the only people to know Henrietta's story. Had she sold it to those dreadful publications? And if so, whose would be next?

Four stiff chicks filed across the table, shapeless and small, their feathers puffed to a dusty yellow-white. Like dandelion clocks waiting to be blown. They perched unevenly on legs fashioned from pipe cleaners, their eyes and beaks barely visible. How had Hester managed to dress and stuff such tiny bodies? There was nothing of them. I wondered how many were wasted and thrown away while she learnt. At least the smell of the rooms had subsided enough to tell me she'd improved her hygiene. And these were certainly less terrifying than her fox.

Angela took one of the chicks and cupped it gently in her palm, holding it out for me. 'I asked her to make one for everyone, but she ran out of time.'

Good heavens, we'd have none left in the run if she made that many. I wasn't at all sure I liked Angela spending time with Hester. She unnerved me. Still, Angela was trying to be kind and the gesture was well meant. Perhaps, after seeing how pleased they were with the biscuits, she wanted to do something else for the children.

'We can share these. Why don't we find a little basket to put them in and you can sit them in the kitchen for everyone to enjoy?' They weren't everyone's idea of table decoration, but they would amuse the children, might give her something to talk about with the others.

'Angela, I must ask you, did you sell Henrietta's story?' I didn't want to believe it, but I'd exhausted every other possibility and she had the book, the opportunity.

Scuffing her boot against the table leg, she refused to meet my gaze.

'I believe that you did. You will have your chance to tell me why you needed money badly enough to betray us. But first I need to explain why it matters.'

Angela listened silently while I recounted our history, beginning with my fall from grace, to show I did not judge, and recounting everything from Maddie's marriage to Lucius to the discovery of the makeshift graves in his garden.

'It's just stories.' Her expression was impassive.

How could she listen to that and not be moved? Unless she'd heard it before. Sophia was quick to share and may very well have told her.

'How does anyone tell what's story and what's fact?' she asked.

'I was here! I lived through it. And I lost my child to them, as did many others.' I struggled to hold my temper. 'If you're to stay, it's important that you understand us. We face many challenges from the outside world, and we must stick together in here. I can't impress on you enough the importance of maintaining privacy for our young ladies.'

'I was given the magazine,' she said sullenly.

'And I am trying to explain why I found it unsuitable.' I took a deep breath; she must know it was me who removed the book. 'You had the casebook in your rooms. Please don't deny that it was you who sold the story. Do you need money? Are you in some sort of trouble?'

'Not everyone is in trouble.'

A tone of disdain, at such a time. *She* was in the wrong here, and yet she made me feel at fault. 'The local news sheets and periodicals love nothing more than sensational tales of women gone bad, mothers on trial, female murderers. We are all on trial every day. If we don't conform to being angels in the house, we are vilified as demons. We work hard to keep ourselves out of the news, and I simply cannot understand why you would do such a thing.'

It suddenly occurred to me that she might have planned to pass the casebook to Mr Lavell, or even Reverend Illingworth, whom she seemed to like. Unthinkable. At least I had prevented that. But I had no idea how many stories she'd read and remembered. Many were worse than Henrietta's, they would all be recognisable, and it was me that the women would blame for breaking their trust. After all, I had written them down in the first place.

'Take this as a warning. If I find that you have shared any more of the stories from the casebook, I will dismiss you immediately.

Without a reference. Whatever you have read, Angela, they're not your stories to tell.'

Angela raised her head then, her face unmoved though her eyes flashed fury. 'I don't need them,' she said. 'I have my own. But you didn't believe that, did you?'

33

Evergreen House

'How is she?' I'd expected Rubina to be asleep, alone in her room, but her eyes were open, and Henrietta sat by her bed, one hand on the patchwork coverlet as though she feared the child might rise up and disappear.

'She's fevered.'

Spots of high colour lay on her cheeks, stark against the waxy pallor of the little girl's skin. Henrietta wetted a cloth from a bowl of clean water and squeezed it onto her forehead, tried to coax a few droplets into her mouth.

'She should drink more.' I knew from Father's work that fevers needed constant quenching.

'She won't open her mouth. Earlier she said it hurt to have anything in her belly, that it was on fire.'

'What does she say now?'

'Nothing.'

The child's eyes were open, staring into the space before the bed.

'Rubina, can you hear me?' It was a fever, nothing more. But it made me uneasy to see her so lethargic. She was a lively girl, sociable, fond of games and always kind to the other children. Only two days ago I had watched her in the garden, soothing Evie who'd fallen and scraped her knee on a stone. She ran here and there to gather leaves and petals that she gently pressed onto the bruise, all the while chattering to soothe her friend and dry her tears. How could a child so full of life change to this in a matter of days?

'She doesn't seem to see or hear.' Henrietta's eyes were bright with tears. She was a good mother, just as kind as Rubina, and still hurting from the way her own family had turned their backs on her. After she was seduced, she'd fought to keep her child, even when her lover tried to kill them both by throwing her onto a train track. If anything happened to her daughter, she would be devastated. 'What ails her? Have you seen the like before?'

I'd seen fever, certainly, the mild kind that came after a cold caught in the rain, or the raving post-partum sweats of the other young mothers when Evergreen was run by Grace and Lucius. Some of them didn't survive. But their fevers were born of infection, the touch of an unwashed instrument to deliver a baby. I'd seen nothing like this. Rubina hadn't cut herself, or caught a chill, or been in contact with anyone who could have passed on something serious. It was possible that one of us could be carrying a disease that affected only children – that happened with scarlet fever or mumps sometimes. In which case, we needed help soon, to detect and contain it.

'I haven't much experience, I'm afraid. But her stillness concerns me, and I'd like to consult a doctor, with your permission.'

Henrietta looked worried. 'I don't have the money for a doctor.'

Neither did I, but we had one downstairs that did little to pay his way. Much as I disliked the idea of being obliged to him, it would be quicker than summoning a specialist.

'I'll ask Dr Threlfall to have a look at her. And if he can't help, I'll find someone who can.' Martha would be of some comfort, with her neat chest of herbs and powders, though it would be awkward to receive her here and I worried about what that might do to our new-found friendship. Compared to her neat rooms Evergreen House was a mansion. I gave Henrietta's shoulder a squeeze and took a last look at Rubina. Eyes glazed, skin white as a funeral lily. First Rose, then Felicia. Would Rubina be the next to leave us?

Just as I reached the back stairs, crossing my fingers in the hope that Threlfall would be in his clinic, I saw him leaving his rooms, dressed for evening, throwing his cloak over one arm as he leant in to lock the door and unimpressed to be stopped as I called for him to wait.

'Rubina is sick, a fever. I hope it will not inconvenience you to take a professional look at her and put our minds at rest?' A flicker of annoyance crossed his handsome features. 'Please. I would consider it a great service.' He carried a number of papers under one arm and was probably in a hurry to get to some society or other and present more of his findings, making his name on the research we helped him undertake. 'I would ensure the girls continued to make themselves available for your studies,' I added quietly, wishing life was not such constant compromise.

With his free hand, Threlfall withdrew a pretty French watch from his pocket and made a show of deliberating over the time. 'I have around a quarter of an hour to spare.'

When Threlfall reappeared, he was clutching a large, black leather bag. The sight of it was reassuring, as was his bedside manner. Standing by the door, still holding his pile of papers, I watched as he moved a finger slowly across Rubina's field of vision, looked inside her eyelids, took her pulse and rested her floppy arm back on the coverlet before questioning Henrietta.

'How long has she been like this?'

'Half a day.'

'Any fall or accident? Head injury? Cold? Any signs of vomiting or loose stool?'

Henrietta shook her head at each question and Threlfall frowned.

'Her temperature is very high. She has contracted a disease of some kind. The symptoms are uncommon. Possibly diphtheria. I read about it last month, though I haven't seen a case. It seems to affect children. The treatment is invasive. It involves making a large slit in the neck to release the toxins and . . .'

'Yes, thank you,' I interrupted, noticing Henrietta's look of alarm. 'If you're unsure, perhaps there's something you can administer to relieve the fever first?'

'Of course. Though this isn't my field, as you know. Presented with a malady of the mind, I would have no hesitation. I can give you something that will help to break the fever, if it *is* a fever, but if there's no improvement in a day or so I would recommend you seek a second opinion.' Threlfall bent down to open his bag, retrieved a roll of brown calfskin and spread it out on the chair. He ran his finger down the phials of tablets and powders attached by little loops, muttering the names to himself as though trying to remember their uses. As he worked, I began to wish I'd waited for Martha; she seemed so much more composed as she searched through her chest of powders. 'Potassium, no, Warburg's . . . possibly . . . mercury and chloride, that might work to purge the stomach, but for a child? No . . . arsenic and iron, hmm, chlorodyne . . . Dover powder, that would be fine.'

He withdrew the phial and requested water, which Henrietta poured into a glass, hands shaking.

'What's in it?' I asked as he stirred it round with a tongue depressor extracted from the bag. The liquid turned milky white. It was certainly stronger than passionflower.

'Powder from the roots and rhizome of the ipecacuanha plant. And ground opium. It will ease the fever and aid sleep for recovery.'

He passed Henrietta a pipette. 'If she won't swallow, you can administer it slowly with this. I'll leave the rest of the phial in case it helps, but I wouldn't recommend more this evening.'

Was opium suitable for a small child? Though I doubted Threlfall's authority in such cases, I was left with little alternative but to trust his advice. I thanked him, and returned his papers.

'Henrietta, I will stay with her – do get some rest, we can take turns. Please. You need to eat something, or you'll be no good to her anyway.'

With patience I managed to get several drops of the tincture into Rubina's mouth, and her eyes fluttered closed. Blue veins crossed the translucent skin of her eyelids. Her forehead burnt against the back of my hand, and I wetted the cloth again, held it to her. What more could I do? Everything we'd established here was to keep the children and their mothers safe. Now it seemed something within our walls wished harm. I thought again of the Everley knife. The finger pointed at Threlfall. Maddie would be the first to believe it. But the tenderness he'd showed in examining Rubina, the courtesy he had shown us. Could a doctor wish such harm? Instantly I remembered Lucius and regretted the thought. Both he and his father were medical men, and both were unimaginably evil.

My thoughts were interrupted by the howl of a dog. Sharp and keening, a long, high yelp to the moon. A bad omen when someone in the house was sick. Difficult to ignore what it might portend. It sounded again and was swiftly followed by a canine chorus, a cacophony of yelps and barks that echoed along the street. I reached down and turned over one of Rubina's indoor shoes, so it lay sole upwards, a superstitious bid to reverse the sign. It did little to still the sense of foreboding that rose in my chest, and so I settled myself in the armchair by the door. Another sleepless night could be used to keep watch.

34

The Royal Playhouse, Barnes

Maddie sat down and immediately stood up again, clapping her hands with delight as the seat sprang back into place. In the next chair along, Tizzy giggled like a child. George and I couldn't help but smile at them. Still so young, with such an awful past to forget. They should be having fun like this constantly, we all should.

'You have really never been to the theatre before?' I asked.

'Only the music hall,' said George, 'the one on Frith Street.' He craned his neck to look up at the chandeliers hanging from gold-painted roses in the red and gold ceiling. 'It's not nearly so grand as this.'

'It's all velvet.' Tizzy ran her hand admiringly over the plush padded balcony, covered in the same red material as the seats and the swagged stage curtain.

The Royal, beautifully decorated with coloured tiles and stained glass in the corridors and stairs, was far smaller than the ones on Drury Lane and Shaftesbury Avenue that I'd been taken to when I worked the streets for Grace. One of my gentlemen loved the theatre so much we would go every week, to sit in a pink-painted box where he could show me off to the world and no-one knew that my skirts were up over my knees behind the gilt-edged balcony. Shading my eyes from the glare of the lights, I looked up to the boxes. Only one on either side of the stage. Both were empty.

Tizzy followed my gaze. 'Are they seats too? Do they tip like these ones? Who sits there?'

'Lords and ladies and la-di-das,' said George and set them off giggling again.

'And anyone they want to impress,' I muttered. 'It's filling up fast.' I spoke to change the subject, but I was pleased for Sophia. She'd worked hard and whatever the outcome, she deserved to play to a full house. A mixed audience, with all kinds of fashion and finery on show. Shakespeare was popular with the well-to-do, who liked traditional drama, and the down-at-heel, who liked the bawdy violence of his plays and the chance to see some mechanical scenery. 'Sophia tells me they have a moving battlement as well as ropes for the ghost to descend on.'

'That sounds dangerous,' said Tizzy.

'I'm sure the actors have practised enough.' Indeed, Sophia had barely been at home in the previous fortnight. Focusing on the play was helpful in taking her thoughts from the unhappy fate of Felicia, and the rest of my fears had been unfounded. Albie was doing perfectly well without his mother there. Once or twice he'd mentioned her, but only with pride and excitement about her acting, and he'd never asked to be taken to see her. His mood was as happy as always and his letters had improved. He seemed more worried about his companion Rubina; her friend Evie was missing her too, but after what Threlfall had said about diseases I was reluctant to allow the other children to visit. We'd gone to her bedside just before leaving for the show, and I was pleased to see that some colour had returned to her cheeks, though the Dover powders left her very sleepy. George read to her while I mixed another dose, because she said it took the 'fire' from her belly. A smaller amount this time, as I worried about the effects of such drugs on her tiny frame. Unable to swallow, she took it in drops from the pipette, leaning back with exhaustion after a few. George managed to raise a smile, at least. He was good with the children – soft on them sometimes with his winks and nudges at my insistence on manners and routine – and always able to win them over or soothe high spirits. He would have made a wonderful father.

'Penny for them.' Maddie nudged me. 'You look miles away.'

'Just thinking of Rubina – she's been quite unwell since she went off to bed at Easter, and not knowing what ails her has left me in rather low spirits. It's hard to know what she needs, or if it may spread to the others.'

'Has anyone seen to her? Francine at the Mews is very skilled with herbs, she may be able to help?'

'Thank you. Martha has given me a mixture of herbs to stem the nausea. Threlfall looked in yesterday and gave her something.' Maddie stiffened at his name.

'Why do you trust him, after all I've told you?' Her voice was a stage whisper, causing a ripple of chatter along the occupants of the seats in the row behind us. They were impatient for entertainment and would be just as happy to get it from the crowd.

I placed a warning finger to my lips. 'You can see her yourself when we get back, and then you can speak with Francine. I agree with you, a herbal tonic would do her some good.'

A hush settled on the crowd as the curtains rose on a lavish set. George's fingers entwined in mine and the sound of the penny whistles faded. Guards walked in front of the ramparts and began to speak while a storm raged behind them. Maddie and Tizzy were transfixed, immediately transported to the court of Elsinore, even though Sophia had already described how the actors' children made the sound effects, rattling dried peas in a box for rain, banging a skin drum for thunder. When the ghost of Hamlet's father was lowered, a diaphanous cape floating behind him and backed by the squeak of a stage pulley, it seemed wholly believable that he had come to seek revenge. Maddie relayed the plot to Tizzy in the scene changes between acts, and the pair of them became increasingly agitated at the unfairness of Hamlet's position. By the time Sophia arrived in the third scene they were fully invested in the story and furious at the way her character was bullied. No expense had been spared on the costumes, and Sophia looked beautiful in Ophelia's courtly gown, remembering all her lines – though she was almost thrown by spotting us in the crowd, especially when George waved.

'Don't distract her,' I berated in the interval. 'She's doing so well and she's on stage a lot more later.'

'Had to do something to entertain myself – the fellow playing Hamlet leaves such long pauses between his words, they ought to play music to fill the gap.'

'He *is* a little melodramatic, isn't he? What do you think of our Sophia?'

George puffed out his chest. 'I always knew she'd be famous; she's got us to thank for that.' Dropping the silly accent, he added, 'Seriously though, I think she's good enough to make a go of it, if she wants to. Don't you?'

I did, but I wanted to see the whole production first. 'And what of her responsibilities?' Wary of eavesdroppers, I turned to look behind, but the seats were all empty, their occupants having wandered off in search of oysters and punch. 'What about Albie?'

George inspected his lapels, brushed at an imaginary speck of dust. 'Albie is very fond of us, especially you. He should stay. And if things go well for Sophia, then we could make that official.'

'Adopt him?'

'Why not?'

George spoke lightly but the weight of his words hung between us. A child of our own. With no risk that he would leave when his mother found a position, or a husband. Someone to receive the love that welled in us. But the words dried in my throat and all I said was, 'What of the others? I wouldn't want them to feel we treated them any differently.' And what of our own ghost, stalking Evergreen with a need for revenge? I pushed aside a sudden vision of the bright red ribbons that bound Lavell's papers. How could we adopt Albie when we couldn't promise to keep the household safe?

'Think on it.' George settled back in his seat as the curtain rose on Elsinore. Through the rest of the play, I did just that. Throughout Sophia's ravings as poor Ophelia, through Hamlet's drawn-out deliberations and Claudius's manipulation. They had modified Sophia's Act IV costume, adding petticoats for modesty and a raft of silk flowers around the neckline that spilt down the sides of the dress in artful chaos. She threw more to the audience, '*there is pansies, that's for thoughts; there's fennel for you, and columbines*'. The scene brought to mind a young woman I'd once seen crawling to pick up leftover single flowers from under the barrows in Covent Garden, a baby tucked under one arm. Gathering them in little bunches and offering them for a penny, with a pin to fix them to lapels. When I asked my gentleman to help her by buying one, he'd laughed and walked straight past. As the other characters ignored Ophelia. The sadness I felt, I realised, was testament to the strength of Sophia's acting, and at that moment I determined to help her succeed if she chose the stage.

'Wonderful!' Tizzy clapped her hands. 'Simply wonderful.'

'I feel as though I've left real life on the stage, and this is the make-believe.' George shook his head as though rousing from a dream. A sweet, sleepy look I'd missed in the broken nights we now shared.

Maddie's eyes were bright with tears. 'Poor Ophelia. None of the troubles were hers.'

She didn't need to finish. We all knew. None of it was her doing and yet she was drawn in, used, faced with a brothel or madness, or both.

'Come,' I said, gathering my things. 'If we hurry, we can take some flowers to Sophia in her dressing room.'

35

All Saints Asylum

Varley brings the mouse on his rounds, and I enjoy the way she squirms when I give her a knowing smile. If he reads my look, he doesn't show it. And I won't waste time amusing myself with his embarrassment; I need his favour today. There are things he can help me with.

'Good morning, Mr Varley. I trust you are well?'

He places the tray gingerly, as though I might throw it all over him, and I sigh.

'No need to be anxious – I am quite recovered, I assure you.' The mouse skitters off with my bucket and I call after her, 'Thank you.' If I knew her name, I would use it. It is a day to use my charm. 'I feel more like my old self. Dr Threlfall was telling me about Evergreen on his last visit and I find myself missing it. I would like to know more, if you are able to help?'

He eyes me cautiously, mistrusting, perhaps wondering how much I should be permitted to know. It's what I expected, but I'm one step ahead because I've been watching him. He's a lascivious man with an eye for the female form, and I know it won't take much to get him onside. I've been up for a while, dressed carefully in green silk that flatters my colouring, bolstered with petticoats that highlight my shape. Difficult to lace them all myself. But

I've learnt. One can teach oneself anything given enough time and determination. All the jewels I have left glitter at my throat, swing from my earlobes beneath the bob of my hair. Their luxury reminds him of my standing, the trouble I could cause for him if, by some chance of fate, I were to be released.

Varley clears his throat and inclines his head, spilling jowls across his collar. 'I'm not sure I'll be able to. As you know, I spend most of my time at All Saints.'

Edward never stops talking, he must have said something. 'Oh, I had thought Dr Threlfall took you into his confidence? Perhaps I am mistaken?'

My words strike his vanity. He puffs his chest and blusters. 'He does, of course – what did you wish to know?'

'He mentioned a change in personnel on the Charity Board, and I was thinking that perhaps he was wrong. He said Mr Lavell was now in charge?'

'I believe that Montgomery Lavell is Chief Inspector for the Board, yes. He has done very well for himself.'

Hasn't he indeed, the little worm. 'I see. Then he would stand much to gain from its demise.' He takes a step back as though I've said something shocking. I must be careful. 'It is a cause very dear to my heart, Mr Varley. As you know very well, the things they said about me in court were simply not true. I was beholden to my brother and father, a mere pawn in their games. Evergreen was my life's work and I would hate anything to happen to it. Would it be possible, do you think, for you to arrange for Mr Lavell to visit me? Just to put my mind at rest?' He hesitates and I strike again. 'No, of course, silly of me, you probably don't have the power to request it now that he has risen to such heights.'

Varley places his hands on his hips, ignores the mouse as she scuttles back with my empty bucket. 'All Saints is the foremost institution of its kind in London, and I am very well connected. If you wish for a visit from Mr Lavell, then consider it done.'

'You are most kind,' I beam. 'I believe a conversation would certainly afford me some peace.'

Edward may not be strong enough to carry out my wishes, and the sooner I can make a back-up plan the better. Rebecca *cannot* be allowed to win. She was a nobody until I trained her; now she marches around Evergreen as though she actually owns the place, and she must be stopped. Will Lavell be tempted? May I rely on his support? He had certainly promised as much when I helped him rise through the lower ranks. Just a lackey when he first visited, carrying bags and papers for inspectors, ogling at our girls with wide eyes and wet palms. He liked my photographs, had probably kept the ones of Rebecca that I caught him stealing. I was right to let him know I'd turn a blind eye. Now he could return a favour.

36

Evergreen House

The moment we returned to the house I knew something was wrong. Expectant silence filled the air, as though the rooms held their breath, and the women in the drawing room sat without talking. We removed our coats, hung them on the stand, changed to indoor shoes and all the while not a sound could be heard from anywhere.

'What is it?' whispered Maddie.

Without answering I took the stairs to Rubina's room, and she followed close behind, gesturing for Tizzy to stay with George. As we reached the landing, I saw Henrietta in the corridor, curled over as though she had slid down the wall, her back rising and falling in anguished sobs. Low voices came from the bedroom.

'Henrietta.' I touched her shoulder gently, wary of startling her, and crouched by her side. 'How is Rubina?'

Dark shadows sat below her eyes and in the hollows of her cheeks. 'She took a turn for the worse. I didn't know what to do. She was screaming in pain.'

Dread set like stone in my stomach. 'Who is with her?'

'Threlfall. He looked in to check on her after yesterday. But she was different. Writhing and screaming. She said she was burning.' Her expression was desperate.

'I'm sure he's helping.' I patted her shoulder and rose to see that Maddie was already opening the door. Was he helping? I could hear the child whimpering, like an animal caught in a trap and making a noise for no other reason than to comfort itself.

From the doorway I saw Julia holding Rubina by the shoulders, to steady her as Threlfall finished stitching her neck with a thin suture, fastened the cotton in a neat embroidery knot and stood back to admire his work. Watery blood filled a kitchen bowl by the side of the bed. Wads of stained cotton littered the floor.

For once Threlfall looked dishevelled, his linen creased and stained, his hair flat with sweat, though he seemed delighted to have an audience.

'I took the advice of a colleague, a new method. It seems likely to us that the cause is diphtheria, and there's only one treatment – to incise the area by the airways at the side of the neck and thus release the toxins. May I have a bowl of water?'

Julia stood by the bed, trembling like a penitent and holding a sharp-toothed implement that I took carefully from her hands and placed onto the cloth by the kitchen bowl.

'Please could you fetch the pitcher and jug from my room upstairs? Maddie, please take Henrietta and Julia to the kitchens and give them some sugared tea and salts.' I tried to make myself sound calm, in control of the situation. In reality, I could not feel less so. I'd never heard of the disease before, let alone its treatment, which appeared to be barbaric. For all I knew, Maddie was right, and he was practising some of Everley's sadistic research.

'I just need to get cleaned up and I'll be out of your way.'

'Did Henrietta give you permission to perform this . . . this operation?'

Threlfall coloured slightly. Of course, he hadn't asked. What right did a mother have? He had his reasons, whether research or simply the arrogance of new medicine, and, as always, those reasons were the first consideration.

'She was quite beside herself when I arrived. Naturally, having administered some help yesterday I wanted to check on the child.' He gave a slow smile that he probably imagined to be winsome. It made him look sly, the points of his teeth glinting foxlike in the dim light. 'Henrietta was hysterical. The others weren't helping to calm her, as you might expect, and the child was in considerable pain. I took enough interest to make a few enquiries about her condition and the advice of colleagues was to open her neck.'

'It's not what I would expect at all. The women are usually very supportive of one another.' My tone was cold, but his words could be truthful. Something had changed the atmosphere in the house and the women were no longer the same. They quarrelled and argued over the smallest things.

'I feel as though I'm on trial.' His face fell to a sulky pout.

'Not at all. We're grateful for your help, of course. But I am responsible for everyone in this house and if anything should happen . . .' Unthinkable. To lose a child in this way. '*If* something happens then the Board will need to be told.' Again. 'And they will want to hear from me what happened. That is all.'

Lavell would be rubbing his hands together. This was surely the last straw.

Poor Rubina would be able to hear, though how much sense it would make to her I did not know. Still whimpering softly, she lay sideways, her eyes closed. The pillow had been removed, presumably to keep her neck and head flat.

'What is your advice now? How should we care for her?' Swelled and angry skin around Threlfall's neat stitches, purplish red, from her ear to the base of her throat. If, by some miracle, she survived, she would bear a thick ridged scar for the rest of her life.

'Is she going to be alright?' Maddie returned with the pitcher of hot water and another bowl, a clean towel folded over her arm. 'I asked them to wait downstairs, I can help to clean up.'

Though she'd addressed me, Threlfall responded. 'She needs rest. Let her sleep as much as she can. Plenty of fluid, when she's ready. Don't try to force it or she may vomit, she's had more powders. Beef stock will fortify her when she's ready to take food. Use the powders sparingly for pain relief.'

Maddie's eyes threw daggers at him.

'Thank you,' I said, 'we're all grateful for your help.'

Plunging his hands into the hot water, he cleaned himself up to the elbows, before wiping his arms, then his tools, on the towels. 'I will see myself out. If anything develops you can call my club.'

The door had closed behind him before I thought to ask which was his club. And then I remembered. It was White's, the same as Lucius – it was where they'd met. Where Lucius had persuaded him that Maddie was losing her grip on reality and hired him to prove it. No wonder she still looked as though she could kill him. No wonder she didn't trust a word he said.

'I understand, Maddie. I know very well why you don't like him, and I am, as always, on your side. But he was lied to by Lucius, a very young and foolish student in thrall to a high-profile name. He is changed. And he's trying to help.' I had to believe that. If he wasn't, and I had not intervened to shield the rest of us, then I'd never forgive myself.

Maddie said nothing. She picked up the cotton wads, swabbed the floor below them, changed the top-sheet for clean linen and replaced the coverlet. All the while her mouth pursing, nostrils flaring, as though considering and rejecting words that could ignite the brittle atmosphere.

'Thank you,' I said quietly, tucking the bedclothes around

Rubina. She was still now, breathing steadily. 'He's not all bad.' Despite working for Lucius, he'd intervened to stop her hanging and it had given us the time we needed to supply proof of their crimes.

'I don't understand why he has to be here.'

'Grace gave him everything. If he wanted, he could make it difficult for us to stay. I cannot set myself against him.'

'Do you even *know* what he's doing in the basement?'

The question seemed never far from my mind. I knew what he *said* he was doing, what he published. 'He's making a study of fallen women, Maddie, you know that. The girls visit him to be measured – the height of cheekbones, brow ridges, the shape of noses – they all apparently reveal someone's underlying moral and behavioural characteristics. Inherited traits. We're not the only ones in the study.'

'A nonsense!'

'You'll wake Rubina.'

'You know it's ridiculous. Since when was it a crime to be cruelly treated? It's not destiny to have to sell yourself. It's how society punishes women for being loving. They are your girls, *your family*.'

The sorrow that had built in my heart for weeks was released by her words. It buckled my knees, brought tears to my eyes. My family. She was right. I hadn't protected them.

'I'm sorry, Rebecca, I didn't mean . . . you're a mother to all of these children and the women besides, you know that. You're a *good* mother. You've never let them down. But you're wrong to trust Threlfall, he's a dangerous man. He was in thrall to Lucius, obsessed by the family name, the background, the money. How do you *know* he's not furthering some horrible mission? The Everleys carried out things in the name of medicine that fooled people before. Don't let him fool you now.'

Was I hoodwinked? With everything I'd seen, I should be quicker than that. I couldn't prevent Lavell pushing his way in, with his sneers and his suspicious red ribbons. But I also let Threlfall come and go like he was one of us. I called him when I could have called another doctor.

As though she read my mind, Maddie continued. 'It's always those close to you, how else do they get away with it? People get close to hurt you. Threlfall is one of those people, wheedling himself into confidences, flattering and sympathising, until he has you in his velvet pocket.'

37

Evergreen House

Gently easing myself from the bed, I made a point of not disturbing George, though I suspected he wasn't sleeping either. We'd both spent the night sighing and turning, watching every shadow, and listening to every creak and stretch as the house sighed restlessly around us. He didn't acknowledge me putting on my robe and slipping away, and I hoped he would finally get some rest. Perhaps this time it was me that unsettled the night. I couldn't stop thinking about Maddie's words, wondering how Lavell came to have Felicia's ribbons, whether Rubina would survive. In all the chaos there'd been no time to speak about George's suggestion that we adopt Albie, and I worried that this silence was his response. Either way there was little point to staying in bed, so I may as well make a start on the books. Sales were down, and Lavell could find that out anytime he liked. At least he wouldn't be in my office at such an early hour.

I felt my way down dark stairs to the gloom of the study. Was it early or late? Dawn hadn't broken, though birds could already be heard stirring: the deep-throated call of corvids and the smack of wings on branches. The door to Angela's room swung slightly ajar, and I wondered how she could sleep in such a cell. Perhaps she didn't. She always seemed tired. Since Hester showed her how to make the chicks, she'd begun to practice her own taxidermy with the skins of animals destined for food. It was deeply unhygienic, and I forbade her to keep anything else in the kitchen, but she liked the attention, the questions, the ability to show off to the others. Perhaps in the hope it might lead to friendship. A better tactic would be to use a kind word more often, to notice people's moods and ask how they felt, as Rose always had.

The chair creaked and sighed as I sat down heavily. Now that I was out of bed, I felt weary, but I knew if I returned my thoughts would crowd my mind, so I opened the sales and orders book, then the accounts book, and arranged them side by side on the desk. Numbers tumbled steadily downwards in the last column. Outgoings remained constant; Angela spent slightly more on food than Rose, but she was not so experienced, not so clever at using every bone or drop of gravy. In any case she spent less on fuel because she didn't keep the stove running all day and night. In a way I wished she would. The cost would be worth it. The old cosy warmth was missing from the kitchen, and we gathered there less often.

Spending on clothes had increased significantly, but the funerals must account for that. Even though none of us needed mourning wear, out of respect we'd all wanted to look our best, with new shawls and stockings instead of mending old. With the exception of boots, nothing was kept from one mourning to the next. It was terrible bad luck to store clothes worn to grieve in; they were bundled and taken to the broker's within days to remove them from the house and mitigate the threat that their presence would pre-empt another death. The funeral expenses themselves were also significant. Dear Rose had the foresight to put away savings for such an occasion and we were grateful to have it, especially given the number that had come to the house. Grief did little to curb appetites. Felicia was young and poor, her death bitterly sad and her life more so. There were few genuine mourners outside of our community, but even without the cost of a reception the expenses were enormous. Sophia, dramatic in grief, had swagged the cart with fine black gauze and a raft of hothouse lilies. It was fitting. But it all added up and it had to be paid for.

With one of Maddie's thin lead pencils, I marked and underscored items, looking for anywhere we could make savings. Grate blacking, boot polish, sugar soap and soda paste – we could lose them all, replace them with a rag and some elbow grease. Thick paper and ribbon for packaging items for sale – they could easily be substituted with something cheaper. It would give me an excuse to visit the haberdasher and put my mind at rest about Felicia's bows. And no-one would really notice the change; customers removed their wrappings immediately the items were brought home. Paints and brushes for the wallpaper – we would have to make the older ones last longer. The stiff paper was hard on bristles but there must be a way to trim and repair them. We wouldn't need any next month anyway. A glance at the orders book showed little to fulfil.

With a deep sigh, I began the process of tallying the orders and reviewing the lists of stock we kept for the basket-weave goods. Four recent markets, and only three baskets sold between them. We used to sell out whatever we took. There was no reason for such a downturn. The workmanship was every bit as good, the shape and style just as appealing. We had begun to thread willow strands dyed various colours around the basket tops, a cheerful look that customers claimed to love. How could our market baskets fall so swiftly in popularity? There was only one reason, the same cause as the lack of orders for our beautiful wallpaper. Our situation was known.

We'd made no secret of Evergreen before. I was happy to talk customers through how we worked, what I hoped for the girls, the life we tried to make for them. Mostly they were interested, positive, supportive. Some of our wealthier clients added extra to their orders and wished us well. But since Lavell had been visiting there were more questions about us. I had the feeling that he liked to smear our reputation, and the penny bloods that linked us to a murky past couldn't be ignored; it was only a matter of time before such stories were common knowledge. Everyone read them. Even those that claimed to ignore such lowbrow gossip would send staff to fetch them so they could devour them in secret, roused by the sensational stories of murder and worse crimes, congratulating themselves at being above it all. The tale of the Everleys would appeal and horrify and, once they knew, they wouldn't want to be close to it. Add to that the orders we'd lost during Lent, another two unsolved murders in the household, with an inspector who seemed happy to share details, and it was a recipe for financial ruin.

Weak light began to show through the window, misted and grey with no sign of sun, though it must be time for the others to wake. I'd been working for a while with no success, unable to conjure hope from the columns of numbers. My shoulders and knees were stiff with cold. I would see if Angela had set the stove, try to speak with her about food. There must be something we could do – fewer meals with meat, padding stews with cheap root vegetables. She must have learnt such methods in Ireland, though she hated to talk about it, for any reason. When I mentioned that her referee had still not responded she scowled and asked if I'd heard what was happening in the country, adding that it wouldn't surprise her if they were all dead by now.

Whilst I was locking the books in the drawer, wondering what I thought I was hiding, a frantic knocking sound made me jump in fright. Immediately I thought of Felicia, white and muddied in a heap by the pond. Had the murderer come for me too? I seized the heavy gas lamp and held it up at head height, hoping the sight of it would scare an intruder, though I knew I wasn't strong enough to wield it properly. Where was George? Perhaps the noise would bring him down.

'Who is it?' I called, my voice wavering. 'I am armed.'

'Is that you, Rebecca?'

It sounded like Amy. I flung open the door to find her standing in her nightclothes, looking at the lamp I held up in alarm.

'You frightened me.' I placed it down. How had she known where to find me? 'Silly of me, we're all quite safe here.'

She looked unsure. 'I went to check on Rubina. Rebecca, I think she has passed. I didn't know what to do.'

We both raced upstairs, two at a time. With my hand on the door handle I paused, sent a message to a God I barely believed in, tried to make a pact that I kidded myself He would keep. I knew it was foolish. Death was in the room. In the sweet-sour smell of fevered sweat, the metal stink of blood, the way the air seemed shrunken. Rubina's skin was cold, tinged with blue like an iced-over pond, livid and weeping around the wound in her neck. Curls stuck to her forehead; her fists were bunched as though she'd died in pain and the sight of them broke my heart.

I couldn't speak to ask Amy to bring a mirror. I went myself to fetch Rose's close-work magnifying glass from the sewing basket, flinching at the initials engraved into its handle. No breath misted the glass when I held it under Rubina's nose, no pulse could be found in her wrist. My whole body curved in the anguish of a silent howl. How had this happened? She'd been full of life just days ago, laughing as she ate her porridge on all fours to keep the kitchen cat company when he hurt his paw. The daisy chain she'd made for me had barely withered on my nightstand. How could she leave us? It felt like losing a child of my own – the grief was the same, like a fist to the stomach, a choking of breath. How would we break the news to Henrietta? Now we would face another funeral, with more questions, and more expense, and I didn't know how we were expected just to carry on existing. I would tell George that my answer was no. How could we think of adopting Albie when we couldn't look after any of them?

Martha Rawlings stood on the doorstep, her kind face full of sympathy. 'I'm very, very sorry for your loss,' she said, folding her vast black umbrella. 'May I come in? It's throwing a gale out there.'

'Of course.' I ushered her inside and relieved her of a coachman's greatcoat, heavy with rain. I was still nervous of how she would view our home, how such perceptions might change the friendship we'd carefully constructed. 'I was hoping you might visit one day but not in such circumstances. I did, in any case, think you were prevented from . . .'

'I'm allowed the secret autopsies.' She spoke without bitterness. 'Wouldn't be right for a woman to be seen doing this in public, of course, but in private, and especially for a child.' She hefted her great leather bag. 'Won't catch many doing this for children. They think it's not worthwhile, as though the little mites are two a penny. But if I can give relief to a mother, I will.'

'Thank you.' It had taken time, and a considerable bribe, to persuade the Coroner's Officer that an autopsy was required. But I had to rule out foul play to understand whether Threlfall had genuinely tried to help, or whether Maddie was right and Rubina was another victim. Something told me Martha wouldn't be impressed to hear of the bribe. She refused tea and cake, asking only for two bowls of hot water.

'Do you have a delicate disposition?' Martha looked me up and down and, before I could reply, added, 'No, I expect not.'

From her it came as a compliment, though I tried not to show my pleasure. 'I'm happy to assist.'

'Not all of it. You won't want to see that. But you can help me set up.'

In Rubina's room we laid out water, towels and rows of instruments for cracking bone and slicing skin. Clamps for holding back the stomach. Wrenches for twisting into cavities to make a body offer up its secrets. Martha cared for the tools of her trade. They were neatly polished, each wrapped in soft cloth, and it took time before everything was set to her satisfaction. Reaching into her bag she brought out six church candles, setting them safely on squares of slate before lighting them and asking me to turn off the lamps. Her way of working was deeply respectful, and I was glad they hadn't sent anyone else. Martha rolled her sleeves to the elbow, fastened a clean white apron over her clothes and began to hum softly to herself. Rubina's hair covered the pillow and Martha started by smoothing it back, brushing it gently and fixing it in a neatly wound plait. She turned the head from side to side, running a finger along the fresh-sewn scar, her brow furrowed as though deep in thought. It was soothing to watch her, and I stayed in the room for a while, observing from a distance, only leaving when she took up the knife to make her first incision.

Helping Albie and the others in the schoolroom, I lost track of time, and when I went back to check on her progress Martha had already finished packing away her things. She was writing on the label of a small glass tube, corked at one end, and filled with something the colour of dried blood.

'Do you know what it was?' I asked and she shook her head slowly.

'Not yet. Not allowed to tell you even if I did know. Have to wait for these to be tested.' She held up two other labelled tubes and then wrapped them all in a piece of soft leather, folding it between them to prevent the glass knocking together in her bag.

Martha stayed to take tea, refused cake, and made a point of explaining the process of autopsy to Henrietta in the kindest terms she could find, to reassure her it was for the best to help the authorities work out what happened.

'If it's a disease that could affect the others, you would all want to know, to take precautions,' she said. Henrietta nodded, eyes raw from tears, and dear Martha held her hands for a long time, as though she could transfer sympathy through skin.

'Thank you,' I said as I handed her back the greatcoat, still steaming with damp.

'I haven't helped yet. Let's see what the results reveal. As a precaution you'll need to burn the bed linen, her nightdress and the cloth toy she was holding. I've removed them all, so you didn't have to, and dressed her in the clothes you left out. She's ready now without anyone else having to see to her.'

Tears pricked my eyes at her kindness. If I could have trusted myself not to cry, I would have seized her in a hug.

'Who sewed her neck?' Martha asked.

'Dr Threlfall, he has a clinic downstairs.'

'Proper doctor, is he?'

'Has he done something wrong?'

'We'll see, won't we? He needs a bit of practise on his sutures, that I will say.'

Martha shrugged on her coat, turned up the collars and opened her umbrella. 'Much as I like and respect you, Rebecca, I do hope it's a long time before you're in further need of my professional services. People will begin to talk.'

38

Evergreen House

Barely two days passed before Reverend Illingworth paid us a call. Ostensibly to offer his spiritual guidance and sympathy. In reality it seemed he had come to gloat. Without removing his hat or coat he marched straight through the house to the garden, and I called Albie over, instructing him to ask Angela to bring a tea tray.

'Straight away please, a special one.' Small sandwiches, two types of cake. Foolish, really, to make a point of lavish refreshments for someone keen to prove your profligacy, but Illingworth would expect some acknowledgement of respect. Though the air was chill, the sun warmed the bricks of the back wall through a layer of wide-leaved ivy and Dr Threlfall was already outside, making notes on a pile of handwritten pages. Relaxed, leaning back, his beautiful leather boots resting up on another chair. I felt a stab of envy for his comfort. When had he ever needed to worry? To face the threat of homelessness and despair? At the sight of us, he jumped up, almost upsetting the inkstand, and offered his hand to the chaplain. Here was a chance for him to fight our corner. If I could steer the conversation to the research we assisted, then Illingworth might put in good words with Lavell.

'I hope I won't disturb you?' Illingworth turned his neck in an attempt to read the notes.

'Not at all. I was just taking some air. I should be leaving really.'

'Don't leave on my account. It's a fleeting visit.' He reached out as if to touch the papers and Threlfall drew the notes closer towards him. 'What are you writing?'

'Reviewing. I've been sent some research through the Ärzteforum in Munich. A physicians' forum.'

'I am familiar with the German language, Dr Threlfall.'

'Perhaps you are also familiar with their focus? They're keen to prove that pain is not imaginary.'

For heaven's sake, the pair were bad as each other, posturing and preening.

'Plainly they are wrong. It's governed by the soul.' Illingworth's face darkened.

'Ah. Well. I'm afraid such thinking is why the German doctors are ahead of us in their theory. That and their ability to test freely on animals.' He tapped his index finger on the pile of papers. Grace's emerald ring glittered. I'd recognise it anywhere – huge and square cut with a row of small, brilliant-cut diamonds around it. Its edges had left scars on many of us when she lashed out in anger. When had she gifted it to him? It was her favourite, and its presence showed how close the pair of them had become. 'This shows quite incontrovertible proof of nerve receptors and their function.'

Were they still colluding? Had Grace *bought* him? She was obsessed with her father, with proving his name and works, repairing the Everley crest. Wearing her ring and discussing pain, her father's special interest. If this was brought about by Grace, then did it follow that he would have an Everley knife? That he'd killed Rose with it? Looking at his handsome features, his elegant fingers, I couldn't imagine him stooping to such crime. But Maddie could, and she knew him better.

'Dr Müller is proposing a theory for pain. He's been working on it for years, gathering observations from various disciplines – physiology, history, pathology and psychology.' Threlfall spoke slowly, as though explaining to a child. 'He's been trying to identify particular points on the skin that respond specifically to one of the four cutaneous sensations: touch, heat, cold and pain. And stimulating his patients with needles, finding that when pressure is applied to the skin with the head of a pin, the subject initially feels pressure, followed shortly by the sensation of pain. It seems that the responses he has documented suggest that pain increases on repeated application of the stimulus in a way quite out of proportion with the intensity of that stimulus. Fascinating. And quite at odds with British research. You may be aware that Dr Everley, who founded this fine establishment, conducted similar studies from the clinic I now use?'

Illingworth inclined his head, but I doubted he had read them.

'If you are, then you will know that his findings were contradictory,' Threlfall continued. 'He found that a repeated stimulus lessened the pain effect, to the extent that his subjects were able to withstand an extreme and accelerated stimulus with no increase in the reported level of pain they felt.'

Everley killed the dogs that were used in that paper – his own wife's dogs – and in the presence of his children. How would such research reach any conclusion?

Suddenly Angela arrived, dumping the tea tray unceremoniously before leaving without serving, and I took the advantage of the pause in conversation to underscore the importance of Evergreen remaining as it was. 'We're helping with your research, aren't we Dr Threlfall?'

Before he could answer, Illingworth banged his fist on the table with such force that the tongs flew out of the sugar bowl. 'You fail to grasp the fundamental concept of the soul!' Flecks of spittle flew as he spat the words. 'To claim that the mind and body are linked in such a way is not only nonsense, it is *unchristian*. The mind is separate from the body, controlled by the *soul*. That is the purpose of the soul, and it is what separates us from animals.'

'My dear chap, do calm yourself. I'm afraid that no-one seems to have studied a soul and I am a scientific man. Where is your proof? *I* have proof that animals *can* feel pain. Now how is that possible if, as you assert, they do not have souls?'

The chaplain loomed over Threlfall, fists still balled on the table, as though he was angry enough to make the discussion physical. He had no reply.

'Do sit down, Mr Illingworth.' I poured a cup of tea and pushed it to him.

Threlfall leant back, thoroughly enjoying himself. 'Did you know that many ancient cultures believed pain and disease to be a punishment from the gods for human folly? That's why they tried to appease potentially angry gods with rituals like votive offerings and scapegoats – the sacrificial animals that carried human sins out into the wilderness.'

'I've heard just about enough of this. Comparing God's True Word with the worshipping of craven gods.' Illingworth rose again, his tea untouched, and placed his hat firmly back upon his head. 'I simply came to see where things stood after the latest scandalous death, but I will return when we can focus on the task in hand. This has certainly brought to light the irregularities in the way this charity is run and I, for one, will be very glad to see the back of such a pack of . . . of pagans and dollymops!'

How dare he speak about us in that fashion? I'd a good mind to report him to Lavell. I hurried to catch him and accompany him out of the house, in case he frightened the children.

'I will do my best to ensure Dr Threlfall is in his clinic when you next visit.'

'You'll be gone before my next visit,' he snarled, and my heart sank.

Someone had put the post on the hall tray. A postcard from Sophia, to tell us she was touring with the troupe and would be back to see us in two months, together with a kiss for Albie and a paragraph cut from the *Mortlake Times* which lauded her performance. There were two more letters, one marked with the stamp of the Royal Academy, which I put aside for Maddie to open herself, and a smaller grey envelope that I recognised as the autopsy report. I opened it quickly, scanning Martha's small, neat script.

Significant amounts of arsenic detected in each section of stomach, concentrated amounts in the larger intestine and liver. Suspected poisoning.

Poison. From Threlfall's powders, possibly? Where else could poor Rubina have picked up such a large dose? I had to check the labels on his phials to know if he had administered too much by mistake or given it deliberately to cause harm. A mistake, surely. There could be no motivation for him to poison Rubina. It made no sense. I placed the report back in its envelope and secreted it in my pocket, determined to spare Henrietta.

When I returned to the garden, Threlfall was back in position, relaxing with his feet up, humming to himself.

'Is he always like that? It doesn't seem a very devout way to behave,' he said mildly. 'We're just doing our best to understand disease and pain. Little wonder we're being overtaken by German medicine if there is to be no room for debate.'

'He is . . .' Would my words be returned to Lavell? 'He is passionate for his faith.'

Threlfall looked amused. 'You are too kind. But is he correct? Are you threatened with leaving?'

'Not through choice.' I took a seat at the end of the table and began to explain our situation, the reputational damage caused by the deaths and the penny bloods, the lack of orders, Lavell's determination to have Evergreen for himself. All the while I watched his face carefully, especially when I mentioned murder, but his expression betrayed nothing. If he was guarding secrets, then he was good at it.

'That seems unfortunate. I've always been supportive of the work you do here, how you help your charges. Some of them have suffered, as you know, and would suffer still in some establishments.' He examined his fingernails, which were beautifully manicured, like little seashells. 'Is there nothing that can be done?'

'They are making their final assessment soon, but I believe their minds are already set. It may help if you could state your position on the work we do? Or the research we help with?'

'I can try. I'm not sure I would hold much sway with the Charity Board, but my name is in favour at the Society. I'd like my work on delinquency to extend to recommendations for the rehabilitation of . . . penitents, for want of a better word.' He cast around as though ensuring we were not overheard. 'Under your watch this place is very different from what Dr Everley intended.'

Should we fear him? Was Maddie right? She didn't even know about the knife, and now there was the poison. None of it made sense. But if he was to be any help to us at all, I had to know if he could be trusted.

'I would like to know more about it,' I said. 'Perhaps you would permit a visit to answer some of my questions?'

Mr Lavell wiped crumbs from his mouth and edged forward on his chair, which creaked dangerously under his bulk. I watched the buttons of his waistcoat strain, fearful they might fly off and injure someone.

'Is this not your workroom?' he asked.

'We've moved things around a little.' Bodies took space, mourners needed to visit.

'And where does the manufacturing take place now? We must see that the women are not cramped, that they have light and space wherever they are working.'

Why? They certainly didn't care about that elsewhere. The workhouse gave each inmate about as much space to work in as a penny postage stamp. Disease and overcrowding were endemic in such institutions, including their beloved hospitals for repentants. I held my tongue. 'We're taking a break from manufacturing, for a week or so,' I replied before Lavell had the chance. 'The women work hard and there are plenty of items ready downstairs, the baskets I showed you. Wallpaper orders are slow at this time of year, so they're focused on learning new painting techniques. Some of them have visited artists.' Lies dripped from my tongue with such ease. A relief that George was not there to hear them and question his trust in my honesty.

'We may as well review the accounts together now, Mrs Harris.'

Smoothing my skirts as I sat back down, I composed myself, clasping my hands together to stop them shaking. It would be a long afternoon, and still there was much to do in preparation for the funeral. Angela grumbled about baking for another wake, and the flowers weren't finished either. We were pinning them ourselves, partly to save money and partly because Rubina was so fond of wildflowers and ordinary plants like dandelions that we'd sent the children all over the lanes and gardens to gather anything they thought would be nice.

'What is this line for?' Mr Lavell held out the book, finger placed on the amount I'd added that morning.

I cursed my own efficiency. There had been no need to add that so swiftly, and the same could be said for the rest of the funeral expenses. For a fee we could ill afford, we'd brought in a photographer from the emporium on the high street to take an image of Rubina that Henrietta could keep. To give comfort in the dark days to come and to serve as a reminder. Rubina had never been photographed before. None of the children had. Photographs were expensive and it was too difficult to take a clear likeness of little ones because they moved so often that they blurred the image, so afterwards George had gathered them together for a group photograph in the garden. It made them happy, made the cost worthwhile. George had to take the trap to fetch the man and his enormous camera, the size of a magician's chest. Albie had tried to climb inside it.

'It's part of the funeral expense.'

'Are these expenses strictly necessary?'

Rubina propped up on the coverlet, a spray of lilies in her stiff hands, hair loose to cover her neck. When they delivered the print that morning, we'd marvelled at how she looked alive, and they explained how they painted the eyes to look open on the glass plate. I didn't tell Henrietta, she thought it was a miracle.

'Are *any* funeral expenses strictly necessary? We could have used the pauper's patch. All of us could. But we don't. Because at such times comfort and ritual are what is needed, the safe knowledge that the souls of beloved departed are at rest.' I did my best to look pious. 'I would rather go without food than manage such things improperly.'

Lavell grunted but he turned the page, and I watched his face turn from incredulity to irritation at the figures, before a smile spread across his fleshy jowls. No doubt the realisation that we were his to take. Between Illingworth's insistence that we stopped work for Lent, and the taint of scandal that attached to our household, there was little business to be had. Without orders and customers, we would have weeks at best. Soon we would only be able to make money by selling our stories. Poking from Lavell's bag I could clearly see red ribbon. When else would I have the chance to challenge him?

'Mr Lavell, I noticed the other day, the ribbons you are using for your papers. They were . . . where did you get them?'

He looked surprised at the question. 'My papers are not your concern, Mrs Harris.'

Though he was permitted to read anything he wished of mine. What was he hiding? 'The ribbons.'

'Angela gave them to me, when I dropped my papers. She said she found them by the side of the coalhouse and washed them to keep for herself, but the coal dust left marks and so she gave them to me, for my papers. Why? Are they yours? I would be happy to replace them.'

'I . . . they were . . . they belonged to one of the girls. No matter. I thought I would ask.'

An answer for everything, a slew of coincidence. I would ask Angela to corroborate his story at the first opportunity. He read in silence for an agonising half hour before looking up. 'This isn't looking in the slightest bit sustainable. This charitable model will be ceased forthwith and the house will be taken over by the Board. Yourself and Mr Harris will be removed from duty, the children will go to the orphanage in Coram Fields and the Magdalen group will add a laundry facility to the downstairs rooms. There is plenty of space. This place will be profitable and purposeful in a matter of weeks, and I would imagine the death rate might slow somewhat with a bit of stability.'

I sat on my hands for fear that their trembling might give way to an urge to slap him hard. 'Would it not be kinder to wait until mourning has finished.'

'I will give you a week for mourning and then two weeks to prepare.'

'But this is my *home*, not your property. I was tasked with managing these women and I was managing it very well until —'

'It is not your property either. As a charitable concern, and with the legal owner inconvenienced, it's the job of my Board to ensure it is managed correctly.'

Three weeks. Where would we go? Maddie's home was tiny, Mother and Father had left Lynton and moved to set up another practice elsewhere. I didn't even know the name of the village. Our sister Isabel claimed we'd ruined her life and cut off all communication years ago. Even if I had somewhere to go, how could I leave them? Send the children to Coram? It was the only place that took illegitimates and its reputation was grim. How was it fair if Threlfall stayed?

'And what of Dr Threlfall?' I enquired. 'He occupies the clinic downstairs by way of a covenant.'

'We're aware of the arrangement. And we are satisfied that he's a fit tenant. He assures us that he has already been of great use to the girls, some of whom he asserts are highly troubled.'

When had the inspectors spoken to Threlfall? And what right

did he have to call our girls troubled? They hadn't asked for his help, they were helping *him*.

'We're involved with ongoing research. And there are other matters to settle. People who may wish to adopt the children if they're to be separated from their mothers, relatives and so on.' I thought for a moment. I needed time. If only I could find some money and change his mind. I could chase orders, George could find work, Maddie may even sell her paintings. 'Allow us six weeks to arrange things properly.'

39

All Saints Asylum

'It's not what we planned, but it's fine.' I struggle to keep my voice calm. Two months on by the marks on the wall and we're no closer to winning. The cook was necessary, and I have some regrets about that. Rose was a good woman, steadfast, knew her place. She worked for Father from the day he opened Evergreen, showing up with no references and only the clothes she stood up in. Gave him loyalty for giving her a chance and never asked questions, turned a blind eye to all the comings and goings, though Father's basement was near to the kitchen and she must have heard something. Her response when asked was always the same, '*I don't know anything about that.*' Keeping everyone well fed was her job, and she took that seriously. A natural in the kitchen, a fondness for gin, and always too soft on the women. Still, she never took sides, she kept things calm and she didn't deserve to go like that, though I'm assured the job was clean.

Felicia's death was never intentional. Foolish girl was just in the wrong place at the wrong time, saw things she shouldn't have seen. Made too much trouble in one way and another. Could never keep her mouth shut and if one of the others told her a secret, it was all over the house within hours. It was she who sold our story, her fault our name got into the penny bloods. But if not her then someone else, and I was happy for our legacy to remain. Still, she was not my target. And now a child. Dispensable of course, unlikely to be missed, but with every death comes closer inspection. To lose three members of the household in such a short space of time means Evergreen will be subject to more scrutiny than ever. More visits, more questions. We may not have much longer to act.

Arsenic is everywhere. It's used to colour so many things – fabric, medicine, wallpaper. Clever to think of it. And if it hadn't missed its target the plan would have worked. But it was only possible to slip it into the kitchen once. Now we'll have to find another way, and from what I know of Rebecca she'll be on the alert – it will become difficult to get anything past her. Anger rises and I turn my face to the wall, compose myself. I need the support; we must remember the objective.

'I imagine the household is unsettled?'

'The girls are fighting. They're prevented from working with nothing to occupy them and their thoughts are troubled by the murders. Rebecca finds things difficult to control. Visits are constantly brought to gather evidence and I don't think it will be long before Evergreen is permanently changed.'

Then we must act quickly, or the chance will be gone. They will disperse. And the chance to punish Maddie and Rebecca will be lost to me. 'And what of Dr Threlfall?' I affect a nonchalant air, but he has missed his visit for the past two weeks and I miss his gaze, the opportunity to discuss Father's work with someone who has a chance of understanding it.

'His research into delinquency continues. He is much at the house and seems to be developing a good relationship with Rebecca.'

Does he? She is certainly pretty, in a garish, rather obvious way. Not the first loose woman he has looked at with a mouthful of flowers. If she has twisted him around her arm, then I was right to find others to help me. Edward seems to be too weak to take things further. Imagine a doctor scared of knives. Unfortunately, I've taken him into my confidence now, and there's a chance he'll tell Rebecca what I planned. He couldn't prove it. But it might make her too careful to trap.

'And his research into pain?'

'We hear nothing of that.'

As I suspected. There is no-one left to finish Father's work and reclaim the Everley name. Now that's gone too, and the only thing left is revenge. It's all that matters. We must stop dithering and act.

'There are many ways to catch Rebecca and Maddie. Watch, wait, catch them off guard.'

Such indifference from someone I have helped, been forced to trust, is infuriating. Even now, after all I have done, no-one understands the importance of the task. I am trapped in here and even my knife is lost. The last thing I owned with the mark of the Everley bees. No-one listens to a word of my story. The house, the crest, our name – they do not care. I will not be weak. *My family will not be weak.* I howl like a banshee and fly across the room, unable to control my anger. Nails connect with flesh, tearing at skin and drawing blood. Their screams will bring the warden and I do not care. Whatever punishment ensues will be worth it.

Before Varley arrives, I manage several vicious blows to the head and face of the one person I thought I could rely on to help. The mouse peeps round the warden's legs and, when he separates us, takes my victim outside. Varley has been waiting for his chance of violence. He's sweating with excitement. Unhooking the truncheon from his belt, he raises it and brings it crashing to the back of my knees until I fold to the floor. There he pins me down, forces my hands into ticking sleeves and closes the buckles behind me before leading me out to the treatment room. What does he imagine could break me in here? Restraints line the walls: a carved wooden shoulder yoke, a leather collar with a silver pin, a set of iron manacles. I'm made to sit in the tin ice bath, which does nothing to calm my anger. But when he wraps me in the shroud, the weight of water feels like relief.

40

Dr Threlfall's Alienist Clinic

Not expecting Threlfall to answer the door himself, I found myself flustered and instead of the speech I had rehearsed in my head I blurted, 'Hester isn't here.'

'You are most observant. And I'm delighted to be blessed with your company twice in one day.' Threlfall spoke with his usual smooth manner, so it was hard to tell if he flattered or spoke with sarcasm. His unkempt hair had been brushed and oiled and he'd changed into fresh linen, a mauve waistcoat embroidered with fleurs-de-lys; he must keep as many clothes here as at his house. 'I've prepared some papers for you but if you'd rather ask questions, I am happy to oblige.'

'I'd like to see the rooms you work in, if I may?'

'I'm afraid I can't offer you any refreshment, Hester is visiting her sister.' Chatting amiably, he led me through to the waiting room. 'Having a baby. Doesn't seem to go smoothly and so she has gone to assist. Wouldn't let me help, for which I was grateful. This is my main consultation room.' He opened the door with a flourish.

High windows covered in a metal grille to shield them from the street. A large desk topped with leather, dyed deep green and fixed with copper rivets like a ship's hull. A huge matching chair on the far side of it, three smaller, upright chairs clustered on the other.

'Are your patients usually accompanied?' I asked the question to buy some time and cast my eyes around the room.

'Yes. They are often hysterical, disturbed, needing the reassurance of family.'

I waited for him to finish explaining how he assessed new patients, eyeing the cases of implements that lined the walls; some small and neat like surgeon's knives, some the size of farmyard tools, each labelled on small cards. Huge metal teeth glinted on something that looked like a gin trap. If it could, it would bite through the glass and latch onto my flesh.

'I see you're admiring my collection.' Threlfall beamed a look of pride.

Why must men hoard and catalogue everything? Animals, plants, shells. Horrors and curios or instruments of torture.

'I assume they are Old Dr Everley's?'

'Some, not all. If you're interested, their provenance is noted on the cards.'

'I wasn't aware you were a surgeon.' Martha thought not. And yet I let him cut Rubina. *It's always those close to you, Rebecca, it's how they get away with it.*

'Oh, I'm not. All my work is with the mind. But sometimes the flesh must be cut to heal the mind. Or to relieve other maladies that I'm asked to treat.'

Fine features, smooth manners. Threlfall was a charming man. But as I looked at the set of his jaw, the cold blue of his eyes, I could believe him capable of great cruelty. I could believe Maddie. He had the look of someone who could fly straight up into the air if he wanted. Standing by these horrible cabinets, shadowed in lamplight, he looked capable of setting his tools to work on me if I crossed him. His black leather bag lay open. A chance to set my mind at rest on everything, or discover evidence that pointed to his guilt.

'Are these your treatments? Would they be the same things you kindly gave to Rubina?'

Pushing the bag open until its frame was almost flat, Threlfall began to remove boxes and rolls of phials. 'Sleep, or lack of it, is a problem for some of my patients. They're troubled by bad dreams and attach all kinds of significance to their meanings. There's a movement in France that would agree with them, but it's my belief that it's usually the digestive system stimulating the mind while the body sleeps – so I give them these powerful sleeping draughts, which blocks the mind from creating stories. Do you dream, Mrs Harris?'

'I sleep very lightly.' And rarely long enough to dream. I couldn't remember the last time I had done so.

'A mother's curse.'

'I'm not a mother.'

'You're a mother to everyone. You must make time to rest properly. It's vital that the mind sleeps. Would you like some of these draughts?'

Though it would do George and I much good to spend a few nights out cold, we needed all our wits at the present time. 'Thank you, but I will manage.' I held up a bottle labelled *Dover powder*. 'Is this the same medicine you gave Rubina?'

He took it, peered at the label, passed it back. 'Yes, that's it.'

Ipecacuanha and opium. No arsenic listed on the ingredients.

'Did you administer her anything else?'

'Some chloroform, to keep her still while I made the incision. Nothing else. Have you noticed any of the others displaying similar symptoms? You must remain vigilant. Diphtheria is a nasty disease.'

No arsenic from Threlfall then. He didn't seem to be lying. He was happily rummaging through the bag and explaining the importance of his medicines.

'This is a new one, valproic acid, apparently highly effective in the treatment of convulsive fitting diseases and those disorders where patients swing between extremes of mood. I have yet to test its efficacy.'

Sounded rather like Sophia. Excitable. I thought of her postcard, all the news of the tour, nothing but a single kiss for little Albie. How could we let him go to Coram? But after the threat of eviction, if we adopted and thereby saved him, we would be abandoning the others. We couldn't treat one so differently. Yet we couldn't adopt them all with no guarantee we could house them. Threlfall was still talking; I must focus, who knew when I would get another chance. With so much running through my head I worried I'd be his next patient.

'Such medicine is extremely exciting at the moment. Did you know the first psychology journal was launched this year? The mind is endlessly fascinating, new treatments are coming through all the time.'

'Would you say that Old Dr Everley was a pioneer? Grace and Lucius certainly thought so.' Brave of me to speak their names out loud, but I had to understand his position.

Threlfall's face fell, and he began to put the medicines back into his bag. 'I'm afraid his field of medicine was very different to mine. He was a surgeon, a skilful one by all accounts, like his son.'

'Yet he did write papers on the mind. Groundbreaking, I heard, what he tried to prove with his forays into understanding pain.'

Threlfall paused, leaning on his bag. 'His research was brutal. Cruel. If I may be honest with you for a moment? I know that this whole field is one that caused immeasurable distress to your family. And I have never apologised for my part in that. I would like to now, whilst we are speaking.'

Amazement silenced me. If this was an act, it was worthy of Sophia.

'I should apologise to Madeleine too, though she seems repelled by my very presence. I was young, you understand, my head was turned. I didn't know what . . .'

'I do realise that, Dr Threlfall. If I did not, I wouldn't have been able to stay.' Was he a brazen murderer or were my instincts right? Either way, I hoped he did not imagine his charms were working on me.

'You are a kind person. May I call you Rebecca? Dr Everley established this house to push his theories of pain to extremes. No longer able to work with animals, he needed human subjects and he needed to find them from those parts of society that no-one would miss. He has written that his subjects were . . . dispensable.'

A cold chill flooded my veins. Dispensable. Felicia, Sophia, Henrietta, myself . . . all those women who came before me, who were here with me.

'I didn't realise at first. I was tasked with continuing, and I tried, but then I realised and . . .'

Who had tasked him? 'May I see the stimulus? The things you were talking of earlier? I would like to see for myself.' Whatever caused Felicia to scream out, it was the last time I heard anything. He must have stopped it then. Did he dispatch her to stop her talking? He sounded so contrite, so genuine, that it was hard for me to carry on, but I had to know.

'There's another room. Behind the second treatment room.' Threlfall's eyes shone as though they harboured tears.

Opening a side door, he ushered us through to a room not

dissimilar to the first. Slightly smaller, with a long sofa and, again, a row of three chairs.

'Sometimes patients do faint. When we uncover painful truths, or the situation is difficult. Sometimes when they recline here, they relax, and we're able to make better progress.'

Reaching into his waistcoat pocket, he withdrew a chain. A half-dozen keys jangled at its end. Slowly he selected two small, ornate keys, like those on the lids of pianofortes, and inserted them into the double keyholes on a narrow door that I'd thought was a cupboard. A musty smell emerged as it creaked open, as though it had been closed for a long time. It was completely dark. Threlfall struck a match to light a gas lamp and carried it over to the entrance, holding it up so I could peer inside. A cramped space, not big enough for much furniture, but shelved on two walls with two wooden benches in front. Rows of wood and metal objects lined the shelving. At first I assumed they were medical implements, but as my eyes adjusted to the gloom, I realised they were instruments of torture, with spikes and sharp teeth. I took a step back.

'Is this . . . when we heard first Sophia and then Felicia scream . . .'

'No.' Threlfall looked shocked. 'I have never used this room. I started to follow the research using a needle stimulus, but I couldn't go through with it. This room is where Dr Everley's research took him, from his pets to his children to anyone he found *dispensable* that he could bring here. It's why he founded the place. Before . . .'

His children. Grace and Lucius didn't stand a chance. I would never forgive them, but to have such a father was unimaginable.

'In his research it is listed as the *oubliette*. From the French 'to forget'. It usually means a kind of dungeon, where people were left and forgotten. But in his research, it seems to also mean the forgetting of the stimulus, that if people are overloaded with pain, it becomes nothing, it lessens.'

'Is that true?'

'I don't know. I would not imagine so.'

'And Felicia . . . ?'

'I know what he did. But I'm not like him.' Threlfall's face was set, serious.

It would be so easy to just believe him. And the knife. Was it a gift or a keepsake? I had peered at everything in his rooms and there was no other sign of the crest or the bees. If he was in the habit of using their things, would he not have more? And if his stomach turned at Everley's research methods, then how could he be capable of worse? His lack of motivation, his mild demeanour – nothing made sense. I thought of Felicia's ribbons on Lavell's papers. The inspector was always impressed with Threlfall, always striving to be accepted in the upper reaches of society; could they be working together? For a moment I wondered whether it was Old Dr Everley, if he haunted us still. If I confided that in Threlfall, he would waste no time in using the treatments from his bag.

41

Evergreen House

Maddie and Tizzy joined us for breakfast, so excited by the promise of the letter that I hadn't the heart to tell them our own news. Or the outcome of my talk with Threlfall. Maddie wouldn't believe that anyway. I'd find a way to explain. I had to. Now that I felt he was above suspicion, I had to talk to someone who might be able to help me understand what was happening. If Lavell was the source of our danger, then I could not keep such thoughts to myself. He was too powerful. Allowed to come and go as he pleased, it wouldn't take him long to find the opportunity to hurt us all.

A waft of the kippers Angela was frying hit my nose and I fought a sudden wave of nausea as bile rose to my throat. They couldn't be fresh. A sweet, rotten smell that brought to mind Hester's taxidermy.

'Are you feeling unwell?' George had noticed. 'You were the same yesterday. I know you are worried about —'

'I'm perfectly well, thank you,' I interrupted. I *was* anxious. But this was something different. A nausea that overcame me early and disappeared by mid-morning. I'd heard that pregnancy took a similar effect on some people. It hadn't affected me like that before, but I was young when I had Elisabeth, and I'd felt perfectly healthy throughout the whole nine months. My body was older now and might react differently if I was with child. Was it possible? After all the years of trying? I tried to remember when I'd last lain with George, when I'd last had my monthlies, but could recall neither. At the first opportunity I would call on Martha; she was bound to have something that might help.

George poured a glass of water and pushed it towards me.

'Drink this, it will help.'

The Royal Academy letter sat unopened, propped against the marmalade pot so that everyone could see it, and Maddie's eyes flicked to it continually.

'Just open it!' Tizzy urged.

'What if it's a rejection? I'm enjoying the idea that it might be good news. Let's eat first, then I'll do it.'

They smiled at each other, let their gaze linger, and I was happy for them. They'd feel no pressure for children, for family life, and were free in ways I couldn't imagine. Henrietta regarded them curiously.

'It's good to see you at the table, Henrietta.' I tried to distract her attention. 'Thank you for joining us.'

She gave a wan smile, and I patted her hand, remembered the autopsy notes. I hadn't the heart to tell her what they concluded. If it wasn't in the medicine, then where on earth had the arsenic come from? Had Rubina somehow got into the paint room and swallowed some of the Paris green? Unlikely. Some women used arsenic wafers to keep their complexions pale, but only Sophia and Felicia would be foolish enough to try such a thing, and neither of them were here. Lavell was the only one in the kitchens with the opportunity to meddle that day. Could he have done so?

'Try to eat something. The hens are laying well and we have plenty of eggs.' I could have bitten off my tongue. Of course she wouldn't want those. It was Rubina's favourite job to fetch the eggs, and the sight of them must remind her of her daughter holding them out in her little basket. 'Or some toast. Angela has put seeds into the bread, it's very good.' I buttered a piece and placed it on her plate, pushing the jar of marmalade towards her. The letter smacked onto the table and Maddie seized it, holding it up to the light.

'The only way you'll know what it says is to open it!' Tizzy plucked it from her hand and, much to the delight of the children, began to dance around the room with it. Holding it up out of reach. She was taller than Maddie, hard work had made her stronger, and she won easily. Holding it between her thumb and forefinger, she pretended to tear the envelope.

'Give it to me,' Maddie squealed and snatched it back. 'You are *so* impatient. Look, I'm doing it now.'

'Don't tear it really.' Tizzy handed her a knife. 'You might want to keep it.'

Slowly, carefully, Maddie pushed the knife under the seal and eased it off. A wax disc embossed with the letters *RA*. She placed it on the table; Albie picked it up and held it carefully in the palm of his hand.

Maddie eased out the letter and began to read, her expression changing from worry to delight.

'They've taken them?' Tizzy guessed.

Maddie hugged her, then me, and then George. '"*We are pleased to inform you that the Council has approved two works from the selection submitted. Medusa and Helen are selected for Gallery 1, in positions 42 and 43. Council decision is final.*" Gallery One! It is more than I had hoped. They'll be the first to be seen and will hang at eye level.'

'Congratulations, dear Maddie. It's no less than you deserve.'

I was so proud of her. 'They're beautiful and the series deserves its own exhibition.' I remembered what George had said about the storeroom. 'You must collect the others back, before they're lost.'

'I'm invited to the varnishing day, a week before it opens, to add the last coat of varnish. If George would be kind enough to come with me, we could collect then.'

'Of course.'

'They're asking if I want to sell them. Should I?'

'We don't have a wall big enough to hold them at home,' laughed Tizzy. 'What did you think you would do with them?'

'I hadn't thought at all.' Maddie stared at the letter in wonder. '"*The prices of the works will be entered in the price catalogues on the table galleries.*" What does a painting like that cost? I've only ever sold small works to publishers before, and they were all commissioned.'

'You can ask when you take your varnish.' I reached over and began to stack the crockery. Whatever the price, it wouldn't be enough to help us. If we were staying, I would buy them myself, the others too, hang them all over the house as a reminder to hold our heads as high as we could. But such plans were impossible. Now George and I must look for somewhere else to live and find a way to break the news to the others. Everything was falling apart so quickly it was hard to know where to start.

Albie stood in front of me and opened up his fist to show me he still had the Academy seal, *RA* embossed thickly in the wax.

'Rubina,' he said.

I swallowed hard. 'Good letters, Albie.' Making sure Henrietta wasn't listening, I added, 'Would you like to keep it, to remind you?'

He put it in his pocket in a gesture that was heartbreakingly solemn. He'd been left by his mother and lost a friend in such a short space of time. I put an arm around his shoulder. 'Could you take these into the kitchen for me, Albie?' I handed him a stack of plates and he staggered a little as he moved away. Poor little mite. George placed the cups on a willow tray. It was one of our new styles, beautifully finished, and I smarted to think of the pile of them unsold.

'We have to help him,' said George, watching Albie's back as he delivered the dirty crockery to Angela's sink.

'We have to help all of them.' Picking up the tray, I followed Albie to the sink, just in time to see him reaching for something on a serving dish that was set on the stove. 'Albie, you have only just finished breakfast, those are for later.'

'No harm,' said Angela, 'I don't mind.'

'But I do. You've spoilt us with your bakery.' I took the biscuit from Albie, intending to replace it, when I noticed the icing was green. Paris green. As ripe and verdant as meadow moss in autumn. A colour I'd seen before. In the toxic paint of our wallpaper rolls and on the biscuit that Rubina had taken, iced with the letter *R*. There were no names on these ones, but the message was clear enough.

'These are very pretty.' I held up the plate to admire the patterns of thick icing. 'Have you used almond paste in the decoration?' Bringing it down, I bent my head and breathed in the scent of vanilla, almond and something bitter, like the taste of a plum kernel, bitten by mistake.

'Doesn't take long,' she muttered, head turned to the stove where she was frying kidneys.

'How do you get such a bright shade? It looks like Scheele's green. Presumably you're not using paint on the biscuits?' I affected a laugh.

'Food colouring,' she replied flatly.

'Can I see the bottle? I'm curious. It's such a wonderful shade.'

Angela turned her head slowly to regard me with suspicion.

'Ruby's favourite,' said Albie sadly. 'I like blue, and Evie likes red, but Ruby liked green.'

'She did. And I'm sure she's enjoying green biscuits in heaven. She wouldn't want to look down and see you sad.' He cheered a little as I tousled his hair.

'Is she with Felicia, and Rose?'

'I'm sure that she is. Run along and play, they'll want to see you happy with the others when they check on you.'

He handed over his wax seal. 'Can you look after this? I don't want to break it.' Then he skipped outside to find Evie.

'Their emotions are so quick to change at his age. So upset and yet so easy to mollify.' Nervous chattering. Angela said nothing in response. 'What were we saying? Yes, green. I'd like to see the food colouring – it might be useful for the wallpaper, or even the willow if the dye is that strong.' And Albie was right, his friend had chosen a green biscuit before, iced with the letter *R*. From Angela's expression it could well have been intended for me. Was she working with Lavell? He'd been there that day, skulking in the kitchen. According to his story, she'd given him Felicia's ribbons too. I had a sudden thought that he had sent her in the first place. It was quite a coincidence that he'd been here when she arrived, even stranger that she opened up to him when she seemed to dislike everyone else.

'It's empty.'

'Then I'll find it in the box.' Still holding the plate, I marched over to the scullery door and pulled it open, searched through the crate where we kept empty glass bottles for refiling or future use. A small blue apothecary bottle was the only likely candidate. Lined and ridged with the unmistakable sign of poison, scented with bitter almonds, and just as I suspected. I turned, ready to ask how many drops would be needed to create such a vivid paste, when a sudden memory of Bessie at Rose's funeral stopped me dead. *She was talking to a youngster before she left.* Angela looked younger than her years, *all skin and bone*, just as Bessie described. Pale skin illuminated by the shaft of sunlight from the kitchen window. We knew nothing about her at all. No references or recommendations other than the one we'd been unable to confirm. Could she have had something to do with Rose's death, too? She certainly knew how to use a knife. The thought brought another wave of nausea. Had she killed Rose? Rubina? With Felicia it was feasible that they'd quarrelled and fought, that she got carried away by her temper. *A whore's dress.* I knew what she thought of some of us, and Felicia had never liked her, never trusted her. But Angela was tiny. And what possible reason could she have to murder a kind old woman or a darling little girl? If I was ever to find out, then I couldn't raise her suspicion now.

'Let me know when you get some more. I'd like to learn how to make the colour,' I said, affecting a light tone. 'I'll take these up to Henrietta for the biscuit tin so that we're well stocked if the inspectors choose to visit.'

Walking out, I felt her eyes on me like the point of a blade. As soon as I could I tipped the biscuits into the coal scuttle, covering them in soot so they couldn't be eaten. No-one would light a fire in the drawing room for a while. If the inspectors had their way, we'd never use the room again.

42

Mr Thomas' Chophouse, South Kensington

Though it was early for supper, the chophouse was already full of people. Couples in Sunday best, groups of young men dressed as clerks, a smart family keen for everyone to overhear that they were celebrating their son starting at Oxford. One table hosted a group of artists whom Maddie knew and acknowledged briefly on the way to our corner seat. Half-empty bottles and used plates littered their tablecloth. Men eccentrically dressed in smocks and long tunics, covered in smudges of coloured oil as though they'd rolled in petals. One wore a turban wound with a silk scarf, like an Arabian knight. Their eyes were glazed as they greeted us, offering to pull up chairs and make room for a party. Maddie politely declined the invitation on our behalf.

'Why didn't you tell them your news?' I whispered.

'Better for them to see the paintings when they hang on the wall,' she whispered back. 'They will first assume they are painted by a man, and when they check it will have far more impact than to show off now.'

I was dismayed to see Mr Lavell at a far table, accompanied by what looked like Mr Tovey from behind and three other men I didn't recognise. Their spirits were as high as the artists'. Probably already celebrating the profit they'd make from our closing. Lavell wore a bright mauve cravat, like something Threlfall would favour, and the sight of him celebrating while we struggled made me furious. If he spotted us and came over I couldn't trust myself not to react, so I sat myself and George facing away from them. He wouldn't recognise Tizzy or Maddie and was unlikely to expect to see us out at a time when the house was in danger.

Our drinks were delivered by a slender girl with yellow hair, whom Maddie confused by calling her a model for Isis. I raised my glass of claret. 'To our famous artist,' I declared, and the four of us clinked glasses.

'We're very proud of you.' Tizzy's eyes shone, and I realised what Maddie meant when she described them as *the colour of happiness*. The pair of them had been laughing all day, playing with the children and teaching the women new techniques in painting. They'd trawled through the orders, looking for patterns, trying to work out whether there were other options we could try to find custom, and had come up with so many ideas that I almost began to believe Evergreen could be saved.

'An amazing achievement,' added George. Treating them to supper was his suggestion. A rare evening out of the house that reminded me how settled we'd become, how full of responsibility. It was just a chophouse, with thick square tables and dark red walls covered in gilt-framed mirrors, but it felt special for us to be there together. Good to be out of the house, though my mind had stayed there. A nagging worry that the children were not safe. I'd asked Henrietta to be vigilant, but I couldn't give explicit instructions without making it plain that I didn't trust Angela. And I needed to be sure.

'It feels unkind to be celebrating paintings when your lives are turned upside down.' Maddie set down her glass. She preferred spirits to wine, which reminded her of Lucius. I wasn't used to it either, but it was needed and warming.

'You shouldn't worry about us.'

'Of course I worry. I wouldn't be here if it weren't for you two.' She looked at George. 'You especially. You've worked too hard to let go of everything now.'

'You should definitely work with the cooperatives. We can go and see some tomorrow,' said Tizzy. She'd always had a good head for business. It was Tizzy who found buyers for Maddie's botanical prints, all the binders and publishers on The Row. She knew which baskets would sell, which patterns for wallpaper were fashionable. 'Morris' can't cope with demand and Hambles just bought another shopfront on Regent Street. Or there's always Walpole's at Strawberry Hill, though they're more craft – but there's no reason the women shouldn't learn to make terracotta tiles.'

'Thank you. You've both had such good ideas. We're very grateful.' In reality, I knew we had barely a hope of surviving the fortnight. Even if these people saw us, liked us, took pity on us, the orders wouldn't pay for weeks and by that time the Board would have pounced. Evergreen was prime property with a high-profile history. Converting it would be a coup for them in proving their governance.

'I like your idea about teaching them landscape painting,' said George.

'Small paintings sell extremely well. Everyone wants them in their homes, so if you finish them quickly and price them cheaply it could be a good source of income. Even if it was only one of the women who could paint them. Henrietta's work is very good,' said Tizzy.

'I wish you'd told me earlier,' Maddie scolded. 'You are always so determined to *manage*.'

'I didn't want to worry you.' I brushed my chest as I raised my glass, and a sudden pain caused a sharp intake of breath. My breasts had felt tight and sore all day, and the bodice of my one smart dress wasn't helping.

'*Now* I'm worried,' said Maddie.

'Indigestion. I'm not used to such rich food.' No point in explaining and raising George's hopes. It would probably turn into nothing. I'd had plenty of phantom symptoms before. I ignored the meaningful look my sister exchanged with Tizzy. Thankfully George seemed oblivious; there'd be time enough to tell him when I was sure it was true.

'There's something that worries me though. I didn't want to say anything until I was sure, but I think Angela had something to do with Rubina's illness.' Why was I speaking like that? I knew she'd done it. And I needed their help to prove it. 'In fact, I know she did.' And I was certain that Lavell was involved. Was he still in the restaurant? I hardly dared to turn my head to check in case he saw me. Safer not to mention his name.

George pushed the empty plates aside and leant closer. 'What is it? We should never have taken her without references.'

He felt guilty just as much as I blamed myself, and we had never even spoken about it. When had that started? We used to discuss everything. 'We couldn't have known. It was a difficult time.'

'What's happened?' asked Tizzy.

Isis arrived to clear the table, confused at the lack of attention this time and slightly huffy as a result. I waited until she left to continue. 'Rubina ate a biscuit she made for Easter.'

'We all ate those,' said George, 'they were delicious.'

'Rubina ate one that was decorated in green icing, in the shape of a letter *R*. It was made of almond paste and coloured with arsenic.'

'Is that safe for food? We use it on the papers.'

'It *is* sometimes used. But not in such quantity. I found an empty bottle in the box. And Rubina's report listed high quantities of arsenic as the cause of death.'

'Not Threlfall's treatment?' Maddie asked, quick to throw blame.

'No. That was my first thought, and I checked all the labels of the medicine he used on her. Arsenic wasn't included.'

'Why on earth would she want to hurt Rubina?' George half rose, panicked. 'What are they eating tonight? Don't we need to get back to make sure they're all safe?'

I put out a hand to stay him. 'I don't think she meant to hurt Rubina. I think it was intended for me.'

'Why would she want to harm you? You gave her a job and a home, you trusted her.'

But I didn't, not really. 'I've never felt that she liked me; she's been cold, difficult. I haven't confronted her because I don't have any proof, just a feeling. And there's more.'

Isis brought us finger bowls, with scented towels, and stood while we cleaned our hands. Without speaking the others waited for me to continue. The artists called for more wine, the Oxford family rose and left, made a fuss about leaving a large tip and swept past our table to collect their coats.

'I spoke to Bessie, from the Half Moon, at Rose's funeral. She said something that I didn't think much of at the time. But she said that, on the night she was murdered, Rose was talking to a young person she hadn't seen before. She asked if Rose had any relatives that I knew of because it looked like a difficult conversation.'

'Confidence trickster?' said George. 'Someone targeting her to walk out with, distracting her while an accomplice came to the attack.'

'That's what I thought at first. You hear about such things and

Rose was friendly to everyone. And I forgot about it. But then there was the report, and the empty bottle of arsenic, and I started thinking about everything else.' I couldn't mention the Everley knife. It would upset Maddie and there was no link as far as I could make out. 'And I remembered that Bessie said the person was sharp and thin. All corners. It's just how I would describe Angela.'

Isis was hovering by the table. A large queue was forming at the door, and she was clearly keen for us to pay and leave. Maddie insisted on taking the bill.

'We're supposed to be treating you,' George protested.

'Your company was the treat.' As a widow she was comfortably off, able to pay. Her brow furrowed. 'But we need to find out more. If it was Angela with Rose that night, then we need to involve the police.'

'What can I get for you? Bessie will be back soon; she's laying Albert out in the bunk.' The barkeep towered over the long wooden bar, a face I didn't recognise, and I wondered why *he* wasn't sorting out the drunks instead. He stood wiping pots with arms like the legs of a horse.

'Bit early, isn't it?' George ordered ginger beers and the man rolled his eyes.

'He's been at it for a while. Buried his wife this afternoon.' He put four stoneware bottles of Batey's on the counter, added four tin cups. 'You're not the Temperance lot, are you? Wasting your time in here if you are.' He covered the bottle necks with his dirty apron to open them.

'Friends of Rose,' I said. 'She was our cook.'

'Big Rose? That was a nasty business. She never deserved that.'

'Who's asking after Rose?' Bessie's voice carried from the back room, and she emerged, straightening her clothes as though she'd been in a fight. A smile spread across her face when she saw us. 'To what do we owe the pleasure? I thought you lot had mended your ways.'

'We have,' said George, pointing to his ginger beer. 'Though we had a few at Thomas' earlier.'

Bessie roared with laughter and poured herself a gin, giving the barkeep a smack on the behind as she squeezed past. Another new conquest. She'd been a fine-looking woman once, her looks overblown now like a late summer rose. Thick dirty-blonde hair was piled up on top of her head like a basket of washing, and a low-cut bodice struggled to contain her charms.

'We wanted to ask you about Rose,' I said.

Bessie surveyed her tavern, two long tables with a younger mixed crowd and several smaller, all occupied with one or two bodies slumped and sinking over pint mugs; a man in the corner tried to rouse the room to song. His voice was surprisingly strong and clear.

'Let's have a bit of peace,' she said and jerked her head to the back. Leaving our bottles, we all followed and crowded into the pot-wash room. Damp cloths hung across the ceiling in crossed lines, like bunting, filling the space with the sour smell of old beer.

'I know it was a while ago, but anything you remember would help,' I said.

'I remember that night like yesterday. Keep asking myself if I could have done anything to stop it from happening.'

'You mustn't think like that – you were a good friend to Rose, she thought a lot of you.'

'That makes it worse.' She took a cloth and blew her nose hard, wiped her eyes. 'Sorry about this, but it always makes me cry when I think about her, and I can't let that lot in there see it. If they think I'm weak, they'll walk all over this place.'

I couldn't imagine anyone thinking that of Bessie. She'd run the Half Moon for as long as I could remember, and it was the kind of place where even the worst sorts didn't cause trouble. Like all taverns, a bubbling threat of violence was ever-present, but it never spilt over because she held her customers' respect.

'Sorry. Don't bloody tell anyone.' She wrinkled her nose and dropped the cloth into the laundry vat.

'What happened that night?'

'In here? It was just odd, a feeling that something wasn't right, I couldn't shake it. Rose came in at the usual time, said hello to the usual people, had a laugh with me at the bar like always. It was a bit quiet. I'd had to throw some ruffians out before she arrived and maybe it was them, waiting around to punish me or my customers for the way I made them look foolish, I don't know.'

'You said she was talking to someone you didn't recognise.'

'That's right, she was. Young girl, all corners if you know what I mean, thin and sharp. Never been in here before and that's odd as well. I know all the girls that come in. The new ones usually get brought by the older ones, introduced to us so we can keep an eye out. Anyway, she didn't look warm enough to be a dolly. I didn't like the look of her, and she didn't buy a drink, I remember that too.'

'What did she do?'

'She asked after the cook from Evergreen, struggled to remember her name, which was odd as well, and when I pointed her out, she walked straight up to the table. Rose moved after that, and they sat at a table on their own. Rose got a bottle and two glasses and they talked for a bit, not friendly but not unfriendly, if you know what I mean, and then Rose up and left at her usual time.'

'What did the girl do? Was she with anyone else?' I was certain she was working with Lavell. He and his party had left Thomas' by the time we did, but I couldn't be sure they hadn't followed us here.

'She sat for a bit on her own, not long, four or five minutes maybe, then she upped and left. There wasn't much in the bottle, but she didn't check it had been paid, or raise a hand or anything. Just walked straight out the front door. Like I said, I didn't like the look of her.'

'Can you remember anything else about her?'

'She had red hair, I should have said that. Beautiful colour really, not the sort of hair you see very often. Clothes were plain, a bit worn and slightly too big for her, like she'd got them fourth-hand or something.'

Angela. An unmistakable description. And from the looks on the others' faces they were thinking the same.

'Thank you, Bessie. Has she ever been in here again?'

The landlady shook her head. 'I'd know. I've been looking out for her. I can't shake the feeling that she had something to do with what happened after.'

'She may well have.'

'Has something happened?'

What could I say? We couldn't be overheard but just voicing my thoughts would make it real, increase the chance that she might run off. I needed to find some way to connect all the coincidence that pointed to Angela. She could hardly be solely responsible. Lavell sitting in the restaurant. He hadn't obviously been watching us, but he could have been. Had the Board placed Angela with us to keep an eye? Had they helped her to violence to unsettle and displace us? I couldn't imagine such a slight girl being capable of murder.

'We're not sure. She fits a description that could tell us more, so thank you.'

Bessie took a gin bottle from its hiding place under the sink, poured a tot into the lid and knocked it back like a cup of tea. 'You sure you won't have one?'

Tempting, but if I started that now I'd never stop. 'When we know more, we'll come back. Have a drink with you then.'

She nodded, drank another, pushed the bottle back into place.

'Don't give up, will you? Whoever did that to Rose, I don't want them to get away with it.'

43

Evergreen House

'What are you going to do?' asked Maddie.

'I don't know. I need to think.'

'Do you think she might have hurt Felicia, too?'

'I've been wondering.' Should I mention the ribbons? Lavell's words circled in my head. What if the others saw patterns I'd missed? I decided to wait until they'd left and talk it through with George, who'd hung back to talk to Albert in the Half Moon, to find out if he'd heard anything. His friend was still trawling the water, full of stories and life. Perhaps George would go back to his old life when we were evicted. Perhaps he'd be happier. 'I don't know what to think. There's no reason for any of it and I'm worried my thoughts may be overreaction, an unkindness to a young woman who's had a hard life.'

'You don't think she's working with Threlfall?'

'They barely see each other. And I honestly can't imagine either of them being capable of such violence. Look, it's getting late – you won't find a carriage this way, go up to the high street and take one from there.'

'Are you sure you'll be alright walking alone?'

'And you accuse me of worry! It's not far, I'll be perfectly fine.'

'Take care. And keep an eye on things.'

When they left, I realised how quiet the streets were and I half thought to call after them. My own footsteps echoed in the empty night, and I hurried a little, unsettled by the evening and eager to reach home. It was dark in the spaces between gas lamps. Wind stretched down the branches of the plane trees like plucking fingers, and a lone nightjar sang a long, sad note. No other signs of life. I started to hum, then thought better of attracting attention, instead making myself as silent as possible, a thief slipping through the blackness.

Relieved to reach Evergreen, I took the low side gate to reach the back entrance, fearful of waking the children with the slam of the heavy front door. Creeper stretched from the wall across the top ledge, the leaves brushing my face as I pushed through. I turned to close it slowly, listening for the soft click as the latch fell. It was a cosy time of day for the house. The women would all be preparing for bed, making cocoa, putting curl papers in one another's hair. Faces washed, nightgowns on, stories read, the children would be fast asleep. I felt a sudden stab of sentimental longing for our lives before everything changed. We'd been happy – I saw it clearly then, standing at the edge of the dark garden. Despite my longing for a child of my own, despite the distance between George and me, we were happy, and I should have known it; should have worked harder to make sure we all knew it. Now Rose was gone, Felicia, Rubina. Something had destroyed it all and I was no closer to finding out what, or who, it was. We had barely any time to break everything apart. As I walked across the edge of the lawn, I began to make lists – visit orphanages, find placements, run inventories of stock, find a new home for George and me. And Albie. I'd already decided we'd keep him with us.

Damp from the long grass spread over my boots to my stockings and I stopped to flatten it slightly. A wet spring with little time to cut the lawn. Soon it would be too high for the children's games; on the first suitable day I'd throw everyone outside to tidy. Mentally I ran through the list of jobs that needed doing in the garden – replanting the fruit canes, trimming the edges, weeding the borders and paths. Would anyone have time to enjoy the garden under Lavell's new regime? Or would the Board dig it all over to put in the huge sunken troughs that would be needed for the lye and ammonia to whiten the laundry? The thought of all our wasted effort pricked my eyes with angry tears. I'd miss sitting here with Amy in the quiet of morning; miss working with George to bring flowers and crops from the fertile soil; miss watching the children chase chickens and collect their eggs. They'd be separated into workhouses; unused to labour, they'd cry into the night until their hands and hearts hardened. The women would disperse, they wouldn't write, and I would worry that their stories had ended badly. Soon everything I loved in life would be gone, and I'd no idea if George and I would survive that after everything disappeared. The only constant at Evergreen would be the stone carving of the Everley crest.

Wiping my eyes on the sleeve of my coat, I turned to go inside the house when a sudden movement by the potting shed caught my eye. The flash of a lamp. Who could be there at such an hour? The light dropped, as though the lamp had been placed on the ground, and the faint sound of a door rattle carried. No-one had been into that shed since Rose disappeared. The sole key was on the set that went missing when she died. My stomach twisted. Whoever was attempting to unlock that door was either Rose's killer or knew who they were. Was it Lavell? He had seemed to know about the keys, he had the ribbons, he'd been in the kitchen when the arsenic was introduced. And he was in the chophouse earlier. My knees buckled and I crouched down, grazing my shin against the low wall and biting my lip to prevent a cry of pain. Steadying myself against the bricks, I listened to the sound of my heart pounding loudly enough to wake the dead. They'd hear me out here, in the still of the night, and there'd be nothing I could do about it except wait for them to come for me. Wait for them to kill me too.

I thought of the wine-dark line across Rose's throat, the vivid weals on Felicia's neck, and it was all I could do not to scream and run. If I could trust myself to outrun them, I would, but I didn't know who I was dealing with. Angela was involved, certainly, and I intended to confront her as soon as I was safe. But there was no way Angela, with her tiny birdlike frame, had so viciously murdered two people. She must be working with someone else. One of London's many thugs for hire, who slipped back into the night as soon as they'd wiped their blades. Or possibly someone closer to home. Lavell or Threlfall. Maddie's warnings about Threlfall rang in my ears. Why hadn't I listened to her? It was the only answer that made sense. Angela couldn't afford to hire thugs, and why would she? Only Threlfall stood to gain from an attack on Evergreen. With us out of the way he could take over the house, build his empire. It was highly possible he was in league with the Board; they seemed to like him well enough. And if that was true then I stood little hope of fighting. The room he'd shown me, the tears he'd almost shed, remonstrating his aversion to the pain research – was all of it falsehood? I'd believed him, come close to sympathy, and now it seemed likely I would die from it. Why didn't I listen to my sister? She, of all people, understood the danger in trust.

Trapped by the wall, halfway between the house and the shed, breathing in shallow, ragged gasps, I was unable to move for fear of attracting the stranger's attention. Across the lawn the light rose again, and I heard another rattle. The lock must be stiff, unused, the door likely swelled in the rain. How long could I stay like this? My knees already ached with the strain of crouching. Slowly I turned my head to the house, sizing up the distance, wondering if it was best to break free and get help. No lights shone from the kitchen, or corridor, though some could be seen through the gaps in the curtains of the upstairs rooms. The women and children were in bed. Even if I made it to the house, the door may be locked and if I was seen, chased, stopped, no-one would hear my screams. Foolish to even try. Bringing danger into the house was the last thing I should do. I'd rather perish outside than risk harm to another of my charges.

No moonlight broke the dark of the night, though stars peeped between clouds in furtive clusters. It was hard to tell how long I'd been hiding. When would George arrive home? Our conversation this evening worried him, I could see that, but in my bid to celebrate with Maddie I hadn't told him Lavell was behind us. He had no idea of the danger I was in, and he was drinking with Albert, his old friend. He rarely spent time out of the house and if Albert decided he'd like a few more drinks, then George may be easily persuaded. It could be hours before he was back.

The light by the shed rose again, then disappeared. The intruder was inside. Staying low, I made my way over, pausing a few feet from the open door. If I pushed it shut, I might trap them, but without a key I couldn't hold them for long. If the trespasser was tall or strong, I wouldn't hold them at all.

I decided to wait for them to emerge, in the hope I might see enough by their lamp to make out their features and identify them to the magistrate. In my position I was too exposed – I couldn't see them without them noticing me, even in the gloom – so I moved, intending to secrete myself behind the large hydrangea.

On stiff legs I crept slowly forward, alarmed at the noise my boots made against the grass. I held my breath. Nothing between me and the shrub to pick up and use as a weapon. All the garden tools were put away, the stone ornaments too heavy to lift. No sound from the shed. The trespasser was engaged in something. I couldn't understand why, if they had keys to the whole house, they'd never been inside anywhere but the shed. Bile rose as my mind threw unbidden images of what might be inside. Had they killed others? Were they keeping weapons, bodies, prisoners in the shed? My imagination ran wild, stoked by memories of the Everleys' crimes. Almost anything seemed possible.

At last, I reached the hydrangea but just as I crept behind it, the shed door opened wider and a figure emerged, dressed in black, a hood or shawl thrown over its head. The material hung so low it was impossible to see a face in the glow of the lamp. It was difficult to see their outline from my crouched position; I couldn't guess their height. They put the light on the ground to fix the lock and I was terrified the halo of the lamp would reveal the hem of my skirts and boots sticking out from the side of the bush. I pulled my feet in. Surely, they'd heard me move? I waited to be asked to reveal myself, holding my breath for fear of making noise, staring at the ground to hide my face below the brim of my hat. Nothing happened. No-one came. They must have caried out their deadly work and then left. I was no closer to understanding who they were, but I didn't care. I would give anything to be safe in the house.

For what felt like an eternity, I stayed hidden until I was sure the figure had left. No noise carried in the still night. As soon as I stepped out from behind the bush, I was struck with something heavy. Even through my hat, I felt a sickening pain and I swung out my arm, attempting to defend myself. All I reached was air. If I could get past, I could run to the house and bang on the windows. Another blow, and then my arms were pinned behind my back. Before I could scream, a cloth was pushed into my mouth, rough wool scraped my tongue and made me gag, closed the back of my throat. It grew difficult to breathe. Struggling seemed to make things worse, so I allowed my body to go limp, knowing it would render me heavier and harder to restrain. All the while I tried to gauge clues. There was a sweet musty scent like old lavender mixed with dead leaves. Small hands but an extraordinary strength of grip. Impossible to shake free.

Could it be Angela? Wearing layers that hid her shape? I remembered her pounding and kneading the bread dough on the kitchen table. George had joked she had the strength of ten men, the forearms of a prize fighter. Was she strong enough to hold me down for long? Enough to kill me? I had to get free and pray that George would return any moment. My arms ached where they were held; the cloth, pulled tight, bit into my mouth. My attacker's arms were thin and strong. Was it her? The cook I'd brought into our home. She had poisoned our food, been the last person to see Rose alive. Had she taken the keys when she killed her? Had she left poor Felicia half out of the pond? Nothing made sense. No cause or motive. No reason for such violent crimes. What could Angela or anyone hope to gain by them? Thoughts and memories flashed through my mind in a jumble. If I died here, I could never tell George how much I loved him. Little Albie would never know we wanted to give him a home. Maddie would never forgive herself for leaving me to walk home alone.

With a huge effort of will I spat the wool cloth out of my mouth and, as the figure's left hand struggled to replace it, bit down hard on the bony flesh. In return I received a punch to the kidneys so vicious that I screamed out in pain, tried to run, barely making two steps before I was tripped and bundled to the floor. In that moment I knew I would die, and if I carried a child inside me, as I suspected, it would die with me, before George even heard the good news. The figure straddled my back, pushing me into the wet earth, pinning me down.

'Who's there?' A voice carried from the door to the basement, strident, with a cut-glass tone. Threlfall, who else. 'Who's out there?'

If he didn't know, then this wasn't planned. Though I feared him as much as I feared Angela, more so, my only chance lay in screaming to attract attention in the hope that others would come. Cloth muffled my cries, my head pushed down to the ground. My attacker didn't answer Threlfall. Why, if they were working together? To avoid being overheard?

Threlfall crossed the garden in long strides, still calling out. Seeing a chance, I kicked out my leg and upset the lamp. Paraffin leaked to the grass and my assailant cursed loudly. Angela's voice. I reached to try to push the flame onto the paraffin on the grass, but she was first, stretching to right it with her leg even as she held me fast. She was strong.

'What the devil is happening?' Threlfall was on us now, he had come. His voice was loud, angry. He was going to help her kill me. Maddie was right all along. Why hadn't I listened? Soon the lawn would be steeped in blood; that was always going to be the outcome of our tale. The stone crest, invisible in the dark of the night, watched over us. The Everleys had won.

As Threlfall reached us, Angela released her vice-like grip on my wrists. She jumped up, and I assumed it was because she had help with dispatching me, someone else to hold me down, but as I lifted my head and struggled to my feet, I saw her launch herself at Threlfall, arm raised as though wielding a weapon. Surprise floored him. As I scrambled to reach them, I saw the blow as Angela smashed a rock hard into the side of his head.

'It's you,' he whispered, before his eyes closed.

Angela turned to face me, still holding the rock, a look of pure hatred spreading across her face.

'What do you want from us?' I cried.

'You took everything,' she snarled, 'every last thing. You and your pathetic sister, your peasant of a husband.'

What did she mean? I racked my brains to think of anyone we'd slighted or harmed since we'd taken control of Evergreen, but there was no-one. We made a point of being fair with our business, kept to ourselves in society. This was more than a jealous spurned lover, a rival for someone's affections.

'You don't even know, do you? You ruined us.'

No sound came from Threlfall. He lay still as the night. Another body in our garden and I was more confused than ever. Could they have worked together in a pact that turned sour? Or had Threlfall always been trustworthy, as Maddie suspected? I breathed deeply, tried to think. If I could talk to her, I would buy myself time. I backed against the shrub, head throbbing, and saw the glint of metal in her left hand, rock still clutched in the right. She had two means of attack, and I was defenceless except for my words.

'Angela. Please. You know you won't get away with this. Dr Threlfall will have people looking for him, and so will I. George was following me home, he'll be here any moment. Put down the knife.'

'You destroyed us. Our whole bloodline gone in a generation.'

I opened my mouth to plead innocence. She raised her arm to strike me, but it was caught above her head by another person.

'Run to the house,' said George. 'I've got her. Fetch the magistrate and send someone else out to help me. Send Amy. Get the bindings from the basket room.'

Tears coursed down my cheeks. I was saved. George had saved me.

'Threlfall's injured,' I said. 'I think he tried to help me.'

'Are *you* hurt?' George had crossed Angela's arms and held her in front of him, pinned like a beetle.

Was I? I didn't know. My head pounded from the blow, my shins and cheeks were scraped and bleeding. But I lived. *We* lived. We'd survive. And we would stay together.

Angela struggled and spat at my feet. Such hatred from a stranger. She'd called George a peasant, the kind of language the Everleys used. Was she really responsible for three deaths? Possibly four. I should get help for Threlfall before it was too late.

'I love you, George,' I called behind me, willing my child to exist, to be safe.

44

All Saints Asylum

'How long has she been here?' The woman in the peach satin dress can barely hide her excitement. An older man with tobacco-stained whiskers smiles indulgently and holds her arm, perhaps as a warning not to get too close, perhaps as a mark of his ownership.

'She's one of our longest-serving residents,' the warden replies. 'Coming up to over ten years now.'

Whiskers leans in, to whisper something to the woman, and she gasps at the mention of the Everley name, stares with open curiosity. Their outing is dangerous; the frisson of fear is what they pay for. Each Wednesday and Sunday afternoon the visitors come, trooping through the corridors to gloat at the degradation, to feel the depths of our suffering. Looking into rooms for the chance to see some violence.

'Without their reason, these inmates descend to the level of animals. Eating, sleeping, attending to their toilet with little decorum and virtually no comprehension of what they do. In the absence of rational thought, they are beasts who have no recognition of themselves over and above their basic needs to survive.'

Mr Varley delivers the same talk twice weekly, though such

tourism is frowned upon. Visits are advertised as a chance to view the buildings, tour the gardens, and be impressed with the way in which the institution is run. Ticket prices are high with further donations expected, only the wealthy are admitted, and they come in great number. Few are interested in the architecture. Philanthropy assuages their voyeuristic guilt – the more they see the worse they feel, and Varley profits handsomely.

'But we are to understand that such conditions may be cured? I read in last week's journal that Bedlam now expects recovery for around half of its patients. Do you find similar rates here?' Whiskers puffs importantly. A frustrated doctor, perhaps, a family man certainly by the looks of his well-fed stomach. I doubt he's ever brought his wife to such a place.

'We are no Bedlam.' The warden inclines his head with a great show of modesty. 'They receive a large number of grants and donations with which we may not compete.' He gives a sly sideways look to judge the effect of his words on the man's wallet. 'And yet the work we do here is similar. On most of our patients we use the gentler methods of treatment – moral instruction, electric therapy or bloodletting to cure the humours and restore the balance of sanguinity. All can be most effective. In many cases they permit recovery of the senses.'

'Fascinating.' Whiskers nods. 'Recovery to normal life?'

'In some cases, yes. Of course, there are many cases beyond hope. And cases, such as this, where life outside the institution will never be permitted.'

The woman listens with rapt attention, eyes and mouth like little *O*s. If I put on a good show, I'll eat well tonight. I snarl up at her, rise to my knees on the bedstead, and claw the fingers of my left hand across the bare plaster wall. She gasps again, takes a step back. What would she like to see? This is not her first time.

She's with a different man but I remember that face, as dull, round and pink as a china doll's. Her fingers flutter around her throat in mock horror, but I recognise a bad one when I see it.

'Pretty lady.' I make my voice crack, beckon her nearer. She moves, holding onto the hand of her temporary amour, and I run my hand over the fabric of her cheap, ugly dress. They've taken my gowns now, all of them – no doubt Varley's wife has squeezed herself into them by letting them out – and I wear nightgowns every day. Regulation off-white cotton, without lace or decoration. 'Pretty dress.' The woman smiles as though I'm something to pet and I stick out my foot and wriggle it, shockingly bare and dirty way past the ankle.

'I think we've seen enough.' Whiskers raises a hand, letting go of hers, and I take my chance to grab her arm, draw her nearer.

'Whore,' I whisper, so only she can hear. I spit on the floor. 'You'll be joining me in here when your looks fade. We are not so very different.'

Varley ushers them away, throwing me a backwards glance intended as a threat, but I don't care what he does to me now. I've lost. First Threlfall, then Lavell refused to help me. Such brutal ambition and yet no stomach for murder. Both weak. What hurts the most is Eloise. My daughter returned from Australia with a story of hardship, degradation, misery. Her new family worse than I'd imagined. It was hard for her to escape, but she was still tough; Everley blood ran in her veins. Disappointing to see how little her looks bore resemblance to mine. Eloise was no great beauty. More like her father, all skin and bone with heavy features. Training her for seduction would never have worked. Instead, we hatched the plan for her to kill Rose, wait a while and then present herself as a cook under a false name, to take Rose's place so she could be close enough to Rebecca and Maddie to finish them. Turns out it wasn't as easy as we imagined. People got in the way, questions were asked, suspicions raised. She began to rush, made careless choices, and in the end Edward – of all people – saved Rebecca from her wrath. She'll be hanged. Such a hard life, such a waste. A mortifying end to the bloodline. She didn't even look like me.

The long nights are unkind, the way time dredges up memories I'd rather not revisit. Cruel memories. But I chose my response, lived it for years, and it almost worked. We almost won, Lucius and I. Two ravens under crossed swords, destined to die by the crest. Does Threlfall still wear the ring? Does he feel its power? I'd imagined him to be a social climber, a man who sold himself to the bidder with the highest standing, but he was only ever impressed with himself. It seems to have served him well.

Without the gaze that fuelled me, I've aged and withered. Gums shrunken and teeth loosened, showing gaps when I bare them at visitors. My hair sticks up in shorn tufts, sores cover my skin. When I try to recall beauty and adoration, the power of my youth and strength, all that manifests is sadness and regret. Our heyday – the beautiful homes with their sumptuous style, all the dinners with their intellect and politics – is someone else's life. All that remains is the pain, the horror, the guilt. In the rough blankets of my cot, I no longer remember the feel of silk sheets. A life of shame and degradation. I can pretend no more. I can live it no more.

When Varley next brings the bloodletting blade, I will press it deep into the vein and he'll be unable to stop me. I wouldn't be the first to die that way. The plan brings peace of mind. I'm ready. No family remains. The crest will wither to a mark in stone or gold that future generations will know only as a picture. The House of Everley is no more.

45

Evergreen House

Threlfall reclined on the sofa against a huge pile of cushions, satin dressing gown open to reveal the front of his yellow silk pyjamas. With Henrietta and Amy fussing around him, settling his position and fetching fruit and wine, he resembled a Turkish sultan in his harem. His skin was a much better colour, his hair newly washed, though the wound on his temple was deep, the bruising livid all the way down his cheek. Swelling drooped his left eye half closed.

'Is it sore?' I passed him a cold compress, scented with rose water as he'd requested, and he breathed in its scent with a satisfied air before touching it to his face.

'It will heal,' he said bravely. 'One should not be too vain.' He flinched as he spoke, and I could see that it cost him dearly to think of his looks fading.

'I'm sure it will heal very well,' I said. 'Dr Melson has promised to look in tomorrow with something to help. You're very lucky to be alive. He says if the rock had hit you any closer to your temple it would have been instant death.'

'She knew exactly what she was doing,' he said solemnly.

Had Angela attacked Rose the same way? Felicia? She insisted she'd never meant to hurt Rubina, but she showed little remorse all the same. It was hard not to think of her as Angela, but by now I knew what Threlfall had realised on the night of my assault: that Angela was really Eloise, Grace's daughter, returned from the colonies and primed for revenge on our family.

'How did you know who she was?' I asked. 'She was so young when she left.' I hadn't seen her much as a child, but with similar colouring I'd assumed she would turn out to look like her mother. Eloise was nothing like Grace now. A plain face and angular frame worlds away from her mother's voluptuous beauty. With her Everley pride and vanity, Grace must have been deeply disappointed.

'I thought I recognised her face, but I didn't know where from. And it troubled me for a while. I assumed she had been a patient, perhaps brought to me as a younger child. I do get young patients from time to time. Once or twice, I met her in the kitchen and there was something about her features that was familiar. A similarity that I couldn't place.' He winced, lifted the compress away from his face and closed his eyes. 'And then it came to me. I'd seen her once as I was leaving All Saints. She was signing the visitors' book, on her way in to see one of the inmates. I was just on my way to tell you when I heard the noise in the garden.'

'You probably saved my life.'

'Probably,' he agreed, wholly unabashed. 'I got a good close look at her face when she attacked me and then I knew for sure it was Eloise. Same eyes and cheekbones as her mother, same hair.'

Same Everley streak of pure evil. Other than that, there was nothing familiar to me in her person. Gone were the chubby limbs and wide eyes, replaced by long legs and slanted cheekbones. A collection of angles in a cheap dress. Her hair the same colour as her mother's but her eyes must come from her father, the unfortunate Matthew – they were the colour of a spring pond.

Eloise had colluded with Grace, planned to catch Rose at her most vulnerable to get close enough to the rest of us to do harm. We should have believed her story.

'I never imagined Eloise would return.' She'd been foiled in her bid to poison me and poor Rubina had suffered as a result. And Felicia. Had she found something out? She'd certainly needed silencing with her disbelief of 'Angela's' story. Or perhaps her death was simply a warning, a way to spread chaos and destroy our community. We'd find out soon enough. The trial was set. Eloise was due to appear in court, and once the evidence was heard, surely Grace would face trial for a second time? She couldn't escape the noose twice. This time, Threlfall wouldn't be there to help her.

'No,' said Threlfall thoughtfully. 'I've been thinking the same. Her life must have been hard to come back like that.'

It was. And we hadn't believed her. We had pushed her closer to her mother. Might we have weakened Grace's hold on her? Perhaps. Though Grace would never have given up. There would have been others. She had tried to use her influence to persuade Threlfall and Lavell to hurt us, that much was clear. She'd almost destroyed us. I was half right when I feared the ghost of Everley was stalking us again. But she was the last of them. And when they both hanged, we might finally be free. Lavell and his Board had given us a reprieve, a stay of leave until the trial was completed, with a pending decision on whether we would be allowed to stay at the house. With all my heart I hoped it would happen. Life, I had realised, is always both heartbreak and love. George's heart was broken too and now that our child grew inside me, now that we were reconciled, I would never take happiness for granted again.

'Try to get some rest.' I picked up the books piled by the sofa. 'You'll hurt your eyes with these.'

'You are a tiresome nurse,' said Threlfall. Though he smiled as if he didn't mean it.

The magistrate peered at the gallery above his lorgnettes, and I was pleased that Maddie hadn't come with us. It was the same man who'd presided over her trial. Serious, weary and difficult to shock. He'd been stopped at the last minute that time, but this case seemed easier to judge. Three murders, three sets of evidence to link the perpetrator, and if that was not enough, a mother in a madhouse who'd already attested to the girl's guilt.

Eloise slumped in the dock as though the proceedings were nothing to do with her. Thinner than ever, her bones jutting painfully through the grey serge dress, her eyes dark hollows.

'She looks ill,' I whispered to George.

He shrugged. 'Her days are numbered anyway.'

'Don't you feel even a little pity? What chance did she ever have?' The previous day we'd heard the full story – the ship that only a handful survived, being allocated to a farm in the middle of the outback, the bullying siblings, the brutal stepfather, the beatings and abuse. Little wonder she felt wronged. Grace would have found her easy to persuade once she returned. No doubt she talked up the glory of the Everley name, promised her the world.

'A sad life story doesn't justify murder,' he replied. 'If it did, half the population of London would be killed off.'

True, but I pitied her anyway. I pitied Grace too, in a way. The papers Threlfall had shown me were evidence of her own violent upbringing. A monster like those in Maddie's paintings, brutalised and punished, a demon in response. Lamia feeding on the souls of the innocent. She was gone now. Out of our lives for ever, though it would still take time for me to recognise it. Threlfall came to tell us just before we left for the court, his face unreadable and his eyes swollen from crying. He'd liked her enough once to be swayed by her charms. A sad end for such a woman. As soon as she heard that her daughter had been arrested and would be tried, that the Everley name would die, Grace had seized a blade from the warden and opened up her veins, while he watched her bleed without lifting a finger to help.

'How do you plead to the charge of murdering Mrs Rose Parmiter?' asked the magistrate. The court clerks both paused their writing to look over to Eloise, to gauge her reaction. She said nothing.

The magistrate read further down his notes, before peering at Eloise again. 'Dr Threlfall has already identified the murder weapon as belonging to your mother. He has claimed that she asked him to use it on the proprietors of Evergreen House.'

I couldn't help gasping, earning me curious looks from the rest of the gallery row. A woman who'd been eating buns from a paper bag stopped mid chew to poke her friend in the ribs and point at us.

'He didn't though, did he?' said George.

'He didn't tell us either,' I muttered.

'What good would that have done? He didn't know Eloise would come back.'

George and Threlfall had struck up an unlikely friendship, thrown together in a house full of women. Something told me they'd be good for one another. George could help him become a little more practical, and Threlfall's unshakeable self-belief might just rub off. In that respect their friendship would be like mine and Martha's, a drawing together of opposites for the better good of each. We had become close enough for her to offer to support me at the trial. Instead, I'd asked her to watch the hanging and was surprised to hear that she was always in attendance at such executions. Because they were often botched, the drop and the weight poorly calculated, leaving the guilty hanging in agony, experiencing drawn-out death when they were cut down. She administered poison to speed the end; a compassionate task at the moment a criminal is most human, and one that would never be considered by a man. It took a woman like Martha to carry out such a duty.

'Dr Threlfall also attested that you had been to visit your mother at All Saints Lunatic Asylum on more than one occasion.' The magistrate paused, looked down at his notes. 'It seems likely, to me, that you colluded to plan the murder of Mrs Rose Parmiter in order to gain access to the household by posing as a replacement cook. Is this in fact true?'

A barely perceptible nod from Eloise caused great excitement among the clerks. The case would be easier than they'd thought.

'And did you also, in cold blood, murder Miss Felicia Barney by strangulation?'

No response.

'We have several witnesses from Evergreen House who attest to your dislike of Miss Barney. I will ask, again, did you murder Miss Barney?'

Another nod so slight it could be missed in a blink. The magistrate signed a slip of paper and passed it to the first clerk, who copied it in his ledger.

'We have also heard from several witnesses that you kept a selection of poisons in the potting shed, situated in the garden at Evergreen House, and that you used some of them in the kitchens, resulting in the death of five-year-old Rubina Cotton. How do you plead to the charge of murder?'

'I didn't do that.' Eloise's chin jutted defiantly. 'I wouldn't kill a child.'

'And yet a child died, by all accounts and testimonies by your hand.'

'It wasn't meant for her.'

'Who was it meant for?'

Eloise remained silent.

'The only possible conclusion I may draw from the evidence presented is that you also murdered Miss Cotton, whether or not that was your intention. In this instance, we do not need to include the attempted murders of Dr Edward Threlfall and Mrs Rebecca Harris on the night you were arrested and charged. There is already ample information to convict you. Miss Eloise Everley, for the three aforementioned murders, I hereby sentence you to be hanged by the neck until you are dead. The next assizes will be two weeks from now; until then you will reside under lock and key.'

Delighted gasps from the gallery, furious scribbling from the newsmen. Another tale for the penny bloods, another mark against the Everley name. Eloise was led away, her hands in iron cuffs with a chain linked between them. It was hard not to think of her as Angela, to wonder if there was something I could have done to change her.

46

The Royal Academy, Piccadilly

Maddie caught both of my hands and started to dance around the room like a child, her face flushed, laughing.

'Becca's dancing,' said Albie, taking Evie's hand and joining in.

'Play piano,' demanded Evie.

'I can't, I'm afraid,' said Tizzy. 'We'll have a proper party later, shall we? These two can play. Can you sing?'

'Yes!' they chorused and broke into a rendition of *ring-a-ring o' roses*.

'Stop, slow down, please. I need to think!' I pulled Maddie to a halt and sat down on the ottoman. 'Albie, run outside and play – go on, both of you, we need to talk.'

'What is there to talk about?' Maddie flopped to the seat beside me. 'It's yours. End of discussion.'

'You can't possibly have had time to think it through. What about Tizzy, doesn't she get a say?'

'Tizzy agrees with me.' Maddie looked over to her. 'Don't you?'

'Explain again, please,' said George, his face serious. 'It's hard to take in.'

'Grace is dead. She committed self-murder at All Saints before Eloise was tried and hanged. They were the last of the Everley blood line. And I am the only living relative by marriage. Everything they once owned is now mine. I inherit it all. Including Evergreen. It's in my power to gift it you, and that's what I intend to do. Tizzy, pass me the bag.'

She lifted up a pretty tapestry bag with a tortoiseshell clasp and began to rummage through its contents. Brushes and charcoals fell onto the floor, along with a teaspoon and several kerchiefs.

'You really are a messy thing, Maddie, I dread to think what your house is like.'

'Tizzy looks after all that,' she said cheerfully, 'she's much better at it than I am.'

'They're all the same, these artists.' Tizzy grinned.

'Here.' Maddie passed George two tickets for the Royal Academy's Summer Exhibition. 'You can use those any time this week. We're going again tomorrow if you'd like to join us?' She searched through the bag again until she found an official-looking envelope, which she pushed into my hands. 'The deeds to this house. They're yours, Rebecca. They are already in your name. Don't look at me like that, I know my mind and it's what I want to do. I wouldn't have a clue how to manage this place, and you and George are doing the most wonderful job.'

Hot tears welled in my eyes and began to spill onto my cheeks.

'Those had better be happy tears.'

'I am happy, Maddie, thank you. If you ever change your mind, you have only to ask.'

'What do I need it for? I already had the money from Arlington Crescent, and I've been given the money from Grace's children, too. We live very simply.'

'We don't have to,' said Tizzy and raised an arch eyebrow, making them both laugh.

'Will this work?' asked George. 'The inspectors are due this afternoon to set up the laundry downstairs.'

For a moment I'd forgotten. Wooden signs had already been sent, marked in white lettering on shiny black paint – *Magdalen Hospital for Penitent Women,* one for the front porch and one for the wall. The sight of them had made me so angry that George took them away before I broke them in two. Even if we owned the building outright, thanks to dear Maddie's generosity, it was still within their power to control how we managed the operation.

'They look after every charitable institution in London. If they don't like how we run things, then I'm afraid it is still very much in their power to change them.'

'Even if it's just your house?'

'Yes. All the women who live here, all their children, are here through charity. We must receive governance from the Board, religious instruction from Illingworth.'

'You said they were going to send the children to Coram?'

They were. But George and I had thought about that. Even before Maddie gave us the house, we had planned to adopt them, all of them. We couldn't choose between them, and we couldn't give them up. If they were all ours, they would have to stay with us.

'They can't,' said George, walking over to the ottoman. He sat on my other side and put a warm arm around my shoulders. 'The children are ours now.'

'You've adopted them all!' Tizzy squealed.

'Yes, so while we're proprietors they're our family and they have to stay put.' As soon as I said it out loud, I realised it was foolish. The Board would never let us get away with it. They'd push us to the attic and bring in new people to manage things.

'Then why,' said Maddie slowly, 'don't you adopt the women too? If you were all just family, the Board would have no oversight in your affairs.'

Before I could reply, a loud pull on the bell rope brought chimes through the hallway and across the house. The inspectors were early. Eager to set up another hospital that would work to death the women it purported to help, whilst generating a nice profit for the Board. Amy, who'd answered, ushered them in and they stood stiffly in front of us, hats in hand. All three wore righteous smirks, the look of people about to get their own way. I did not invite them to take seats.

'You haven't hung the signs,' admonished Lavell.

'I didn't care for them,' I replied. 'I don't think they will do.'

He looked taken aback. 'There will be a new regime here on Monday whether you like it or not, and . . .' A sudden squeal from the garden raised his eyebrows even further. 'Are there still *children* in this house, Mrs Harris?'

'Yes. There are. My children.' I squeezed George's hand. '*Our* children. They are all ours now, we have adopted them.'

'That is most irregular. There will not be room for such a large quantity of infants in a hospital of this nature; they will overrun the place and get in the way. The laundry may be dangerous for them.'

'Then we won't have a laundry,' I replied. The others exchanged looks.

'We have discussed this at length, Mrs Harris. The Board's decision is final. If you do not comply, you leave us little alternative but to establish alternate management.'

'We don't need managing.' I rose to my full height and looked down on the lead inspector. 'And there's no longer any need for your interference. *All* of the inhabitants of this house are now our children, all the women as well as their offspring. We have adopted them all.'

Tizzy clapped her hands. Mrs Beckwith opened and closed her

mouth like a rat trap; Lavell and Tovey grew so red and swelled that it looked as though they might explode if I poked them hard enough in the waistcoat.

'I will see you out.' I swished before them in what I hoped was a majestic gesture. 'You may collect your signs on the way.'

Though we arrived early, crowds were already gathered outside the Academy, queuing down both sets of wide steps and spilling into Trafalgar Square. So much finery on show. Men brushed and polished, their whiskers waxed and curled, gold glinting from chains and jewellery. Women in silks of every colour, long dresses swagged with ribbons and curlicues, hair in elaborate ringlets or hats drowned in feathers. I pulled at my new dress, conscious of the way it strained across my stomach. Before long I would be letting it out again, to accommodate the growing life inside me. A boy, I felt it, the nubs of his little heels drumming hard as soon as I stopped moving. George had felt them too, the delight on his face making me love him all over again. He said the same of me too, after the way I stood up to the inspectors. They were talking about it again, making me redden and squirm.

'You were amazing,' said Maddie. 'You should have seen their faces. So brilliant. And when they had to pick up those signs and walk away with them.' She turned, eyes narrowed. 'What will you do about Threlfall?'

She wouldn't like it. No matter how many times I explained about that night, the way he saved us, the way he'd changed. She insisted that if he hadn't used his alienist claims to save Grace from the noose in the first place, then none of it would have happened – Rose, Felicia, Rubina would all have lived. But life didn't work like that. Not really. And he was just a boy then, in thrall; he'd thought he was in love. I'd made my own mistakes that way. So, I didn't bear grudges. I couldn't. 'He's going to stay. You should get to know him, Maddie, he's changed. He will help us. And the money he'll pay in rent will cover things until the business gets back on its feet. He's been very generous.'

'He's not so bad,' George agreed. They'd been spending time together, finding common ground. 'Needs a new tailor though.'

'You're looking like a dandy yourself today,' I said. 'I like it. Threlfall may be rubbing off on you more than you think.' George drew himself up and hooked his thumbs into his plum-coloured waistcoat, affecting a society air.

Suddenly all the doors opened in a row, and the crowd surged forward. We followed the people in front, taking small halting steps, stopping as each party's tickets were checked and the viewers waved through to the galleries.

'I think that's Oscar Wilde,' whispered Maddie, pointing out a tall man wearing a flamboyant checked suit with a huge fur collar. For some inexplicable reason he was carrying a riding crop, which he flicked at members of his group from time to time. 'He has the most beautiful face.'

'He does,' I agreed, earning a playful dig from George. 'No-one else could carry off such an outfit.'

Tizzy pointed out other well-known faces: a composer of stage music; Holman Hunt, whom I recognised as the artist with a turban from the chophouse; and the poet Robert Browning, who looked thoroughly miserable.

'Poets are always the same,' said Tizzy darkly.

'They are indeed,' said a voice behind us. We turned to find Sophia, looking beautiful in a green brocade dress and coat trimmed with sable. Curled hair, caught at the sides with tortoiseshell clasps. She looked every inch the actress, and her clothes were expensive, her head held respectably high. She introduced us to the man whose arm linked through hers, the producer who owned her theatre troupe and a dozen more besides.

'We start on Drury Lane tomorrow with a run of *As You Like It*. I'm to be Rosalind. Do come.'

The producer fished into his pocket and held out a card, lavishly edged in gilt. 'You will have a box,' he said. 'Sophia has told me how much she owes to your kindness.'

'How is Albie?' she asked, her cheeks turning pink.

'He's happy. Come and see us. He'll be so pleased to see you. You know it's possible for him to love us all,' I said. Sophia threw her arms around my neck while I told her the news, that Evergreen was safe.

'We're next,' said George. We straightened ourselves while the doormen took our tickets, then we were inside the entrance hall with its white columns and glass, high ceilings like a cathedral. Although this was the private viewing, weeks ahead of the public show, they were staggering entrance, allocating galleries by ticket, and we started in one further away from Maddie's paintings. A room hot with bodies, the scent of wool suits, the heady smell of rose and violet perfumes. Everyone talked constantly, attempting to impress their friends with a knowledge of colour and brushstroke. George particularly liked the Turners, three of them that he said captured the early evening play of light on water, and which gave him a nostalgic look. By the time we reached Gallery One, I was almost ready to go home, when I overheard a woman exclaim, 'Medusa! What an extraordinary and original piece.' Above the heads of a gathered crowd, I saw Maddie's glorious snakes, that expression in the portrait's eyes. The Medusa was powerful, vengeful and triumphant.

'She's beautiful,' breathed Tizzy.

'She is,' I agreed. We moved closer, waiting for the admirers to move away one by one until we stood before her in all her glory. Easily twice the size of the next largest canvas, she dominated the entire wall. 'You were right to paint her so big. She deserves it.' So much was captured in the painting that it was hard to look away, and I found myself standing firm against the viewers that tried to crowd in behind me. Captured in her gaze was a vindication, a martyred refusal to agree that all the evil in the world was somehow women's fault. She was darkness and light together, at peace with both to survive. Wronged and traumatised, but the painting had healed her.

Someone had marked the name plate with a single stroke of orange paint. 'What does it mean?' I asked Maddie.

'Someone has bought it. I can find out who if I check the catalogue.' She smiled, delighted, and we turned to move away.

The Medusa had been hung on the opposite wall to Helen. I imagined that when the room was finally empty, they would contemplate one another in triumph, two wronged women made good.

Acknowledgements

When I completed *The Small Museum* there remained a sense that the stories of some of its characters were unfinished. Rebecca and Grace, in particular, continued to call me in dreams. So I am grateful to my agent, Charlotte Seymour, and to Wendy Bough at The Caledonia Novel Award, for the faith and encouragement that prompted this companion novel. Many thanks, also, to the army of readers, bloggers and booktokkers who took *The Small Museum* to heart and kept me writing.

As always, I am grateful for the honest support from my first readers, Jacqui Seymour and Becky King. Both Charlotte and Susie Dunlop, Publishing Director at Allison & Busby, made suggestions and recommendations that have immeasurably improved this book and I am deeply grateful for their insight and experience. Allison & Busby's team of copywriters, proofreaders, designers and publicists are exceptionally talented and I am thankful for the care and attention they have given my text.

There are times when writing takes over every sphere of life and I am forever indebted to my amazing family, Matt, Ben and Ted, for their support and understanding. I could not love them more.

JODY COOKSLEY studied literature at Oxford Brookes University and has a Masters in Victorian Poetry. Her debut novel *The Glass House* is a fictional account of the life of nineteenth-century photographer, Julia Margaret Cameron. *The Small Museum*, Jody's third novel, won the 2023 Caledonia Novel Award. Jody is originally from Norwich and now lives in Cranleigh.

jrcbooks.co.uk
@jcooksleyauthor
@jodycooksleyauthor